CHASING DREAMS AT HEDGEHOG HOLLOW

HEDGEHOG HOLLOW BOOK 5

JESSICA REDLAND

Boldwood

First published in Great Britain in 2022 by Boldwood Books Ltd.

Copyright © Jessica Redland, 2022

Cover Design by Debbie Clement Design

Cover Photography: Shutterstock

Every effort has been made to obtain the necessary permissions with reference to copyright material, both illustrative and quoted. We apologise for any omissions in this respect and will be pleased to make the appropriate acknowledgements in any future edition.

A CIP catalogue record for this book is available from the British Library.

Paperback ISBN 978-1-80162-435-0

Large Print ISBN 978-1-80162-434-3

Hardback ISBN 978-1-80162-433-6

Ebook ISBN 978-1-80162-436-7

Kindle ISBN 978-1-80162-437-4

Audio CD ISBN 978-1-80162-428-2

MP3 CD ISBN 978-1-80162-429-9

Digital audio download ISBN 978-1-80162-432-9

Boldwood Books Ltd
23 Bowerdean Street
London SW6 3TN
www.boldwoodbooks.com

To fellow Boldwood author Samantha Tonge for some amazing advice just when I needed it xx

RECURRING CHARACTERS FROM A WEDDING AT HEDGEHOG HOLLOW

Samantha Alderson, aka Sam or Sammie
Owner and full-time manager of Hedgehog Hollow. Recently married to Josh

Josh Alderson
Veterinary surgeon and partner at Alderson & Wishaw Veterinary Practice. Recently married to Samantha

Jonathan Wishaw
Samantha's dad. Lauren's lodger. Veterinary surgeon and partner at Alderson & Wishaw Veterinary Practice

Debs Wishaw
Samantha's mum. Aspiring gardener. Identical twin to Chloe's mum, Louise

Lauren Harbuckle
Josh's auntie. Non-identical twin to Connie. Head of Health and Beauty at Reddfield TEC

Connie Harbuckle
Josh's mum. Trainee counsellor. Non-identical twin to Lauren. Engaged to Alex Williams

Chloe Turner
Samantha's cousin. Married to James

James Turner
Samantha's ex-boyfriend. Married to Chloe

Samuel Turner
Chloe and James's young son

Louise Olsen
Samantha's auntie. Chloe's mum. Identical twin to Samantha's mum, Debs

Simon Olsen
Samantha's uncle. Chloe's dad

Paul Alderson
Josh's dad and former business partner. In remission from cancer. Lives at Hedgehog Hollow with Beth, Archie and Lottie

Beth Giddings
Paul's girlfriend. Josh's ex-girlfriend

Archie Alderson
Paul and Beth's young son

Lottie Alderson
Paul and Beth's young daughter

Thomas Mickleby

Elderly widower befriended by Samantha. Left Hedgehog Hollow to Samantha in his will on the proviso she ran it as a hedgehog rescue centre

Gwendoline Mickleby
Thomas's wife, whose dream it was to run the hedgehog rescue centre

Rich Cooper
Good friend of Samantha. Partner of Dave. Ambulance paramedic

Dave Williams
Good friend of Samantha. Partner of Rich. Builder

Alex Williams
Dave's uncle. Engaged to Connie

Hannah Spiers
Samantha's best friend. District nurse

Toby Spiers
Hannah's husband. James's best friend

Amelia Spiers
Hannah and Toby's young daughter. Samantha's goddaughter

Tariq
Josh's best friend from university. Vet

Fizz Kinsella
Volunteer at Hedgehog Hollow. Trainee veterinary nurse

Yasmin Simms
Fizz's girlfriend. Artist/sculptor

Barney Kinsella
Fizz's older brother. Farmer at Bumblebee Barn

Natasha Kinsella
Fizz's mum. Runs events and catering business

Hadrian Kinsella
Fizz's dad. Police sergeant

Phoebe Corbyn
Accountancy student at Reddfield TEC (2nd year). Volunteer book-keeper at the rescue centre. Lives at Hedgehog Hollow

Darcie Flynn
Seven-year-old neglected by the Grimes family and adopted by Phoebe. Lives at Hedgehog Hollow

Hayley Grimes
Darcie's biological mother

Rosemary Norris
Good friend and former neighbour of Phoebe's. Has a guide dog called Trixie

The Grimes family (Tina, Jenny, Cody, Brynn and Connor)
Relatives of Gwendoline's with a vendetta against Samantha. All currently in prison

Terry Shepherd
Good friend of Samantha's. Has brought in several rescue hedgehogs/hoglets

Zayn Hockley

Animal Care student at Reddfield TEC (2nd year). Volunteer at Hedgehog Hollow rescue centre

THE STORY SO FAR...

After an amazing first Christmas as the owner of Hedgehog Hollow, the year ahead looked rosy for Samantha Wishaw. She'd settled into a routine at the hedgehog rescue centre, had some great volunteers to support her work, and was excited about her wedding to fiancé Josh.

A couple of days after Christmas, she was shocked to learn that volunteer accountancy student Phoebe was part of the Grimes family – a family who'd made Samantha's life hell over the past year, believing they should have inherited the farm.

When Samantha discovered the charity's bank account had been emptied, Phoebe seemed the obvious perpetrator and Samantha feared the only way to keep the rescue centre afloat would be to scale back her wedding plans and cancel her African Safari dream honeymoon.

Phoebe's stepmother Tina Grimes and her sister Jenny had stolen the rescue centre cheque book from Phoebe, defrauding Hedgehog Hollow without her knowledge. They went on a Caribbean holiday, leaving Jenny's then six-year-old granddaughter Darcie at Tina's house for Phoebe to care for. With little money for food, Phoebe searched for loose change but found large quantities of cash and suspected drug-dealing paraphernalia under the floorboards in Tina's and Jenny's houses.

Fizz's dad Hadrian, a police sergeant, led the case and Samantha rushed to the police station to support Phoebe, who she discovered had suffered years of physical, verbal and emotional abuse. With the approval of Social Services, Samantha invited Phoebe and Darcie to make Hedgehog Hollow their home. Darcie's mother, incapable of providing care herself, agreed to Phoebe privately adopting Darcie.

Thanks to generous donations from friends, family and the community, there were enough funds and supplies to keep the rescue centre running, so Samantha and Josh were finally able to have the wedding of their dreams at Hedgehog Hollow on the one-year anniversary of the rescue centre opening. The day was made extra special for Samantha when her estranged mum Debs agreed to attend.

With the evening do in full swing, Samantha and Josh stepped out of Wildflower Byre and witnessed another relationship being rekindled. Samantha's parents, currently going through a divorce, slow-danced then kissed before heading in the direction of the holiday cottages.

And they weren't the only ones who saw this...

1

LAUREN

Samantha and Josh's wedding

I fastened the ankle straps on my sandals and stood up, teetering for a moment.

'How did I let her talk me into heels?' I muttered.

When my twin sister Connie dragged me out shopping for an outfit for her son Josh's wedding, it was with the assurance that she was only there to offer a second opinion and I could have the final say. But somehow the trouser suit and ankle boots I'd chosen were still in the shop and I was wearing the wraparound flowery maxi dress and strappy sandals Connie had loved. I'd had to get my razor out for the first time this year and even slap on some fake tan. If she'd still been around, our mum would have been thrilled to see me looking like this. She never had understood my preference for comfort and practicality.

I pulled on the bolero jacket that hung on my wardrobe door and rolled my eyes at my reflection in the mirror. Raspberry, my arse. The jacket was pink. I'd been duped!

Shaking my head, I tossed my hairbrush into my overnight bag and zipped it up. Josh and Sam were getting married at their farm and hedgehog rescue centre, Hedgehog Hollow, and close friends and immediate family were staying overnight in the holiday cottages there.

There was a knock on the bedroom door.

'Just a second,' I called to Jonathan, father of the bride and my temporary lodger – if you can call nearly fourteen months temporary. He'd moved in after separating from his wife Debs and seemed in no rush to move out, which suited me just fine. He was great company and a brilliant cook, saving me from death by takeaways and ready meals. I didn't do cooking – another thing that had disappointed Mum.

'I'm going to put my bag in the car,' Jonathan called. 'Is yours ready?'

I pulled the door open. 'All packed, thanks. I just need to...' I tailed off and frowned at him, perturbed by his open-mouthed, wide-eyed stare. 'What's up? Is it too much? Too pink?'

I dropped the bag on the floorboards with a thud and smoothed down the dress. 'I *knew* I should have gone for the trouser suit.'

'No! The dress is great. Honestly, Lauren, you look amazing.'

'You're just saying that because I don't have time to change.'

He gave me one of his warm smiles, where his dark brown eyes softened and crinkled at the corners.

'I'm saying it because it's true. You always look great, but this must be the first time I've seen you in a dress. You scrub up well, Ms Harbuckle.'

Reassured, I returned his smile. 'So do you, Mr Wishaw. Tie's a little wonky, though.'

'Would you...?'

As I reached out to straighten the knot, my fingers grazed against his freshly shaved chin and the butterflies in my stomach did a loop-the-loop thing that I hadn't felt for... actually, I couldn't recall when the last time was. Many years ago.

I stepped away a little too quickly, wobbling on those damn sandals again. Jonathan's strong arms steadied me, and the butterflies did another loop. What the hell?

'Bag's ready.' I picked it up and thrust it at him, eager to maintain some distance. 'My car keys are… what am I saying? You know where they are! Two minutes and I'll be down. Just need to…' I couldn't actually remember what else I needed to do but getting away from Jonathan was a priority.

'See you shortly,' he said, flashing me his brilliant smile again.

I closed the door and leaned against it, gulping down deep breaths, but the fluffy dressing gown hanging on the back of the door hugged me, sending a hot flush from head to toe. Curses to being a woman of a certain age. Escaping from its embrace, I shrugged off my jacket and grabbed the wedding invitation off my tallboy.

'What was that all about?' I muttered, frantically fanning my face.

I peered out of the window to see Jonathan on the drive, loading our bags into the back of my car. It was the suit. It had to be. Even though I wasn't a fan of playing dress-up, I had to admit that certain men looked mighty fine in a suit and Jonathan Wishaw, at six foot four, with broad shoulders and what I suspected were impressive abs under that shirt, was one of them. He wasn't used to seeing me in a dress and I wasn't used to seeing him in a suit and there was nothing more to my unexpected reaction than that. Which was just as well because anything else would be immensely inconvenient, not to mention cheesy. Father of the bride and auntie of the groom? Absolute no-no.

I wafted the bodice of my dress as another hot flush flowed through me.

After a little more fanning with the invite, I felt cooler and more composed. I applied lipstick, grabbed my clutch and went downstairs. *Just the suit. Nothing more.*

* * *

It was only a fifteen-minute drive from Amblestone to Hedgehog Hollow.

'Do you want to practise your speech again?' I asked as we left the village.

'I think I've cracked it. Thanks for your help.'

'Sam's going to love it. How are you feeling?'

'A bit emotional. It seems like no time since we brought this tiny little pink bundle home from hospital and now she's all grown up and getting married. Where have thirty years gone? It's scary how quickly time flies.'

He could say that again.

'The last wedding I went to was Chloe's,' Jonathan continued. 'Fingers crossed Sammie's will be less dramatic.'

I crossed my fingers on the steering wheel. 'Let's hope so.'

Chloe was Jonathan's niece and Sam's cousin, and she'd ostracised Sam following a major drama on her wedding day nearly two years ago. They'd settled their differences but there'd been several incidents since then. No way would I have forgiven Chloe for all the crap she'd put Sam through, but I wasn't generally a forgiving person. I used to be, but it's tough to stay that way when life drives a great big dumper truck full of manure right up to you and deposits it on your head. Twice.

'When were you last at a wedding?' Jonathan asked.

I stiffened. 'Eight years ago.'

'Whose was it?'

My hands clenched the steering wheel, and I kept my focus straight ahead. 'That would be mine. Second one.' I didn't recognise my own voice, dripping with bitterness.

'And, no, I *still* don't want to talk about it,' I added, sounding a little more like myself.

I *never* wanted to talk about it. Or the time before. Jonathan knew I was twice-divorced – no point trying to hide that – but I never discussed the details with him, or with anyone else for that matter. Talking about it wasn't going to change what had happened and I'd learned my lesson not to go down that road again. My second marriage to Glen hadn't even lasted a year and I'd been resolutely single ever since, which worked for me.

Despite my own negative experiences, I wasn't completely cynical about love and willingly helped chase that dream of happy ever after for others. When Sam started tutoring at Reddfield TEC after Chloe's wedding, I was convinced she'd be perfect for my nephew Josh, and I'd been right.

My marriages hadn't lasted but I was convinced that, if anyone could make it, that pair could. That dumper truck of manure had already visited them several times, mainly courtesy of the Grimes family and their vendetta against the farm, and they'd shovelled their way through it all and come out the other side stronger than ever.

* * *

Connie and her fiancé Alex arrived as we were unlocking the door to Snuffles' Den, the holiday cottage where the four of us were staying overnight – one of four holiday cottages beautifully converted from two stone barns.

'I'd better go and find the bride,' Jonathan said after we'd taken our bags inside. 'I'll see you all later.' He paused, smiling at me. 'You really do look fantastic. So no changing outfit.'

'We've got thirty minutes before Josh wants us for photos,' Connie said after he'd gone. 'Just enough time for a coffee, or I may have something a little stronger in my suitcase.'

'I'll get the glasses,' I said, grinning at her.

Connie, Alex and I took our glasses of bubbly out onto the patio.

'So,' Connie said as soon as we'd all settled. 'You and Jonathan. Has something happened?'

'God, no!' But those butterflies stirred in my stomach, just like they'd done earlier. 'Why would you say that?'

She shrugged. 'You've always been close, but you've seemed closer than ever recently and, just now, there was something in the way you were looking at each other.'

'We're just friends,' I insisted.

'Sometimes friendship develops into something more.' She raised her eyebrows. My first husband Shaun and I had started off as friends and so had Connie and her ex-husband Paul. Both relationships had been amazing. At first.

It was tempting to retort, 'And look where that got us,' but I smiled sweetly instead.

'And sometimes sisters invent things that don't exist. There's nothing going on between Jonathan and me.'

'But you wish there was?' she teased.

'No, I don't! Seriously, Connie, where's this sprung from?'

She glanced at Alex, who looked mortified and held his hands up in surrender. 'It didn't come from me!'

'No, but you agree with me, don't you?'

'It's okay,' I said, saving Alex from embarrassment. 'I know it's all Connie. I really like Jonathan but only as a friend. And even if I did have feelings for him – which I don't – I'm too old and far too jaded for all that.'

'Don't say that!' Connie cried. 'You're never too old and it's never too late for love.'

She glanced at Alex, who gazed back at her adoringly. 'I'd echo that.'

'Yeah, well, you two are an exceptional case and one I personally take credit for.'

Connie laughed. 'And how do you work that one out?'

'You met when I was out celebrating my divorce from Glen. If I hadn't been stupid enough to marry him in the first place, you'd never have had that moment where your eyes met across a crowded bar.'

'As I recall, our eyes met because I was apologising for my extremely drunk sister bashing into Alex and spilling his drink.'

'I did all that just for you, you know.' I struggled to say it without laughing. 'You know full well that you weren't ready to accept it was over with Paul. You needed more time and I afforded you that. Now look at the two of you. Destined to meet again when the time was right, planning your wedding, and deliriously happy. You're welcome!'

Connie and Alex made such a great couple and I was delighted they'd reunited. My sister deserved to find happiness.

'In that case, something good *did* come out of your relationship with Glen,' Connie said.

I shuddered. 'Something had to.'

We sipped on our drinks in silence for a moment. I closed my eyes and tilted my head back, letting the sun warm my face, and cast aside the unhappy memories of the marriage that should never have happened.

When I opened my eyes, Alex was looking at me, a gentle smile on his lips. 'For someone who says she's too old and jaded for a relationship, it's funny that you mentioned destiny.'

'She's a romantic at heart,' Connie said. 'Aren't you?'

I was ready with a sarcastic comment, but I caught Connie's expression. She looked so hopeful, and I could tell it meant a lot to my sister to believe that, one day, I might let someone in again. And I could see why she'd think that. After all, I'd never let her know how deep the scars ran and likely never would. That was my secret pain.

Today was her son's wedding day – a day about love – so I'd play along for now. I wouldn't ruin the moment by telling her the destiny comment was a joke and I didn't buy into any of it.

I looked around furtively as though checking there was nobody else in earshot, and leaned towards Alex. 'I have my moments. But if you tell anyone, I'll have to kill you. I have a reputation to uphold.'

Alex's smile widened. 'Your secret's safe with me.'

Connie drained her drink and stood up. 'Best get organised and find the groom.'

* * *

As Sam walked down the aisle a little later, looking absolutely stunning in a cream lace dress covered in tiny flowers, I glanced at Josh, standing by the wooden wedding gazebo. Their eyes were locked, their expressions full of love, and I experienced a flashback to when I married Shaun. He'd looked at me just like Josh was looking at Sam now and I'd believed nothing would tear us apart.

Shaun had been my best friend, my one true love... and was now the reason I no longer believed in destiny.

2

LAUREN

Thirty-nine years ago

I poked my head round the kitchen door to find Connie sitting on a wooden stool in the middle of the floor, wearing a pink ballet leotard, bolero, and net skirt, clearly trying not to wince each time Mum jabbed a hairgrip into her bun.

'I'm going to see Dad,' I said. 'Good luck, Connie.'

'Thanks. See you later.'

Mum momentarily paused the torture to look me up and down, and there it was – that familiar look of dismay.

'Oh, Lauren, what on earth are you wearing?'

I glanced down at my frayed denim shorts and answered honestly. 'Shorts.'

Mum tutted. 'I can see that. Where did you get them?'

'I cut the legs off the jeans you told me to chuck.'

She clapped her hand to her throat, her eyes wide. 'The ones you ripped on your bike? Whatever next?'

I shrugged apologetically. 'All my other shorts are too small and I know money's tight...'

She looked like she was going to object, but how could she? Money *was* tight and had been since Dad lost his job at the local pet food factory four years ago when Connie and I were eight. I didn't really understand what his job had been – something to do with the electrics – but I knew he was a manager and they'd decided they had too many of those. He'd loved his job and I could tell he was gutted. I'd cuddled him that night and told him everything would be all right, just like he told me whenever I fell off my BMX or skateboard. It always made me feel better, so I'd hoped it would help him. I don't think it did.

Mum and Dad argued a lot after that. Connie and I would lean on the banister upstairs, listening to them. Mum wanted him to go back to the factory to do a different job, but Dad refused to 'step down', whatever that meant. He spent a lot of time in the pub, which made Mum angry too.

At the start of last year, his old boss had offered him a job as a supervisor so he returned but only lasted a few months before they sacked him for drinking at work. We only found that out because we were woken up one night by them shouting at each other about it.

Dad had done some labouring on a building site, so he returned to that but, as Christmas approached, the atmosphere in our house was definitely not festive.

'Sacked again?' Mum yelled when Dad arrived home early from the building site at the start of December. 'Happy Christmas to us!'

Connie and I leaned over the banister, exchanging pained looks.

'It wasn't my fault,' Dad yelled back.

'Whose was it? Mr Vodka's, Mr Gin's or Mr Bourbon's? You need help, Doug. Your drinking is out of control, just like your dad's.'

'Don't bring *him* into it.'

'Why not? Because the truth hurts? Your dad was an alcoholic and he made your poor mother's life a living hell. You're following in his footsteps, and I will *not* let you ruin my life like he ruined hers. The girls and I deserve better.'

'I'm *not* an alcoholic.'

'Says the man whose first action on arriving home via the pub was to pour himself a drink. No, doesn't sound like an alcoholic to me.'

'Most men I know have a drink after work to unwind.'

'But do they also have a drink for breakfast, elevenses, lunch and afternoon break, because their team won, because their team lost, because it's Tuesday, because there's a full moon?'

The lounge door opened, and Connie and I ducked away from the banister so Mum couldn't see us.

'You're destroying this family, Doug, and you're destroying yourself and I won't stand by and watch. It's three weeks till the big day and my Christmas gift to you is an ultimatum. You either decide you want to remain part of this family, admit you have a problem, enrol in AA and approach Christmas sober, or you and your liquid family can live unhappily ever after without us.'

'Is that a threat?' Dad shouted.

'No. It's a promise.'

And Mum kept her promise. We spent Christmas at Mum's sister's, returning to our house on the outskirts of Reddfield the day after Boxing Day. Dad was drunk. Their marriage was over. He spent a week sleeping on the sofa before moving into a tiny flat in town above a hairdressing salon, which was where I was going this morning while Connie was in a dance show. If he'd remembered. If he wasn't already in the pub.

'Well, don't wear them when you're out with me,' Mum said, scowling at my shorts. 'And stop slouching like a boy.'

Connie rolled her eyes at me, and I gave her a weak smile in return.

I nipped out onto the back patio, retrieved my skateboard from the shed, and steeled myself against another comment as I walked past the kitchen with it.

'You're never going into town on that thing, are you?'

'It saves the bus fare.' It was a risk to play the money card twice, but I had nothing else.

She released an exaggerated sigh and must have taken out her frustration at me on my sister with her pin-jabbing because Connie squealed before I stepped into the hall.

Most of the time, I got on well with Mum. She was caring and attentive and she'd done her best to keep us in our family home by getting a job in the local newsagent's while we were at school and taking in ironing on a weekend. But there was one thing we clashed on – her disappointment at me for not behaving in the way she thought a young girl should. She was always making digs at me for slouching, nibbling my nails, refusing to wear skirts or dresses outside of school and 'acting like a boy', as she put it.

When she'd dreamed about having a family, she'd wanted two girls because she'd loved growing up with a sister. Twins were a bonus. In all the photos of us as babies and toddlers, Connie and I were dressed the same but, as we got older, we didn't like that. We weren't identical twins, so why dress us identically?

We also developed different interests – another source of disappointment for Mum. She enrolled us both into dancing lessons when we were five. Connie was graceful and excelled at all styles but after two years of frustration, the teacher suggested to Mum that I might like to try something a little less delicate. Dad bought me a skateboard, swiftly followed by a BMX. Mum was disgusted. She believed that little girls should do ballet and leave boards and bikes for the boys, but I agreed with Dad that we should do what interested us. And why splash out good money for dancing lessons and costumes when I had two left feet, didn't enjoy it and even the teacher declared me a hopeless case?

So we settled into a pattern where Mum took Connie to dance shows and exams and got to be the proud mum of the dream daughter, and Dad and I went out on our bikes. The added bonus was the impracticality of wearing dresses while cycling, so I got to live in jeans and jogging pants while Connie wore pretty outfits.

* * *

I jumped off my skateboard, stamped on it to flip it into my hand, and squinted up at Dad's flat. The curtains were drawn.

The doorbell didn't work, so I banged on the door and waited. I banged again a couple of minutes later and sighed. Glancing into the window of the hairdressing salon, I caught the eye of the hairdresser doing a perm closest to the window. She pointed down the road and mouthed, 'He's in the pub.'

I stuck my thumb up to thank her. It was ten past eleven, meaning the pub had only been open for ten minutes, so at least he wouldn't be drunk yet. When he finished his drink, we'd have a day together, as promised, with a trip to the park and fish and chips.

I hesitated by the door. The scary pub landlord had repeatedly told me kids weren't allowed in, but I was going to have to brave it, or how else would Dad know I was here?

'Out the way, kid,' a man growled, shoving past me. I took my opportunity and followed him inside, reeling at the stale smell of beer and wafting the cigarette smoke.

'Out!' The landlord stopped wiping a nearby table and glared at me.

'I just need to—' I scanned the pub, searching for Dad, but there were too many nooks and I couldn't see him.

The landlord towered above me, his face purple. '*Out!*'

Trembling, I ran outside and flopped down on the doorstep to Dad's flat. I'd have to stay there until he came out – *if* he came out. Mum and Connie would be out all day. Mum had offered to leave me a key, but I'd been stubbornly adamant that I didn't need one as Dad would keep his promise to me this time.

A knock made me jump and I looked at the salon window. The hairdresser who'd helped me moments ago was beckoning me.

As I stepped inside the salon, I was hit by a wave of heat from the hairdryers and a weird chemical smell.

'Jimmy didn't let you in?' she asked as she continued to roll tresses of an elderly lady's hair onto small plastic rollers.

'No.'

'What ya gonna do?'

'Sit on the step and wait for him?'

She glanced at the board in my hand. 'You like skateboarding?'

I nodded.

'Why don't you go to the skatepark instead?'

'Dad wouldn't know where I was.'

She shook her head slowly. 'Sorry, love, but we both know he's in there for the day.'

I gulped and lowered my eyes to the floor. Connie had stopped visiting. It was easier for her to break ties because she'd always been closer to Mum, but I'd been closer to Dad, and it hurt that he didn't seem to care anymore. Like Mum said, he'd chosen his liquid family over us.

* * *

I'd never been to a skatepark before and hadn't even known there was one in town. I stood near the ramps, watching a mixture of kids, teens and adults skating up and down the slopes. Some wore knee and elbow pads, but most didn't. The tumbles looked painful and I glanced down at my bare knees, wincing at the thought of falling.

I must have been there for at least fifteen minutes and I had no nails left to chew. A spotty lad who'd kept looking over in my direction pointed at me, flapped his arms and made chicken noises. His mates laughed. I thought about leaving, but where would I go? Sit on the doorstep at home, tummy rumbling, waiting for Mum and Connie to return?

Confident I'd watched enough to work out the technique, I made my way to the edge of one of the smaller ramps. I'd skated down slopes before – drives, streets and paths – and I'd landed jumps from various heights, but skating up and down a ramp was new.

Don't fall! I repeated the phrase over and over in my head as I stood at the top, the end of my board sticking out into the open space. Another chicken squawk gave me a boost of determination.

Somehow I didn't fall and made it up to the other side. Heaving a sigh of relief, I turned round and prepared for another drop-in. I'd planned to do that single journey several times to build my confidence, but the spotty kid and his mates were watching me, flapping their arms and laughing.

I ignored them and did a single journey back to the start, but the volume of the squawks intensified. I felt the pressure to do a return journey without stopping but I hadn't thought it through. It meant riding backwards on the second leg, which disorientated me. I did make it back to the start, but I lost my footing at the top. Sprawling full length onto the concrete, I stifled a scream. I lay there for a moment, trying to catch my breath, cheeks blazing with embarrassment as laughter mingled with chicken squawks came from every direction. Nobody came to help. Nobody asked if I was all right.

My palms were scraped and tears burned my eyes as I pressed my hands on the ground to push myself up to a kneeling position. I whimpered as pain shot through my bleeding knees.

'Let me,' a lad said.

His arm slipped round my waist as he helped me to my feet. I looked up into a pair of warm brown eyes and tried to give him a grateful smile, but every part of me hurt and all I wanted to do was cry.

'Do you live nearby?' he asked.

I shook my head.

'My mum's a nurse. She'll clean your cuts.'

'Are they bad?' I glanced at my palms but didn't have the guts to look down.

'There's a lot of blood. Do you think you can walk? It's five minutes.'

'Okay. My board?'

'I'll get it.'

While he retrieved it, I braved looking down and whimpered again. Blood had trickled down my legs into my socks and both knees were a bloody, gritty mess. Mum would kill me and I'd get another lecture on the dangers of skateboarding.

Knowing we were being watched, I tried to walk straight and tall as

I left the skatepark but, as soon as we were round the corner, I slumped onto a bench and burst into tears.

The lad put his arm round my shoulders. When the worst of the tears had passed, I wiped my cheeks on my T-shirt.

'Thank you for helping me,' I said to him. 'What's your name?'

'Shaun. What's yours?'

'Lauren.'

I looked up at him. He had thick, mousy brown hair, a spattering of freckles over his nose, and flecks of gold in his brown eyes. He looked vaguely familiar.

'Do you go to Lord Lennerby's?' I asked.

He smiled as he nodded. 'I think I've seen you around. Do you have a twin?'

'Yeah, Connie.'

'I thought it was you. Do you think you can walk again? You can lean on me. Or you can stand on your board and I'll pull you.'

I shuddered at the thought of getting on my skateboard straightaway. Shaun put one arm round my waist, tucked both our boards under his other arm, and I limped to his house with his help.

'Mum?' he called, pushing open the front door of a terraced house with colourful window boxes.

'That was quick. Did you...' A petite woman with dark brown hair pulled back into a high ponytail rushed towards me. 'Oh, my goodness! What have we here?'

'This is my friend, Lauren,' Shaun said. 'She fell off her board.'

'Oh, sweetheart, that's a bit of a battering you've had. Come through to the kitchen and I'll get you cleaned up. My name's Ivy. I'm a nurse and I promise to be as gentle as I can.'

Ivy pointed to a step and told me to use it to hop onto the unit beside the sink. Between them, they cleaned me up, Shaun working on my hands and arms and Ivy on my knees. Shaun talked to me the whole time, asking where I lived and which subjects and teachers I liked best, which helped take my mind off the pain.

'I can't believe nobody else came to help you,' Ivy said, handing me a beaker of juice when they'd finished. 'Lucky you were there, Shaun. I thought you were going to the park.'

'I was, but I changed my mind last minute.'

'And you say it was your first time on the ramps?' Ivy asked me.

'First time at the skatepark. I was meant to be spending the day with my dad but...' I paused, too embarrassed to say where he'd been. 'Something came up.'

'So neither of you had planned to be there?' Ivy grinned at us both. 'Must be destiny. I have a feeling you two are going to be the best of friends. Why don't you take Lauren up to your bedroom, Shaun, and I'll fix you both a sandwich?'

I thanked her as I slid down from the unit and followed Shaun upstairs, wincing with each step.

He had a big room at the back of the house and his walls were covered in posters of bands, mainly out of *Smash Hits*, including all my favourites like Duran Duran, Madness, The Police and The Human League.

'Do you like ELO?' he asked, holding up a cassette.

'I only know "Mr Blue Sky" but that's brill.'

'They all are. Listen to this.'

We sat on his bed all afternoon, listening to cassettes and talking non-stop. I'd never had a good friend who was a boy before. I'd mainly hung out with Connie and there'd been a circle of girls we were friendly with, so this was new, but I loved it.

As teatime approached, I knew I'd have to leave, and I felt quite tearful about saying goodbye.

'I'll drop you home,' Ivy said. 'Can't have you skating across town and taking another tumble when those knees are only just starting to heal.'

Shaun sat in the back of Ivy's car with me and we chatted all the way to my house.

Ivy turned to us as she stopped outside. 'I'm working the next few days, but I'm taking Shaun to the beach on Tuesday. Would you like to join us?'

Shaun and I looked at each other and grinned. 'Yes, please!'

'I'd better introduce myself to your mum and check she's all right with that.'

I went to bed that night with stinging knees but a big smile on my face. I had a new best friend. It was going to be the best summer ever.

3

LAUREN

Present day

'Where are you sneaking off to?' Connie asked, falling into step beside me as I headed away from Wildflower Byre – the converted dairy shed where the wedding reception was being held.

We were in the downtime period between the reception and the evening do, and it remained warm and sunny. Some guests were still at their tables, chatting and drinking, while others were playing games in the field near the barn, which Darcie had christened Fun Field. I'd already played the giant versions of Jenga and Connect Four and had even beaten Jonathan in a space hopper race – not particularly digni-fied in a dress – and would have stayed longer, but Debs had appeared. She and Jonathan were acting all flirty with each other, which made me feel a little uncomfortable when they were meant to be getting divorced.

Debs wasn't my favourite person. As far as I was concerned, she hadn't been kind to Sam or Jonathan and I wouldn't have been as forgiving as they both seemed to be. Having said that, I was aware that something bad had happened to her in the past and she was getting help to deal with it and change her ways. I hoped she appreciated how amazing they both were for supporting her through that.

I'd made my excuses to catch my breath and freshen up and think I managed to pull it off without it being obvious that Debs was the reason for my departure.

'I fancied a moment alone to celebrate my space hopper victory,' I told Connie.

'Completely alone or can I join you?'

'You're welcome to join me.'

We smiled at the guests we passed and paused for a moment to watch Josh and Sam posing for photos on the gazebo, commenting on how beautiful Sam looked.

I slipped my arm through Connie's. 'On a scale of one to ten, how proud are you of Josh right now?'

'Twelve,' she said. 'They're so perfect together.'

'Which I knew from Sam's first day.'

'I remember you saying. Josh was in such a bad place back then. I was worried he'd never move on. Time's a great healer.'

'For some.' I hadn't meant to say it. I hoped Connie had been too distracted watching the happy couple to notice.

She narrowed her eyes at me. 'Are you talking about Shaun?'

'No! Of course not! That was a lifetime ago. I was talking in general.' My voice sounded a little too high.

'Hmm. Let's go somewhere quiet and you can tell me why you're still carrying a torch for your ex-husband who walked out on you with no explanation more than two decades ago.'

'Twenty-five years, seven months and three weeks ago.'

Connie's mouth dropped open. 'Oh, Lauren, why didn't you say anything?'

'I'm joking. I have no idea how long it really is.'

She wiggled her fingers, presumably counting in her head. 'Liar!

You know *exactly* how long ago it was. We're going back to the cottage and you're going to explain yourself.'

'You're not going to turn counsellor on me?' Connie was nearing the end of her training and would soon be qualified.

'Unofficially, perhaps. Depends what's going on up there.' She tapped her finger against my forehead.

'You don't want to go rooting around in there. Messy place.' I didn't add that it was full of dark thoughts and regrets. She'd be so hurt if she knew how much I'd shut her out.

'I do,' she said gently. 'Because I'm your sister and I love you.'

I gazed beyond the meadow, beyond the fields, where the sky gave teasers for the sunset ahead. Bands of lemon and gold kissed the horizon. Above them, light grey and white wispy clouds floated lazily in a pale-blue sky. It was so relaxing and peaceful – the perfect place to talk.

Was it finally time to open up to Connie? I hadn't managed to resolve anything by keeping it to myself. Laughter from Josh and Sam reminded me where we were. Maybe it *was* time to start sharing, but not tonight.

'Let's enjoy the wedding today. You can play Freud another time.'

'Lauren!'

'I mean it. Not today.' I sat on the nearest bench.

'Are you sure?' she asked, sitting beside me with a sigh.

'Another day. I promise. Tell me about your wedding plans instead. Have you picked up some inspiration from today?'

'Loads. Alex and I love everything they've done, but it's the same venue and lots of the same guests, so we need to make sure ours is different. We're meeting Natasha next week to go over a few ideas.'

Natasha Kinsella – the mother of rescue centre volunteer Fizz – ran an events management business and had recently partnered with Sam to hold more events at the farm.

Connie was in the middle of running through some of her ideas when something soft brushed against my ankles, making me gasp. I looked down, laughing at Misty-Blue, the farm's grey and white tabby cat, weaving between my legs. I bent down to scratch behind her ears which she took as an invitation to jump up onto the bench between Connie and me.

'Who's beautiful?' I asked her as she nuzzled against my palm before settling in my lap, purring loudly.

'I didn't realise you two were such good friends,' Connie said.

'I've never really been around animals, so it's a friendship that's steadily developed, but we love each other very much now, don't we, Misty-Blue?' I blew her a kiss.

Connie didn't miss a beat. 'Speaking of friendships that have steadily developed…'

'Jonathan? Seriously? Are you ever going to drop this?'

'No. Come on, Lauren! Please tell me you find him the teeniest bit attractive.'

'Okay! I'll admit he's good-looking and maybe there've been a couple of teeny-weeny moments today.' I held my thumb and finger a couple of millimetres apart to indicate exactly what I meant by teeny-weeny. 'But it's only because he scrubs up well, we're at a wedding, and you and Alex have planted the suggestion.'

'Are you going to do anything about it?'

'No, because I think it'll have blown over by tomorrow and, even if it hasn't, I'm pretty sure Jonathan isn't interested in more than friendship.'

'I beg to differ. I've seen the way he looks at you. I reckon he'll make his move tonight.'

The suggestion thrilled and terrified me in equal measures. There'd been nobody since Glen. Seven years in a wilderness of bitterness and celibacy thanks to that man. Home alone in Chapel View on several evenings before Jonathan moved in, I'd started the process of registering on dating apps, wondering if a meaningless one-night stand or a short-term casual fling would be a good way to exorcise my demons, but I'd always come to my senses. It wasn't the way forward for me.

'You're sure it's not your rose-tinted glasses because you're so loved-up?' I asked.

'I'm sure.'

Misty-Blue turned over onto her back and I stroked her warm belly.

'Sorry, Connie, but it's not a good idea. He's still married—'

'But getting divorced.'

'And he's still hurting from that. I like him living with me and I don't want to jeopardise that. What if one of us made a move and it all went wrong?'

'What if one of you made a move and you found your true north?'

'Shaun was my true north.' And I believed I'd been his. It killed me that I didn't know what changed for him.

'I thought Paul was my true north, but I realised he wasn't when I met Alex. Maybe you'll discover that Shaun wasn't really yours either.'

No chance.

Josh and Sam had disappeared into the wildflower meadow with the photographer, but they were back now and walking towards us, Sam holding her train over her arm. All day, she'd glowed with love and happiness, and it warmed my heart.

'Getting some peace and quiet?' Sam asked as she paused beside our bench.

'Recovering from thrashing your dad in a space hopper race,' I said. 'I hope you're going to have a go later.'

'I don't have much choice. As soon as we've finished the photos, Fizz has organised a bride and bridesmaids race. I haven't been on a space hopper since I was a kid.'

'Don't listen to her,' Josh said. 'When Natasha brought the space hoppers over on Friday, the first thing the pair of them did was race each other round the barn.'

Samantha pressed her fingers to his lips. 'Ssh! I was lining up my excuse for losing the race.'

'You don't need an excuse,' Josh said. 'Darcie's got it in the bag. She's like Tigger without a space hopper, so she's going to leave you all for dust.'

They headed off again with the photographer and I smiled at Connie. 'He chose well.'

* * *

While Josh and Sam danced for the first time as husband and wife a little later that evening, I had a lump in my throat and my eyes grew misty. This was ridiculous. I didn't like weddings and I wasn't one for crying, but I'd teared up several times today. It had to be because of what the bride and groom meant to me. Josh was an amazing nephew and Sam was like a daughter to me. I was like a proud parent.

As the track changed, I took a deep breath in an effort to pull myself together.

'Mr and Mrs Alderson would like to welcome the wedding party and other guests to join them on the dance floor,' the DJ announced.

He didn't need to ask twice as several guests eagerly joined them. Jonathan led Sam round the room in the obligatory father/daughter dance. I'd never seen him on a dance floor before and had anticipated an awkward shuffle so was taken aback by his impressive rhythm and how suave he looked as they waltzed together.

Terry – a good friend of Sam's, who she'd adopted as her surrogate grandfather – cut in partway through the track and Jonathan headed off the dance floor. I had no intention of dancing myself, but a light shove in the back propelled me to Jonathan's side. Connie was still dancing with Josh, so that threw me, until I spotted Alex grinning at me from the sidelines. The cheeky meddling pair!

'I was just coming to look for you,' Jonathan said. 'Care to dance?'

'I've got two left feet.'

Jonathan took my hand, stirring my butterflies. 'I don't believe that for a minute.'

My heart raced as he slipped his arm round my waist and waltzed me round the floor. I tried my hardest to keep up with him, but I kept treading on his feet. It didn't seem to bother him as we whirled in fits of giggles. It felt good to laugh like that. Shaun used to make me laugh all the time and I'd been sure that our ability to laugh at whatever life threw at us would help keep us together. It had never been like that with Glen. Looking back, I sometimes wondered if I'd been attracted to him for being the opposite of Shaun.

When Jonathan entered my life, it had been so refreshing to welcome back proper side-aching belly laughter and to feel that there were still good men who could be trusted.

The next few hours whizzed by in a haze of drinking, dancing and chatter. Every so often, I'd catch Jonathan's eye across the room and he'd smile, nod or raise his glass, making me wonder if my sister could be right about us. It could have been the drink – probably was – but the idea of something happening between us was steadily becoming more appealing. I already knew how good it felt to be in Jonathan's arms from a million hugs before tonight and it didn't take much effort to imagine one of those hugs progressing to a kiss. A hot flush raced through me as my mind wandered and I put my half-empty wine glass on the side. I needed some air and a sobering coffee.

Rows of white lights illuminated the pathway from Wildflower Byre. Laughter reached me from Fun Field, which was also well lit so guests could continue to play all evening.

Music followed me from the barn – a slower track I recognised but couldn't place. I hummed softly as I approached the benches in front of the wedding gazebo. A couple were slow-dancing in the aisle and I smiled as I slowed my pace, not wanting to disturb their romantic moment.

A few more paces and my smile slipped as butterflies swirled in my stomach. It was Jonathan. With Debs.

I hesitated, unsure as to whether to flee back to the barn or sneak past and hope they wouldn't spot me.

Debs tilted her head up towards Jonathan and my breath caught in my throat. No way. They weren't going to…

But they did. He slowly lowered his head and their lips met. I half-expected them to pull apart and laugh about it but their bodies pressed closer together as the kiss intensified. I clapped my hand across my mouth, barely able to believe what I was seeing. It was meant to be over. How many hours had I spent with Jonathan while we discussed divorce details and his plans for the future? A future without Debs in it.

Unable to watch any longer, I hung my head and scurried towards the holiday cottage. So much for Jonathan having a thing for me. He clearly still held a torch for his soon-to-be-ex-wife.

Not that I had any right to pass judgement on that when I still held one for Shaun.

4

SAMANTHA

Aware of being watched, I opened my eyes and smiled at Josh, propped up on his elbow beside me.

'Good morning, Mrs Alderson,' he said, his eyes sparkling in the dappled light as he pushed a lock of hair back from my face.

'Mrs Alderson.' I sighed contentedly. 'I wonder how long it'll take me to get used to being called that.'

Josh had asked whether I wanted to change my name when we married, but being at Hedgehog Hollow with him had been all about new beginnings for me and it felt right to embrace the future with a new name.

'Considering how quickly you perfected your new signature, I'm guessing not long. So, how excited are you about our honeymoon?'

'Off the scale! I can't believe we'll be in Tanzania tomorrow. Do you know what I'm looking forward to the most?'

'I reckon it's a toss-up between lions and rhinos.'

'Nope. I'm most looking forward to slowing down and spending some quality time with you.'

'Aw, Sammie.' His lips lightly brushed mine.

'I mean it. Since we met, it's been one thing after another – setting up the rescue centre, your dad and Beth moving in, Chloe turning up with Samuel, all the problems with the Grimes family, taking in Phoebe and Darcie and planning our wedding. Add in the demands of hundreds of hedgehogs and hoglets and we've barely had a minute to ourselves. This is such a gift.'

'I feel the same. And you know what else is a gift? Being alone right now. Listen to that.'

I cocked my head and listened. Absolute silence. We'd stayed overnight in the smallest holiday cottage – Meadow View – so we could have an undisturbed night and a lie-in this morning while Dad saw to the hedgehogs.

'Peace and quiet,' I whispered.

'I'm thinking we should take advantage of that. What do you say?'

'I say you have the best ideas.'

* * *

Stepping out of Meadow View shortly before eleven, blinking in the sunshine, felt so indulgent.

Phoebe and Darcie had gone to the small coastal resort of Fellingthorpe for the day with Paul, Beth, Archie and Lottie. I'd been tempted to join them, but the packing needed to be done and there were a few administrative loose ends I wanted to tie up before we left.

Immediate family and close friends had stayed in the holiday cottages but most of the cars were gone from the parking area, which surprised me. Last night, Rich and Dave had told me they'd be spending the morning in Fun Field, but maybe they'd had their fill of games last night.

'I'll take this lot over to the farmhouse if you want to see how your dad's doing,' Josh said as we approached the barn. He hitched our overnight bag onto his shoulder and relieved me of the carry cases containing my wedding dress and his suit.

A burst of laughter reached us through the open window by the sink and Josh and I smiled at each other.

'Sounds like Dad and Lauren are having fun,' I said.

But when I stepped into the barn moments later, it wasn't Lauren who was with Dad.

'Mum!'

I pictured them slow-dancing then kissing last night and now they were huddled together over the treatment table, laughing. Curiosity burned inside me as to what, if anything, was going on between them. How could I broach that subject? *I saw you two getting very close last night. Anything you'd like to tell me?* Perhaps I could channel Chloe and get straight to the point: *Did you two have sex last night and was it a one-off or are you trying again?*

'You've got to see this,' Mum said, beckoning me over.

'New admission this morning,' Dad announced. 'It's pretty special.'

There was a large plastic crate in the middle of the table. As I stepped closer, I gasped.

'Oh, my gosh!'

'Isn't it the most adorable thing?' Mum gushed.

Lying on her side in among the folds of a tartan picnic blanket was a black cat with five tiny hoglets suckling on her.

'They were brought in together?' I asked.

Dad nodded. 'Barney brought them in. He heard a cat mewing in the stables this morning and this is what he found in among the hay. He had a quick look round and couldn't see a mother hedgehog or any kittens but Fizz, Yasmin, Rich and Dave followed him back to the farm to do a proper search. They said to apologise for not saying goodbye.'

'Aw, bless them. I wondered where everyone had gone.' Barney was Fizz's brother and owner of Bumblebee Barn – a farm which had been passed down through the generations.

I couldn't peel my eyes away from the crate. I'd once read about a case of a cat adopting orphaned hoglets, but this really was the most incredible sight.

'Have you had a chance to check them over?' I asked.

'Yes, and the cat. They all look healthy.'

The cat was watching me through the most beautiful yellow eyes.

'Who's being a good mum?' I asked, stroking her ears back. 'Thank you for looking after the hoglets. What's your name?'

'We thought you'd like to name her,' Mum said.

'Luna,' I declared. 'Those beautiful eyes make me think of the moon.'

'It's perfect for her,' Mum agreed. 'We've named the hoglets, but you can change the names if you don't like them.'

'We decided to go for a wedding theme in your honour,' Dad said. 'There are three girls and two boys.'

'The girls are Confetti, Lacey and Bridie,' Mum said.

'The boys were harder,' Dad added, 'so please forgive the lack of creativity. We've got Whisky and Groom.'

'Very cute.' I sat down. 'I wonder what happened to Luna's kittens.'

Dad shrugged. 'Could have been anything from stillbirths to an animal attack. Even though she's being a great mum to the hoglets, she might have rejected her own kittens. We'll probably never know unless they find something at the farm.'

The hoglets appeared to have finished their feeds and Luna was licking the belly of one of the girls.

'It's like she knows exactly what to do,' I marvelled.

'She must be part cat, part hedgehog,' Dad joked. 'We'll help them with the toileting now. Grab some gloves, Debs. Time to get hands-on.'

Although Mum didn't look disgusted by the idea, I thought I'd better give her a get-out clause. 'I can do it if you prefer.'

'Thanks, but I'm happy to give it a go. I learned loads about the adults from you in the summer and your dad's been educating me on hoglets this morning. I'm so impressed with everything you do here.'

'Thank you. You're welcome any time you'd like to learn more.'

I watched for a few minutes while Dad showed Mum what to do. It was weird seeing them together like this – so close and clearly enjoying each other's company – after a lifetime of tension and hostility.

Last night, I'd pushed their kiss out of my mind and focused on celebrating my wedding. Mum and Dad were adults, capable of making their own decisions and responsible for their own mistakes, if indeed last night had been a mistake. Looking at them together now, it appeared to be far from it. If they had decided to try again, I knew I should be happy for them, but I couldn't help feeling a niggle in the pit of my stomach.

'Looks like everything's under control here so I guess there's no excuse not to crack on with the packing.' I pushed the chair back to murmurs of seeing me later for lunch.

Josh was approaching the barn as I stepped outside, and I steered him round to the back of the farmhouse.

'Mum and Dad are really cosy and I don't know what to make of it,' I blurted out as soon as we sat down on Thomas's bench.

Misty-Blue emerged from the meadow and sprinted up the garden towards us, leaping onto the bench.

'Do you need to make something of it?' Josh asked as our cat settled across my knee.

'It's strange seeing them being friendly, although it's also strange not having Mum snapping at me all the time. I just...' I shrugged. 'I don't know. If they're trying again, I'm not sure whether that's a good or bad thing.'

'They might not be trying again. We saw them kissing last night and we saw them go off together, but we don't know what happened after that and probably never will. It could have been a combination of the drink and the emotions of seeing their only child getting married that drew them together for one night only. It could have been a for-old-time's-sake-never-to-be-repeated night of passion. Or they might have made a coffee, sobered up and talked.'

I'd been focusing on stroking Misty-Blue as Josh spoke, but he tilted my chin so I had to look him in the eyes. 'If they did try again, what's the worst thing that could happen?'

'She could break Dad's heart all over again.'

'And he could break hers. They've got to make their own decisions and, if they go for it and it doesn't work, they'll get over it in time and they'll move onto something so much better, like we both did.'

I smiled at him. 'You're right. It's pointless me stressing about something that may or may not have happened. I should focus on how lovely it is to see them together without the tension.'

'Cup of tea?' Josh asked, standing up.

'Sounds like the perfect excuse to put off the packing for a bit longer.'

'Back soon.' He bent down and gave me a gentle kiss. 'Try not to worry about your dad. Focus on how amazing yesterday was and how fantastic our honeymoon's going to be.'

Feeling comforted by Josh's words, I relaxed against the bench and looked towards the wildflower meadow. I loved the meadow all year round, but spring brought such an abundance of colours. Rhys Michaels, a landscape gardener from Whitsborough Bay, took care of the grounds including the maintenance of the meadow. I'd asked him if he could add even more colour to it without straying too far from what Thomas and Gwendoline had originally sown. He'd mainly stuck to the same plants but in greater concentration. There were more pink, purple and blue flowers than last year, which contrasted beautifully with the yellows and whites. My favourite was the cornflower – such a rich majestic blue – but I also loved the beautiful simplicity of butter-cups and daisies.

Butterflies and bees flitted between the blooms, and I could hear the gentle chirp of birds in the trees. I knew I was going to love Tanzania, but I couldn't imagine feeling happier or more content anywhere in the world than I did when sitting on Thomas's bench, stroking Misty-Blue, gazing out at the meadow and knowing all the people I loved were close by.

'I hope you enjoyed the wedding,' I whispered to Thomas and Gwendoline. 'Wish you'd been here in person, but I felt you in spirit.'

Josh returned a few minutes later with tea in my favourite hedgehog mug and a basket of warm croissants.

'Thought you might be hungry,' he said, placing them down beside me. 'I've got to love you and leave you.'

'You've been called out?'

'Emergency surgery on a dog. Not sure how long I'll be but I'll text you when I'm leaving. What will you do?'

'Enjoy my breakfast and then I should probably see if I can find the others before starting on the packing. Was anybody in the house?'

'No. Completely empty. See you later.' He brushed his lips against mine, helped himself to a croissant and disappeared round the side of the house.

By the time I'd polished off a couple of croissants, Misty-Blue decided she'd had enough attention and jumped down from the bench. As she weaved her way back into the meadow, my thoughts turned to our new feline arrival in the barn. I knew that Barney had a couple of cats at his farm but it sounded as though Luna was a stray. Would Barney want her back or could she make her home here? Misty-Blue had been a stray when Thomas found her in one of the barns here and she'd soon become domesticated. Could Luna do the same? I liked the idea of a second cat at the farm, and I could imagine the squeals of delight from Darcie and Phoebe if we had another pet. The pair of them were animal-mad.

I returned my mug and the basket to the kitchen and set off towards Fun Field in search of my family. Beyond the barn, I spotted Lauren sitting on the front bench by the wedding gazebo with her back to me.

'I was beginning to think you'd all been abducted by aliens,' I said, approaching her.

She turned and smiled. 'Your parents are in the rescue centre and Chloe and her family are playing Jenga, boys versus girls. Happy first day of married life.'

'Thank you.' I sat beside her. 'Did you enjoy yourself yesterday?'

'Best wedding I've been to. It made me very happy seeing you and Josh getting hitched, and don't forget who called it about you two.'

'I won't. And I'm very grateful to you for not setting us up when neither of us were ready, even though I know you were very tempted.'

'You can't force these things. Sometimes the timing isn't right and sometimes the person isn't right, no matter how much we wish it was different.'

There was more than a hint of melancholy to her words, and I pictured her expression last night when she saw my parents kissing. Was she thinking of Dad and her? Just like earlier in the barn, I had no idea how to broach it. *Josh and I were hiding behind the flowers last night and we saw what happened. Do you fancy my dad?*

'You've got the perfect set-up here for functions,' Lauren said, changing the subject. 'Should be a great success. Will Connie's wedding be the next event, or do you think you'll try to squeeze in others?'

'We'll start advertising when we're back from our honeymoon. We might pick up a few parties, but I'd imagine any wedding enquiries will be for next year or even the one after. And, of course, we have the Family Fun Day at the end of June.'

My stomach lurched at the thought of it. I'd had exciting plans for last year's event, especially with it being our opening weekend, but the arson attack had scuppered them. This year I'd wanted to go bigger and better but, with a wedding to plan and an unexpected extension to the family, the Family Fun Day had shifted right down my priority list. If we ended up simply copying what we'd done last year, it would still be a good event and a reasonable fundraiser, but it had much greater potential.

'So much to do, so little time,' I said, rolling my eyes at Lauren.

'Is there anything I can do while you're away?' she asked.

'No, but I appreciate the offer. The basics are sorted and I'll catch up with Natasha when I'm back. She's the events expert, so I'm sure she'll have some ideas for extra things we can do. I'll pack a notebook and do some planning on the flight.'

A manly cheer drifted over from Fun Field.

'Sounds like the men have won Jenga,' Lauren said.

'Chloe's not going to like that. I can pretty much guarantee she'll be demanding a re-match right now.'

'You two seem to be getting on well at the moment.'

'We are. She's made a big effort with everyone recently, which I've really appreciated, and I think James has too. They seem a lot happier. If she starts being demanding and whiny again, I'll tell her.'

'Good. Keep her in line, Sergeant Sam.'

I laughed as Lauren saluted at me. 'So what's your plan for the rest of the weekend?'

She shrugged. 'I was planning to help your dad with the hedgehogs today, but he's got your mum so I'm superfluous to requirements. I might go to the garden centre for some hanging baskets and come back for your dad later.'

'A trip to the garden centre sounds lovely.'

'And then it's back to college tomorrow and the *big meeting*.' There was clear disgust in her tone as she uttered those last two words.

'What's the *big meeting*?' I asked, emphasising the last two words in the same way she had.

'Oh, it's nothing.' She wafted her hand. 'We had some consultants in before Easter and they're presenting their grand proposal to the staff tomorrow. Tell you what, there'd better be biscuits – good ones covered in thick chocolate – 'cos I'll be fuming if I have to stay late for some weak coffee and a couple of plain digestives.'

'What have they consulted on?'

'God knows!'

'But you're head of department. Weren't you involved?'

'Nope. None of the heads were, which has been a right bone of contention. It'll be a launch of some new values or ways of working, messing with what isn't broken.' She sighed as she stood up. 'I'll say goodbye and get to Bloomsberry's. Can you ask your dad to give me a ring when he wants picking up?'

I stood up too. 'I'll drop him back at yours later. You relax and enjoy the rest of your day.'

We hugged goodbye.

'Welcome to the family, by the way,' she said, stepping back. 'You were already part of it but it's legal now. You're bound to us forever, God help you.'

'Can't think of another family I'd rather be part of.'

I watched her wander over to the holiday cottages, thinking it was a little strange that she wasn't going to pop into the barn herself to say goodbye to Dad. Or was I reading something into that? As for that consultancy thing, she might have casually dismissed it, but her voice was a little higher-pitched than usual and I sensed she was worried about it. I was about to run after her to check she really was all right when Terry pulled into the farmyard.

I'd met Terry a year ago at the Family Fun Day when he brought in an injured hedgehog and, after he brought in several more admissions, a friendship built. Aged eighty now, he had no family, so he'd adopted us and, with no grandparents between us, Josh and I had adopted him too.

After the Grimes family emptied the charity's bank account over Christmas, the community rallied round and were exceptionally generous with their donations of food and money. The local newspaper set up a crowdfunding campaign but what made the biggest difference was the exceptional generosity of Terry, who replaced the stolen £30,000, telling us the rescue centre was the named beneficiary in his will and we might as well make use of the funds when we needed them.

'Time for a cup of tea?' I asked when he got out of his car.

'I'm not stopping. I'm on me way back from t' beach with our Wilbur. I wanted to say I had a right good time yesterday. Thanks for making me part of your special day.'

'Aw, Terry, it wouldn't have been the same without you. I'm glad you enjoyed it.'

'I've got a request for your honeymoon. If you can get on your email, can you send me a photo of some elephants? They were one of Gwendoline's favourite animals.'

It had taken a bit of coaxing, but Terry had finally admitted last year that he'd been in love with Gwendoline since school but she'd only been interested in friendship and then she'd met Thomas, her soulmate. Terry had never found anyone who compared to Gwendoline so had remained unmarried. I loved hearing his stories about her as a girl and young woman and nearly all of them included animals. Setting up a large-scale hedgehog rescue centre had been her dream, which Josh and I had fulfilled.

'Bit bigger than hedgehogs,' I said.

He smiled. 'Just a tad. She'd always dreamed of seeing elephants in t' wild but it weren't to be. She drew a picture of one at school once. She were always getting told off for drawing when we were meant to be doing our sums but she hated maths. Teacher ripped t' elephant out and chucked it in t' bin but I took it out and gave 'er it back and said it were right good. She told me I could keep it.'

'Have you still got it?'

'Nah. Don't know what happened to it.'

'Well, I'll be sure to get you plenty of elephant photos.'

I hugged Terry and waved him off, smiling. A passion for elephants? How lovely to learn something else about Gwendoline.

5

LAUREN

Before I pulled off the farm track and onto the road, I glanced in the rear-view mirror and sighed. I probably shouldn't have driven off without saying goodbye to Jonathan, but it was done now. No point sweating over it. Sam would pass the message on and it'd do me good to get some space to clear my head.

I pulled onto the road and drove towards Bloomsberry's. Yes, space was definitely a good plan to give myself a damn good talking-to. Starting right now.

'You're a fifty-one-year-old woman who is happy in her own company and doesn't need a man in her life,' I muttered. 'The last thing you need is a stupid crush on one of your best friends. Get over it. Now!'

I wasn't even sure it was a crush. I wasn't sure what it was. I'd definitely felt something when I saw Jonathan kissing Debs last night, like a punch in the gut, but was that because I was jealous or because I was worried for a friend? That was the quandary that had kept me tossing and turning most of the night.

As I neared the garden centre, ELO's 'Mr Blue Sky' came on the radio. If ever there was a piece of music designed to make the world seem a brighter place, that was the tune, despite it reminding me of

Shaun. I turned it up, wound the window down and sang at the top of my voice – very likely with all the wrong words. Just like in the song, the sun was shining, it was a beautiful day and I was going to stop behaving like a jealous teenager. So that last bit definitely wasn't in the lyrics, but who was around to quibble?

Arriving at Bloomsberry's, I reversed into a parking space alongside a swanky convertible, music still blaring. A man with messy blond hair was sitting in the driver's seat and, although he was wearing sunglasses, I could feel him staring at me. Clearly he didn't appreciate good music played loud. Sighing inwardly, I buzzed the windows up and turned off the ignition, psyching myself up for a lecture on noise pollution.

'Not waiting until the end?' he asked when I exited the car.

'The end of what?'

'This.' He smiled at me as he pressed a button on his steering wheel to increase the volume of his music. He was listening to the same radio station.

'Great track,' he said. 'But infinitely better at the volume you had it.'

I returned his smile. 'I agree.'

'Don't you just love the orchestral bit at the end?' he added, his smile widening to reveal a single dimple on his right cheek.

'It's all good. Snapped me right out of a bad mood just now.' I closed my door and locked it, frowning. 'Sorry. Bit of oversharing with a complete stranger. Don't normally do that.'

'Then let's not be strangers. I'm Riley. Pleased to meet you.'

'Lauren.'

'Brilliant! We're not strangers anymore. And if it helps, I'll even things out. I was seriously pissed off earlier, but "Mr Blue Sky" has lifted my mood too.'

The track slowed. 'Your favourite bit's coming up, so I'll leave you to listen in peace. Perhaps we'll meet again by the geraniums.'

'Perhaps we will. Bye, Lauren.'

A few paces past the car, I turned and shouted back. 'Riley! Turn it right up. Life's too short for quiet music.'

Next moment, the car park was filled with choral and orchestral melodies. Full volume was definitely better.

* * *

My flatbed trolley creaked under the weight of several sets of ceramic pots, a couple of bags of compost and enough plants to fill a green-house. I'd only come in to buy a pair of pre-prepared hanging baskets but, with an afternoon alone looming ahead of me, I had decided to keep busy by making my own and adding some new pots to the back garden. My debit card was going to take a bigger hammering than planned, but it was worth it. I always felt relaxed and at peace with the world while doing a spot of gardening. Mum had been delighted that I loved flowers but, of course, lectured me for not wearing gloves. *Why do you have to get mud all over your hands, Lauren? You'll ruin your nails.*

I paused by a water feature in the middle of a large round plinth, surrounded by garden ornaments. They weren't to my taste – far too cutesy – but I could imagine Sam loving the hedgehog ones.

'We meet again.'

Riley – the blond man from the car park – was at the other side of the water feature, smiling at me. He'd pushed his sunglasses onto the top of his head, revealing the most startlingly bright blue eyes, like Daniel Craig's, although nothing else about him resembled the Bond actor. He was tall, but not as tall as Jonathan – probably just over six foot – and slim, his build more reminiscent of a runner.

'Not quite the geraniums,' he said. 'But hedgehogs are good. Are they both going home with you?'

I glanced down at the stone hedgehogs, one in each hand, and shrugged. 'My nephew's wife runs a hedgehog rescue centre. I thought she might like one, but I can't decide which. Not really my thing.'

He seemed to take that as an invitation to scoot round the water feature to join me. As he did, a smell from my childhood hit me with a wave of nostalgia. Was that rhubarb and custards? Dad used to love them, before his only love became the bottle. We always took them on our bike rides.

Riley cocked his head from side to side, making tutting sounds as he surveyed the two hedgehogs.

'It's going to have to be both. It would be cruel to separate them.'

'You're no help!'

'I mean it! Look! They've bonded already. They're kissing.'

I glanced down at the hedgehogs. Although they were set in different poses, they both had their noses raised and the way I was holding them did look like they were kissing.

'They're destined to be together,' he added.

I carefully placed them both inside one of the pots. 'I can't believe you've just made me feel guilty about rejecting an inanimate object.'

He bent down and covered the pair's ears. 'Ssh! They'll hear you and you'll upset them even more.'

I couldn't help laughing at that.

'No trolley?' I asked. Unless he'd stayed in his car way beyond the end of the ELO track, he'd spent a long time in the garden centre without buying anything.

'Not today. Just browsing.'

'You have better restraint than me. I love a garden centre and especially this one. Would you believe I had no plans to come here today? One heaving trolley later...'

'But just think how amazing your garden's going to look and how happy your nephew's wife will be with her pair of deeply-in-love hedgehogs.'

'Whatever you say. I'd best get to the till before I spend any more. Nice to see you again.'

'Likewise.' He fished into his jacket pocket and held out a cellophane bag. 'Sweet for the road?'

I grinned. 'Rhubarb and custards! I thought I could smell them.'

'That'd be me. They're my kryptonite.'

'Thank you.' I popped one into my mouth.

'I probably should have paid for them first,' he said.

'Riley!'

He burst out laughing. 'Sorry! It's okay. I know the owners. We're not about to be arrested. They're just through that door if you fancy your own packet. They've got sherbet lemons too. Not my kryptonite but still a weakness. Three-for-two on bags of sweets just now. I spotted the sign when I got mine.'

'When you stole yours.'

'To be paid for later. Tell you what. How about I join you at the till? You can be my witness as I pay for these and, in payback for making you an accessory to my criminal activities, I'll help you load that lot into your car.'

It was on the tip of my tongue to say no, but I glanced down at the pots. Sod it! They were heavy. I'd loaded them onto the trolley and I'd have them to unload at the other end, so if some petty criminal with bright blue eyes and one cute dimple wanted to waste ten minutes of his life doing my heavy lifting, he could be my guest.

I wasn't sure why Riley was being so friendly. Men didn't normally strike up conversations with me, which suited me just fine because I wasn't interested. Connie always attracted attention. Even though we aren't identical twins, we do look very similar. On a night out with Connie once, after she'd turned down a third unwanted advance, I commented on how odd it was that she was frequently approached and I never was. She found my observation hilarious. 'Hmm, let's see, could that be something to do with the enormous *fuck off* you have tattooed across your forehead?'

My sister's blunt response had shocked me, partly because swear words never passed her lips and partly because I realised it was the truth. I couldn't help it. I'd put up a self-protection wall after Shaun, which I'd built even higher after Glen, and I wasn't willing to take it down. And if I ever did, it certainly wouldn't be for some sleazoid who thought it was acceptable to interrupt two women when they were deep in conversation.

Maybe Riley's dark sunglasses had stopped him seeing my special 'tattoo' when I'd parked next to him. Maybe he was just bored. And if he hadn't picked up on the *don't touch, don't even look* vibes and was hoping to get my phone number at the end of this, he was going to be sorely disappointed.

'Were you browsing for anything in particular?' I asked Riley as we waited in the queue. 'Other than sweets to slip into your pocket.'

He laughed at my dig. 'You know I said earlier that I was pissed off but ELO lifted me? I've recently moved back to the area and I'm looking for a short-term let. I had two viewings lined up today, but both were a waste of time. One landlord wanted a year's rental, which the agency had failed to tell me, and the other had already found a tenant and not bothered to tell the agency, so I found myself at a loose end and decided to kill some time.'

'Sorry to hear about the houses. That's a pain.'

'What about you?' he asked. 'Why were you in a mood?'

'It's complicated. Combination of being worried a good friend might have made a big mistake and dreading some crappy work thing tomorrow.'

'Ah! The dreaded "crappy work thing". I feel your pain.'

We'd reached the front of the queue.

'You first,' I insisted. 'I need to make sure you really do pay.'

Riley rolled his eyes at me, stepped forward and placed the open bag of sweets on the counter.

'Hi, Cassie, just these please.'

The sales assistant – a curvy white-haired woman – squealed. 'Riley! So the rumours are true!'

She dashed from round the till and flung herself at him. 'I hope you're back for good this time.'

'I am. Especially if there's more hugs like that on offer.'

She laughed as she took her place behind the till once more. 'For you, always.'

Riley handed her a twenty-pound note but she batted it away. 'Don't be daft.'

'I insist. I want to pay for these.'

With a sigh and a shake of her head, she scanned them in and took the money before handing over his change. He lifted up a charity box chained to the till and read the label, glancing at me. 'Hedgehog Hollow. Is this your nephew's wife's place?'

'It is.'

'In that case...'

He dropped the coins into the box then folded up the ten-pound note and shoved that in too. I appreciated the generosity, but not if he was doing it to impress me. Then he made me laugh again.

'It's for the upkeep of Hogmeo and Hogliet there. I feel guilty for adding in a couple of extra mouths to feed. Right! Let's get you through the till and packed up.'

'It's going to be easier if I come round with the scanner,' Cassie said. She lifted it off its perch and wandered round the trolley, zapping each item. She barely paused for breath the whole time with compliments about my choices, interspersed with gardening tips. I couldn't decide if she was always like that or whether she was trying to impress Riley.

When they hugged, I'd noticed he wasn't wearing a wedding band. I reckoned he was about my age and Cassie had to be at least fifteen years older than him, not that age should make any difference. And why was I even having this conversation in my head? I'd never see Riley again after he'd loaded up my car, so what did I care?

A little later, I closed the boot while Riley wheeled the flatbed to the trolley bay.

'Thanks for your help,' I said when he reappeared.

'Absolute pleasure.'

I braced myself, ready to say no if he asked for my number but, instead, he opened his car door and I felt surprisingly disappointed. So he really was just being friendly. No agenda at all. Refreshing but... strange. Definitely strange.

'Hope the "crappy work thing" isn't as bad as you're anticipating,' he said, sliding into the driver's seat and closing the door.

'Zero chance of that.' I clambered into my car, started the engine and wound the window down. 'Thanks again for your help today.'

'Thank you for humouring me with the hedgehogs. As I said, they were destined to be together.'

'I'm sure Sam will love them.'

'Lauren?'

'Yes?' I inwardly sighed. This was it. This was the agenda moment. What would he go for? Number? Drinks? A meal? All a bit clichéd.

'You've got great taste in music, plants and sweets. You've made me laugh today and I think I did the same for you. Neither of us were planning on coming here today but we both showed up in the same place at the same time after being pulled out of a downer by the same piece of music. What if, just like Hogmeo and Hogliet, we were destined to meet?'

'Wouldn't that be something?' I said, readying myself to say no to whatever he suggested next.

'It would. And if it's destiny, then it'll bring us together again, won't it? So I may see you around or I may not. Destiny will decide.'

Wow! He was deadly serious. If I'd been interested in a relationship, I might have protested and claimed destiny had already done her bit, but this was perfect. No awkward moment while I turned him down. And the chances of bumping into each other again were so slim that we could both walk away, dignity intact.

'Let's do that,' I said, smiling.

'Enjoy your rhubarb and custards.'

'I forgot to buy some.'

'You'll find a packet in one of the pots.'

'Riley!'

He laughed. 'Don't worry. I'm going back in to pay for it.'

'Pleased to hear it. I could do without being pulled over by the police on the way home. Thank you for the help, the sweets and the donation to Hedgehog Hollow. I hope you manage to find somewhere to rent.'

He held up his crossed fingers and smiled at me.

With a wave, I pulled out of the space and left the car park, chuckling to myself as I caught sight of him in my rear-view mirror exiting his car and waving his wallet in the air to prove he was going back in to pay for my sweets.

I was still smiling when I pulled onto the drive at Chapel View. That had been an unexpectedly pleasant hour. I didn't believe in all that rubbish about destiny – especially after what happened with Shaun and me – but I couldn't help wondering whether I would bump into Riley again. It wasn't an altogether unpleasant thought.

6

SAMANTHA

'I wish I could come,' Darcie said, snuggling up to me on the sofa on Monday evening. 'I'll miss you.'

I brushed her dark curls back from her face and kissed her forehead. 'Aw, sweetheart, I'll miss you too. But I don't think I can squeeze you into my suitcase.'

'Will you blow a kiss to the animals for me?'

'I'll blow them lots of kisses.'

'Princess Darcie's bath's ready!' Phoebe announced, poking her head round the lounge door. 'And your new boat's ready for launch.'

With a final squeeze, Darcie clambered off the sofa and ran to Phoebe. I smiled as I heard them clattering up the stairs.

'Thanks for taking them out today,' I said to Beth and Paul, who'd already settled their two to sleep.

'It was a pleasure,' Beth said. 'They were such a help with Archie and Lottie, so it was the most relaxing trip to the beach I've ever had.'

Josh entered the room with a tray of mugs and distributed the drinks before sitting beside me.

'I know you said there was no rush to make a decision,' Beth said, 'but we had a good chat about your offer while we were out.'

Dave's team had recently completed the refurbishment of Alder

Lea, the house at Josh's veterinary practice. The intention had always been to offer it to Paul and Beth, but we hadn't wanted to do that until Paul was well on his way to full recovery in case they took it as a hint that we wanted them out. With Paul greatly improved, we'd put it to them a couple of days before the wedding and told them to discuss it while we were on honeymoon. Josh had also offered his dad a position as a veterinary nurse, with a phased return to suit him.

'We'd love to move into Alder Lea,' Paul said. 'Thank you for that and for everything you've done for us over the past year.'

'Good decision,' Josh said, looking relieved. 'When are you thinking?'

'After half-term?' Beth suggested. 'If that's okay with you and with Dave.'

'I'm sure that'll be fine,' I said. 'It's going to be so strange not having you all here.'

'It's going to be strange not being here.' Beth's voice caught in her throat and I noticed her eyes glistening.

'What about the job?' Josh asked.

Paul put his hand out palm down and rocked it, indicating it could go either way. 'I'm interested, but can we revisit that after we've settled in? I'm not sure how much the move will take out of me.'

'The offer's open as long as you need,' Josh said. 'It's got to be the right time for you.'

'We're so grateful to you both,' Beth said. 'Any time you need a favour, no matter how big, we're on it.'

'There's no need,' I said.

'Oh, I don't know.' Josh's eyes sparkled mischievously. 'By half-term, you'll have been here for thirteen months. I reckon that's thirteen months of cleaning out hedgehog crates.'

'It's the poop soup that's the most special,' I added. Some of our hedgehogs were particularly messy and did dirty protests in their food and water bowls, which led to an attractive concoction we referred to as poop soup – a term which reduced Darcie to hysterical laughter every time she heard it.

'Honestly, if that's what you wanted, that's what we'd do, ten times over,' Beth said.

I smiled at them both. 'I think we'll settle for making sure you come back to visit us regularly.'

'Try and keep us away.'

* * *

'That's such good news about your dad and Beth,' I said to Josh as we got ready for bed a couple of hours later.

'I'm glad they've made their decision before we go away. It would have been at the back of my mind otherwise.'

'I thought they might say no.'

'Me too. I thought his stubborn streak would kick in.'

We clambered into bed and I snuggled up to Josh, resting my head on his chest. 'Do you feel like things with your dad are finally back to how they were before?'

Josh and Paul had been exceptionally close, working in partnership at the practice, until Paul's long-term affair with Beth came to light when she was pregnant with Archie. Josh severed all ties after that and it was only when Beth turned up at the farm last year, pregnant with Lottie, that he discovered his dad had non-Hodgkin lymphoma and needed a stem cell transplant. Being back in touch had initially been rocky, but they'd worked through it.

'I don't think it could ever be how it was before,' Josh said after a moment's contemplation. 'It's a good relationship now, but it's different. I can't forget what he did or erase the pain he caused, but I'm happy to make a fresh start. A bit like you are with your mum.'

The mention of Mum made me think of Lauren and whether she was upset about seeing Mum and Dad so cosy together.

'Lauren didn't seem her usual perky self today,' I said. 'Did she mention anything to you about a big meeting at work tomorrow?'

'No, why?'

'I'm not sure. She mentioned it then brushed it off, but I got the impression she's worried.'

Josh hugged me to his side. 'If she wants to talk, she's got Mum, but I'm sure she'll be fine. You know Auntie Lauren. Nothing's a drama and she takes everything in her stride.' He kissed the top of my head. 'We'd better get some sleep. Early start in the morning. I love you.'

'I love you too.'

We switched off our bedside lamps and settled down to sleep, but I couldn't shift the feeling that all wasn't well in Lauren's world. She was loud and confident and always on the go. Sitting on a bench on her own, staring into space, wasn't her style. But as Josh said, she had Connie to talk to. They were close. Connie would be there for her if there was a problem.

7

LAUREN

My Tuesday so far had been the day from hell, and I still had that blasted meeting to face in half an hour.

Ninety-five per cent of the time, I loved my job. It played to my planning and organising skills as well as my ability to deal with the unexpected, and this morning had certainly thrown the latter at me. One of the hairdressing tutors had taken ill in the middle of an assessed lesson, then a window had shattered in the childcare classroom. I'd calmly dealt with both situations, but the afternoon had been full of the five per cent crap that I hated: breaking up a fight, acting as mediator between a couple of bickering students, and dealing with a tutor complaint.

'You look like you could do with a stiff drink,' said Alice, dumping some files on her desk.

I'd interviewed Alice at the same time I interviewed Sam for the role of health and social care tutor. If I'd had two roles, I'd have recruited them both so, when Sam left to run Hedgehog Hollow full-time, I'd gone straight back to Alice.

'I could do with several,' I admitted. 'Seriously grim day.'

'Soon be home time. And I have news. I've just walked past the hall and they were putting out biscuits.'

'Interesting. What type?'

'Posh ones from Bloomsberry's.'

At the mention of the garden centre, my heart did an unexpected leap and I pictured Riley standing by the water feature, those brilliant blue eyes fixed on mine. Where had that come from?

'You're not just saying that to cheer me up?' I asked Alice, trying to dislodge the image of Riley.

'Hand on heart. I recognised the boxes because they're my favourites.'

'Things are looking up! Thanks, Alice.'

Sure enough, when we headed into the hall twenty minutes later, we were greeted by plates full of chocolate and shortbread biscuits from Bloomsberry's. I helped myself to a strong coffee and three biscuits then Alice and I shuffled into a row alongside some of the rest of my team. The large screen on the stage was ready for a presentation but was blank at the moment.

The college principal, Judith Janis, stepped up to the stage to a collective hush from the audience.

'Good evening,' she said. 'I hope you all enjoyed the bank holiday weekend.' She smiled as she looked round the room, her expression giving away nothing as to whether we were about to receive good news or bad. She apologised for the intrusion on our time and positioned the evening as the outcome of the consultancy visit and an opportunity to ask questions.

She paused and looked down for a moment, as though composing herself, and I had a feeling in my gut that I wasn't going to like what she said next.

'As some of you are aware, I've experienced a few health challenges over the past year and the upshot of that is that I'm taking early retirement. This term will be my last.'

A collective gasp went round the room, along with several murmurs of disappointment. Judith had worked at Reddfield TEC for about twenty years and had been the principal for the past eight, and a damn good one at that. I'd be sorry to see her go.

'That's not the only change. From September this year, Reddfield TEC will officially be part of the Think Future Skills Academy and—'

The shocked response stopped Judith in her tracks. Alice glanced up at me, an obvious question in her expression: *Did you know?*

I shook my head. 'I had no idea,' I mouthed to her and the rest of my staff. But I was fuming. A takeover? Where had that sprung from and why had I found out at the same time as everyone else?

'Can we have some quiet?' Judith called.

It took her four attempts to bring the room to order and I couldn't help feeling sorry for the poor woman. She was likely just the messenger here.

'Thank you,' she said. 'I know that's a shock.'

'We didn't even know the TEC was up for sale,' someone shouted.

'I appreciate that and I understand there will be many questions but that's why we're gathered here tonight. It's timely for me to hand over to the person who'll be able to explain what this all means. Please welcome the transition director of the Think Future Skills Academy, Mr Riley Berry.'

A blond-haired man in a sharp suit ran up the steps and joined Judith on the stage, and my heart leapt into my mouth. Riley from the garden centre. Wow! I hadn't seen that coming.

'Thank you for the introduction, Judith,' Riley said as Judith made her way off the stage. 'I'm delighted to be here tonight and I very much look forward to managing a smooth transition. I know that the first reaction to an announcement like this is usually shock and—'

He'd been looking round the room the whole time he spoke and, at that moment, his gaze rested on me and he faltered. His eyes widened and his mouth gaped open before he gathered himself together.

'—and shock... already said that... worry, fear, concerns about your job, so let me address that outright by saying that there *will* be changes needed to bring Reddfield TEC in line with the way Think Future Skills Academy operates, but this is *not* an exercise in massively reducing headcount. I therefore ask that you put those fears aside for the moment and remain open-minded as I explain a little about who we are and the amazing benefits that we'll bring to you and your learners.'

He caught my eye again and threw me a weak smile, no dimple this time. He'd got his wish. Destiny *had* just brought us together again, but not in a way either of us would have expected.

* * *

I slammed my car door closed, yanked the seat belt across me and turned the keys in the ignition. Pharrell Williams's 'Happy' filled the car and I jabbed at the button to silence it. Happy? Far from it!

I'd tried my hardest to listen carefully and remain open-minded during Riley's presentation. I was impressed by the statistics rolled out around the academy's prior successes. I admired their values and their way of working. Hell, I even loved their proposals for taking Reddfield TEC forward. But what I hated was the way they'd done this. None of us had any inkling we were on the radar for a takeover.

Some of my direct reports had stormed out of the hall as soon as the presentation finished. The rest of them had surrounded me. *Why didn't you tell us? Why didn't you warn us? Am I going to lose my job?* And I had no answers. How was I supposed to provide comfort, reassurance, guidance and all those things you'd expect from your manager when I was as much in the dark as they were?

I felt like some sort of diplomatic management puppet as I reeled off the sort of statement I knew would be expected of me: 'I'm hearing it at the same time as you but it all sounds really positive. Let's not jump to any conclusions about restructuring or job losses. I'm sure it will all become clear this week, and we'll deal with whatever that means together.'

I sat in my car for several minutes, my whole body tense, staring ahead at the college entrance and fighting the urge to storm back into the hall and demand to know what the hell they were all thinking.

The door opened and Riley ran down the steps and across the paved entranceway, looking towards the car park. His eyes connected with mine and he sped up, but that was my cue to leave. Grateful that the car park's one-way system meant I didn't need to drive past him, I pulled out of my space and accelerated up the hill. In my rear-view mirror, I saw him running into the road and flinging his arms into the air. He'd wanted to speak to me. He'd probably wanted to apologise, but I wasn't ready to hear it.

I'd found Riley entertaining yesterday and, last night, I'd allowed myself to admit that there'd been a slight possibility that I might even have given him my number if he'd asked. Just as well he'd left it to destiny because how awkward would it have been if I'd agreed to a date? From now on, the only contact I'd have with him would be in a professional capacity, which was fine by me. Riley had a job to do, and they could throw a posh job title at it – director of transition, no less – but we all knew he was the hatchet man. He was here to make some cuts. Some jobs would go, others would combine and there might even be a couple of 'new' roles created around whatever was their current tick-box exercise.

I'd been round the block enough times to know how these things worked. Riley and his team would instigate the changes, be congratulated on their brilliance once the new structure was in place, and then they'd withdraw troops and throw their grenade into another unsuspecting workplace. We'd be left on our own, picking up the pieces: the guilt of survivor syndrome for those who stayed, hostility towards those who secured promotions, bitterness from those whose jobs changed. And typically there'd be more work to do, fewer hours in which to do it, more responsibility and less pay.

I'd been right about it being a crappy work thing and I didn't care that I'd said that to Riley at the garden centre before I knew who he was. Tomorrow, I'd happily say it to his face.

* * *

By the time I reached home, I felt a little calmer. Sitting on the garden bench with a strong mug of tea, I gazed at my new flowerpots and sighed. Like I'd once told Sam, shit happens and it's how you deal with it that makes you happy or miserable. I could roll in whatever shit the Think Future Skills Academy threw my way or I could spray the air freshener and move on.

I suspected I was going to need an enormous can of air freshener.

8

LAUREN

I selected my smartest trouser suit on Wednesday morning – the power suit my team joked I only wore when I meant serious business – and strode purposefully towards the college entrance.

Judith must have been watching out for me from her office at the front of the building because she headed me off in the reception.

'I need a quick word, Lauren.'

Even though I was fuming at being blindsided yesterday, I wasn't going to take it out on Judith. She'd have had her instructions. Poor woman looked shattered and, knowing her, she'd likely have had several sleepless nights worrying about the impact on her staff, which wasn't good for her health.

'Before you say anything, I must apologise that I couldn't forewarn you,' she said once we'd settled in her office.

'I presumed your hands were tied.'

She sighed. 'Off the record, I begged them to permit me to let the heads of department know but it was on-off until the eleventh hour so we couldn't risk it.'

'I understand. I'm fuming about it, but not with you. Do you know what their plans are?'

'I honestly don't know and I'm afraid that'll continue to be the case for another couple of days.'

'You're kidding. They're not coming back today?'

'Riley's priority for today was one-to-ones with you and each of the other department heads, but something urgent has come up.'

I tutted loudly. 'What could be more urgent than sorting out this?'

'I don't know, Lauren. I arrived to an email with a profuse apology and a promise he'd be here on Friday.'

'He'd better have a damn good excuse for throwing in the grenade and fleeing.'

She gave me a weak smile. 'He sent the email at half three this morning, so I'd imagine he does.'

'I suppose you want me to keep everyone placated in the meantime?'

'Yes, please. I know that's hard when you're as frustrated as them.'

'Don't worry. I'll be Mrs Professional as always. Level with me. It sounded impressive last night but is this *really* a good thing?'

'I genuinely believe that being part of the academy is a good thing for the college and the learners but – and this comes from a hunch and not from a place of knowledge – I think there'll be some uncomfortable disruptions to the staff.'

'By which you mean redundancies?'

'Have you ever known a takeover to result in an increased headcount?'

'What level do you think they'll cut?'

Judith held my gaze, and she gave me the weakest of apologetic smiles.

My shoulders sank. 'Oh. Okay. Cheers for the heads-up.'

'I hope I'm wrong.'

'I hope you are, but I bet you aren't.'

As I made my way back to my office, all I could think about was how I'd been correct last night about needing a huge can of air freshener.

* * *

The rest of the day was as horrendous as anticipated, with a constant trail of staff members seeking reassurance. All day, I'd trodden that fine balance between toeing the party line and being a sympathetic friend and I was drained. I understood they were worried about their jobs and frustrated by the delay, but so was I. Would it have killed them to ask how I was feeling? Maybe they didn't believe me when I said I knew nothing. Maybe they just assumed that I'd be safe because I was management.

Even though I wasn't usually one for talking and I didn't yet have the full picture about the work situation, I had the strongest urge to speak to Connie about it.

I took a detour via Little Tilbury and pulled up outside Primrose Cottage. Connie's car was on the drive but, as I approached her front door, she stepped out, pulling on her jacket.

'Lauren!'

'Are you going out?' I asked, a little pointlessly.

'Alex and I are seeing someone about a wedding cake.'

'Oh. Have you set a date?'

'Not yet.' She glanced at her watch and winced. 'Sorry. I'm running late.'

'Off you go. I'll catch you another time.'

She gave me a quick hug then jumped in the car and pulled off her drive.

'That went well,' I muttered to myself as I pulled away shortly afterwards.

I still wanted to talk, but there was no way I could have insisted Connie stay home and hear me out when she had plans – especially when losing my job was speculation. I felt a slight niggle that she hadn't asked if I was okay, then I shook my head in disgust. What was I thinking? I'd spent years wearing a *nothing to see here* face so there'd been no reason for Connie to suspect anything could possibly be wrong. It wasn't fair of me to expect her to pick up on signals when I wasn't giving any. She was a trainee counsellor, not a mind reader!

Jonathan would be home tonight. He'd listen and he'd understand what I was feeling. As well as filing for divorce from Debs, a trigger for him moving in as my lodger had been his unexpected redundancy from the veterinary practice where he worked in Whitsborough Bay, after the brothers who ran it had decided to sell the building to a property developer. That had been a bolt from the blue, just like yesterday's news.

I'd barely seen Jonathan since Monday morning. Josh had dropped him back at Chapel View quite late in the evening and I was ready for bed by then, so we had a quick cuppa then said goodnight. Just as well because that stopped me from quizzing him about Debs. Last night, he'd stayed over at Hedgehog Hollow as he was on hoglets duty, so tonight would be our first chance to talk. I knew he didn't have plans, as he'd texted me earlier, checking I'd be home for tea. He loved cooking and I hated it – mainly because I'd never learned, refusing to bow down to Mum's gender stereotypes that the woman should cook and clean – so part of our rental agreement was for Jonathan to be chef whenever possible.

I wasn't going to ask him about Debs. Whether or not I had any feelings for Jonathan was neither here nor there in the current circumstances. All I wanted to do was have the rant I hadn't been able to have at Connie's.

The smell of chicken curry – one of Jonathan's specialities – greeted me as soon as I opened the door and I inhaled it with a contented smile. Loud music was coming from the kitchen with Jonathan's enthusiastic but not quite on key accompaniment.

I leaned against the kitchen doorframe, watching him bobbing his head while he stirred the curry and reached the final crescendo of Queen's 'Somebody to Love'. Everything about the scene before me – even the many bum notes – made me feel joyful. I could almost forget the past couple of difficult days.

'Nice one, Freddie Mercury,' I said, applauding him.

He turned round, laughing. 'You've caught me too many times for me to be embarrassed. Curry's nearly done. Five-minute warning if you want to get changed.'

I was bound to slop food down my best suit if I didn't, so I ran upstairs and returned minutes later in jeans and a dark T-shirt.

'Do you want to eat outside?' I asked, picking up my plate of food.

'Just in the kitchen, if you don't mind. I'm going out again shortly, so I need to wolf it down.'

'Hedgehog Hollow?'

'No. I'm driving over to Whitsborough Bay.'

That joy I'd felt earlier bolted out the back door and leapt over the garden wall. I couldn't help myself. 'To see Debs?'

'Yeah.'

I should have stopped there but the words were out before I could stop them. 'You two looked very cosy at the wedding.'

Jonathan's eyebrows shot up, and who could blame him for looking surprised? I sounded like a suspicious girlfriend.

'We've buried the hatchet.'

'Not heard it called that before.' I wasn't prone to blushing, but a hot flush rippled from head to toe as my dignity bolted down the garden too.

Jonathan was one of the most easy-going people I'd ever met, but even the kindest most patient individuals have buttons that can be pressed, and I'd just found his. His expression darkened and his jaw tightened as he laid his fork down and rested his elbows on the table, his eyes fixed on mine.

'If you have something to say,' he said sharply, 'I suggest you just come out and say it.'

I put my plate down on the side, my appetite gone. 'Forget it. It's none of my business.'

'If you genuinely thought it was none of your business, you wouldn't have said anything, so you might as well get it off your chest.'

'Okay. I saw you two kissing.'

'That's it?'

'And I went back to our cottage and saw you and Debs go into hers.'

'Which had to mean we slept together? Couldn't possibly have been for a coffee and a chat?'

I hugged my arms across my chest, feeling really stupid. 'I'm sorry. I shouldn't have said anything.'

'So why did you?'

'Because I...' I faltered. It wasn't the moment to bring up my personal feelings about everything that was happening at college or my turmoil about potential feelings towards Jonathan, but there was no reason not to share my fears for him.

'Because I'm worried about you.'

His expression and his voice softened. 'Why?'

I sank down into the chair opposite him. 'Last year, you were really cut up about the divorce, but after the New Year, you seemed more at peace with things. I'm worried that rekindling something with Debs could set you back again.'

He reached for my hand across the table and a tingle of electricity rippled up my arm, sending the butterflies flitting in my stomach.

'You don't have to worry about me, but it's sweet that you do.'

I felt a sliver of disappointment when he released my hand and ran his fingers through his hair. 'We didn't sleep together at the wedding. I know you said it's none of your business, but the subject's been raised, and I don't want any misunderstandings. Sunday night was unexpected and the reason I'm going across to Whitsborough Bay tonight is to talk about it now that we've had a couple of days apart.'

'Do you think you'll get back together?'

'Not sure. I don't know if I want to, I don't know if Debs wants to, and there are probably a million reasons why we shouldn't. All I know is that I enjoyed her company at the weekend. I saw glimpses of the eighteen-year-old I fell in love with, but neither of us are eighteen anymore and there hasn't just been a lot of water under the bridge since then – there's been a fast-flowing angry torrent. So we're talking and we're finding our way back to friendship and that might be as far as it goes.'

'Please be careful.'

He took my hand again and squeezed it. 'Thanks for caring. I'd better hit the road.' He shook his head at his plate. 'I thought I was hungry but I'm too nervous to eat. You're worried about me, but I'm worried about Debs. She's made amazing progress this year and I'm scared of saying the wrong thing and being the one who causes her a setback.'

'You'll be fine. If it helps, I've never yet heard you say the wrong thing.'

He grinned at me. 'You're a good friend. Thank you.'

'I'll sort the dishes. Go! Good luck.'

He kissed me on the cheek then ran upstairs to finish getting ready. I brushed my fingers down where his lips had touched my skin. It was so weird because my heart had reacted when he'd touched my hand but not when he kissed my cheek just now.

Although there could be a good reason for that. I was thinking about Shaun again.

9

LAUREN

Twenty-six years ago

Sometimes the commute from the market town of Wilbersgate, where Shaun and I lived, to Hull Royal Infirmary, where I was a nurse, did my head in. It was only twelve miles but could take up to an hour if the traffic was particularly bad. But on days like today, I loved the drive. It was a Friday, a week into September, and I'd come off nights – my last shift before a week off – so even some heavy traffic wasn't going to dampen my spirits.

Even though it was only just past 8 a.m., it was already warm and sunny, so I wound the windows down in my battered old white Metro and opened the sunroof. With the wind whipping my ponytail, I screeched along to Blur's 'Country House' on the radio. They'd beaten Oasis to the number one spot a fortnight earlier in an epic Britpop battle for the top.

As I drove, I mentally ran through the things I needed to do when I got home. Shaun and I were celebrating our seventh wedding anniversary tomorrow in style with a week in Tenerife, and I couldn't wait.

Money had been too tight while I was training to be a nurse and, once I'd secured a permanent role, we'd stretched ourselves to come out of rented accommodation and buy our own home, so I was extra-excited about our first trip abroad together.

Seven years married and thirteen together and I couldn't be happier. Not bad for a couple of kids who weren't meant to have been in the skatepark that day.

Shaun and I saw each other most days that first summer together. His mum, Ivy, took us on day trips between shifts and we spent the rest of the time skateboarding, out on our bikes, or listening to cassettes in one of our bedrooms. As the end of the summer holidays approached, I felt sad about time away from Shaun. Although we attended the same school, we weren't in any of the same classes, but we did our homework round each other's houses and met up every weekend. Shaun had promised me nothing would change between us, and it didn't. At first.

For Shaun's fourteenth birthday in late November, sixteen months after we met, I wanted to get him something special but I didn't have much money, so I decided to record a mix tape of all the songs that made me think of our friendship. Listening carefully to the lyrics, it hit me that I didn't just see Shaun as a friend. Somewhere along the way, I'd fallen in love with him, and I wanted him to know that. I was too scared to just blurt it out, so I chose a recent song we both loved – 'Hold Me Now' by the Thompson Twins – and wrote a note on the cassette sleeve:

Listen carefully to the chorus of the last song on side A.

I was really nervous when I presented him with the tape that evening before we went to the cinema. The message was clear and I hoped he'd feel the same way and act on it. If he said or did nothing, I'd know my feelings weren't reciprocated.

I deliberately hadn't written out the song listings, but Shaun read my message out loud.

'What's the song?' he asked.

'I'm not telling. You'll have to listen and find out.'

I couldn't concentrate on the film. I kept thinking about that song and whether I'd made a mistake.

The following day, Shaun was waiting for me after school. He grinned as soon as he saw me.

'I liked the song,' he said as we set off walking home. 'Did you mean it?'

'That depends. Would you like me to mean it?'

'I would. Very much.'

'Good, because I *do* mean it.'

He slipped his hand into mine and my heart leapt. Once we were clear of the school crowd, he pulled me down a quiet street and kissed me for the first time. It was a little hesitant – neither of us knowing what we were doing – but practice made perfect, and we had plenty of that.

Shaun proposed to me on my seventeenth birthday and we married in September the following year. Connie and Paul had married in the spring with a big white wedding, but Shaun and I only wanted something small – a registry office followed by a pub meal. 'Hold Me Now' played as we signed the register. It had remained our special song ever since.

I stopped off in town for a few last-minute holiday purchases and it was approaching lunchtime when I arrived back at our house in Osprey Close – a 1960s-built three-bedroom semi on a housing estate on the outskirts of town. It wasn't the prettiest of buildings, but it was home and we both loved it. Eager to get into holiday mode, I went straight upstairs to pack.

With a summer hits CD playing on the stereo in the bedroom, I sang along while I piled up the clothes I wanted to take on the bed, trying on a couple of outfits to be sure of my choices. By the time that was done, my stomach was rumbling so it was time for a lunch break, after which I'd start on Shaun's clothes and dig the cases out.

Leaving the CD playing, I went downstairs and into the kitchen where I did a double take as I spotted today's post on the worktop. The post usually arrived way after Shaun had left for work.

I reached for the envelopes. On top of the pile was a folded piece of paper with my name on it in Shaun's handwriting. We often left notes for each other round the house with reminders of things to do or declarations of love, so I unfolded the note, wondering which this would be. My stomach lurched as my eyes scanned down the short paragraph.

Dear Lauren

I'm so very sorry but I can't do this anymore. I know my timing's awful and what I'm doing is unforgivable. I should have been honest with you a long time ago. I'm such a coward and you deserve so much better. I wish you nothing but happiness.

Shaun xx

I grabbed onto the worktop as my legs threatened to buckle beneath me. Was this a 'Dear John' note or – I clung on tighter at the thought – was it a suicide note? It couldn't be. Shaun had really strong views about people taking their own lives. 'Long-term solution to a short-term crisis,' he'd say. 'There's always hope.' He'd even said it at the weekend. There'd been a story in the paper about someone we'd known at school who'd disappeared and was found hanging in the woods a few days later.

My stomach lurched once more. What if him reading out that newspaper story had been a cry for help? What if he'd hoped to open up a conversation about how he was feeling about God knows what? All I'd done was express sympathy for the man and his family before asking Shaun whether he thought two bikinis would be enough for Tenerife.

Heart thumping, I dashed into the lounge. All clear. I ran back upstairs. We usually kept the bedroom doors open to let light and air through, but the boxroom door was closed. The CD had ended, and the house was eerily silent except for my rapid breathing.

My hand shook as I slowly lowered the door handle. I scrunched my eyes tight shut as I pushed the door wide and took a deep, shuddery breath before I opened them.

Nothing.

I slumped against the wall, relief flowing through me momentarily. But I still didn't know if Shaun was safe and alive. All I knew was he hadn't done whatever he'd done in our home.

I frantically scanned down the note again, hoping to find answers. What should I do? Phone the police? His mum? I couldn't think straight.

My eyes rested on the new suitcases we'd bought for our holidays and my hand tightened on the note. There weren't suitcases plural anymore. There was only one.

Back in the bedroom, I yanked open Shaun's drawers. Nothing. Empty hangers were all that remained in his single wardrobe. I slammed the wardrobe door shut and sank down to the floor, staring at the letter in my hand, a whirlpool of emotions inside me. He hadn't taken his life, thank God, but he'd left me, and I had no idea why.

What I'm doing is unforgivable. Yes, walking out on me without warning or explanation was unforgivable! And what was that about honesty? What did that mean? That he'd been thinking of leaving for a long time and hadn't had the courage to tell me? It made no sense. We were happy together. We were best friends and soulmates. We loved the same things, shared the same outlook on life, and laughed constantly. He was affectionate and passionate and neither of those things had waned recently.

My gaze lifted to the pile of clothes on the bed. If he'd been planning on leaving me, why suggest the holiday? That made no sense either.

I needed to speak to him. I crawled across the carpet, reached for the phone on my bedside drawers and dialled his work number. It rang and rang. Shaun often moaned about how his colleagues never answered his phone. I was about to hang up when the call connected.

'Good afternoon, Planning Department. Jackie speaking.'

Jackie? Who was Jackie?

'Hi, can I speak to Shaun?'

'Just a second.'

I could hear a mumbled conversation before Jackie came back on. 'Can I ask who's calling?'

'It's Lauren. His wife.'

'Hang on.'

Another mumbled conversation while my mind raced. Shaun hadn't said anything about a Jackie joining the team and he always shared details like that.

'Hi, Lauren, it's Eddie.'

I'd met Eddie at a Christmas party a few years back. Nice guy.

'Hi, Eddie, is Shaun about?'

'Erm... he doesn't work here anymore.'

'What?'

'He resigned. It was his last day yesterday. Didn't he tell you?'

What? *What?*

'Lauren? Are you still there?'

'Yeah. Sorry. When did he resign?'

'He's been working his notice, so three or four weeks ago.'

'Has he got another job with the council?'

There was a pause. 'No. He told us he was leaving the area. I presumed you were both moving. He never said anything about the two of you...'

The unspoken end to that sentence hung heavily in the air. Eddie's discomfort in every word was obvious and I could imagine him and his colleagues glancing at each other, cringing at the awkward conversation. He'd probably put me on speakerphone, hoping someone would pipe up and throw him a lifeline. I'd better do that.

'He's maybe won the lottery and is planning a big surprise for our wedding anniversary tomorrow. Thanks, Eddie. Take care.'

I disconnected the call. The handset slid onto the carpet as I pulled my knees to my chest and wrapped my arms round my legs. I tried to gasp for air, but a low, guttural sound bounced off the walls as I rocked back and forth.

He'd left me. No warning, no signs, no explanation. What the hell was I supposed to do now? How was I supposed to live without him?

10

SAMANTHA

After landing in Tanzania on Tuesday night, we'd stayed in a hotel near the airport and set out yesterday morning on a 125-mile sightseeing drive to a small town called Karatu – our base for travelling into different National Parks during our safari week. We'd passed through villages and countryside, the landscape forever changing, excitement building in me for the week ahead each time we spotted any wildlife.

Today, at the recommendation of our tour guide Obuya, we'd risen early to catch the morning mist over the coffee fields.

'It's so beautiful!' I exclaimed, breathing in the freshness of the air.

Josh put his arm round my waist as we stood on the hotel terrace, taking it all in.

'Just think, there might be hedgehogs asleep in those fields right now,' he said.

I'd been so focused on seeing the big five that I hadn't thought about the smaller mammals. When he heard I ran a hedgehog rescue centre, Obuya had said he'd join us towards the end of breakfast, bring some photos with him, and tell us more about the native breed. I was almost as excited about that as I was about our trip into our first National Park today.

'What are you thinking about?' Josh asked after a while.

'How different my life was two years ago. I thought I'd lost every-thing, but I could have saved myself a few tears if I'd known that what I have now was at the other side of the rainbow.'

Back then, I'd been busy trying to organise Chloe's wedding while secretly nursing a broken heart and, even though I'd lined up a new job and intended to relocate, my only focus had been on what I was running from. I'd never paused to consider that I could be running to a better life.

Josh squeezed my shoulder. 'Same here. Maybe not the tears, but I did a lot of angry stomping and swearing. Could have saved myself a lot of stress if I'd known.'

We'd both spent so much time getting worked up about the past and chasing dreams that weren't ours anymore. My nanna used to say *the past's in your head but the future's in your hands*. Being in this magical place on my honeymoon, it really did feel like all the bad stuff from the distant and not so distant past could be packaged up as memories and the future really was in our hands – a very bright future.

Josh tilted my face towards his and, as the mist steadily rose, I kissed my husband in a moment of complete and absolute content-ment. We hadn't even ventured into the National Parks and already our trip to Africa was better than anything I'd dreamed of.

* * *

'Hedgehog time!' Obuya announced, pulling out a chair at our table after breakfast.

He opened up an iPad. 'You recognise this little creature?'

I smiled at the photo of a European hedgehog. 'We've rescued hundreds of those at Hedgehog Hollow. They're adorable.'

'Very cute,' he agreed. 'What about this one?'

It looked similar to our native hedgehogs back home, but the hedgehog's face and underbelly were white and the spines appeared to be white with dark brown tips.

'The North African hedgehog,' Obuya declared. 'Almost twins but some differences. Lighter colouring.' He pointed to the areas where I'd spotted the differences. 'Smaller and lighter than the European hedgehog too and you see the face?' He enlarged the photo. 'No spines on the crown.'

He flicked back to the European hedgehog and enlarged the same area so we could compare the two.

'Oh, yeah,' I said. 'You can see a lot more of the North African hedgehog's face.' I looked up at Obuya. 'Do you find this species in Tanzania?'

He shook his head. 'No, no, no. The North African hedgehog is native to the far north – Morocco, Algeria, Libya, Tunisia and is even found in Spain and Malta – but we have our own.'

He tapped the iPad and I recognised the African Pygmy hedgehog which had increased in popularity as a pet over recent years.

'Four-toed hedgehog,' he said, 'also known as the African Pygmy. Everything is smaller, even the number of toes! There are many of them, mainly in grassy areas, open woodland and where there's rocks for shelter. Beautiful animal and—'

Obuya's radio burst into life, interrupting him. 'I am needed so goodbye for now, but I can answer more questions later.'

We thanked him as he closed the iPad and left the dining room.

'It would be amazing if we saw one while we're here,' I said.

'We'll have to ask Obuya if there's a good place to spot them. In the meantime, we have something a bit bigger to search for.'

We returned to our room to freshen up, ready for an exciting day exploring Tarangire National Park. The sixth largest National Park in Tanzania and with a hilly landscape, we were expecting stunning views, amazing vegetation and, hopefully, an abundance of elephants. We'd seen lots of wildlife on our drive yesterday, including elephants, but only at a distance, so we hadn't taken any photos for Terry.

In the en suite, I rummaged in my toilet bag for my birth control pills which I always took on a morning, but they weren't in the front pocket where I'd expected. Frowning, I checked both side pockets, then the inside one but there was no sign of them. I tipped everything out onto the floor and scrunched the empty bag, but they definitely weren't there.

'Josh!' I called. 'Have you seen my pills?'

He appeared in the doorway. 'I saw you take one yesterday morning, but I haven't seen them since.'

I shrugged. 'They're not in my toilet bag. We don't have time now but I'm going to have to go through all the luggage when we get back.'

* * *

Tarangire National Park was incredible. When I'd imagined seeing herds of elephants, I'd pictured maybe thirty together but there were hundreds of them, all different sizes and shades of grey, and what a delight they were to observe, especially the playful calves. I took stacks of photos and videos for Terry.

There were wildebeest, gazelle, impala, buffalo and so many beautiful zebras. Colourful exotic birds called from the treetops and I was captivated by the varied vegetation, particularly the giant baobab tree, its enormous canopy providing the animals with shelter from the sun.

With it being early May, we were still in the rainy season and were caught in the most tremendous downpour during the afternoon. It was such an experience to see the landscape change during and after.

We returned to the hotel in the afternoon, buzzing from an amazing day, ready for a couple of hours of relaxation before dinner. I checked my toilet bag one more time in case my pills had miraculously reappeared but no such luck. I checked my make-up bag too in case I'd put them in there in error and then I stopped, clapping my hand against my forehead as I realised what had happened. Over breakfast yesterday morning, Josh had mentioned having a headache. He wasn't going to take anything for it but, as we were leaving the hotel room, I reminded him of the long journey to Karatu and he relented. I'd heaved my case back onto the bed and removed my toilet bag. The box of paracetamol was at the bottom of a zipped compartment, so I needed to remove my other first-aid supplies to get to it but, in my haste, I managed to knock everything onto the floor.

'You know where they are?' Josh asked.

'In the airport hotel. I thought I'd picked everything up, but I never checked under the bed. I think they might have bounced under there. I can't think where else they could be.'

Josh wrinkled his nose. 'Oh. That's not ideal.'

I sat down heavily on the bed, my mind racing. 'We have a few choices. We could have a sex-free honeymoon.'

Josh pulled a shocked face, making me laugh.

'Yeah, I didn't think you'd be up for that one and, to be fair, neither am I. The second choice is to check out the public toilets to see if they've got a condom machine or wander into town. There's bound to be a pharmacy.' My heart raced at the other possibility. 'Or...'

Josh sat beside me and took my hand in his and I knew from the tender way he stroked it that he was on the same wavelength as me.

'Or we just see what happens?' he suggested. 'How would you feel about that?' Josh's eyes had lit up, indicating how he felt.

I pondered for a moment. 'Pretty excited, actually. I know I said we'd leave it a bit longer, but I was thinking on the flight over how empty the house is going to be when Paul and Beth move out. I know we've still got Phoebe and Darcie but there won't be any more babies and that's going to be strange.'

'I was thinking the same. I've got used to them being there.' He drew my hand to his lips and gently kissed it. 'But this is a big decision, Sammie. I want you to be sure.'

'I am sure. A honeymoon baby would be pretty special.'

He ran his hands through my hair and kissed me. As his kiss deepened, it was clear he agreed.

11

LAUREN

✉ From Judith
Riley Berry is definitely back today. See you later

I placed my phone back in my bag on Friday morning and loaded my breakfast pots into the dishwasher. So this was it! We'd *finally* find out what the future looked like for Reddfield TEC – and our jobs.

I'd re-thought the power suit this morning. That initial fury had burned off and I didn't feel the need to go into battle.

'I'm on hoglets duty tonight,' Jonathan said, entering the kitchen and tipping his coffee dregs down the sink. 'So I'll see you at some point tomorrow.'

'Do you fancy going out for a drink tomorrow night?' I hadn't told Jonathan what was going on but, if it was the bad news I expected, I could probably do with a distraction.

He wrinkled his nose and I felt silly for asking. Of course he'd have plans.

'I'm going over to Whitsborough Bay for the day and stopping over. Sorry.'

I smiled brightly. 'I'll see if Connie's free or I might just take advantage of being in charge of the remote control.'

'Oi! I don't hog the remote.'

'Yeah, right.'

We left the house together, laughing. I loved our banter and was relieved that the moment of tension I'd caused earlier in the week had been brushed aside. I wasn't sure how it had gone between Jonathan and Debs on Tuesday night as I'd been in bed when he returned, he'd been seeing to the hoglets on Wednesday night, and he'd been on an emergency callout to a farm last night. But if he was seeing her again tomorrow night, presumably it had gone well.

Driving to the TEC, I had no sense of how I felt about Jonathan seeing Debs again because all I could focus on was me seeing Riley Berry once more. He hadn't been far from my thoughts over the past few days, and it was confusing as hell. Every time I thought about the work situation, he inevitably drifted into my mind, but I always pictured the way he'd looked at me across the water feature at Bloomsberry's – those mesmerising eyes, that single dimple, that cheeky smile – and butterflies stirred in my stomach. Then I pictured his shocked expression when he'd clocked me from the stage on Tuesday and that excitement turned to anxiety. Just like now.

'Oh, well, pointless getting worked up about it. What will be will be.'

* * *

I arrived a little early for my 10 a.m. meeting with Riley and peered through the glass panel in the office door. He was pacing up and down in front of the window with his mobile phone pressed to his ear. From the tension in his body and the frequent shaking of his head, it didn't look like a good conversation. I stepped back from the door so my presence wasn't obvious.

When he disconnected, he rested his elbows on the windowsill and held his head in his hands. From my lurking position, I could see his side profile. He had the appearance of a broken man, and I felt a strange compulsion to rush in and hug him. I pushed that swiftly aside.

That man was very likely about to give me my marching orders. A hug was the last thing he deserved.

Pushing back my shoulders, I rapped on the door. Riley straightened up, flattened his dishevelled hair and called, 'Come in.'

I couldn't bring myself to make eye contact with him, but I felt his eyes on me as I closed the door and took the ten or so paces over to the round meeting table – no edges so no barriers. I caught a whiff of his body spray as I passed. I couldn't place the scent, but it was delicious, and butterflies stirred in my stomach again.

I settled myself into one of the four chairs.

'You can look at me, you know,' he said softly.

I looked up and the butterflies soared. He was looking extra good today in a charcoal suit and a deep blue shirt which made his eyes seem even brighter. *Argh! Stop looking at his eyes!*

'Looks like destiny reunited us after all,' I said. Not sure where that came from.

He smiled but not enough for that dimple to appear. 'Not quite the circumstances I'd hoped for.'

'Life, eh?' I shrugged. 'So, hit me with it. The explanation can come afterwards. What I want to know right now is whether I've still got a job.'

'Okay. We *will* be restructuring and as part of that, your current role as head of department will disappear.'

Even though I'd been expecting news along those lines, it still hit me like a punch to the gut. My throat burned and tears pricked my eyes. *Do not cry. Don't you dare cry!*

'Just mine?' I managed.

'No, not just you. My apologies. I should have made that clear. There won't be a head of department role anymore, so all five of you are in the same position.'

My lips felt dry, but my palms were sweating and I was still trying to fight back the tears. I opened my mouth, but I had no words.

'I can imagine that's come as a shock,' he said gently. 'How about I give you a moment? Would you like a water or a coffee?'

'Strong black coffee, please.'

'Back in a moment.'

I released a long, shuddery breath as soon as the door closed behind him. I thought I'd been prepared, but I hadn't been. Deep down, I'd hoped Judith and I had both been wrong. I loved my job and I was bloody good at it. I didn't want to do another role here – if that was even an option – but I didn't want to leave the TEC either. I had no interest in further progression. Judith had suggested I apply for the vice principal position when it came up a couple of years back, but the role hadn't interested me. I'd envisaged doing exactly what I was doing now until I was sixty, at which point I'd planned to retire early and maybe travel the world. Now everything was in jeopardy.

I'd managed to compose myself – initial shock subsided – by the time Riley returned with a couple of coffees.

'How would you like to do this?' he asked once I'd taken a sip on mine. 'Do you want to fire questions at me, or would you like me to explain the structure?'

'You might as well explain it.'

Take the emotion out of it and what Riley presented sounded like a logical and sensible approach to the college's structure. It would ensure consistency and resolve some of the communication issues that arose occasionally. But it left me stuffed. My layer of management had been wiped out completely – just like Dad's had in the pet food factory all those years ago.

'As you can see, there'll be two vice principal roles instead of one,' Riley concluded, 'and, with Judith retiring, the principal role will also get advertised.'

'Which Harvey will get,' I said. Harvey Wyatt was the current VP – driven, ambitious, prone to being overzealous at times, but good at his job.

Riley shook his head. 'No roles have been earmarked. Harvey can express his interest in any or all three roles and he'll be interviewed alongside other suitable candidates. I've had several lengthy conversations with Judith, and we don't want to lose your talents. We hope you'll apply for the vice principal *and* principal roles.'

'Principal? Me? Do you need your head read?'

I winced at Riley's shocked expression at my unprofessional outburst, but then he burst out laughing. 'That's one of my mum's favourite phrases.'

'Then your mum and I are on the same wavelength, but me and the role of principal? Not so much.'

'What would make you think that? Judith believes you're more than capable and, from looking at your performance reviews and hearing about the great work you've done here, I agree.'

I gave him a weak smile while shaking my head. 'I'm flattered. Honestly, I am, but it's not for me. I take great pride in any job I do, and I give it my all, but that's because I love what I do. For me, it's never been about striving for the top or earning the big money. It must 100 per cent be about job satisfaction and, although there would be elements of the principal and VP roles I'd enjoy, there wouldn't be enough of those to light a fire in my belly. So thank you, but no thank you to any of them.'

'Why don't you take some time to look through the job descriptions over the weekend?' Riley suggested, sliding a cardboard folder across the table. 'The roles are changing so you might find they appeal after all.'

I took the folder and briefly flicked through the information inside. This was one occasion where being stubborn wouldn't do me any favours.

'Okay, I'll take a look over the weekend, but I very much doubt I'll change my mind. For what it's worth, I think Harvey would make a good principal. He's proved himself as VP and he's hungry for it.' I pushed my chair back. 'Was there anything else?'

'No, that was it,' Riley said. 'Can't say I'm not disappointed, but your honesty's appreciated.'

'I'm not a game-player. I don't see any point in messing anyone about.'

'It's refreshing.'

He held my gaze and my stomach did an unexpected backflip.

'It's just those eyes,' I muttered under my breath as I plonked myself down at my desk a few minutes later, fanning my flushed cheeks with a pamphlet. *And the suit. And he smelled good.*

I tried to do some work, but I couldn't concentrate on anything. The job I loved was disappearing and all my current projects felt a little pointless. I needed some uninterrupted space to think and, as break was approaching, the only place I had a chance of that was my car. I drove up to the very top of the car park and stopped on a patch of scruff land containing a couple of skips and some recycling bins.

Turning the ignition off, I pushed open the door to let some air in and sat back in the seat, looking towards the building that had been my second home for a decade. A wave of sadness swept through me.

Throwing myself into my career had been my way of coping with life after Shaun and, even though I'd moved into teaching long after he left me, it was because of Shaun and, more specifically Ivy, that I'd chosen nursing in the first place. My move into teaching had kept me committed to the same subject area which had been my way of keeping them both close to me, even though they were no longer in my life.

With that taken away from me, what was I supposed to do now?

12

LAUREN

Twenty-six years ago

Connie and Paul offered to stay with me the night Shaun left, but there was no point. They'd already helped me practically – between us, we'd rung round everyone we could think of, but nobody had seen or heard from Shaun – and now I wanted to be alone with my thoughts to try to make sense of things.

'Are you going to tell Mum?' Connie asked as she hugged me goodbye.

'No. Not yet, anyway. She'll blame me and I could do without that right now.'

Mum really liked Shaun. Any time I called round, the conversation was always dominated by her asking how he was and when he'd be visiting next. She was never so excited about my visits. We'd chat and it would be lovely at first, but the conversation always ended up going down the same tired, worn path: *Have you learned to cook yet? What sort of wife makes her husband iron his own shirts? Isn't it about time you started your family?*

When I told her that Shaun and I weren't planning on having children, she assumed we'd discovered we couldn't have them and wittered on about how we should consider adopting. Once I'd put her right – that we'd chosen together not to have kids – she told me she'd never heard anything so ridiculous, and I felt another tick go on her ever-increasing list of ways I disappointed her. I didn't want to add my husband walking out on me to that list. Not yet. *What did you do to make him leave? Were you neglecting him? It's because you insisted on working full-time, isn't it?*

'He'll be back soon,' Connie said, grasping my hand. 'He'll realise he's made a stupid mistake and everything will be back to normal.'

I didn't trust myself to speak in case the floodgates opened again so I held up my crossed fingers and waved goodbye.

A few minutes later, I lay on our bed on top of the duvet, cuddling the soft fluffy lamb which Shaun had given me on our first wedding anniversary. Lambs had been a recurring theme with cards and gifts from Shaun due to L. A. M. being my married initials – Lauren Amy Marfell. Shaun called me his little lamb and sometimes Ivy did too. Would he ever call me that again?

Even though Connie said he'd return soon, I knew she didn't believe it any more than I did. If it had just been a case of packing his things and doing a runner, I might have clung onto that hope, but he'd worked his notice at the council. This hadn't been an impulsive mistake that he'd regret. He'd planned this for at least a month – very likely longer – and I had no idea why.

Did Ivy know? Shaun was exceptionally close to her – we both were – and he might have confided in her. She'd been the only person we hadn't contacted this evening. She'd moved on from nursing and was now an emergency call operator. I knew she was working nights across the weekend, and I didn't want to worry her in the middle of a night-shift – assuming she didn't already know her son was leaving me – when she did such an important job requiring the utmost levels of concentration.

We'd been round to Ivy's house for a meal on Wednesday evening and she'd been her normal bubbly, chatty, attentive self. She'd been eager to know all about our holiday plans and had joked that she might hide in one of our suitcases. I'd done the lion's share of talking – not unusual – but Shaun had chipped in and had appeared excited himself. An act?

At the end of the night, Ivy had hugged us both goodbye, wished us a happy holiday, and said she was looking forward to seeing us on our return. It had been a relaxed, laughter-filled evening and, if she'd known what was coming, it wouldn't have been. Could he have told her since then?

* * *

Having barely slept a wink, I showered, pulled on some fresh clothes, and drove over to Ivy's house early on Saturday morning, aiming to catch her as soon as she arrived home from her shift. A combination of my eagerness and zero traffic on the roads meant I was far too early. I parked up outside her house and must have dozed off, as a knock on the window scared the life out of me.

I looked up to see Ivy frowning at me.

'What are you doing here?' she asked when I pushed open the door. 'Why aren't you at the airport?' She peered past me to the empty passenger seat. 'Where's Shaun?'

From her bewildered expression and tone, it was obvious she hadn't a clue.

'Shaun's left me,' I managed, before bursting into tears.

* * *

'He's not here, love, and there's no sign of him staying last night.' Ivy sank down beside me on the sofa and put her arm round my shoulders, drawing me close. 'I'm so sorry.'

I'd spilled out what had happened as soon as were inside and she'd rushed upstairs to see if Shaun was here, not that I'd expected him to be. There'd been no sign of his car on the street.

'I don't understand,' I said. 'I thought we were happy.'

'So did I. I thought you two were made for each other from that first day he brought you home after you fell off your skateboard.'

'Then why did he leave me?'

'I don't know, love. He's never said or done anything to suggest this could be on the cards.'

We huddled together on the sofa for several minutes, both lost in our thoughts.

'Have you got the note with you?' Ivy said eventually.

I fished it out of my jeans pocket and handed it to her. 'It's a bit crumpled.'

Her brow furrowed more deeply as she read the note. 'I never imagined he'd behave like his father.' She sighed deeply as she handed it back to me. 'Although at least I knew why Max left.'

Following a diagnosis of endometriosis in her late teens, Ivy was told she couldn't have children. At twenty, she met Max Marfell and they'd married two years later. He'd never wanted kids, so they were both shocked when, at thirty-two, she discovered she was pregnant. At eight months pregnant, she'd returned from a check-up to find a note: *Can't do this. Never wanted kids. Hope you're happy with your choice.*

'Can you think of anywhere he might have gone?' I asked.

'I've been racking my brain, but I really can't. We haven't got any family and you've already tried his friends. We haven't even got a special place like somewhere we regularly holidayed.'

'I keep thinking I must have said or done something to make him leave, but what?'

'If you had, it could only have been in the last couple of days because he was fine on Wednesday.' She frowned and shook her head. 'Although how would that explain him putting in his notice at work?'

'That part makes no sense at all. So did I say or do something a month or so ago to upset him and trigger all of this? Or has it been building up for years?'

'It doesn't have to be something you've said or done, love. I know it's easier to blame ourselves.'

I couldn't help it. 'Has Shaun ever said anything to you about wanting children?' I asked. 'We agreed that we didn't, but could that be it?'

Ivy shrugged. 'I once made a flippant comment about looking forward to being a grandma and he told me that children weren't part of your plan. We didn't discuss it any further but, from the way he said it, it was clear to me it was a joint decision and one that he was happy with.'

'The not knowing is killing me,' I said. 'I just wish I knew where he was. If I could talk to him, I'm sure we could work something out.'

'We're going to have to be patient. When he's had some time and space to work things through, I'm sure he'll get in touch and explain everything.' The words were positive but her frown and the worried look in her eyes conveyed her concern.

'And what if he doesn't?

'I don't know, love. I'm finding it hard to accept that my Shaun would walk out on you like this.' She shook her head. 'He loves you. Keep holding onto that.'

13

LAUREN

Present day

Following my meeting with Riley and my time out in the car park, I somehow made it through the rest of the day, returning to my office and going into business mode. The news affected me, but it also affected my team, and my priority was not to prolong the uncertainty for them for any longer than necessary. I managed to catch most of them at lunchtime so they could hear the news from me rather than via the rumour mill.

The overriding reaction was shock, especially when I told them that – as I'd already told Riley – I wouldn't be applying for any of the senior roles. The questions came thick and fast: *What will you do? Could you go back into nursing? Will you leave the area? Will you be okay? Would it help if we complained?* I had no answers.

By the end of the working day, I felt drained from dishing out smiles and reassurances when I felt anything but happy and reassured myself. The future I'd had mapped out had been unexpectedly taken away, and I hadn't coped well the first time that happened – when

Shaun left. It was going to take all my strength to get through it this time, although hopefully it wouldn't be quite so difficult. After all, I knew why I'd lost my job and I could ask questions.

* * *

Driving home from college, that urge to talk to someone about losing my job was overwhelming, but who could I turn to right now? Everyone was away or preoccupied. Jonathan had whatever he had going on with Debs, Josh and Sam were on their honeymoon, and Connie never seemed to be free. I'd tried to pin her down for a coffee this week, but every evening had been filled with something wedding-related, running cubs or scouts with Alex, or seeing his large family. So much for wanting to sit down and explore why I was still hung up on Shaun. Had that been a drunken promise at the wedding, already forgotten?

Did I really only have four people I could turn to in a time of crisis? How? I knew loads of people. The guest list for my fiftieth birthday last year had been huge, but the truth was that none of them knew the real me. They saw this loud, confident woman through whom they vicariously lived adventures. I'd fulfilled a long-term ambition in celebration of my fiftieth birthday last year – a tandem skydive – and had previously tried a stack of other activities including: paragliding, wing walking and microlighting. My first adventure had been a weekend in the Peak District, a few years after Shaun left, climbing and abseiling. It was a last-minute thing with a colleague at the hospital after a friend cancelled on her. I'd loved the adrenaline buzz, but it had also given me something to talk about, diverting conversation from my disastrous love life, so I'd sought out other thrills.

I was the one who friends called on when they wanted a good laugh. But who could I call on when the laughter stopped? It wasn't their fault. I was the one who kept everyone at arm's length, who kept relationships superficial, who made out that everything was fine when it never really was.

Back at Chapel View, I clicked into Facebook on my phone and typed 'Shaun Marfell' into the search bar. No results. There never were. I don't know why I tortured myself with it, but it was a compulsion I fed every few years. I'm not sure what I'd do if I found a profile in his name.

I put my phone aside, tutting. Some wounds were best kept closed.

Or were they?

I ran up the stairs and opened the hatch to the attic.

'Is this really a good idea?' I muttered to myself, staring up into the darkness.

Probably not. But I was going to do it anyway. I pulled down the extendable ladder and climbed into the space between the eaves.

I hardly ever went into the attic. I stored the Christmas decorations and my suitcases in there and that was pretty much it. Except for one box I'd shoved into a corner.

My heart thudded as I crouched down beside it, batted away some cobwebs and blew off a layer of dust, bringing into clearer focus the word 'UNEXPLAINED' scrawled across the top in thick marker pen.

I chewed on my lip. 'Sod it! What's the worst that could happen?'

I grabbed the box and carried it down the ladder. Downstairs, I plonked it on the dining table and, before I could talk myself out of it, I ripped off the packing tape, opened the flaps and reached inside, heart racing.

Even though I'd packed it all away more than two decades ago, I knew exactly what I'd find on the top. I lifted out the plastic ring binder pocket containing Shaun's 'goodbye' note, my stomach on spin cycle as I scanned down the familiar words, everything about that day so vivid in my mind. Putting the note aside, I unpacked the other items: the boxes containing my wedding and engagement rings, a silver scroll containing our marriage certificate, the tickets for the holiday to Tenerife we never had, and the passport in my married name. I lifted out a carrier bag and removed my soft lamb. The Christmas of the year Shaun walked out on me, the Aardman Animations character Shaun the Sheep first made his appearance in the film *A Close Shave*. Shaun would have laughed his head off about that and we'd have tried to outcompete each other over the years with our sheep-buying. If we'd still been together.

My fingers sank into the lamb's fur, and I cuddled it to my chest for a moment, a wave of sadness sweeping over me with the memories. It had sat on my bedside drawers until the day the divorce papers arrived and I was forced to accept that it was over, Shaun was never coming back, and I'd never find out why he'd left.

There were two more items at the bottom: a box file full of photos of us from when we'd met right up until the weekend before he left, and our wedding album. I lifted them out and carried them over to the sofa.

In the weeks following Shaun's disappearance, I became obsessed with looking through the photos of days and nights out, events, Christmases, parties and UK holidays, searching my memory for any clue as to why he might have left, but I couldn't find anything.

I ran my fingers down the navy-blue cover of the wedding album, then opened it to where I'd written our names and wedding date in an appalling attempt at calligraphy. I poised to turn to the first photograph and shook my head, closing the album. What was the point? So many old memories had already been stirred and this was going to mess with my head even more.

With everything returned to the box, I left it in the corner of the dining room to return to the attic tomorrow. For now, I'd make a coffee and watch a film. There were no answers and I needed to accept that. For reasons known only to himself, Shaun had walked out of my life for good that day and no amount of re-reading that note, stroking my soft lamb or looking through photos was going to give me any closure.

I missed his friendship and had never let anyone take his place as my best friend and confidante – not even Connie. I missed his love because, until the day he left me, I'd never been in any doubt how much he loved me. I'd felt it in every look, touch and conversation and I'd returned it wholeheartedly. And I missed Ivy.

* * *

Twenty-six years ago

Ivy was waiting outside our house in Osprey Close when I returned from a shift at the hospital in late October, seven weeks after Shaun left. The rain was torrential, so I hadn't noticed her and nearly smacked into her as she exited her car.

'He's been in touch,' she said, her voice barely audible over the downpour.

I ushered her inside and peeled off my coat, my heart thumping. It was Ivy's birthday and, as Shaun was her only family, he'd always made a fuss of her on special days. I'd wondered if he might make contact.

'A card or a call?'

'Just a card.'

I could hear her heart breaking in those three words. They'd had such a strong bond and I didn't understand why he'd cut her out of his life too. He'd walked out on our marriage, so surely it was me he wanted to cut out of his life, not his wonderful mum.

She removed the card from her the pocket of her waterproof coat and handed it to me. I barely glanced at the picture in my haste to see what he'd written, but my heart sank at the short note:

I'm sorry I can't be there to share your birthday and I'm sorry I can't explain why or tell you where I am. Please look after my little lamb for me and tell her I'm sorry xx

'That's it?' I asked turning the card over in the hope that there was a full-page explanation on the back.

'That's it,' she said, her eyes filling with tears. 'But the poem's lovely.'

Ivy had been so strong for me but now it was her turn to crumble. I held her petite body as she sobbed and could imagine that she'd been holding on all this time convincing herself that he'd turn up on her birthday with a gift and a cake and whisk her away for a meal or a day out, like he'd always done.

'At least we know he's okay,' I said, stroking her back.

'Do we? He doesn't say he is.'

I didn't like to voice what I'd really meant: *At least we know he's still alive.*

* * *

Ivy received another card from Shaun that Christmas – still no explanation – but I received nothing. None of his friends had heard a peep out of him either.

On Mother's Day in mid-March, I invited Ivy to join my family for Sunday lunch. She declined at first but phoned me a couple of days later, saying she'd made a decision to stop moping and pick her life up again, just like she'd done when Max walked out. It was the first time I heard her use the line about spraying the air freshener and I felt inspired to take that strong approach too.

She was on the phone in the hall when I arrived to collect her for our meal. The excitement in her voice was clear as she closed down the conversation with declarations of love and promises to see the caller soon. My heart thudded. That could only be one person.

'That was Shaun!' she exclaimed as she opened the door. 'I'm going to meet him next week.'

'That's wonderful,' I said, hugging her. 'Did he say anything about me?' I asked when I released her.

Her smile faltered. 'He asked how you were.'

'But he doesn't want to see me.'

'I'm sorry, love.'

'Not your fault,' I said brightly. 'Ready to go?'

I laughed and smiled my way through that meal while my heart broke all over again. He'd sent birthday, Christmas and Mother's Day cards to his mum and was meeting her next week. I'd had nothing.

'I'll find out why he did it,' Ivy promised when I dropped her back home later that afternoon. 'And I'll let you know.'

But the only explanation I got after she met him was, 'It's complicated.'

What the hell did that mean? I bombarded her with questions, begged her to talk Shaun into meeting with me so he could explain why it was complicated himself, but she stood fast.

And then she lost her patience with me – something I'd never seen her do before. 'Shaun has asked me not to say anything and I need to respect that. He's my son, Lauren. I don't want to choose sides but, if you're going to make me, I have to choose Shaun.'

'What sides? I'm not asking you to take sides. This isn't a fight.'

From that moment, it felt like one. A fight I wasn't going to win. I couldn't bear the tension every time we met. I couldn't stand that she knew what was going on but wouldn't tell me, even though I did understand the difficult situation she was in. I couldn't deal with the anguish in her eyes every time I mentioned Shaun. So I eventually took myself out of the game. I stopped calling and I stopped visiting and I waited for her to make contact with me.

But she never did. She let me go and that broke my heart all over again.

14

SAMANTHA

All was silent except for the occasional blast from the burner as our hot air balloon steadily rose through the darkness early on Saturday morning. A ride in a hot air balloon had been on my bucket list and I'd always assumed that, if I ever got the chance, it would be over the English countryside. I'd never dreamed it would be across the Serengeti.

From the ground, the herds of animals had been impressive, but looking down on them from the air, as the sun peeped over the horizon and the sky gradually lightened from pale lemon and peach to blue, was breath-taking.

We glided over a river with an astonishing number of hippos in the water and on the riverbank. It made me a bit teary seeing so many of them together and I blew them kisses, as I'd promised Darcie.

As we neared the end of our flight, the balloon pilot alerted us to the right. A cheetah was chasing an impala, but a lioness was chasing the cheetah. It was captivating viewing, seeing nature in action, even though I couldn't help hoping all three of them would come out of the chase alive and uninjured.

'That was incredible,' I gushed, hugging Josh once we'd landed safely. 'Better than I could ever have imagined.'

While Josh took a few more photos of the balloons, I hugged my arms across my chest, feeling so grateful again for the life I now had and the exciting future Josh and I had stretched out in front of us, potentially adding to our family.

All I needed to make things perfect back home was for Chloe to keep up with her village activities and steer clear of the drama and for my parents to find love. Preferably not with each other, harsh as that sounded. And for Lauren to find someone special too. Whether that special person was my dad, I wasn't so sure, but I wanted to believe there was someone out there for everyone, including those who claimed to be jaded and cynical like Lauren.

* * *

Tonight, Obuya had something special lined up just for Josh and me – hopefully introducing us to the native hedgehog. He'd asked around the village and a friend had said that he sometimes saw one emerging from a field near his farmstead so had invited us over.

'Oh, my gosh!' I whispered. 'Look at it!'

'The moon is good tonight,' Obuya said. 'Meet the four-toed hedgehog.'

I crouched down to get a closer look and tears pricked my eyes. We'd spent the past week seeing animals in their natural habitat – a mixture of large, majestic beasts, some of which were sadly too rare – but seeing a single hedgehog made just as strong an impact on me.

'It doesn't matter that it is smaller than the lion, slower than the leopard and abundant, unlike the rhino,' Obuya whispered, as though reading my thoughts. 'It is still special, yes?'

'Very special. Thank you so much, and thank you to your friend.'

From what I could see in the limited light, the colouring was closer to the browns of the European hedgehog than the white of the North African one. Although the hedgehog was smaller, the legs appeared to be longer.

'It can run fast,' Obuya said. 'As you see now.'

The hedgehog, which had been snuffling along the edge of the undergrowth, took off like a rocket down the dirt track.

'It always amazes me how fast they can run,' I told Obuya. 'Maybe it's faster than the leopard, relative to its body size.'

Obuya laughed. 'Interesting thought. Sadly, I cannot arrange a race for you but I'm happy we saw him tonight. Most guests would not be so bothered about the small ones but all creatures, from the largest elephant to the smallest rodent, warm my heart.'

As Obuya drove us back to the hotel, my thoughts turned to Hedgehog Hollow. I didn't want our honeymoon to end but, at the same time, I couldn't wait to get home to see everyone again and be back in the barn with my hedgehogs. Every day in Tanzania brought stunning scenery, amazing animals and new experiences, but so did every day at Hedgehog Hollow. It was only day five, but I already missed that tingle of anticipation when a vehicle pulled into the farmyard with a new admission. I missed stroking the spines on a curled up adult hedgehog and seeing them unfurl for the first time, gazing into their dark eyes and sending a silent promise that I'd do my utmost to make them better. And I missed the most precious moment of all – releasing a healed hog back into its natural habitat, knowing that I'd played my small part in helping save a vulnerable species.

Tears pooled in my eyes, and I wiped them away.

'Are you okay?' Josh asked, his voice full of concern.

'Yeah. Ignore me. Seeing that hedgehog has made me homesick.'

His fingers entwined with mine. 'You're enjoying it here, though?'

'Gosh, yes! It's been the best experience ever – especially the hot air balloon this morning and the trip to... actually, it's all been outstanding. So I feel really ungrateful saying I miss home, but I can't help it. It doesn't mean I don't want to be here, though. Does that make any sense?'

'Perfect sense. Hedgehog Hollow is a big part of both our lives and it's been such an intense first year. It's bound to feel strange being away from it.'

'Thanks for understanding,' I whispered, wiping another tear away.

'It's a given. You can tell me anything, you know, no matter how silly or insignificant you might think it is. We'll get through it together.'

It wasn't just words. He'd proved that so many times already and it had worked the other way round too. I loved the partnership we had and couldn't imagine anything ever coming between us.

15

LAUREN

I squinted at my reflection in the bathroom mirror on Saturday morning and shook my head.

'Good grief, woman, what the hell are you playing at?'

Even though I hadn't given in to the tears – something I'd sworn never to do again after a meltdown when my divorce from Glen came through – my eyes were bloodshot with dark bags under them. My hair stuck out in all directions from tossing and turning for most of the night and my head thumped. How had I let myself get into such a state?

I slipped off my nightie and stepped into the shower, the hot water cloaking me like a hug, and felt a lot more human when I emerged. By the time I'd downed a large mug of strong coffee and eaten some toast, I looked a lot more human too.

The whole day lay ahead of me. The sensible thing to do would be to update my CV and start job-hunting, but what would I hunt for?

I stood by the back door, looking out onto the garden. After a glorious fortnight, the weather had turned. The wind was strong and dark clouds threatened rain, so doing something spontaneous outdoors was out of the question. After potting those flowers last weekend, I was itching to do some more work on the garden, but I wasn't stupid enough to attempt that in the rain.

I FaceTimed Connie, hoping she might be available for that cuppa.

'Have you got any plans for the weekend?' I asked, after we'd exchanged greetings.

She rolled her eyes. 'It's going to be a manic one. Melissa and Gareth are moving house today and their new place is a mess, so we're helping them clean and paint.'

Melissa was the youngest of Alex's three grown-up children.

'All weekend?' I asked.

'Yeah, and probably next weekend too. How's your week been?'

Connie sounded weary and I could see she was moving around the house as she spoke, presumably getting ready to leave.

'Bit of a rubbish one but it's the weekend now so all's good. Hope the move goes well. Give me a shout next week if you have five minutes.'

'Okay. Will do.'

'How typical is that?' I muttered to myself after the call ended. For years, Connie had asked me if I wanted to talk about Shaun and, later, about Glen and I always said no. Now that I did want to talk, she wasn't available.

With Jonathan in Whitsborough Bay, I didn't want to spend the day alone and, even though there was nobody else I could talk to, I did have an idea about how to spend the day which would give me some company, a welcome distraction and hopefully make two youngsters very happy too. I scrolled through my phone contacts and called Paul.

* * *

'Auntie Lauren!' Darcie ran along the path in front of the farmhouse at Hedgehog Hollow and threw herself into my arms, wrapping her legs round me like a koala. 'I've missed you!'

I squeezed her back. 'I've missed you too. Are you excited about seeing all the fish?' I was taking them to The Deep in Hull, which was a huge aquarium I'd heard good things about but had never visited.

'She's most excited about seeing the sharks, aren't you, Princess?' Phoebe said, joining us as I lowered Darcie to the ground.

'Sharks!' Darcie cried, running across the grass with her hand resting on the top of her head like a shark's fin.

Archie – Paul and Beth's young son – was clinging onto Phoebe's hand. I crouched down in front of him, struck as always by his strong resemblance to Josh, his half-brother.

'Hi, Archie, are you looking forward to our day out?'

With a smile and a gurgle, he lunged at me for a cuddle.

'Aw, thank you for that. That's very nice.' *And needed more than ever this morning.*

He relaxed into my hold for a moment before toddling after a butterfly that flitted past us.

'He's very cute,' Phoebe said as we watched him. 'And he gives the best cuddles.'

'*I* give the best cuddles!' Darcie planted her hands on her hips with indignation.

'Sorry, Princess,' Phoebe said, ruffling Darcie's hair. 'Archie gives the best cuddles of any nearly-two-year-old I know. And you give the best seven-year-old cuddles, as well as being my favourite person in the whole wide world.'

Darcie wrapped her arms round Phoebe's waist and squeezed her. I loved their relationship. There was only a twelve-year age gap between them, but Phoebe had managed to create a unique role of being mum, sister and best friend to that little girl. They weren't blood-related but that didn't stop them having an exceptional bond, just like I'd had with Ivy.

Beth and Paul stepped out of the farmhouse, Paul pushing a double buggy while Beth held their daughter Lottie.

'You're sure you don't mind us tagging along?' Beth asked.

'You're more than welcome.' When I'd phoned Paul, he'd thought the trip was a great idea but had asked whether I'd mind Beth and the two little ones joining us. He'd made great progress in his recovery after a stem cell transplant last year, but the wedding had taken it out of him and, even though they were all really considerate, having the farmhouse to himself would give him an opportunity to properly rest.

We headed over to the farmyard, Darcie holding my hand and telling me how much she'd loved helping Beth bathe Archie and Lottie last night and how Beth had let her choose Lottie's outfit this morning. I loved listening to her chattering and it struck me how different everything was since Sam had come into our lives. I'd never been much of an animal person before, but I'd fallen in love with Misty-Blue and the hedgehogs and I no longer crossed the road to avoid dogs. I knew how to feed hoglets and had helped clean crates and give medication. Perhaps more surprisingly, I was enjoying the company of children. If somebody had told me a year ago that I'd be looking forward to a day out with a baby, toddler, child and teenager, I'd have told them they needed to get their head read. It wasn't that I didn't like kids; I just hadn't had them in my life until now.

Connie had always wanted children. Growing up, she'd practised being a mum with her dolls and soft toys, taking such good care of them. I preferred cars and construction kits and, from an early age, I was fairly sure I didn't want kids of my own. Shaun and I had agreed we'd revisit our no-children decision when we hit thirty, but he'd been long gone before then.

I'd loved playing the auntie role to Josh – still did – but he'd been the only child in my life. I'd therefore been surprised at how quickly I'd taken to being surrounded by babies and children at Hedgehog Hollow, and had been really touched when Phoebe told me that Darcie would love to call me Auntie Lauren if I didn't mind. Of course I didn't!

I was past the age when having a child of my own was a physical possibility, and I was comfortable with that – no regrets about my choices there. Occasionally the thought popped into my head that I would have liked to be a grandmother, but I brushed it aside. If Josh and Sam had children, I'd be their great-auntie and that would be a privilege and, in the meantime, I had everyone at Hedgehog Hollow. As

Phoebe and Darcie had proved, families were so much more than blood connections and family trees.

'Thanks for doing this,' Paul said as he secured Darcie's car seat in the back of my car while Phoebe and Darcie helped Beth strap Archie and Lottie into her car, parked at the other side of the farmyard.

'You're welcome. I've never visited The Deep so, don't tell the others, but this is as much for my benefit as theirs.'

He smiled as he straightened up. 'It'll be our secret.'

'You take it easy while we're gone.'

'I will. I want to be fully recovered for Lottie's first birthday next Saturday. It's so frustrating because I felt on top form last weekend, but I did too much and I'm paying for that now.'

I squeezed his arm reassuringly. 'Recovery's a slow process but you'll get there. Just keep remembering how far you've come since August. Could you have imagined doing space hopper races at your son's wedding back then?'

'No chance.'

'Beth's ready!' Darcie called, running towards us.

She scrambled into the back and Phoebe checked she was fastened in before getting into the front passenger seat.

Paul walked round the car with me. 'While I've got you on your own, I wanted to thank you for how you've been with me. You had every right to give me a hard time and you didn't.'

'I wasn't the one you hurt, Paul, so if Connie and Josh could forgive you and move forward, then so could I. It was awful at the time but, as they say, you've got to have rain to see a rainbow. It's worked out for the best for all of you now.'

'It has. And what about you? Any sign of your rainbow?'

Beth drove past and waved at us.

'That's my cue,' I said, welcoming the opportunity to swerve the question. A few droplets of rain hit the car and I glanced up at the dark clouds. 'Get inside before that cloud bursts and get some rest.'

'Okay. See you later. Have a great day.'

We set off down the farm track behind Beth, with Darcie excitedly chattering about all the sea creatures she couldn't wait to see at The Deep and how she hadn't seen any of them in real life.

'I've never been to an aquarium before either,' Phoebe said as we pulled onto the main road. 'Thank you for taking us.'

'It's a pleasure.' And it really was. No child should ever have to go through what that pair had experienced at the hands of the Grimes family, and taking them out somewhere special was the least I could do. I'd make sure I made time for plenty more days out in the future and, given this week's turn of events, time was something I'd soon have in abundance.

* * *

The Deep was fantastic. Each area we walked through elicited excited squeals from Darcie and a new favourite sea creature. We picked up takeaway pizzas on the way back and, after she'd had a bath, Darcie insisted I read her a bedtime story, although she'd come on so much with her reading since escaping from the Grimes family that it was more a case of her reading the book to me. I hadn't cosied up to a child with a bedtime story since Josh was little and, once more, that grandparent pang was there.

'Do you think Samantha and Josh are missing me?' Darcie asked as she snuggled down to sleep, cuddling the soft seahorse I'd bought her.

'I'm sure they're missing you loads.'

'They've been away forever.'.

I smiled at her exaggeration. 'They've only been away for five days, but they'll be back before you know it.'

She wasn't the only one looking forward to their return. I hadn't appreciated how often I stopped by Hedgehog Hollow on my way home from college for a quick cuppa and a catch-up with Sam, and I'd missed that more than ever during this tough week.

I said my goodbyes shortly before eight and was about to get into my car to drive back to Chapel View when I paused and looked over to the barn. It had been such a good day, full of noise, excitement, laughter and hugs, and I didn't feel ready to go home to an empty house.

Fizz was on hoglet duty tonight. We'd picked up a pizza for her earlier, but Phoebe had taken it into the barn, so I hadn't seen her myself. I'd call in and see if she needed a hand with anything.

Fizz was sitting cross-legged in the middle of the barn, teasing a black cat with a feathered stick.

'Hi!' she said, looking up and smiling. 'Thanks for the pizza. It was awesome.'

'You're welcome. I was about to go home but thought I'd pop in and say hello first and see if you could use any help.'

'I could, actually. We've had a litter of hoglets in and they'll be awake soon if you want to help me feed them.'

'Count me in. Who's this then?' I crouched down and gave the cat a scratch behind the ears and was rewarded with a loud purr.

'This is Luna. Isn't she beautiful? Barney found her in one of his barns, feeding a litter of hoglets.'

'The cat was feeding the hoglets?'

'Yep. Isn't that amazing? A few of us searched the farm for her kittens but we didn't find any. They could have been anywhere. She's been a great mum. We lost one of the girls, Bridie, but the other four are thriving. They're asleep at the moment, cuddling up to a soft toy, so I thought I'd play with Luna for a bit.'

She picked up the cat and kissed the top of her head. 'You're such a good girl, aren't you?'

Some tiny squeaks came from the direction of the treatment table.

'That's our newbies awake so let's settle you back in with your adopted babies, Luna.'

Fizz removed a soft panda from a crate on the side and gently laid Luna in its place. The cat shuffled to curl herself protectively around the four hoglets in there.

'Not something you see every day, is it?' Fizz said, grinning at me. 'Right! Let's feed the newbies.'

'Could Luna not feed them too?'

'In theory, yes, but it wouldn't be fair to use her as a milking machine. Plus, there's a risk she might reject the new ones or even reject the existing ones once new hoglets are introduced, so we'll hand-rear any newbies.'

We washed our hands and prepared some formula for the latest admissions.

'There are four of them,' Fizz said. 'One was spotted in the middle of someone's garden during a family barbeque – nearly got stood on – and they heard squeaking and found three more among the shrubs.'

These were the first hoglets I'd fed since the intake of autumn juveniles, but it didn't take long to get back into it.

'We need to give them names,' Fizz said as we each fed our first hoglet. 'I've got a new theme of safari animals. Think of the animals Sam and Josh will see on their honeymoon and whether there are any famous ones. For example, I had an adult hedgehog admitted earlier and I've called him Dumbo after the elephants.'

'Ah! I see! So what sex have we got here?'

'You've got the two boys and I've got two girls.'

'Simba and George,' I said after a moment.

'I'm getting Simba from *The Lion King*, but George?'

I laughed. 'I'm showing my age here. When I was little, I used to watch a kids' TV programme called *Rainbow* and there was a puppet on it called George. He was a pale pink hippo with big eyes and even bigger eyelashes.'

'Oh, my God! He sounds awesome. I'll have to Google him later. For the girls, I'm going to go lion and hippo too – Nala from *The Lion King* and Gloria from *Madagascar*.'

'How old do you think they are?' I asked.

'Just a few days.'

'I can never get over how tiny they are.'

'I know! It's a miracle any of them survive.'

After I'd fed and toileted George, I moved onto Simba.

'Isn't it early for hoglets?' I asked Fizz. 'I could have sworn it was

June last year when they started coming in because that's when Sam stopped working at the TEC.'

'Hoglets season is usually June and July, but we've had a mild winter which brings mating season forward as they come out of hibernation earlier and, in some cases, don't even go into hibernation. Oh! Do you hear that? Luna's hoglets are awake. Take a look.'

I peeked into the crate and saw the hoglets clambering over each other to suckle on the cat. 'Wow! That's not something I expected to see today.'

'It's one of the reasons I love working with animals. They're so awesome. Just when I think I've seen it all, there's a special moment like this. And every day is so rewarding, knowing I'm making a difference.'

* * *

As I drove back to Amblestone a little later, I pondered on what Fizz had said about working with animals being rewarding. I'd felt that way about my nursing career and in a different way when I started teaching. Job satisfaction came from helping young people find their way in the world, encouraging those who were struggling, and supporting others through career choice doubts. But as I'd dropped my teaching hours to become management, those moments were few and far between. I loved my job and I was good at it, but was it rewarding? No. I hadn't realised that until now and it unnerved me.

If someone had asked for a list of things that were important to me in a job, 'rewarding' would have been at the top. So how had that disappeared without me noticing? Had I got myself into a rut – albeit a comfortable one – at Reddfield TEC? I was going to need to do some soul-searching over the next few weeks about what I really wanted from my next career move. Oh, to be young again like Fizz and to have it all worked out.

When I arrived back at Chapel View, the cottage felt empty and far too quiet. After making a mug of tea, I sat on the sofa and scrolled through the stack of photos on my phone, smiling at how wide Darcie's and Phoebe's smiles were in every posed picture and the captivated expressions on their faces when I'd caught them unawares gazing into the tanks or watching the penguins.

If Shaun had stuck around, would we have reconsidered having children when we were thirty? Was he playing happy families with someone else now? At the time he left, I'd wondered if he might have a secret family hidden away somewhere or a pregnant girlfriend who he'd chosen over me. It remained a possibility, even though it didn't feel like something Shaun would do. Although running away hadn't seemed like something he'd do either.

16

LAUREN

As promised to Riley, I took some time on Sunday to carefully read through the job descriptions for the three senior roles. They were challenging and exciting jobs... for someone who wanted to climb that ladder. There was no fire in my belly thinking about any of them, not even a flicker. I was extremely committed to any job I did – always throwing myself in with passion and conviction – but there was no way I could do a job that didn't excite me, as that would mean a half-hearted effort which wasn't me. With everything I did – work and personal life – I was either fully in or fully out. There was no halfway. I'd tried that once and it had been disastrous.

First thing on Monday, I checked the college diary system to see if Riley had any time free to confirm face to face that it was a pass from me, but he was booked out solid, so I sent him an email instead.

'Lauren!'

I was almost at my car when Riley shouted my name at the end of the day.

He ran and caught up with me. 'Can I walk you to your car?'

'If you insist, but it'll take about thirty seconds, if that.'

'Then can you spare me five minutes?'

There were some raised flowerbeds at the end of the car park enclosed by a brick wall, so I suggested we perch there.

'Did you get my email?' I asked when we sat down.

'Yes, I did. Thank you.'

'Please tell me you're not going to try to talk me into changing my mind.'

'No, don't worry. I wanted to ask you what your ideal job would be.'

'Head of Health and Beauty at Reddfield TEC,' I deadpanned.

Riley smiled. 'I walked into that one. If that role didn't exist anywhere in the world, what would you do?'

'Ah! The question I've been asking myself since Friday. I don't actually know. All I keep coming up with is what I don't want. I don't want a more senior role here and I don't want to return to nursing.'

'You were a nurse?'

'First job after school. Went through my training, got a job at Hull Hospital and loved it.'

'If you loved it, what made you leave?'

'I was seeing a consultant there and we decided it would be easier if one of us moved on. Well, he decided it would be easier for me to move on but, as we ended up getting divorced, it turned out to be one of his better ideas.' I frowned, not sure why I'd just shared that bit of personal information.

'Anyway, I'd been doing an outreach thing with the TEC and they were advertising for a health and social care tutor. It sounded interesting so I applied, got the job, and worked my way up to department head where I'd have happily stayed until retirement, but...'

'But I came along and ruined everything,' he finished for me.

'If the cap fits... Look, I'm not angry at you. Well, not anymore. The air was blue last Tuesday! You're doing your job and, even though it's not ideal for me, I do believe in what you're trying to do here.'

'Thank you.' There was a moment's pause before he asked, 'Did you listen to ELO last Tuesday?'

'On full volume with my own sweary lyrics, but even that couldn't lift me.'

'Really bad, then.'

'The worst. And I crunched my way through most of that packet of rhubarb and custards and had a scary moment when I thought my teeth were welded together.'

'I can top that. I never used to eat sweets, but they became my pick-me-up when I was going through my divorce – a messy one. I was eating a chocolate eclair after a particularly bad encounter with my ex and I managed to pull a crown out.'

'Nasty!'

'It was! And you'd think I'd have learned from it, but I did the exact same thing a few months later, so that's when I gave up on toffees and turned to boiled sweets, although I have to make sure I suck them instead of crunching. Speaking of which...'

He dug in his jacket pocket and held out a bag of rhubarb and custards.

I took one with a smile. 'Thanks. I'd better get home. Was there anything else you wanted to ask me?'

'Yeah, one more question. What is it about your job that you love so much?'

'The variety. It has a bit of everything – planning and organising, teaching and managing a team. I like them all, but a role where the main focus is only on one of them really doesn't appeal.'

He nodded slowly then smiled. 'I appreciate you giving me the time. Have a good evening.'

'You too. Bye.'

As I started the car, I noticed that Riley was still sitting on the wall, looking thoughtful. I sucked on my sweet and smiled. I should hate him, but I didn't. There was something endearing about him, and I felt surprisingly comfortable in his presence. The only other men I'd felt so at ease around were Jonathan and Shaun.

Riley was making his way back to the college entrance as I pulled out of my parking space. He stopped and waved and my stomach did that backflip again.

'Stop it!' I cried, turning the radio up. 'He's the hatchet man.

Nothing more.' But I couldn't help thinking there was so much more to him than that. He genuinely seemed to care, which really didn't fit with the role he had.

* * *

An unexpected outcome of my present work circumstances was that my evenings were now my own. I was used to working for a few hours at home – catching up with emails or marking assignments – but now I didn't need to do any of my planning activities and my team were temporarily reporting to Judith. This meant I could fit in all my student-related work during the normal working day.

I might have relished being free every evening had Jonathan been around, but I'd barely seen him, and I really missed him. Every evening he was either at Hedgehog Hollow, on call, or over at Whitsborough Bay seeing Debs. That's where he was tonight.

Connie had texted to say she'd be helping out at Melissa's new place most evenings but to shout if I needed her. I *did* need her, but I had no right to think that my needs were more important. We'd hopefully have a proper catch-up next week.

Which left me unable to put off job-hunting any longer. I opened my laptop, logged onto an education job site and half-heartedly scrolled through the adverts. I couldn't face the idea of starting over again in another college. I felt too old to be the newbie. Reddfield TEC was comfortable. Easy. And I was still worried about that desire to do something rewarding. Would I get that doing the same job elsewhere? I had a lot of thinking to do.

17

SAMANTHA

The safari stretch of our honeymoon ended, and we flew to the exotic island of Zanzibar on Tuesday evening, where we were staying in the most gorgeous thatched bungalow on the beach. So far, we'd been on an island-hopping boat trip where we'd seen dolphins, we'd snorkelled over the stunning coral reefs and had swum with turtles, which had been pure magic.

Today we'd decided to take things at a more leisurely place with a day on the beach by the bungalow. Early afternoon for us was mid-morning in the UK and time to call home.

'I can't believe Lottie's one already,' I said to Josh as we sat on our shaded terrace, waiting for the FaceTime call to connect to Beth.

Lottie's face appeared on the screen, and Josh and I sang a chorus of 'Happy Birthday'. Her little face crumpled and she released a wail.

'Was it that bad?' Josh asked when Beth appeared on screen instead.

'Bit pitchy,' she joked. 'But I think the cry was less about the singing and more about us taking her away from the horses. Just a second.'

The crying faded. 'That's better. I've come out of the stables. We're at Bumblebee Barn. Natasha's thinking of running children's parties where they get a hands-on experience with the animals, so we're the guinea pigs. Phoebe and Darcie are here and so are Samuel and Amelia, with Chloe and Hannah, of course. There are little people everywhere!'

'I bet that's a shock to the system for Barney,' I said.

'I don't think he knows what's hit him. So how's the honeymoon? The photos look amazing.'

'It's the best experience ever. We're—'

A shout interrupted me and Beth turned away from the camera for a moment. 'I'm going to have to go. Archie's managed to sit in a water trough. I'll put Phoebe on.'

'Sounds like it's chaos,' I said when Phoebe appeared on screen.

'It's Archie! He can't be left alone for two seconds. He's already on his second outfit.'

'How are you and Darcie?' Josh asked.

'We're both good. Darcie's been invited to a birthday party over half-term so she's really excited and I got a distinction on my last two assignments so I'm on track for an overall distinction.'

'That's fantastic. I'm so proud of you.'

'Me too,' Josh said. 'That's brilliant work.'

I could see by Phoebe's big smile that she was proud of herself too and rightly so. It was a fantastic achievement anyway but to have managed to excel academically after what she'd been through was quite astonishing and took a special kind of determination.

'Has Lauren told you about the TEC being sold?' Phoebe asked.

Josh and I exchanged confused looks.

'They made a big announcement on Thursday that an academy has bought the college. It was in the paper too. It won't affect me, as I'm leaving this year, but there'll be a few changes next year for the current first years.'

'I didn't know the college was up for sale,' I said.

'Nobody did. The heads of department have lost their jobs.'

Josh gasped and grabbed my arm. 'That's Auntie Lauren.'

'Has Lauren said anything to you?' I asked Phoebe.

'I haven't seen her since last weekend when she took us to The

Deep and she didn't say anything then, although I don't know when they found out.'

I chatted a little longer to Phoebe before Darcie came on, desperate to tell me all about the birthday party she'd been invited to and how much she missed us and couldn't wait to see us both next week.

After disconnecting the call, I turned to Josh and sighed. 'That's a nightmare about Lauren.'

'She's going to be gutted,' he said.

I suddenly felt a very long way from home and a bit helpless. Lauren wasn't fazed by anything and took bumps in the road in her stride, but having reported into her for a couple of terms, I knew how passionate she was about that job. There was no way she'd be able to easily shrug it off and move on.

'I might just try Lauren.' I attempted a FaceTime and then a normal call, but it just rang out.

'I'm sure she'll be fine,' Josh said, heading into the bungalow. He paused by the door. 'She's not facing it alone. She's got my mum and your dad to talk to if she needs a sounding board. It's not like she won't be able to walk straight into another job with her skills and experience.'

I had no doubt he was right about that, but I'd always got the impression it wasn't just about the job itself for Lauren. There was something about being at Reddfield TEC she absolutely loved. She'd once joked that she'd move in if they let her. I suspected this would have hit her really hard – and, if I knew Lauren as well as I thought I did, she probably hadn't told anyone how hard.

'I'm going to attempt the hammock again,' Josh said, emerging with a beach towel and a book. 'But you're not allowed to film me this time.'

'Why would you spoil my fun like that?' I cried, hands on hips in protest.

Colourful hammocks were strung between trees on the white sandy beach and we'd made several attempts to clamber into them, but each had resulted in fits of giggles after the hammock twisted and unceremoniously dumped us on the sand. There was definitely a technique which neither of us had mastered.

'Fancy joining me?' Josh asked.

'I might stay in the shade for a bit. Good luck.'

I went inside to retrieve my Kindle but dug out my notebook and pen instead. I hadn't done any planning for the Family Fun Day on the flight over to Tanzania as intended and the downtime now would be the perfect opportunity.

* * *

With a frustrated cry, I ripped another page from my notebook and scrumpled it into a ball to join the others on the table. I wasn't short of ideas, but I was short on time. Everything I thought of required longer than we had or talents I didn't possess. Feeling the panic rising, I closed my notebook and went inside for a cold drink.

I held the bottle of chilled water to my forehead and cheeks before gulping it down, but it didn't calm me in the slightest. I paced up and down the room, trying to calm my erratic breathing.

'There's nothing you can do about the Family Fun Day now,' I muttered to myself. 'It's not worth stressing about. Control the controllables.' That was another big learning from my counselling sessions; that there were some things in life over which we had no control and investing all our energy into trying to control or influence them was fruitless.

I was thousands of miles from home and realistically there was nothing I could do about adding to the Family Fun Day plans. The essentials were already in place and time was too tight for anything more. Next year, I'd go bigger and better and I'd start planning it much sooner.

Finally feeling calmer, I took my Kindle outside, but my mind was in work mode and I couldn't concentrate on the book. I opened my notebook again. I couldn't do anything about the Family Fun Day, but I could start a to-do list of all the things I needed to do when I got back so I could hit the ground running.

The list grew and grew. By the time I started my fourth page in the A5 book, my eyes burned with unshed tears. I flicked the pages back and forth, shaking my head in despair. This wasn't even a complete list – just the short-term needs. If I considered longer term, I'd fill another six pages at least. And that was without all the work around the holiday cottages and promoting Wildflower Byre as a function venue.

My stomach lurched as a thought hit me: *if I have a baby, how will I manage it all?*

I closed my eyes, willing myself not to cry. My right leg bounced up and down, knocking against the table, and I felt beads of sweat trickle down my back as nausea took hold.

I glanced at the date on my phone and my stomach lurched once more. One year ago yesterday, I'd fainted at college after taking on far too much. I'd barely recovered from my coma when Hedgehog Hollow opened for business and I'd underestimated how much work would be needed, particularly as we were straight into hoglets season. Running the rescue centre alongside a full-time job had been too much, but wasn't having a baby also a full-time job?

Feeling lightheaded, I pushed the notebook aside and pressed my fingers to my temples as I stared at it. How could I do all of that and raise a baby? It wasn't possible. I struggled to gasp for air as panic gripped me.

'Not here,' I whispered, calling on all the advice from my counsellor to control my reactions. *Not on my honeymoon. Calm down. Breathe. Relax.*

* * *

Before dinner that evening, Josh and I strolled hand in hand along the ocean's edge as the sun dipped in a blazing orange sky.

'You're quiet,' Josh observed, concern in his voice.

'Just a bit tired,' I said, not wanting to worry him. Everything had been back under control by the time he'd returned from his hammock, and I hadn't told him I'd been working after promising to relax.

'Me too,' he said. 'I think it's slowing down today that's done it. We could skip the entertainment tonight and get an early night.'

'Sounds good.' I sighed contentedly as I gazed at the horizon. 'It's so beautiful here.'

'It is. Any more feelings of homesickness?'

'No. Well, teeny moments but I'm having the best time.' And I really was apart from earlier. I'd given myself a stern talking-to about the homesickness and had pushed aside those feelings, determined to make the most of this once-in-a-lifetime experience, especially when it very nearly hadn't happened.

Further down the shoreline, we paused to watch a family a little way ahead of us. A boy who appeared to be about Archie's age was holding hands with a girl a couple of years older and they were splashing in the shallows while the woman took photos and the man watched, laughing. It was a picture-perfect family moment which warmed my heart.

Josh wrapped both arms round my waist and rested his head against mine. 'That could be us in a few years.' His hand brushed across my stomach. 'It's amazing to think our first child might be in there right now.'

That statement should have filled me with excitement but, instead, a wave of panic swept through me just like earlier. My stomach churned and beads of sweat prickled on my forehead and top lip. I thought about that enormous list of things to do and how I barely had enough hours in the day as it was.

'Of course, it might not have happened yet,' Josh continued. 'But imagine if it has.'

I *was* imagining it and I could feel my stress levels rising rapidly. Terrified of triggering a PTSD episode, I closed my eyes and concentrated hard on the gentle lapping of the waves until the tension eased.

Josh mused over what he might like to eat as we ambled back

towards the bungalow, but I couldn't think about food right now. My stomach was churning and I felt dizzy.

'I'll just nip to the loo before dinner,' I said as we reached our bungalow. 'You go ahead and get us some drinks.'

Inside, I flicked the bedside lamp on and slumped down on the edge of our bed with my head in my hands, my heart racing once more, feeling sick and shaky. As I pictured that family, I struggled to catch my breath and had to fight hard to regulate my breathing and prevent a full-blown panic attack.

'It's too soon,' I whispered.

When I'd presented Josh with his special wedding gift – the news that I'd worked through my fears, had accepted I wasn't going to be a carbon copy of my mum and was ready to have a family – I'd meant it. I wanted to be a mum, I wanted Josh to be a dad, and I could absolutely picture us raising our family at Hedgehog Hollow. I'd suggested trying for a baby after Paul and Beth were settled in Alder Lea and Phoebe had a job, but I hadn't thought through the reality of how soon that really was – potentially the start of the summer. I'd had a vague notion of us trying next year, maybe even the year after, but that wasn't what I'd said to Josh. No wonder he'd barely challenged me when I'd lost my pills and suggested we just go with it. We'd already had a deep conversation about whether I was sure about starting a family so, as far as he was concerned, we were only bringing what I wanted forward by six to eight weeks.

The timing was wrong, with far too much going on at home and at the rescue centre. I should have taken a step back and considered the practicalities and not allowed myself to get carried away by the romance of a honeymoon baby conceived in this incredible place.

I stared at my hands, lying loose in my lap, and blinked back tears as I ran a finger over my wedding and engagement rings. A few nights ago, when I'd shared my feelings of homesickness with Josh, he'd said I could tell him anything and he'd understand, but how could I tell him this? How could he understand this? I might already be pregnant. If I shared that it was too soon and we found out I was expecting, it would be like me saying I didn't want the baby. Which would, despite everything I'd worked so hard to overcome, make me just like Mum, who hadn't wanted me. The circumstances were completely different, but the feeling was the same.

I sat up straight and ran my fingers through my hair. If I didn't go to the restaurant soon, Josh would be worried and would come looking for me. Hopefully it was just a silly blip brought on by fatigue and I'd be fine in the morning. Although, in the morning, that to-do list wouldn't be any shorter.

18

LAUREN

I sat on the patio with a coffee on Saturday morning, trying to decide what to do with my weekend. The students now knew about the takeover and the local newspaper, *Wolds Weekly*, had carried the story. During a teaching slot yesterday afternoon, I'd been bombarded with questions about me leaving. A couple of the students offered to start a petition begging for my role to be reinstated, which was touching but unnecessary.

I felt more at peace about leaving since realising that the role was no longer rewarding, although I was still confused because I had no idea what would bring me that job satisfaction again. I'd hoped an idea would present itself as the week progressed, but my mind remained bank.

Riley had given me my redundancy quote yesterday which confirmed what I'd suspected – that I was now in a financial position not to need to work again. The redundancy payment on its own wouldn't have been enough to give me that freedom but the decent thing Shaun had done for me was to transfer the mortgage on our house into my name only and to relinquish rights to any profit if I sold up. Presumably that was his way of appeasing his guilt.

Despite the financial security, not working wasn't an option for me.

I was struggling to find a way to fill this weekend, so there was no way I could cope with all the days spread out ahead of me and nothing to do. I probably should get myself a regular hobby instead of thrill-seeking a couple of times a year.

I'd expected Connie to get in touch after the story broke in the paper and felt miffed when she didn't, before reasoning that maybe she hadn't seen it. That urge to talk had eased, so I'd wait until I could have her undivided attention next week.

* * *

I decided to spend the day in the garden and, by teatime, the garden waste bin was full, but I was still drawing a blank on my next job move, which was disconcerting. I didn't usually do indecisive.

My phone showed a missed FaceTime and missed call from Sam this morning. I clicked into my emails and there was a message from her:

We've just spoken to Phoebe and heard the news about the college takeover and your job. We're so sorry. I know how much that place means to you. Thinking of you xx

While the kettle boiled, I tapped in a response to thank her, reassure her I was fine and to say we'd catch up when she was back. I didn't want her spending any of her honeymoon fretting about me.

Curling up on the sofa with my coffee, I reflected on how funny it was that the news about the college hadn't reached my sister a few miles down the road but it had reached Zanzibar, nearly 7,500 miles away!

'Stop blaming Connie,' I muttered to myself. I knew she didn't read the paper and none of Alex's family were of college age, so the only way she could know what had happened would be if I'd told her. Although it wasn't like I hadn't tried to, this time.

I glanced across at the bookshelves in the alcove to the right of the fireplace and my eyes rested on a photo of Connie and me, laughing at our fiftieth party last year. Anyone who saw us together would think we were exceptionally close, and they'd be right, but I'd felt an undercurrent since childhood, thanks to Mum, and I'd never felt able to talk to my sister about it.

It was usually little things but there'd been enough of them over the years to position Connie as the firm favourite and me as the disappointment. Mum would comment on how shiny Connie's hair looked, then glance at mine with a frown and a little shake of her head. She bought a scrapbook for Connie to stick all her dance certificates in and said: 'I didn't get you one, Lauren. You don't have anything to put in it.' It was the delight at teaching Connie how to bake and cook and frustrated sighs when I said I'd rather go and visit Dad.

Fortunately I'd had Shaun by my side, understanding my frustrations and reassuring me he loved me just the way I was. Ivy showered me with love and attention too, which helped me adopt the smile-politely-and-change-the-subject approach with Mum.

While my parents' divorce was going through, Mum had found love again with her first boyfriend, Kelvin. They'd met by chance at the solicitor's office – Kelvin was also getting divorced – and had gone for a coffee to catch up on old times. Neither of them could remember why they'd split up and the spark was still there. Kelvin moved in with us when both divorces were finalised. I wanted to dislike him because he wasn't my dad, so I kept him at arm's length at first, but how do you keep pushing away someone who is genuinely kind and decent? He made Mum so happy too.

My gaze shifted to my favourite photo of Dad and me, the day he bought me my BMX. Before he lost his job. Before he started drowning his sorrows. Three weeks today, on 5 June, would be thirty years since he died. He'd only been fifty-four – three years older than I was now. I hadn't cried at his funeral or any time afterwards. We'd lost him many years before and I'd shed all my tears then. I didn't know that self-absorbed bitter man in the coffin. The drink had taken away my wonderful dad.

Mum hadn't liked me spending time with Dad but I knew it was mainly because he was so unreliable and she didn't like seeing me upset. I appreciated that she was careful not to badmouth him around Connie and me but I only had to look at her and Kelvin together to see how tough her marriage had been, even before Dad lost his job and started down the road of self-destruction. Some people should never be together. Like Glen and me.

My colleagues at the hospital had been buzzing with excitement about Glen Fairclough – the new consultant who'd transferred from Nottingham at the start of summer thirteen years after Shaun left. Brilliantly efficient, recently divorced, and drop-dead gorgeous, they said. I was intrigued to see what all the fuss was about but knew there was no way he'd have any effect on me. Aged thirty-eight at the time, I'd given up on men after a handful of dates post-Shaun – all set-ups from well-meaning colleagues – had been disastrous. It wasn't their fault. It genuinely was a case of *it's not you, it's me* – they weren't Shaun, so I wasn't interested.

And then I met Glen and I understood what the fuss was about. With his dark hair, permanent five o'clock shadow, high cheekbones and a strong jaw, he could have been a model. Looks were superficial but when they came with confidence, intelligence and kindness, they made for a compelling package.

Glen was charming and flirty, and I got the impression he liked me, but I was determined to keep our relationship strictly professional. But the more time I spent with him, the more that conviction waned. I had tremendous respect for how good he was at his job, managing to make his patients feel valued and heard while still running a tight ship. I relished the shifts when I was able to work alongside him, telling myself it was because I was learning so much from him and pushing aside those feelings of deepening attraction.

He asked me out to dinner on several occasions, but I always declined. I expected to hear he'd moved onto someone else but there were never rumours of him dating any of my colleagues. Not a player, then.

At the Christmas party the year I turned forty, we found ourselves standing under the mistletoe. We both looked up and laughed about it then he asked my permission to kiss me. I couldn't think of any logical reason to refuse. He cupped my face and gave me the softest kiss that left my lips wanting more.

'I've wanted to do that for the past eighteen months,' he said, running his thumb across my cheek. 'I wish you felt the same.'

With a resigned shrug, he left me and, at that moment, I *did* feel the same. I couldn't take my eyes off him for the rest of the night and, even though I knew that playing doctors and nurses usually ended badly – I'd seen it go wrong for colleagues so many times – I couldn't resist pulling him under the mistletoe in a dark corner at the end of the night and inviting a more passionate kiss.

When I woke up the following morning to find myself alone in his bedroom with my clothes in a neat pile at the end of the bed, I shook my head, cursing my stupidity. He wanted me gone. Last night, it had been a line to get me into bed and it had worked.

I started dressing, ready to do the walk of shame, and was stunned when he appeared holding a couple of mugs of coffee and wearing nothing but a smile.

We stayed in bed all weekend. It was new, passionate and exciting, and I think that's why it worked. At first. He was nothing like Shaun in looks, personality, attitude or outlook, so there weren't constant reminders of what I'd lost.

I hadn't expected it to last. Glen could have chosen any woman and I'd fully expected him to realise that and move onto someone younger or better looking, but he didn't, and I think it was because I was nothing like his ex-wife.

Relationships at work were complicated and, after a few months, Glen suggested that 'one of us' might want to put in for a transfer. I knew that by 'one of us' he meant me. I'd have dug my heels in, but I was ready for a career move. I'd been a sister for some time and the next step at the hospital was matron, which didn't appeal, but the role of tutor sounded like an interesting new challenge. The unplanned and unexpected change of direction had worked perfectly.

Shame the same couldn't be said for our marriage.

19

LAUREN

Eight years ago

The Easter holidays had arrived but, as I drove across to Glen's apartment in Hull on Friday evening, I didn't feel the buzz of excitement which usually accompanied time off and I knew exactly why.

Glen would be celebrating his fiftieth birthday on Wednesday, although 'celebrating' wasn't a suitable adjective. We'd been together for over two years now and, at his request, we hadn't done anything to even acknowledge his previous two birthdays. I understood his reluctance, after finding his wife Juliette having her own private celebrations with her tennis coach on his forty-second birthday, but it saddened me that he'd ignored his birthday ever since. I'd suggested going big for his landmark year, thinking it might help push aside that Juliette-shaped shadow. He'd mulled it over, had booked a week off work and had conceded to going for a meal on his actual birthday and perhaps a couple of days out, although he hadn't wanted to commit to when or where, in case he didn't feel like celebrating when the time came.

Again, I understood his thought process and was happy to support him, but it wasn't ideal for me. I liked to make the most of my time off and it didn't sit comfortably with me that next week was so up in the air. Tonight, I was going to have to get Glen to choose which days he might like to go out, even if how we spent them remained unconfirmed and even if he cancelled last minute. That way, I could plan the rest of my week around him.

'I've been thinking about what you said about going big for my fiftieth,' Glen said as he poured me a glass of wine a little later. 'I haven't celebrated my birthday for nearly a decade and, this year, that changes.'

'That's brilliant! What do you want to do?'

He sat beside me on the sofa. 'I want us to go on holiday. In fact...' He removed something from behind a cushion and held it out in front of me.

'Plane tickets? You've booked somewhere?' I couldn't hide my surprise. Glen was *never* spontaneous, which was frustrating at times but was another difference between him and Shaun and therefore a good thing.

'I have.'

'Where?' My guess was a European capital city full of history and culture. He was much more sedate and serious than Shaun, into art galleries, museums and plays.

'Las Vegas,' he declared.

'Yeah, right. Where are we *really* going?'

'Las Vegas.' He passed me the tickets and there it was in bold typeface, flying on Monday, returning on Friday.

'You said go big. I don't think it comes much bigger than that, and you said you've always fancied going.'

'I have, but...' I lowered the tickets. 'It's your birthday, not mine. It's about what *you* want. I didn't think Vegas would be your kind of place.'

He looked at me tenderly. 'I want to make you happy, and I don't want what Juliette did to affect my life anymore. A week away in the party capital will achieve both.'

I glanced down at the ticket once more, excitement welling inside me. 'It's going to be amazing, Glen. You've done the right thing. We'll make this your best birthday ever.'

* * *

On the flight over to Las Vegas, Glen seemed different – more touchy-feely, more excitable – and I liked this 'new' version of him. I hushed the voice in my head that whispered, *you only love this because it reminds you of Shaun.*

Glen was extremely cautious with money, so I wasn't surprised when he announced that he'd set a gambling budget. What did surprise me was how generous it was. He'd spared no expense, with a suite booked in a hotel just off the strip and tickets for a couple of shows.

On his actual birthday, we started the day with a champagne break-fast in our suite. We visited the botanical gardens in the Bellagio Hotel, after which Glen had booked a gondola ride in The Venetian Resort. He seemed agitated as we waited for our turn, frowning and fiddling with his watch strap.

'Are you okay?' I asked. 'You look nervous.'

His cheeks reddened. 'All good. I was thinking about missing the step and ending up in the water.'

As we boarded our gondola, my heart started racing. We were about to be serenaded on a gondola in a hotel inspired by the city of love – all very romantic – and Glen was nervous. Was it possible that he was planning to propose? We'd never discussed marriage. I'd assumed he was dead set against it after his marriage to Juliette ended so badly, and I wasn't convinced I was ready to go down that road again either.

Now it was my turn to be nervous. My legs felt unsteady as I stepped into the gondola and took my seat, and my mouth felt dry. I wanted to sit back, relax and enjoy the experience, but now that the idea of Glen proposing had entered my head, it wouldn't go away. What would I say if he did? I really cared about him, and we'd had a great relationship so far. But marriage?

A little later, I could see the end of the ride ahead of us. If Glen was going to pop the question, he was cutting it fine. But he didn't ask. As he took my hand to help me off the gondola, I felt oddly disappointed. Maybe I was ready after all.

We stayed in The Venetian Resort for lunch before making our way to Caesars Palace Casino. I felt lightheaded from a few glasses of wine and, as Glen kissed me after a small win on roulette, I imagined what it might be like to be his wife, seeing him every day, kissing him every day, and it gave me a warm glow inside.

'Tequila!' Glen announced, pulling me towards the bar.

We smiled at each other as we each licked our hand, sprinkled on some salt and raised our shot glasses.

'Happy birthday!' I said. 'Go!'

We raced each other, licking off the salt, downing the tequila and sucking our limes. Glen grinned at me with his lime wedge still in his mouth.

'Vegas suits you,' I said, laughing at him.

'It's not Vegas that suits me. It's you.'

It was right up there with romantic moments and, as he kissed me once more, I wished he had proposed earlier. There was still time.

An hour and several more shots of tequila later, we won big on craps and that was when it happened. In the busy casino in front of everyone, Glen got down on one knee and took my hand.

'We've won big on craps but there's a bigger win I'd like – your hand in marriage. Lauren, will you be my wife?'

At that moment, it felt right. 'Yes!' I cried, hurling myself at him. 'Yes!'

* * *

'I never thought I'd do this again,' Glen said as we sat in the ostentatious wedding chapel reception, his hands clasped round mine, waiting for Elvis to legally bind us together. 'But from the first moment I saw you, I knew you were special. You made me work for it, though.'

I smiled at him. 'I wasn't ready. But, as they say, the best things come to those who wait.'

'You were definitely worth the wait.' His speech was a little slurred. I'd never seen him drunk before. It brought out his soppy side, which was endearing.

He kissed me softly and stroked my cheek as he pulled away.

'But you're ready now,' he said, nodding at me.

'I am.'

'That ghost from your past is laid to rest, isn't he? Ready for a new life with me.'

My heart thudded and my stomach did a loop-the-loop. No! That ghost would never be laid to rest. Why did he have to mention Shaun at a moment like this?

Glen patted my hand. 'I'm nipping to the gents. Don't do a runner on me.' He laughed at his own joke as he staggered towards the toilets.

I gulped as I watched him disappear and glanced towards the chapel door, his final words ringing in my ears. What would happen if I did do a runner? No! I couldn't do that to Glen. He was a good man, and I couldn't put him through what Shaun had put me through. Nobody deserved that.

I smoothed down the bodice of the cream lacy shift dress I'd spotted in a shop window after picking up our wedding licence. Feeling uncomfortable about getting married in jeans, Glen had bought it for me, and I'd had a chance to retouch my make-up back at the hotel while he changed into a suit that I hadn't even known he'd brought with him. Had he planned this all along? Had he meant to propose on the gondola but the nerves got to him?

I glanced round the reception. Opposite me, a young couple in full wedding gear were gazing at each other lovingly. Beside them, a very drunk-looking couple wearing jeans and *I Heart Vegas* T-shirts were locked in a passionate embrace and needed to get a room. Guests chatted and I could feel the excitement and anticipation.

Could I really marry Glen? While I admired him greatly and enjoyed his company, I didn't love him. He wasn't Shaun. I'd given that man my heart when we were kids and had never got it back. But Shaun was gone and, even if he miraculously reappeared wanting me back, it could never work. I couldn't forgive him for what he'd done, and I'd always fear him doing it again.

The last couple of years with Glen had been really good. We were definitely a case of opposites attract, but it had worked so far. Our relationship was nothing like mine with Shaun had been but, considering how that ended, surely that was a good thing. It wasn't like Glen and I were a pair of inexperienced teens rushing into the first throes of love. We were sensible, mature adults who knew who we were and what we wanted from life. Glen wanted loyalty and I wanted company. I'd enjoyed being half of a couple after so long on my own. It would be fine. It would last.

Glen emerged from the toilets as a cheer and a burst of music emitted from the chapel.

'Glen and Lauren, your wedding is next,' the receptionist gushed. 'Are you both ready to say I do?'

Glen held out his hand to me. 'I am. Are you?'

No! Yes! I don't know! There were so many reasons why I should pull out but there were many in favour of going ahead. He wasn't one for talking about feelings, but I knew Glen loved me. I cared for him deeply and, if we went through with it, I would wholeheartedly commit myself to making our marriage work because that's the sort of person I was.

'Lauren?' he prompted, his voice a little squeaky.

I placed my hand in his. 'Yes. I am. Definitely ready.'

He pressed his hand across his heart. 'You had me worried for a moment.'

But even as Elvis conducted our ceremony, a voice inside my head was screaming *stop this madness!*

* * *

One year later

My mobile phone rang as I spooned mince onto the layer of pasta sheets and I knew without looking at the screen that it would be Connie, making a final attempt at convincing me to join her, Paul and Josh for a meal to celebrate our birthday.

'The answer's still no,' I said as soon as I put the pan down and connected the call, trying to keep my voice jovial. 'Glen will be back too late to go out so we're celebrating at home.'

'But we always see each other on our birthday.'

'I know, but please don't pull a guilt trip on me. It's just for one year.'

'Okay, no guilt trip, but you tell Glen that we're celebrating together next year whether he likes it or not.'

'I'll tell him. Now finish getting ready and leave me to my cooking. I need to concentrate. You know how rubbish I am in the kitchen. Bye.'

I forced down the lump in my throat as I resumed my layering of the lasagne. Next year? It would be a miracle if Glen and I were still together then. Our first wedding anniversary was only a fortnight away and even making it to that was hanging in the balance.

He wasn't the man I'd thought he was. Story of my life.

With the lasagne prepared and in the oven, I poured myself a glass of wine, took it over to the window and sipped on it as I looked out over the lights of Hull city centre.

Looking back, it's ridiculous that we'd tied the knot without having a conversation about living arrangements. We were on the plane home when Glen asked if I was going to sell or let out my house in Osprey Close. I stared at him for a moment, wondering what he was wittering on about before reality hit. We could hardly continue living apart now that we were married. When I challenged him on moving into Osprey Close instead, he laughed.

'I work longer hours, so it makes more sense to live nearer the hospital. And there's no way I'm living somewhere you chose with another man.'

The first statement made sense, but a distant alarm bell sounded at the second. As we settled into married life in his apartment, letting my house out, that alarm bell got lounder: *Who's that text from?*

And louder: *Who are you talking to?*

And louder: *Where've you been? Who with? Were there men there?*

Until it reached a crescendo: *You're seeing somebody else. Who is he?*

I understood that he had baggage from his previous marriage. Didn't we all? But just because Juliette had been shagging her tennis coach didn't mean I'd be tempted to stray. It hurt that he didn't trust me and that he believed I could behave that way, although I was acutely aware of my hypocrisy when, truth be told, I was effectively being unfaithful to him by still holding a torch for Shaun.

The tension over the past few months had been unbearable. He'd invited me to his work Christmas party and it had been lovely to catch up with all my old colleagues, but Glen was suspicious of every male. Protests that we were just friends, they were happily married, they were gay, they were old enough to be my father all fell on deaf ears. Disgusted with him, I slept in the spare room that night.

I'd slept in the spare room most nights since. Our first Christmas as a married couple was hideous and New Year was worse. We went to a dinner party with Connie and Paul, and the host decided to mix up the couples, seating me next to Paul. He was my brother-in-law and we'd been friends since our teens, so naturally we chatted and laughed. Partway through the meal, I became aware of Glen glowering at me across the table.

The accusations he hurled at me back at the apartment were so loud that the neighbours called the police, fearful for my safety. I was mortified when the officers left and I started tossing my clothes into a suitcase, but Glen broke down and begged me to stay. Stubbornly determined to make it work, I read him the riot act about the behaviour I expected going forwards or I'd walk.

The following day, he was like a reformed man, full of apologies and, as the weeks passed with no more interrogations, I decided that the police visit had been the wake-up call he needed and the jealousy crap was behind us.

Until this morning.

'We're not going out with your sister tonight,' he said as we left the apartment together. 'I know it's your birthday, but Paul is *not* your birthday treat, no matter how much you wish he was.'

I was so stunned, I couldn't actually find any words to respond. He kissed me on the cheek, got into his car and drove away and I was still rooted to the spot.

No way was he telling me what I could and couldn't do. Relationships were meant to be about compromise, not control. Driving to college a little later, I recalled a million other ways he'd taken control. There were the biggies like me changing job and moving in with him, but there were so many others, like 'suggestions' about what I wore and how I styled my hair to his choice of places to dine out and TV programmes to watch. In a desperate attempt to make it work – and appease my guilt for letting my guard down and saying *I do* – I'd let him have his own way.

It was tempting to pull a sickie – something I'd never done in my life – and run straight back upstairs to pack, but I couldn't do that. Even though Glen would know why I'd left, I wasn't willing to put him through what I'd been through. I'd make an excuse and tell Connie we couldn't make it, I'd prepare one of the few meals in my repertoire, and we'd sit down and talk. I didn't want my forty-fourth birthday to be the day I ended my marriage, but my hand might have been forced.

I'd never have believed Glen could be so jealous and controlling. But I hadn't believed Shaun could walk out on me without explanation. Did we ever really know people?'

Feeling melancholy, I sat in the tub chair by the window and scrolled through my phone to the photos from Las Vegas. We'd had an amazing time there and, had life after marriage continued like that – or even close to that – I might have woken up one day realising that I'd fallen in love with the man I'd married.

Looking at a photo of us dining out on cheesy nachos, I remembered that I hadn't put a layer of grated cheese on top of the lasagne. I wandered over to the kitchen and removed the lasagne from the oven, breathing in the delicious cheesy, garlicky smell. A text pinged on my phone as I opened the fridge.

✉ From Paul
Sorry you can't join us tonight. Miss you. Have an amazing birthday and see you soon x

I quickly tapped in a response:

✉ To Paul
Thank you. Miss you too x

I grabbed the container of grated cheese I'd put aside earlier and closed the fridge door as I sent the text.

'Who are you texting?'

I squealed and dropped the container on the floor.

'Glen! I didn't hear you come in.'

'I said who are you texting?' His voice came out like a growl.

'Nobody.'

'Let me see.' He lunged for the phone.

'Get off!' I gripped it more tightly as I backed away.

'Let me see!' he yelled.

'No!'

He lunged for the phone again, but I was too quick for him and sprinted round the island.

'It's him, isn't it?'

'Who's him?'

'Paul.'

'There's nothing going on between me and Paul.'

'You expect me to believe that?'

'Yes! Because it's true!'

'Then show me your phone and prove it.'

There was no way I could show him our text exchange because, while completely innocent, the declarations of missing each other and the kisses would be proof of guilt to my jealous, suspicious, paranoid husband.

He chased me round the island, trying to snatch the phone. I changed direction but he was too quick for me and managed to wrestle it out of my hand. The screensaver hadn't kicked in, so our text exchange was there in full view.

'I knew it!' he yelled. 'How long? Does your sister know?' He scrolled further up. I couldn't remember what other messages there were, but we always ended our texts with a kiss. It was a friendship thing; nothing more.

Glen's face was a terrifying shade of purple. Beads of sweat trickled down his forehead and his normally immaculate hair stuck on end.

I stood a couple of feet away, stomach churning, psyching myself up for another explosion but praying he'd come to his senses and break down in tears once more.

Whether it was a specific message that caught his eye or one kiss too many, I don't know, but he hurled my phone across the kitchen where it ricocheted off the wall, landed on the hard tiles and smashed to pieces.

With a guttural cry, he swept the Pyrex dish off the worktop onto the floor. The glass shattered and dollops of boiling lasagne splattered over the tiles and units.

'Glen! What the f—'

'I'm sorry. I'm so sorry.' Looking mortified, he took a couple of steps closer to me, arms outstretched, but I backed away, shaking my head.

'I won't hurt you,' he cried.

'Damn bloody right you won't.' I stormed round the other side of the island and retrieved the pieces of my phone. I held my hands out to him. 'Look at the state of this. What the hell's wrong with you?'

'It's you! You drove me to it.'

'Bullshit! This is all you, Glen. You have a horrific temper and major trust issues. You need to get some help and fast.'

'I'm sorry.'

'Do you know how many times you say that word? Do you even know what it means? If you were genuinely sorry, you'd have done something about it.'

I shot him a withering look before marching towards our bedroom.

'Where are you going?'

'To pack.'

'You're leaving?'

'It's over. I mean it about you getting some help, but it's too late for us. I will *not* be yelled at. I will *not* have my every movement monitored. I will *not* be stopped from celebrating my birthday with my family. And the only way that's going to happen is if I'm *not* married to you.'

'Please don't go. I love you.'

'Empty words, Glen. Don't cut your hands while you clean up that mess.'

I retrieved my suitcases from under the bed in the spare room and hastily shoved in as many clothes as would fit.

When I wheeled my cases into the living area, Glen was sitting on the kitchen floor next to the lasagne, his head dipped.

'I'll need to come back for the rest of my stuff tomorrow.'

He looked up and I had a flicker of empathy for him. He looked broken, but that hadn't been my doing. It wasn't my job to fix him.

'Can I trust you not to damage anything or do I need to—'

'I won't touch your stuff.' His voice was small. Defeated. 'What time? I'll make sure I'm out.'

'Ten. Give me two hours.'

'Okay.'

'Goodbye, Glen.'

'Goodbye, Lauren. And I know you think I don't mean it, but I really am sorry. I just… never mind. I never used to be like this.'

I wasn't sure what he wanted from me. Understanding that his behaviour was all Juliette's fault and nothing to do with him? Reassurance that he was a wonderful person who'd lost his way? I couldn't say either of those things, so I said nothing.

With a feeling that this had been inevitable from the start, I loaded my cases into the boot of my car and drove back to Osprey Close. When my last tenants had moved out after Christmas, I hadn't looked for new ones. I'd told myself it needed painting and some fresh carpets before I rented it out again, but that wasn't strictly true. I'd known, deep down, that it was only a matter of time before I moved back there myself.

The house had that stale musty smell from not being lived in for two months. I'd set the timer on the central heating to avoid pipes freezing in the cold snap we'd had, but there was still a chill in the air.

I perched on the edge of the sofa and ran my hands down my face, sighing. It might be cold and smelly, but it was home. For now. I'd have a fresh start without Glen, but it was probably time I had a fresh start altogether. I thought back to the comment Glen had made on the plane back from Vegas about not moving into a house I'd chosen with my ex. I could never have full closure on my relationship with Shaun while I remained in the dark about why he left, but I could do the next best thing by selling the home we'd chosen together.

With no food or drink in the house, I poured myself a glass of tap water.

'Happy birthday,' I muttered.

* * *

I turned up at the apartment to collect the rest of my belongings the following morning and was relieved that Glen had kept his promise to go out. The kitchen was a mess. The lasagne hadn't been cleaned up and there were squashed empty cans of lager strewn across the work-top. I could imagine him crushing them in a drunken rage.

I packed as quickly as I could, dropped everything back at home, drove into town to get myself a new mobile phone then did a super-market shop.

When I returned to Osprey Close later, my heart sank as I clocked Glen's car parked outside the house, with Glen in the driver's seat.

'Where've you been?' he demanded, getting out of his car as I lifted my shopping out of the boot.

'Where do you think?' I held up the supermarket carrier bags. 'Not that it's any of your business.'

'All afternoon?'

'Also none of your business.'

He grabbed my arm. 'You're my wife. Of course it's my business.'

I yanked my arm away. 'Not anymore I'm not. It's over.'

'You don't mean that.'

He followed me across the front garden. I placed the bags on the doorstep and turned to face him. He looked terrible – unshaven with dishevelled hair and bloodshot eyes. I didn't like seeing him hurting but he'd brought it on himself.

'Yes, I do,' I said gently. 'Go home. Please.'

I thought for a moment that he was going to cry again but he narrowed his eyes at me. 'It's him, isn't it?'

'Who?'

'Paul.' He practically spat the name.

'No! It never was and it never will be.'

'But there's someone else.'

I shouldn't have hesitated. Yes, there was someone else, but I wasn't having an affair like Glen believed. The someone else was Shaun.

'You'll be sorry,' he hissed, storming back to his car and screeching out of the street.

* * *

I was still awake at 1.30 a.m., curled up on the sofa in the dark, reflecting on what a terrible mistake I'd made marrying Glen. Why hadn't I had the courage to say no in Vegas? There'd been red flags about his jealousy before we married, but I'd pushed them aside. Why?

There was one thing I kept coming back to: the fear of being alone. I'd lost three of the most important people to me in the whole world in the space of five years – Dad, Shaun and Ivy – and then I'd lost Kelvin and Mum, one month apart, shortly after I'd started seeing Glen. All I had left was Connie, but she had Paul and Josh, so I'd clung onto Glen, needing his comfort like I'd needed Shaun's when Dad died. It hadn't been the same, but it had been enough. Or at least that's what I'd convinced myself. The truth was that Glen had *never* been enough... because Glen wasn't Shaun.

I hated myself for being so weak. I'd known how much Juliette hurt Glen and I'd resented her for that, wondering how somebody could be so cruel to a good man, but it seemed I was just as guilty of disloyalty as she'd been.

A car pulled up outside the house, the headlights momentarily dazzling me. I rose sleepily, peering into the darkness. The car door opened, and a dark figure emerged. Next moment, the lounge window shattered, and I screamed as something flew past me, grazing my arm. I was rooted to the spot, shaking, my bare arms and legs stinging from where the glass had pierced my skin, as the car wheel-spun out of the street. Glen.

* * *

The police caught him a couple of miles away after he ploughed onto a roundabout, testing a whopping four times over the legal drinking limit. He was dazed but not seriously injured and thankfully nobody else had been involved.

His fingerprints were all over the brick that so nearly hit me. There was no way he'd have expected me to be in the lounge – especially with no lights or TV on – so I knew it hadn't been an attempt to physically hurt me, but that didn't stop me being shaken to the core. I kept telling myself that he was the one who'd chosen to drink and drive and he was the one who'd chosen to put a brick through my window, but I still felt guilty for marrying a man I could never fully give my heart to.

Glen had already ruined his career and I didn't want to make things worse than they already were by pressing charges. I offered to let it go providing he sign a legal agreement to pay for the window, never come near me again, grant me a divorce without objection and get professional help for his anger and jealousy issues. To be fair to him, he played ball. It was over.

* * *

Present day

I ran my hand down my left arm. There was only a faint scar where the brick had sliced me, barely noticeable unless you knew where to look. The glass cuts had all healed, but the emotional scars hadn't.

Connie had repeatedly asked if I wanted to talk about it but that would have meant telling her I'd never got over Shaun. I didn't want her shock, sympathy or disappointment. I didn't want her guilt either – I had a suitcase full of my own.

The day my divorce was finalised, I insisted on a girls' night on the town to celebrate being free. Connie suggested a dignified meal or even a night in with a takeaway instead but, no, I knew best. I wanted shots, cocktails, loud bars and a club. But a few drinks in, it hit me that there was nothing to celebrate about the end of a marriage that should never have happened in the first place. There was nothing to toast about a man whose career hung in tatters because the two women he'd loved both loved someone else.

I probably should have opened up at that point, but I kept the drinks coming instead and made out that everything was great. It was far from great, and it was only when we got to the club that I finally admitted to myself that I was grieving, but not for the end of my second marriage. I was still grieving for the end of my first one, for losing my husband and best friend and not knowing why. I was grieving for Dad, for Ivy, for Kelvin and Mum. And I was grieving that, somewhere in the midst of it all, I'd lost myself.

So I drank some more and ended up in the toilets in a sobbing, vomiting mess. I told Connie that I felt like a failure but, even in my inebriated state, I only talked about Glen. When I sold the house in Osprey Close and moved into Chapel View, I'd physically and metaphorically packed my life with Shaun away in that box marked 'unexplained' and shoved it the dark recesses of my the attic and my mind, never to be opened again.

If only I'd left it that way.

20

SAMANTHA

Present day

'I feel like we've been travelling forever,' Josh said as we settled into our seats on the train at London King's Cross on Wednesday morning after staying overnight near the airport.

'Me too. I wish we could click our fingers and be home instantly.'

'What are you most looking forward to?'

'Everything,' I said. 'Seeing everyone again, seeing the hedgehogs, having a cup of tea in my favourite mug on Thomas's bench. What about you?'

'The same. And I'm ready for a night in our own bed too, although I have a feeling I put myself down for hoglets duty so it could be a night in the barn for me.'

'Bad move.'

'Yeah, I didn't think that one through.'

I shifted down in my seat and rested my head on his shoulder, the exhaustion from all the travelling catching up with me as well as the restless nights worrying about whether I might be pregnant.

Josh and I weren't the sort for spending days on end relaxing on the beach or by the pool, so we'd spent the rest of our honeymoon exploring the islands and it had been amazing, but that feeling of panic was never far away. I felt on edge all the time and the effort of keeping that from Josh had been exhausting. I kept telling myself that, once I got back to Hedgehog Hollow with Fizz, Phoebe, Zayn and all my other wonderful volunteers around me, the pressure would ease and I'd realise I'd made a mountain out of a molehill while I was away. I didn't allow myself to think about what would happen if it didn't.

I felt the train pull out of King's Cross and heard the conductor's welcome as I rested my eyes.

'Sammie! We're nearly there.'

I opened my eyes as Josh shook me. 'What?'

'We'll be in Hull in five minutes.'

I glanced round me, blinking, feeling disorientated. I could have sworn I'd only closed my eyes for a couple of minutes. How had two and a half hours passed?

'You must have needed the sleep,' Josh said, brushing my hair back from my face. 'Final stretch now.'

We'd booked a private transfer back to Hedgehog Hollow, and we both settled into the back seat. I couldn't believe I'd slept for the entire train journey. It was probably from a combination of travel fatigue and lack of sleep, but extreme tiredness was one of the earliest signs of pregnancy. Nervous butterflies swarmed in my stomach, and I felt nauseous.

Travelling closer to home, I gazed out of the window at the rolling countryside. The lush green fields – some dotted with animals and others devoted to crops – were so different to the wide-open spaces of the savannah teeming with wildlife, but they were equally beautiful.

My heart leapt as the taxi driver turned onto the farm track at Hedgehog Hollow and a feeling of warmth enveloped me as we made it over the brow of the hill, revealing the ivy-clad farmhouse to our left and my beloved rescue centre in the barn to the right. Josh squeezed my hand and we both smiled at each other, excited to be home.

While Josh and the driver lifted out our cases, I stood in the farm-yard and breathed in the fresh country air. It was early afternoon, and the sun was smiling down on us from a blue sky streaked with wispy cloud trails. Tanzania had been phenomenal, but there really was no place like home.

Fizz's electric-blue Mini was parked by the barn alongside Phoebe's pink moped. They both had Wednesday afternoons off from their stud-ies. The barn door opened and there was a squeal of excitement as Phoebe and Fizz ran out and across the farmyard, arms outstretched. I hugged Phoebe then Fizz and, the moment I released her, Misty-Blue shot across the farmyard and launched herself into my arms.

'Aw, it's lovely to be missed,' I said, showering our cat with kisses. 'How is everyone?'

'All good here,' Phoebe said, 'but it's been strange without you both. Darcie kept begging for the day off school so she could be here when you got home.'

Josh glanced at his watch. 'We'll be picking her up in about ninety minutes so not too much longer for her to wait.'

'We've got loads of new patients,' Fizz said. 'We'll introduce you to them later.'

'Have you had any lunch?' Phoebe asked.

'We were going to get a sandwich on the train, but someone fell asleep,' Josh said, smiling at me affectionately.

Phoebe smiled. 'Perfect. Beth's made a feast.'

'We said we'd wait for you,' Fizz added, 'and I'm so hungry now, I could eat a scabby donkey.'

That phrase always made me laugh but most of the things Fizz said made me laugh. She'd been a breath of fresh air since the moment she'd phoned me almost exactly a year ago to say her cat Jinks had brought a hoglet into her cottage to play with. I was so grateful to Jinks for bringing Fizz into our lives that evening.

As we walked over to the farmhouse, Fizz and Phoebe filled us in on how 'Luna the amazing hedgepuss' was doing with her litter of hoglets. They bounced off each other, adding bits of information in. It struck me how much Phoebe had grown in confidence since January and how big a part Fizz had played in that. I loved how close the pair of them had become and I knew how grateful Phoebe was to have found a good friend. She'd told me it had been a struggle to maintain friendships while studying and meeting the demands of the Grimes family.

* * *

I took a sip of my lemonade, a feeling of contentment flowing through me as I took in the hive of activity on the back lawn. Over lunch, Paul had mooted the idea of a barbeque for tea, and it had taken on a life of its own. Everyone was eager to hear all about our honeymoon so we'd thought we could invite a few friends and family members round and tell them together. Being mid-week, most people didn't have other plans, so it had become a pretty big gathering. My mouth was dry from repeating the same stories, not that I minded. It was a pleasure to revisit those memories.

What made me especially happy was seeing Rosemary sitting on Thomas's bench, deep in conversation with Terry. I'd seated them next to each other at our wedding in the hope that, being a similar age, they might enjoy each other's company, so it warmed my heart to see it had worked. Even more adorable was that Rosemary's guide dog, Trixie – a gorgeous dark golden retriever – had befriended Terry's springer spaniel, Wilbur. The pair of them were lying side by side, occasionally playing with one of the nearby dog toys.

'How cute are they?' Phoebe said, joining me. 'Terry took Rosemary out for tea and cake last week and the week before.'

'On a date?'

She giggled. 'No. They clicked at the wedding and they're friends, but you never know what the future holds.' She made a heart shape with her hands.

'Friendships can grow into something more,' I agreed. It would be lovely for them both to find love again, but I was equally happy for them to have found a friend because they'd both lived fairly lonely existences, just like Thomas had after losing Gwendoline, and I couldn't bear the thought of anyone being lonely.

'My parents were friends for a long time first,' Phoebe said, sounding wistful. 'My dad loved my mum, but she was engaged to someone else before she realised he was wrong for her and Dad was right. Sometimes it needs time and patience but, if it's meant to happen, it will.'

I turned my gaze away from Rosemary and Terry, expecting Phoebe to be looking in their direction, but she was looking across the lawn at somebody else and suddenly several things she'd said over time clicked into place. Of course! How could I not have realised before?

'I take it Fizz doesn't know how you feel?' I asked gently.

Phoebe gasped and her eyes locked with mine. 'How did you know?'

'You were looking right at her as you spoke just now and there was something in your voice that suggested you were talking from personal experience. Plus, I'm a hopeless romantic and I recognise love when I see it.' I gave her a gentle nudge. 'You've got good taste.'

Phoebe gave me a grateful smile. 'Thank you. She doesn't know. She's with Yasmin, so it would be unfair to say anything.'

We both looked towards where Fizz and Yasmin were talking to Chloe at the far end of the garden. Phoebe had been with Fizz when she met Yasmin – they'd rescued a hedgehog from a drain on Yasmin's drive – and I knew from Fizz that there'd been instant chemistry. That had to have been tough for Phoebe to witness but, as with every challenge in her life, she seemed to be facing it with maturity and dignity.

Phoebe hadn't mentioned any previous relationships, but I'd assumed that, if friendships had been too challenging to hold down, a relationship would have been impossible.

'If you want to talk about it any time, I'm here for you,' I said.

Connie and Josh waved me at me, trying to grab my attention.

'Looks like you're wanted,' Phoebe said. 'But thanks for the offer. I'd like that.'

She wandered over to Rosemary and Terry while I joined Connie and Josh.

'I was asking Mum if she and Alex had thought about a wedding date yet,' Josh explained.

'I wasn't going to bring it up tonight,' Connie said. 'Not when you've only just got back from your honeymoon. But Josh said you'd want to know.'

'Definitely! It's not stealing our thunder, if that's what you're thinking. When do you have in mind?'

'Saturday, 4 September, if that suits you.'

'Consider it booked. We've got nothing in the diary except the Family Fun Day. So that'll be...' I started counting off on my fingers.

'Fifteen weeks on Saturday,' Connie declared. 'A scarily short time when I think of it in weeks.'

'We pulled ours together in about the same time,' Josh said. 'It'll be great.'

'Have you spoken to Natasha?' I asked. 'Not that you have to use her, of course.'

'She did a brilliant job of yours, so we definitely want to use her. I wanted to confirm the date with you before I call her.'

'Let me know if you want to use the holiday cottages so I can block them out for that weekend.'

Darcie ran up to me with Misty-Blue by her side and grabbed my hand and Connie's.

'You have to come and see all these ladybirds.'

We ran across the lawn with her. On one of the fenceposts by the meadow, there were a couple of dozen ladybirds.

'They're called a bloom,' Darcie said. 'We've been learning about it in school, but Miss Penny says some people call them a loveliness of ladybirds and I think that's prettier. Don't you?'

'It's perfect for them,' I agreed.

She rattled off a load of other collective nouns she'd learned.

'Misty-Blue and Luna are friends now,' she said. 'Can Luna be my cat and sleep on my bed?'

I knelt down beside her. 'Luna's very welcome to do that when the hoglets are bigger, but she might not want to. Some cats like living in houses with people like Misty-Blue but others are used to being on their own in the wild. We think Luna was one of those cats, so we need to give her the choice to live where she wants. Is that okay?'

Darcie nodded solemnly. 'I'll ask Misty-Blue to invite her to stay.'

'That's a good idea.' I crossed my fingers in front of Darcie. She copied me, as did Connie.

A burst of laughter drew my attention towards the barbeque. Dad, Rich, Uncle Simon and James were all huddled round it, nursing bottes of lager. Mum was several feet away from them, talking to Hannah.

I had no idea whether my parents had met up since the wedding. They'd arrived separately this evening, although that didn't signify anything other than convenience. Mum had travelled from Whitsborough Bay with Auntie Louise and Uncle Simon. Dad had come on his own after insisting on taking Josh's hoglets shift so we could have a proper catch-up with everyone and enjoy our first night at home together.

I'd spoken to them both separately but they'd each kept the focus on the honeymoon, which was understandable, as it was the purpose behind the gathering. Every time I'd steered the conversation onto how the past fortnight had been for them, I'd had some vague response, followed by another question about Tanzania.

The food was dished up and I continued to mingle but I kept my eye on my parents throughout the evening. Any time Mum and Dad were together, they looked comfortable and there was laughter, so the good news was that whatever had happened at the wedding hadn't caused any friction between them or, if it had, it had been resolved.

'What are you staring at?' Josh whispered in my ear later that evening, slipping his arm round my waist.

'Trying to work out the relationship between my parents,' I whispered back. 'Do they look like they're back together to you?'

Josh watched them for a moment. 'I haven't a clue. I'm hopeless at this sort of thing. They're not touchy-feely, but who is at a family event?'

'Good point.'

'If it's killing you that much not knowing, why don't you join your dad in the barn later tonight? You can interrogate him then.'

I thought about it for a moment and shook my head. 'I barely gave it a second thought while we were away, so I'm not going to start obsessing about it now. If there's something going on, I'm sure they'll tell me when they're ready and, if it was a wedding-only thing, I'd probably rather not know.'

'Very wise.' He kissed the top of my head. 'How's the fatigue, by the way?'

'Okay at the moment but it'll probably catch up with me when everyone's gone.'

'Am I right in thinking exhaustion's an early sign of...' There was nobody within earshot, but I appreciated him not saying 'pregnancy' out loud just in case.

I stiffened. 'One of the earliest, so it's possible. But travel's exhausting too.'

'Is it too early to take a test?' His voice was full of excitement, and I hated that I didn't feel the same.

'There's no point until I've missed a period and we're not at that stage yet.' Butterflies swirled in my stomach. We'd know soon enough, and I was either going to have to get my head round being a mum sooner than I'd hoped and somehow work out a way to balance that with the hedgehogs or I was going to have to have a difficult conversation with Josh about putting off trying again until much later. Both scenarios filled me with dread.

'I didn't get a chance to say earlier, but I got a pack of those early-predictor tests while I was getting the barbeque stuff this afternoon, and I've got some folic acid so you can start taking that.'

Tears pricked my eyes. He wanted this so badly and he deserved it. I was going to have to play along for now. I put my arms round his neck and hugged him. 'That's so thoughtful. Thank you.'

'You want to go back inside and take a test, don't you?' he whispered.

'I really do,' I said, truthfully, 'but we need to be patient for a little longer. I'm due on again on Sunday so, if that doesn't happen, I'll give it a few more days then take a test.'

I hated lying. If my period didn't return on Sunday, I'd be taking a test on Sunday night because, if it was positive, I'd need those few days to get my head in the right place. The day I announced to Josh that we were expecting a baby, I had to do so with excitement and conviction. I couldn't ruin that moment for him. I couldn't ruin what we had together. It wasn't like I didn't want a baby. I just didn't want one yet. But with so much to do in the rescue centre, when would be a good time?

21

LAUREN

When I picked up Josh's voicemail inviting me to the barbeque, I should have gone with my gut reaction and said no. Desperate as I was to see them both, I wasn't in the mood for socialising, and I especially wasn't in the mood for being around Connie.

I understood that she had a lot on at the moment with finishing her studies and planning her wedding and I was fully supportive of that, but what I was struggling with was how she managed to fit in seeing Alex's family but didn't seem to have time for me. We usually caught up at least once a week but I hadn't seen her properly since Josh and Sam's wedding.

I'd called her a few times over the weekend and at the start of this week but got voicemail each time. Yesterday, I'd received a text: *Sorry I've missed your calls. May's been crazy. Promise to catch up properly soon xx*

'When?' I'd shouted at my phone before tossing it onto the sofa in disgust.

I knew my frustration with her was unreasonable, but I couldn't help it. For the first time in my life, I wanted to talk about everything – not just my work situation but Shaun and Glen and the cloud that still hung over me – and Connie wasn't there for me. I had a feeling she never would be again. She'd always dreamed of a big family, and it hadn't happened for her and Paul, but she'd been warmly welcomed by Alex's three adult children, six grandchildren and even his ex-wife, from whom he'd had an amicable split. Connie helped run cub and scout packs with Alex and some of his kids and she was in her element with it all. Definitely a more appealing way to spend her time than with me – the person who never quite let her in.

She'd greeted me with a hug when I arrived at the farmhouse, repeated that we must get together soon, but I got whisked away by Darcie and we barely crossed paths for the rest of the evening. Was she avoiding me? Was I avoiding her? At one point, I was standing close enough to hear her confirming her wedding date to Josh and Sam and my stomach lurched. It was the first I'd heard of it. It felt like she was slipping away from me.

I'd had a headache all day, but it was pounding now so it was time to take my leave. I didn't want to make a big fuss out of going but I wasn't rude enough just to slip away. I said goodbye to Josh and managed to catch Sam on her own.

'You do look a bit pale,' she said, looking at me with concern after I'd told her why I was leaving early. 'Do you want some paracetamol before you go?'

'I'll take some at home. I've got something in the car for you if I can steal you for a few minutes.'

She followed me across the farmyard.

'I'm so sorry about your job,' she said. 'How are you feeling?'

'I've been through every emotion under the sun, and I'm left with confused. No idea what to do next.'

'I can't believe they're letting you go. You're brilliant at your job.'

'They tried to convince me to apply for the vice principal and principal roles, but I wasn't interested.'

'Judith's leaving too?'

'Oh, yeah, it's all change at the TEC. Long story.'

'Which you know I'm more than happy to listen to. When are you free?'

My throat felt tight. Connie had given me empty promises, yet here was Sam only home a few hours and already making a firm arrange-ment. I was so desperate to be able to spill it all out.

'They've set me up with a career development counsellor and I've got my first appointment on Friday morning. I've got the rest of the day off to job search or have interviews. How about I bring lunch over?'

'Sounds perfect, but if you want to talk before then, you know where I am.'

My throat tightened again, and I felt tears rushing to my eyes. Sam had to be the kindest person I'd ever met.

'Thank you, but Friday's good.'

We'd reached my car, so I opened the boot and unwrapped the stone hedgehogs from an old towel.

'I saw these in Bloomsberry's after your wedding and couldn't resist them. Meet Hogmeo and Hogliet.'

Sam picked up one of the hedgehogs. 'Oh, my gosh! They're gorgeous. Thank you so much. Did you make up the names?'

'No, it was...' I pictured Riley and smiled. 'It was a friend.'

'They're genius.' She picked up the second one and inspected it. 'I think I'll put them outside the barn. They'll look—'

'Lauren!' Connie's shout interrupted Sam. She ran across the farm-yard. 'Are you leaving?'

It was on the tip of my tongue to say *like you care*, but I managed to stop myself. That would be unfair and unreasonable.

'I've got a headache,' I said instead. 'I hear you've set a wedding date. Congratulations.'

I'd tried to keep the edge out of my voice but mustn't have succeeded because Connie looked taken aback and sounded defensive.

'I would have told you, but we wanted to make sure the date worked for Samantha and Josh first.'

'Which it does,' Sam chipped in. 'Very excited for the second Hedgehog Hollow wedding. Have I convinced you to go on safari for your honeymoon?'

'It sounded amazing and it's definitely on the bucket list, but we're going to British Columbia in Canada. The plan is to fly out to Vancouver...'

As Connie ran through all the places she and Alex planned to stay and for how long, my jaw tightened. The last time I'd had a conversation with her about their honeymoon had been over breakfast, the morning after Josh and Sam's wedding, and Canada hadn't been mentioned. They'd been keen on one of those overwater bungalows in somewhere like the Maldives or Fiji but couldn't make a definite decision until they'd decided on their wedding date because of the weather. Which meant that at some point since the wedding, they'd not only decided on a date but had done a complete about turn on the type of honeymoon they wanted and had planned it all out. That would have taken a lot of research and time during a fortnight when Connie hadn't been able to spare me five minutes for a cuppa.

I knew I shouldn't make an issue of it but, the more she talked, the more annoyed I got, and I couldn't stop myself.

'Sounds amazing,' I said when she'd finished. 'So when did you decide all this?'

'At the weekend. Melissa and Gareth decided we'd done more than our fair share at their new place, so we were shooed out and told to have the weekend off.'

'And you didn't think to ring me?'

Connie frowned. 'What for? To help plan our honeymoon?'

'Of course not! For a catch-up. Other than two minutes outside your house, I haven't seen you since the wedding. I might have had stuff I wanted to talk about.'

'Well, I'd like to think you'd have said if you did.'

'How could I when you were rushing off with a paintbrush in your hand every time I contacted you or your phone was on voicemail?'

'Do you have something to talk about?' she asked, an edge to her tone.

'I might have.'

'Lauren!'

I was aware of Sam glancing nervously between us and could

imagine how uncomfortable she felt right now. I handed her the other hedgehog and closed the boot.

'I've lost my job,' I snapped, glaring at Connie. 'Which you'd have known if you'd bothered to return any of my calls.'

Connie's jaw dropped and she clapped her hand to her heart. 'Oh, Lauren, I'm so sorry.'

'Shit happens. I'll see you on Friday, Sam. Thanks for tonight.'

'Thanks for these,' she said in a small voice, holding up the hedgehogs.

'We can talk now,' Connie offered, her tone apologetic.

'I've got a headache. I'm going home to bed. Enjoy the rest of your evening.'

In my rear-view mirror, I saw them standing in the middle of the farmyard, likely both bewildered as to what had just happened. I shouldn't have snapped at Connie like that, and I definitely shouldn't have done it in front of Sam. I'd ring her and apologise, but it would have to wait until tomorrow. I was too riled to do it tonight. Best let the dust settle.

22

SAMANTHA

By lunchtime on Thursday, I was back into the rhythm of things at the rescue centre, and it already felt as though I'd never been away.

The latest hedgehog names category of 'famous safari animals' had me amused, although, looking down the names already used, I wasn't sure I could think of any others, so it was probably time for a new category.

'It's spring,' I muttered to myself. 'Let's make that a theme and see what we come up with.' I typed it into our database, the Hog Log, and added it to the Happy Hog Board – a whiteboard showing how many hedgehogs we'd treated and released since opening – before taking a mug of tea over to the sofa bed.

There was a knock, followed by the door opening.

'Is it safe for Wilbur?' Terry asked.

'No hedgehogs out and you've timed that perfectly,' I said, standing up. 'I've just made a brew.'

Wilbur trotted down to give me a fuss, did a couple of laps of the barn, sniffing out the new arrivals, then lay down beside the sofa bed. He was such a good dog.

'Did you enjoy the barbeque last night?' I asked Terry when we sat down with our drinks.

'Oh, aye. Thanks for having us over.'

'It wouldn't have been the same without you. Like I always say, you're part of the family now. I see you and Rosemary are friends.'

'She's a good woman. I usually struggle to talk to new folk, but there's summat about Rosemary that reminds me of our Marion. Feels comfortable.'

Marion was Terry's older sister, but she'd passed away last autumn. If Rosemary reminded Terry of his sister, it was unlikely there was much chance of a romantic future for them, but friendship was good.

'I noticed Wilbur and Trixie had made friends too.'

'That they have, which is nice.'

He took a sip on his drink and scratched his nose a few times. I was familiar enough with that mannerism to know he was building up to saying something but needed a little more time before he was ready to spit it out.

'After half-term, Josh and I would like to take you out for a meal – just the three of us – to thank you again for the generous contribution to Hedgehog Hollow.'

'There's no need for that,' Terry said. 'I had no use for the money and you did. It were the least I could do.'

'But we really do appreciate it. Our honeymoon was incredible, but we'd have had to cancel it and donate that money to the rescue centre if you hadn't been so generous. So have a think about a date that's good for you and where you'd like to go.'

'Thanks, lass. That'd be nice.' He scratched his nose again.

'I'm glad you liked the elephant photos,' I said.

His face lit up. 'They were so special. Gwendoline would have loved them.'

'Tell you what else she'd have loved.'

I scrolled through my phone to show him the photos I'd taken of the African Pygmy hedgehog and explained the differences between it and ours.

'She'd definitely have loved that,' he agreed.

One more scratch of the nose and then he reached into the inside pocket of his jacket. 'You know I said I'd lost that elephant drawing? I had a right good sort out while you were away and I found it.'

He handed me a crinkled piece of paper and I glanced down at a simple but beautiful pencil drawing of an elephant.

'Aw, Terry, it's lovely. She was obviously a very talented artist.'

I handed it back to him, but he shook his head. 'You can have it. Thought you might be able to iron out some of the creases and put it on your noticeboard.'

I smiled down at the picture. 'Who drew the love heart in the corner?'

'That'd be me.' He gave a weak shrug.

'I'd love to put it on the noticeboard. Thank you. Do you want to stay for lunch?'

'No. Wilbur and me'll head off now. Leave you to settle back in.'

I walked them to the door and waved them off. Terry never stuck around after he'd shared something about Gwendoline. He'd build up to saying something and then he'd be keen to leave, presumably to be alone with his memories.

When Terry's car disappeared from view, I went over to the farmhouse and found Paul in the kitchen, making sandwiches.

'You've just missed Beth,' he said. 'She's gone out the back with the kids. We thought you might like to join us for a picnic in the garden.'

'Aw, that's a lovely idea. Anything I can do to help?'

'Just about finished but you could take the plates out.'

* * *

'That was perfect, thank you,' I said, wiping my hands on a paper napkin after I'd finished eating. 'I used to have picnics all the time when I stayed with my Nanna and Gramps in Little Tilbury. Nanna loved them. If the weather was bad, she still packed everything into a basket, laid a blanket down in the lounge and we sat on the floor to eat, pretending we were in a meadow.'

'An indoor picnic sounds like fun,' Beth said.

'It was. I loved their picnic basket and always wanted one. It was one of those proper old wicker ones with all the plates and cutlery packed into it.'

I started gathering the plates together, smiling at the happy memories.

'Leave them,' Paul said. 'I'm sure you have stacks to catch up with. And I might fancy seconds.'

'Good to see you with your appetite back,' I said.

Paul looked better than I'd ever seen him, with a light tan and a small weight gain, taking that gaunt look from his face. He'd told me yesterday that he'd struggled with exhaustion following the wedding, but he'd had plenty of rest and had really turned a corner this past week.

They'd met Dave at Alder Lea and had chosen paint colours ready for their move. I was excited for them moving into a place of their own for the first time since having Lottie and I knew it would be good for them, but I was going to miss them so much. It would certainly be quieter around here. At least we weren't going from having a houseful to an empty property, thanks to Phoebe and Darcie, as that would have been very odd.

I was about to stand up and head back to the barn when Lottie crawled over to me and settled on my lap.

'I'll have to show you the photos and video from her birthday,' Beth said. 'They had a great time at the farm. I can't believe she's one already.'

Lottie shoved a teething toy in her mouth and chomped on it.

'I can't either,' I said. 'Where's that year gone?'

'Time goes so quickly when you have kids,' Paul said, keeping a watchful eye on Archie, who was running up and down the lawn.

'Do you remember the panic we had about me being pregnant with Lottie so soon after having Archie?' Beth said smiling fondly at Paul.

'You had a panic?' I asked.

'Huge one! We knew we wanted a brother or sister for Archie, but we were thinking we'd wait until he was two or three. The thought of two kids with less than a year between them terrified me.'

'How long did it take you to adjust?'

'A couple of months, I think.' Beth looked to Paul for confirmation.

'About that,' he agreed. 'By the time we had her first scan, we were both really excited. Most things in life don't happen the way you plan them, and you just have to go with the flow.'

I cuddled Lottie to me and stroked her soft hair. What Paul said made sense. If I was pregnant, I would just have to go with the flow, but my situation wasn't the same as theirs. I wasn't going to be unexpectedly pregnant with a second child earlier than planned. This would be my first and I'd categorically told my husband I was ready when I wasn't. And they hadn't had a rescue centre to run.

Time. It was always about having time but, unfortunately, I didn't have much of that. The clock was ticking.

I'd hoped that what Paul had said about going with the flow would relax me a little, but I woke up in the barn on Friday morning after a night on hoglets duty feeling more tense than ever.

Josh picked up on it when I joined him for breakfast but one of the most recent hoglet admissions hadn't made it through the night, so it hadn't taken much to convince him that was why I was sad and on edge.

After he left for work, I returned to the barn to continue cleaning out the crates and found Melman – named after the giraffe in *Madagascar* – hadn't made it either. He'd been admitted on Monday while we were still away, riddled with the worst case of parasites I'd seen. I therefore wasn't surprised we'd lost him, but it didn't ease the pain.

Around mid-morning, a car pulled into the farmyard and a middle-aged woman got out.

'Three hedgehog babies,' she said, thrusting an ice cream container at me, full of scrunched up kitchen roll.

'Where did you find them?'

'In our garden. We tried to feed them but they won't eat or drink anymore, so I thought I'd better bring them to you.'

'When did you find them?' I asked.

'A couple of nights ago.'

My grip tightened on the box. What was wrong with people? If they found an injured cat in the road, would they think they could nurse it back to life? No! They'd take it to the vet. So why did they think they could treat wild animals themselves?

'Can I ask what you fed them?'

'Exactly what you're meant to feed them. Bread soaked in milk.'

My stomach sank. If any of them were still alive, it would be a miracle.

'Hedgehogs can't eat bread and they're lactose intolerant so they can't have milk either.'

She planted her hands on her hips and glared at me. 'Since when?'

'Since it was discovered bread and milk can kill them.' It was so hard not to snap at her, especially with the dark mood I was in already. 'If you do find any others, especially babies, it's best to get them straight to me.'

'Like I have time to do that.'

'I can collect them if that's easier. It's really important to get them professional help as soon as possible.'

'Screw you!' she said, giving me the filthiest look. 'I won't bother next time.'

Shoving past me, she clambered back into her car and sped away down the track. I released a deep, shaky breath before returning to the barn, almost afraid to peel back the kitchen roll.

One of the hoglets was already gone and the other two were in a bad way. I warmed them on a heat pad and did my best but, within thirty minutes, they'd both joined their sibling. I removed the soiled kitchen roll from the ice cream container, lined it with some fresh pieces and gently placed the three siblings side by side. Tears rained down my cheeks as I covered them with another few sheets and whispered goodbye.

It was so senseless. If they'd been brought in on Wednesday when the woman found them, there was no guarantee of survival, but we'd have done our best. Was it my fault? I'd been so busy organising the wedding that I hadn't run a spring campaign to remind the villagers of what to do if they found abandoned hoglets or hedgehogs in trouble.

My sobs came so thick and fast that I could barely catch my breath and I knew it wasn't just the loss of the hoglets and Melman; it was the fear of being pregnant. It was the worry about the mounting workload. It was the panic at being back to where I'd been last year, pulled in two directions to the point where I collapsed.

Aware that Lauren could arrive at any moment, I dashed to the bathroom and splashed water on my face. My eyes were red and puffy, but I could easily explain that away. Lauren would understand if I told her my day had started with five bereavements.

When I emerged from the bathroom, I jumped as I spotted someone seated at the treatment table.

'Chloe! You scared me!'

'Sorry. Didn't mean to.'

'I'm expecting Lauren for lunch,' I said as I unplugged the heat pads. 'Had we made plans too?' With the mess my head was in at the moment, it was plausible that I'd double-booked.

'No. Samuel started at nursery today and I was at a loose end so—'

'You were bored,' I interrupted. 'So you thought you'd turn up and expect me to entertain you.'

She shook her head vigorously. 'No, it wasn't—'

The sensible approach was to take a deep breath and count to three, but I didn't do that.

'Do you ever listen to anything I say?' I winced at the harsh tone.

Chloe pushed back her chair and stood up. 'Yes, I do actually,' she snapped. 'You told me you've got a job to do so you can't always give me your undivided attention, but you said I was still welcome here. Clearly I'm not. Clearly I should have made an appointment.'

She grabbed her bag and stormed down the barn.

'It would have helped,' I shouted after her. 'Did it not even enter your head I might have a stack of things to catch up on when I got back from honeymoon?'

She paused, hand on the door. 'Yes, it did and if you hadn't bitten my head off, you'd have known that the end of my sentence was that I was at a loose end so I thought I'd stop by and see if I could help you with anything. But no, you had to assume the worst of me as always. Thanks a lot, Samantha.'

'Chloe!'

'Too late!'

I rested elbows on the table, my head in my hands, cursing under my breath. That was horrible. She'd barely uttered a word and I'd unleashed all my anger and frustration on her. This wasn't who I was. I didn't recognise this person who shouted at and kept secrets from the people she loved. Before the wedding, everything in my life had finally felt in control. Now it felt like it was falling apart.

24

LAUREN

Chloe's car was parked in the farmyard, and I heard raised voices from the barn as I walked towards it. Next moment, the door was flung open and Chloe strode across the yard.

'What's going on?' I asked.

'I didn't make an appointment, so I'm not welcome,' she snapped.

'What?'

'Ask Samantha. She's just yelled at me for no reason. She's in a foul mood. Better hope it's only with me, or it'll be a short lunch.'

She slammed her car door closed and shot off down the track.

Yelled at for no reason? Foul mood? That didn't sound like Sam. What had Chloe done this time?

I pushed open the door. 'Hello?'

Sam was squirting antibacterial spray onto the treatment table and wiping it vigorously but, as I got closer, I could see she was crying.

'I saw Chloe outside,' I said, gently.

Sam sniffed and wiped her cheeks. 'What did she say?'

'Not much, but I heard the shouts too.'

She put the spray and cloth down and slumped back onto a chair. 'It was awful. She came to help but I didn't give her a chance to explain that. I assumed she was bored and wanted entertaining as usual, and I let rip. I took everything out on her.'

I lowered myself onto the chair beside her and lightly touched her arm. 'Everything?'

'Melman died and one of the hoglets and this horrible woman brought in three that she'd tried to feed on bread and milk and they're all dead now. I've got the Family Fun Day to sort out and not enough time to make it the sort of event I wanted and, even if I had the time, I can't think straight because...' She paused and looked up at me, her expression fearful.

'Because there's something else going on, isn't there?' You didn't get to hide things for as long as I had without recognising when someone else was doing it.

'I can't...'

'There's only us here. I won't tell. I doubt the hedgehogs will either, although I've heard Misty-Blue's a voracious gossip.'

She gave me a weak smile.

'How about you take a moment while I put the kettle on and then you tell me all about it and, to even things up, there's something I could do with talking about too.'

* * *

'Aw, Sam,' I said after she'd told me about her possible pregnancy and her fears about it being too soon. 'I'm so sorry. But you know what I'm going to suggest, don't you?'

'That I tell Josh.'

'He needs to know. I've been that person kept in the dark and it's a lonely place to be.'

'What if he hates me?'

'This is Josh we're talking about. He loves you unconditionally, but you have to let him in. I know you're worried it could cause some damage but, believe me, there's greater damage to be done if you shut him out. What are your plans for tonight?'

'He's on hoglet duty.'

'Then join him and tell him everything. I bet you those fears won't feel quite as strong after you do.'

Sam sipped on her tea in silence for a moment before nodding. 'You're right. I'm only delaying the inevitable. I'll do it tonight.'

'Good.'

'My turn to listen,' she said. 'This is about more than losing your job, isn't it?'

'Yep. So much more than that...'

I stayed at Hedgehog Hollow all afternoon, helping to feed the hoglets in between sharing my life story and discussing more about Sam's situation. I told her all about Shaun, Glen and even the undercurrents in my relationship with Connie caused by Mum's favouritism, although I squirmed initially talking about that – Connie was, after all, Sam's mother-in-law.

'I'd never have guessed that about you and Connie,' Sam said. 'You seem so close.'

'We are! Always have been. I've worked hard not to let it come between us, but I always feel it.'

'I can relate to that. Chloe could do nothing wrong in Mum's eyes and I could do nothing right. It could easily have come between us, but we were both determined not to let it. It wasn't Chloe's fault that Mum treated us differently, just like it wasn't Connie's fault that your mum reacted differently to you two.'

'But it must have frustrated you.'

Sam nodded vigorously. 'Drove me mad and sometimes I could feel the tension building and had to get away. I loved staying with my grandparents in Little Tilbury because it gave me valuable time away to calm down and get perspective again. Sometimes Chloe stayed too and, even though they were careful not to show any sort of favouritism, I knew

Nanna and Gramps found my company easier than Chloe's, which helped me accept that, even though Mum didn't like me, it wasn't me. I wasn't this problem child who nobody wanted to be around.'

'How my mum was with me sounds like a walk in the park compared to how your mum was with you,' I said, piecing together the snippets I'd heard over the past year.

'Doesn't mean what you went through wasn't challenging. It sounds to me like your mum loved you both, but she struggled to relate to any choices you made that didn't sit with what she knew and understood. Parents can struggle when they don't have all the answers. Hardest job in the world, they say.'

'And one I think you and Josh will excel at.'

She raised her eyebrows, looking doubtful. 'You think?'

'I know.' I gave her a reassuring smile. 'And do you know what else I know? Very little in life comes with perfect timing, but wouldn't it boring if it did? The unexpected happens all the time and we deal with it. If you are pregnant, you and Josh will find a way to balance raising a baby with keeping this place running and you've got a stack of people around you who'll be more than willing to help. You're not alone in any of this. Never forget that.'

* * *

Phoebe and Darcie had been invited to Fizz's for pizza and a film, so Sam and I had an uninterrupted afternoon until Josh arrived home from work shortly after six.

'I wasn't expecting you still to be here,' he said, giving me a hug after he'd kissed Sam.

'We had a lot to talk about,' I replied, giving Sam a meaningful look. 'But I'll head home now and leave you in peace.'

Sam walked me to my car while Josh went to the farmhouse to change.

'Thanks for today,' she said, squeezing me tightly.

'Right back at you. It felt good to offload.' As we stepped apart, I added, 'You're going to talk to Josh tonight?

'After we've eaten. And you're going to talk to Connie?'

'I'll drive home via hers.'

We hugged again and I set off down the track. It really had felt good to offload and, in giving Sam some advice, I'd helped myself too. Losing my job wasn't the end of the world and I needed to stop moping around as though it was.

As for Connie, Mum had been gone for a decade and I needed to get over it. She'd made hurtful comments and made me feel like I was a disappointment but, those niggles aside, we had enjoyed a good relationship. I needed to focus on the positives, stop dwelling on the bad stuff, and close that distance between Connie and me. After all, Mum hadn't created that; I had.

I was about to turn off to see Connie, but there was someone else I wanted to see first. Sam would apologise to Chloe for her outburst, but she had other priorities tonight. Perhaps I could help calm things a little in the meantime.

* * *

I hadn't been to Chloe and James's house in Bentonbray before, but I knew roughly where it was in the village and had seen photos. Approaching a double-fronted Victorian property with the name 'Dalby House' on a stone plaque, I spotted Chloe's car on the drive.

Chloe answered the door, holding Samuel, who was drinking from a sippy cup.

'Lauren!'

'Can I come in?'

'Sure.' She shrugged as she stepped back into a grand entrance hall with beautiful Victorian floor tiles and a dado rail.

'I was just about to give Samuel his dessert. Do you want to come through to the craft room?'

There was a craft room?

'It was the dining room,' she said as I followed her into a room at the back of the house, 'but we've got a kitchen-diner, so I snaffled it.' She lowered Samuel into a highchair, removed the lid off a fromage frais and handed him a spoon.

I looked round the light and airy room. White cupboards, shelving and cubby holes full of crafting materials ran alongside the longest wall. There was a large dining table and desk against the opposite wall and a window seat with pretty floral cushions on it. Chloe must have been mid-project when I arrived, as what looked like bunting was resting across a sewing machine on the table.

'I wasn't at Hedgehog Hollow because I was bored,' she said, sitting on one of the dining chairs and indicating I should sit on another.

'Sam knows that. She's got a few things going on and she didn't mean to take it out on you.'

'Nice of her to apologise in person.'

'She doesn't know I'm here.'

'So why are you?'

'Because I wanted to make sure you're okay. You looked upset.'

She shrugged dismissively but I noticed her eyes filling up.

'I honestly was there to help,' she said. 'I know I've got form, but I'm trying to change. I wanted to show her something. Can I show you?'

'If you like.'

'I've joined a craft club in the village and this week we were asked for ideas for community projects the group can support over the next few months. I put Hedgehog Hollow forward and they all approved.'

She lifted the lid off a plastic crate. 'Our last project was making fidget muffs and blankets for dementia patients, and it got me thinking about the comforters Samuel likes with ribbons on them. I thought we could make some hedgehog-themed ones to sell at the Family Fun Day, like this.'

Chloe passed me a piece of soft material about the size of a face-cloth. A large hedgehog touching noses with a hoglet had been appliquéd onto it, there were satin ribbons sewn round the edges, and it made a scrunching noise.

'You made this?' I asked Chloe, running my fingers across the neat stitching.

'It's just a rough version I threw together, and I haven't added the clip to it yet. It could have been neater if I wasn't rushing, but I wanted to try a few things. I've made some bunting.'

A string of colourful hedgehog-themed bunting was thrust into my hands.

'And some felt hedgehogs. Again, they're only quick ideas I've knocked together. The ones we sell would be made with more care.'

I stared down in astonishment at the pile of crafts on the table. 'Chloe! These are all amazing.'

She twirled a lock of hair round her finger and shrugged. 'It's a while since I've used my sewing machine. I'm more used to paints and glitter. You really think they're okay?'

'I didn't say okay, did I? I said amazing. Honestly, if these are your quickly knocked together attempts, your care and attention pieces must be phenomenal.'

'I know the Family Fun Day is next month, so it's tight, but I haven't found a job yet, so I could devote all my spare time to it and the other crafters will do as much as they can. If we run out on the day, I can take orders and deliver them after the event and I can build the stock up ready for next year.'

I loved how enthusiastic she sounded but couldn't resist playing devil's advocate. 'And what would you get from it?'

She looked surprised at the question. 'It's not about me. Don't get me wrong, it'll be nice to have something to do – I'm sick of feeling like a spare part – but this is about helping Sammie and the hedgehogs. I was going to show her them this afternoon but that didn't quite go to plan.'

For the first time, I saw why Sam kept giving her chances. This was clearly the kind, thoughtful side to Chloe that Sam had sworn existed.

'Sam was just saying earlier how she'd wanted to make this year bigger and better than last but she's running out of time. She's going to love these.'

'I've got other craft ideas, but I didn't have time to make samples of them all.' Chloe packed the items back into the crate. 'There's a mother and daughter team in the village who have a face-painting business. They do a handful of charitable events each year where all they charge is the cost of the paints, so the charity gets to keep the profits. They're available for the Family Fun Day but have had a request for a paid gig on the same day. I've got first dibs, but they need a decision by the end of the weekend.'

'If they're good, I'd confirm it. Can they do hedgehogs?'

'They hadn't done any before, but they've been practising. Look! How cute are these?' Chloe showed me a couple of designs on her phone. 'The one on the mum is a quick one and the one she did on the daughter is more complex.'

'They're both brilliant. Definitely book them.'

'Okay. I'll call her tonight.'

Samuel had finished his fromage frais and was busy smearing some dribbled bits across his highchair tray. Chloe whipped out a couple of baby wipes and swiftly cleaned up.

'I love both designs,' she said, 'but I was thinking it would be best to stick to the simple one and offer four or five others – maybe all with a nature theme – that are quick to do. That way, we can get through more children and make more money.'

'Good plan. Why didn't you just go ahead and book the face painters?'

She twiddled her hair again. 'I was going to, but I started doubting myself. I've messed up too many times with Sammie. I didn't want her to think I was trying to take over or make the event more complicated than she wanted it. She's my best friend. I don't want to lose her.'

She looked really vulnerable – something I hadn't seen before either – and I kicked myself for being so quick to judge her at the barn, assuming she'd caused the problem.

'I think you'll make her very happy with these ideas.'

'Thank you,' she said, beaming at me as she removed Samuel's messy bib and lifted him out of his highchair.

'I might be able to help with some of the crafts.'

'You're good at sewing?'

'Crikey, no! I can sew a button on and re-hem some trousers, but I've never used a sewing machine. You might want to speak to Connie. She's great at that sort of thing. I was thinking more along the lines of cutting out pieces of felt or lengths of ribbon to save you from doing the monotonous stuff.'

'That would be really helpful. Will you be in tomorrow morning? I could drop some stuff off then.'

We exchanged phone numbers and I pulled away from Dalby House, smiling. Wonders would never cease. Chloe Turner was capable of doing something for others. Sam would be so chuffed. A craft stall and face-painting would build on what she'd had last year and solve one of her current concerns. I just hoped I'd been right about her biggest worry being resolved by a conversation with Josh.

Driving into Little Tilbury, I felt a little less cheerful. I'd advised Sam to tell Josh everything, but was I ready to completely open up to Connie? Telling her about the work situation was easy, confessing everything about Shaun and Glen was a little harder, but discussing why I'd kept her at a distance – even if she'd never realised it – was going to be an extremely difficult conversation. But, as Sam had pointed out, if I didn't tackle it now, it would continue to fester and one day it could well blow up and irrevocably damage our relationship.

Her car wasn't outside Primrose Cottage, so I parked up and took out my phone.

✉ To Connie

Called round to yours in the hope of a catch-up. Probably should have rung first! Don't suppose you're free tomorrow night for a takeaway and wine round mine?

✉ From Connie

Throw in an apology and I'll be there x

✉ To Connie
I can do that. See you at 7 xx

* * *

Back at Chapel View, I reflected on a busy day. The career development counselling meeting had been form-filling, followed by an explanation about how they could help, so it had hadn't been particularly effective, but hopefully future meetings would be. The afternoon had been good and the early evening visit to Chloe had been unexpected.

The cogs were now turning about whether there was anything that I could do myself to help Sam create a bigger event, proving to her that support was available and she could balance a family with the needs of the rescue centre. I could get some of the hair and beauty students to do demonstrations, but that had no connection to hedgehogs and was therefore a bit random. Maybe there was something the art and design department at college could do instead. If the students needed a real-life project to work on, this could be the answer.

25

SAMANTHA

Beth had prepared a delicious meal for us all on Friday evening, but I struggled to eat. Lauren was right about me speaking to Josh, but my stomach was in knots about it. Last year when I'd thought I didn't want children – before I understood why I had the fear – I'd been terrified he might walk away. That wasn't a risk anymore, but it didn't stop me feeling nervous.

Phoebe and Darcie offered to clear away after we'd eaten, so I made drinks and suggested Josh and I take ours to Thomas's bench.

'Not hungry?' he asked when we sat down.

'Not really.' I glanced towards the meadow, willing Thomas to give me the strength to get through this conversation. 'There's something I need to tell you but it's going to be really hard to say.'

'Okay.' He drew out the word. 'Bit worried now.'

I wished I could reassure him, but he had every right to be worried.

'On Saturday, when we stayed at the bungalow and you lay on the hammock, I couldn't concentrate on reading so I got my notebook out to plan the Family Fun Day but I got myself all worked up about lack of time, so I wrote a to-do list instead, which panicked me even more. Later, when we saw that family playing in the sea and you made a comment about that being us, it should have filled me with excitement, but it didn't.'

Josh's eyes widened then his expression softened. 'You're not ready for a baby,' he said softly.

'I'm so sorry. I really thought I was. I *do* want us to have a family and I've worked so hard on my fears with my counsellor and with you but I'm scared this is too soon, but I don't know when the time will be right. There's so much to do here. I shouldn't have got carried away on our honeymoon.'

Josh took my hand in his. 'You can't take the blame for that. We both got caught up in the moment. What happens if you're pregnant now?'

'I have until they're born to get my fears under control and to work out how to balance running Hedgehog Hollow with a baby. I'm scared of going back to how things were this time last year.'

He tenderly ran his other hand down my cheek. 'I'm right here every step of the way. You must know that by now.'

'I do, but aren't you annoyed with me?'

'Why would I be annoyed?'

'Because I keep changing my mind about something as huge as having a baby.'

'I don't see it like that. You took your time, got help, and only said yes to a family when you knew for sure it was what you wanted. The situation on our honeymoon was unexpected and, as I say, you weren't the only one who got carried away. I should have insisted we take more time to talk about it. It's you who should be annoyed with me.'

I shook my head. 'This is *not* on you.'

'But it's not just on you either. What stopped you from telling me sooner?'

'I was fine with it at first, but something triggered that day and then I was ashamed. If I said I had doubts but we discovered I was pregnant, that would suggest I didn't want our baby, which would...' I lowered my eyes.

'Which would make you just like your mum.' He tilted my chin and gently kissed me before resting his forehead against mine. 'I get it. You'd be exactly what you'd worked so hard to avoid. Only there's one big difference between you and your mum. She'd been through a serious trauma and her feelings towards you were connected to that and had changed her as a person. You've been through some serious traumas too but you're still the same person – a kind, caring, generous baddass hedgehog saviour.'

I loved how Josh could always make me laugh, even when I felt at my lowest. He kissed me again, a slow and tender kiss which stirred the butterflies in my stomach and reassured me that saying he wasn't angry with me wasn't just words.

'You might not be pregnant,' he said as we snuggled together on the bench.

'I know. I was going to wait until I knew for sure, but Lauren said I should tell you.'

'Lauren knows?'

'I had a meltdown earlier...' I explained what happened this afternoon with Chloe's visit and my talk with Lauren, although I didn't share what she'd confided in me.

'I'm glad she was there for you,' he said. 'And she speaks sense. It's good that I know. If you are pregnant, we'll take each day as it comes and book some extra sessions with Lydia if that would help, and we'll sit down and work out how best to run this place because you're not alone there either. If you're not pregnant, we can keep discussing it and try again when the time feels right for both of us. But...'

He adjusted position so he could see into my eyes.

'You have to promise me two things. Firstly, don't bottle up anything else. Talk to me. We'll face whatever it is together. Agreed?'

'Agreed.'

'Secondly, we don't have to have a family. I love you and what we have already is more than I ever dreamed of. I don't want to add children into the mix if it's not right for you.'

I'd managed to keep the tears at bay so far, but they broke through with his unconditional love and understanding. 'I really do want a family with you. I meant it on our wedding day, and I still mean it. It's the timing thing – not the family itself – that's panicked me.'

He brushed aside my tears. 'Keep talking to me and we'll get there.'

26

LAUREN

'The face-painters are booked, and they've suggested these designs,' Chloe said when she called round late on Saturday morning.

She scrolled through her phone, revealing the simpler hedgehog design I'd seen before, a butterfly, ladybird, badger, fox and rabbit.

'They look brilliant. Sam's going to love them. And I've got some news for you too.'

Last night, I'd emailed Javine Dafoe, the head of art and design. She'd responded immediately, saying she was a massive hedgehog fan with a garden full of hedgehog houses and feeding stations and would be delighted to help.

'One of my colleagues, Javine, is a talented artist. She's offered to create a range of hedgehog-themed artwork in different styles – pencil sketches, watercolours and brighter paints – which she'll donate to the rescue centre in return for us handing out her flyers.'

'Oh, wow! That's amazing!'

'She reckons some of the students on the art and graphic design course will be interested in creating and gifting designs so she'll talk to them on Monday. She's also going to speak to the costume design course tutor to see if the students who've already finished their portfolios would be up for making baby and children's clothes with hedge-hogs on them.'

Chloe's mouth dropped open. 'Sammie's going to be made up by that. Thank you.'

'I'd never have thought of it if it hadn't been for you, and I'll make sure she knows that.'

Her eyes clouded over and, for a moment, I thought she was going to cry. I wasn't good with tears, so a subject change was needed.

'What's in the box?'

She smiled and patted the lid, blubbing averted. 'Supplies. You're still happy to help with the prep?'

'Definitely.'

The box was full of felt, material and ribbons, and an envelope containing templates. Even though she'd prepared written instruc-tions, Chloe showed me what to do and gave me some tips on getting the maximum use from each felt square. Once more, I saw a side to her that I'd never seen – a patient, encouraging teacher – and she went up in my estimation a little further.

'Did you never want to become a teacher?' I asked as we packed everything away.

'I briefly considered primary teaching, but I love arts and crafts and was more drawn to creative play and early development. Preschool suited me better.'

'How's the job hunt going?'

She curled her lip up. 'Not good. I've had three interviews and I had my heart set on one of them but, typically, that's the one I didn't get. I turned the other two down. I might have been spoilt by having the perfect job back in Whitsborough Bay. The way they ran things was spot on, the physical set-up was ideal and the staff were lovely. With the two I turned down, at least two of those things weren't quite right. It's hard to feel enthusiastic about working somewhere new when I know it's going to be too different. Or do you think I'm being too fussy?'

She'd echoed my thoughts exactly from my recent job search. Nothing seemed quite right. 'No, I'm with you there. I love my job and where I work, and I'd have happily stayed there until I retired, but that's not going to happen.'

'I saw the news about the takeover in the paper. Does that affect you?'

'The new owners are stripping out a layer of management – *my* layer. I can apply for more senior roles, but they don't appeal, so this term is my last.'

'I'm sorry. That must be tough.'

I shrugged. 'It is, but these things happen. I've been looking at similar jobs to mine in other colleges and, just like you, I'm struggling to muster the interest for something new when what I have now is so good.'

'Could you re-train and do something different?'

'I've thought about that, but I don't know what I'd do. I would have said it's late in life to re-train but Connie's proof that it isn't. She's never been happier in her career. And it's not like I haven't done it before, moving from nursing to teaching, but nursing was the thing I always wanted to do and teaching was an unexpected fork in the road which happened to work out for the best. I'm drawing a blank on a third career. All I know for sure is I want it to feel rewarding.'

'Welcome to the unemployed and confused club.'

We both looked at each other and burst out laughing.

'I can't believe I said that,' Chloe said when we'd composed ourselves. 'Makes us sound so pathetic.'

'Could you re-train?' I asked.

'Same thoughts as you – re-train as what? I can't think of anything I'd rather do.'

I hadn't heard his key in the lock so was surprised when Jonathan called, 'Hello?'

'In the lounge,' I called back. 'You were quick.'

He'd been called out to a farm to see to a goat in labour difficulties but had been gone less than an hour.

'The goat needed some help, but...' He stopped short, clocking Chloe. 'Hello. Wasn't expecting to see you here.'

They hugged each other.

'I needed to drop some things off for Lauren. She's helping me with some crafts for the Family Fun Day.'

'Crafts? Lauren?'

'I'm just cutting things out,' I said. 'I can manage that.'

'I need to get back,' Chloe said. 'We're taking Samuel to the beach. See you later, Uncle Jonathan.'

I walked her to the door.

'I'll be spending tomorrow crafting. You're welcome to come over and have a go with a needle.' She giggled. 'We could officially establish the unemployed and confused crafting club.'

'Love it! I might just take you up on that.'

I waved her off, smiling. Who knew an hour in Chloe's company could be so much fun?

Jonathan was halfway up the stairs when I stepped back into the hall. 'Do you fancy a pub lunch?' he asked.

'Sounds good.'

'Give me ten minutes to get freshened up.'

* * *

'I love Chloe when she's like this,' Jonathan said, after I'd brought him up to speed in the pub. 'The great thing about her is that, when she decides to do something, she really takes a hold and follows it through, so if she says she'll have a craft stall full of gifts, that's exactly what she'll deliver.'

'I've seen a different side to her these past couple of days. I'm starting to understand why Sam puts up with all the crap.'

'She's been a good friend to Sammie, especially when they were growing up. I know she's been her worst enemy too, but she was always there for Sammie when she'd had a run-in with Debs, and it helped massively.'

'Speaking of Debs, how's it going? I haven't seen you to ask.' We'd been like ships that pass in the night again. The most I'd seen of him lately was at the barbeque, but Debs had been there, so I could hardly ask then.

'Hard to say. We went out for a meal with Louise and Simon last night and it was a good evening with lots of laughs, but...' He paused, scrunching up his face, '... something didn't quite feel right and I'm struggling to pinpoint what it was.'

'Did you talk to Debs about it?'

'No. I didn't know what to say. It was probably just me being tired. I've been dashing from one place to another since the wedding and what I really need is a night in – or out – with you. We've barely spoken, and I've missed you.'

The sincerity of his tone and the sad look in his eyes was really touching. He reached across the table to squeeze my hand, but I felt nothing. No zap of electricity. No butterflies. That strangeness at the wedding had thankfully gone.

'I've missed you too,' I said.

'Other than befriending Chloe, how's it been going?'

'Not so great.'

'Why? What's happened?'

I told him all about the work bombshell and everything that had happened since, although I missed out the part about meeting Riley at Bloomsberry's. It wasn't relevant.

'I wish I'd been home when you found out,' Jonathan said.

'Can't be helped. You had other priorities and so did Connie. It's not like I was a blubbing wreck.'

'I still wish I'd been there for you.'

'Honestly, I was and am fine. I just need to re-think a few things.'

Jonathan's phone rang and he answered it, apologising that it was probably a call out.

'It's okay,' I said when he hung up, having caught that he needed to leave. 'We've eaten, so just drop me home and you can head off.'

As he dropped me off outside the house, he lightly touched my arm as he apologised for abandoning me, but I felt no reaction. It was such a relief that I didn't have feelings for Jonathan after all. It would have been far too messy if I had, especially when he was trying again with Debs, although he'd sounded very uncertain about that over lunch. Maybe it would fizzle out soon. Debs aside, I could definitely do without any romantic inclinations to anyone.

* * *

I grimaced as I poured the last drops of wine into Connie's glass that evening. 'That's the second bottle done.'

'It ruins it when you count.'

'I'll stop counting then.'

'Good.' Connie patted the sofa beside her. 'Now that I know all about work and you've admitted that you should have told me earlier...' She waggled her finger at me sternly, '... can we finally talk about Shaun?'

So she hadn't forgotten after all.

'Do we have to?' I said, curling my lip.

'Yes! And it's a long overdue conversation. Spill!'

I took a deep breath. 'Don't get mad with me, but what you said at the wedding was right. Shaun's still the one.' I'd already said as much to Sam, but saying it to Connie was so much harder because it wasn't just admitting how I still felt; it was admitting that I'd kept it from her for all these years.

Connie gently touched my arm. 'What does "still the one" mean to you?'

I closed my eyes for a moment, gathering the strength to articulate it. I was going to have to say it. Straight out. We'd deal with the fall-out from there.

'I still love him.'

'Aw, Lauren.' Her voice was gentle and full of sympathy that tears rushed to my eyes.

'I know what you're thinking. *After all these years? After what he did to you?* I ask myself those same questions constantly, but the truth is I fell in love with my best friend when I was thirteen and I never fell out of love, and it kills me that he did, and he cared so little about me that he didn't bother to tell me himself.' The tears brimmed over and trickled down my cheeks. 'Why did he do it? Who walks out and leaves a cryptic note? What did I do so wrong to deserve to be treated like that?'

I swiped angrily at my tears but, as fast as I wiped my cheeks, more tears fell.

'Argh! I don't want to cry over him again. I knew this would happen if I opened Pandora's Box.' I'd managed to hold it together while telling Sam, but I hadn't had any alcohol inside me then and I hadn't had Connie looking at me with pain in her eyes.

Connie held out the box of tissues from the table beside her and I snatched a couple of them. 'I know I should hate him, but I can't. I hate what he did and how he did it, but I can't hate him. It's Shaun! He was everything to me.'

Connie took a tissue from the box and dabbed her eyes too.

'Sorry,' I said. 'I didn't mean to make you cry.'

She shook her head. 'And I didn't mean to make this about me, but it breaks my heart that you've been feeling like this for all these years and you've never said a word.'

'I couldn't. I knew it made no sense to feel this way, so I tried hard not to think about it or talk about it. Hell, I even re-married in an effort to get over him and I would have done everything possible to make that work if Glen hadn't turned into a bunny boiler.'

We both blew our noses at the same time and laughed.

'So there you have it,' I said. 'Hopeless basket case.'

'You're not. You're just someone who fell very deeply in love with the... I was going to say wrong person, but I'm not sure he was. Anyone who saw the two of you together could see how much you loved each other.'

'Then why did he leave?'

'I wish I knew. I wish you knew. Remember when I told you that, as part of my training, we spent a lot of time exploring and dealing with our own baggage?'

I nodded, recalling how cathartic she'd told me it was to talk about

all the challenges she'd been hit with over the years like her miscar-
riages, Kayleigh's stillbirth, her lack of career, things falling apart with
Paul, Paul's affair with Beth, and her accidental overdose.

'I didn't tell you that one of the things that we explored was Shaun.'
She shot me a panicked look. 'Please don't think I was talking about
you. This was about me and how I felt about it.'

'It's fine. Keep going.' I was intrigued as to what she was going to
say. At the time, she'd expressed surprise and disappointment, but I
could tell she'd been careful not to say anything too negative in case he
came back and it made things awkward between us.

'I knew I was angry and hurt about what he'd done to you, but I
hadn't realised how I felt about what he'd done to our friendship. It
had been the four of us together for so long and the ripples affected
Paul and me too. Our best friend hadn't shared whatever was both-
ering him and he'd also walked out on us without saying goodbye,
which really hurt. The pain we were feeling must have been escalated
a hundred-fold for you, so I can understand why it was so hard to
let go.'

'Try a thousand-fold.'

She took a sip on her wine. 'I can't help thinking that you wouldn't
be in this position today if you knew why he'd left. Have you thought
about tracking him down and demanding he explain himself?'

'Constantly. I've searched for him on social media, but I've never
found him. I've searched for Ivy too.'

'That's another thing!' Connie cried, waving her arms and slopping
wine over her hands. 'You lost Ivy too and I know how close you were.'

'I miss her so much. She'll be eighty-three now, if she's still alive. I
don't even know that. Shaun could even be dead for all I know.'

Until I uttered those words, I'd never actually considered that
possibility about Shaun, but none of us knew how long we had.

I took a big glug of wine. 'Shaun might not have made it to fifty. He
might not even have made it to thirty. That would explain his absence
on social media.'

'Plenty of people aren't on social media, so it's a big leap to conclude that no Shaun Marfell on social media means Shaun Marfell RIP.'

I ran my hand through my hair, sighing. 'What am I going to do?'

'What do you want to do?'

'Turn back the clock to 1995 and ideally stop him leaving or at least get some closure.'

'Is it worth contacting his divorce solicitor again and seeing if he can put you in touch? I know they wouldn't help at the time, but policies might have changed.'

When the divorce papers first came through, I'd written several letters begging the solicitor to put me in contact with Shaun and, when he wouldn't do that, I'd written further letters which I'd asked him to forward on. Each letter was returned to me unopened. Connie already knew that, but I hadn't told her about my other attempts since then.

'I've already tried. I wrote to them every year on the anniversary of Shaun walking out. I even did it when I'd married Glen because I thought some answers might help me properly throw myself into my marriage.'

I took another gulp of my wine. 'I even... and don't judge me on this as it was the early days... I even travelled to Sheffield, waited for the secretary to come out for her lunch break and...' I hung my head, embarrassed by my behaviour. 'I offered her money to slip me his address. Obviously it was a no. I can't believe I did that now, but I was so desperate to have him back, to have my life back, to have my hopes and dreams back.'

I expected a declaration of shock from Connie, but tears had clouded her eyes once more. She gently took my wine from me, put both glasses down then drew me into a hug.

'I'd probably have done the same,' she whispered, rocking me as we sobbed together. 'Some dreams are worth chasing.'

'Shaun was. He still is.'

* * *

I could see why people went for counselling. Getting it out in the open after all these years felt like a weight lifted.

We opened our third bottle of wine and Connie declared that she had a brilliant idea. Maybe I'd put Shaun on a pedestal and had only been focusing on the good times. If getting the closure I needed directly from him wasn't an option, why didn't I try to get it myself by taking him down from that pedestal?

I was willing to give anything a try but, between us, we couldn't think of anything negative about him.

'What about his inability to tie a tie?' Connie suggested. 'What grown man can't do that?'

'I know we took the piss, but that was endearing.' It had also been one of our little things. I'd tie it for him before work then give it a little tug and draw him in for a kiss.

'I've got one!' Connie cried. 'He cheated at Monopoly. He used to insist on being banker and would slip himself extra notes when he passed Go!'

'I think you'll find that was Paul, not Shaun.'

'Oh, yeah.'

And so it went on. We drew a blank on the negatives, but it was reassuring to talk about so many positives because it proved to me that, even though I knew I'd wasted years pining after him, he'd been worth pining for.

'Do you remember when we first moved in together and we invited you and Paul round for dinner?' I asked.

'The curry!' Connie cried.

Shaun had decided to make a chicken tikka masala from scratch rather than using a jar of sauce. He'd been so proud of himself, and it looked and smelled delicious. A couple of mouthfuls in, the four of us had streaming noses and eyes and were glugging the water. When he'd shopped for the ingredients, he'd forgotten to buy a small chilli so had substituted that with chilli powder: a tablespoon of the stuff!

While Connie and I were still laughing about the curry, Jonathan arrived home from an engagement party for one of the veterinary practice's receptionists.

'Sounds like I've missed a good evening,' he said, his wide smile and slurred speech suggesting he'd had a good evening himself.

'Join us for a nightcap?' I asked.

'Probably shouldn't, but what the heck.' He disappeared into the kitchen and emerged with a wine glass.

After another hour of laughter, Connie declared that she could barely keep her eyes open and headed upstairs to bed.

'It's good to see you smiling again,' Jonathan said, slipping into Connie's vacated space on the sofa beside me.

'We've had a good chat and set the world to rights. I didn't realise how much I needed to offload.'

'I should have been here for you.'

I shook my head vigorously. 'You had responsibilities at Hedgehog Hollow. Besides, it wasn't just the redundancy thing. I really am okay with that. It was other stuff.'

He raised his eyebrows questioningly.

'It was Shaun and Glen. But mainly Shaun.'

'You never talk about them.'

'I'm not a talker. I mean, I'm a big talker but I'm not... you know what I mean. I don't do the deep and meaningful stuff. Too deep and too meaningful.'

'And painful?' he suggested.

'Very painful.'

We were silent for a moment as we sipped on our wine.

'Did you know Debs is seeing a counsellor?' Jonathan asked.

'Sam mentioned it, but she didn't give any details. None of my business.'

'It's really helping her, but she asked me whether I thought it would be a good idea for us to go back through some issues we had before we were even married.'

'That's a long time ago. What did you say?'

'That I wasn't sure, and she should probably explore the idea with her counsellor first. I'd hate for any conversations we have to jeopardise the great progress she's made.'

'But even if her counsellor gives the green light, you'd rather not have those conversations?'

'I can't help thinking we'll be waking up some ghosts that were best laid to rest and we could end up hating each other.' He rolled his eyes at me and sighed. 'That's a bit cryptic when you don't know what's gone on. Let's just say that, once I was qualified and returned to Whitsborough Bay, things weren't as perfect as they'd been before, and I've sometimes wondered how different things would have turned out for both of us if one of us had called it a day at that point. Before other things happened. I can't personally see any benefit in going back that far, but I'll do it if Debs and her counsellor reckon it'll help.'

I swirled the last of my wine in my glass, trying to think what Connie would say if she hadn't gone to bed.

'I'm going to ask you an either/or question and I want you give your gut reaction about what *you* want. Not what Debs might want or what you think the *right* answer is.' I did air quotes – not easy when holding a glass of wine – to emphasise the word 'right'. 'Remember, it's what *you* want.'

'Okay. Hit me with it.'

'What would you rather have? You and Debs back together with some past issues unresolved... or everything out in the open and the divorce going ahead. Be honest.'

Jonathan grimaced. 'Divorce.'

'And is that because you don't want to rake over the past or because you don't think you have a future with Debs?'

He emitted a low whistle. 'Oh, crap, what a mess.'

'You know you're going to have to tell her how you feel, don't you? And you should probably do that sooner rather than later.'

He ran his hand down his face and sighed. 'I'll give her a ring tomorrow and see if she's free. How did you realise before me?'

'I know we've barely seen each other recently but you were buzzing after the wedding and you weren't at lunchtime. You said something wasn't quite right when you had your meal with Louise and Simon, and I wonder if it was having a slice of your old life back and realising you don't fit into that space anymore.'

He nodded slowly. 'God, you're good! That's exactly it! I don't fit.'

'It might not be as bad as you expect. You might find she's feeling the same.'

Jonathan gave me a cheeky smile. 'You're saying she could resist this?' He pointed his thumb towards his chest. 'How's that even possible?'

'I can't begin to imagine. Fine specimen of a man like you.'

His eyes held mine and it was potentially a moment for the air to crackle with electricity but, once more, I felt nothing.

'I think it's time I headed up to bed too,' I said, standing up. 'I'll see you in the morning.'

'Night, Lauren.'

As I closed my eyes a little later, I pictured Shaun. I turned on my side and buried my face in the pillow. Jonathan had been worried about waking up ghosts from the past. My ghost had never left my side.

27

LAUREN

'Wish me luck,' Jonathan said as he loaded his breakfast pots into the dishwasher on Sunday morning, ready to drive over to Whitsborough Bay to call time on his relationship with Debs.

'Good luck. I'm sure she'll understand.'

'What are your plans for the day?' he asked.

'I'm not sure. There's no point job-hunting until after my second career counselling session on Friday when I'll hopefully have some guidance on what to look for. Chloe invited me over to do some crafts. I might do that.'

When Jonathan left, I made another coffee while I mulled over my plans for the day and decided that an afternoon with Chloe was infinitely more appealing than moping round the house on my own. I'd enjoyed cutting out the felt hedgehogs yesterday and it might be fun to have a go at stitching some of them together.

✉ To Chloe
If the inaugural meeting of the unemployed and confused craft club is still planned for this afternoon, I'm in!

✉ From Chloe
It is! James is making a roast and he always over-caters so you're welcome
to join us for lunch first and we'll craft with full tummies

✉ To Chloe
Tin of vegetable soup with stale bread bun or home-cooked Sunday roast?
Life's full of tough choices. See you for lunch

✉ From Chloe
Sounds like you're as competent in the kitchen as me! See you at 12.30 x

* * *

'Finished!' I declared, cutting the thread and putting my needle down
later that afternoon.

'Let's see it.' Chloe took the felt hedgehog from me and released a
low whistle as she turned it over to examine the back, then returned to
the front. 'You've honestly never done any sewing before?'

'Nothing more adventurous than buttons or a hem. Is it any
good?'

To me, it looked like a match to the sample hedgehog Chloe had
made and my stitching seemed neat, but I wasn't the expert. I couldn't
believe how nervous I felt awaiting her verdict.

'Good? It's brilliant! You're a natural. I can't believe you've never
done this before. The stitches are so neat and consistent. Did you
enjoy it?'

'I loved it, which was unexpected, and I feel this amazing sense of
achievement thinking *I made that*.'

Chloe's eyes lit up. 'Welcome to my world! I can't imagine a better
feeling than taking some raw materials and turning them into something beautiful. Do you want to do another, or do you want to try something else?'

'I'll do another and see if I can do it faster.'

James, who'd taken Samuel to the village playground after lunch, poked his head round the door. 'We're back but Samuel's fallen asleep in his pushchair. Do you want me to leave him in it?'

'Yeah, that's fine, but see if you can slip his coat off and drape a blanket over him.'

James returned a little later with coffees and a packet of biscuits.

'Looking good,' he said, admiring our creations. 'Did Chloe show my attempt?'

'Oh, my God!' Chloe cried. 'You have to see this!'

She rummaged under a pile of material and handed me a lump of brown felt. I glanced at it then looked up at James, wincing. The back and front didn't match, the stitches were uneven, the stuffing was hanging out and the face was menacing.

He laughed. 'I know. It looks more like roadkill.'

'I had to hide it under here because it gave me the fear,' Chloe said, shoving it back under the material. She caught James's hand and looked up at him adoringly. 'But I love that you tried.'

James planted a gentle kiss on Chloe's forehead then left us to it.

'You two seem happier,' I observed.

'We are. James loves it here and halving his commute has made a big difference. I'm feeling more settled, and Samuel now sleeps through most nights, so we're finally getting some sleep ourselves. I was worried we'd made a big mistake moving but I think it's going to turn out for the best. All I need now is to find the right job in the right place with the right people.'

'The easy part,' I joked.

'Something'll come up. We're fortunate enough not to need my salary, but I'm not the sort of person who can't work. I'd only planned to take a year's maternity leave and we're well past that, but at least I have Project Hedgehog to keep me occupied until the end of June. Sammie FaceTimed me yesterday, by the way, and apologised for Friday.'

'Did you tell her about your ideas?'

'No. She seemed a bit stressed and then someone turned up with a hedgehog, but she texted me later to see when I was free for a catch-up.

I'm going round on Tuesday evening after Beavers and I'll take all the stuff with me.'

'Do you want some moral support?'

'Are you free? I'd love it. How about I pick you up at six?'

The rest of the afternoon flew past, and I was surprised at how easily the conversation flowed with only occasional pauses while Chloe showed me something she was making and encouraged me to have a go. I was impressed with how clearly she explained everything. It was a shame she had no interest in becoming a teacher as she had a natural gift.

Being the daughter of a twin herself, Chloe was interested in my relationship with Connie and what it had been like growing up with a twin sister who was the opposite of me in so many ways. She told me about the similarities between her mum and Debs but how Louise would often pull rank as the first-born. That was something I'd never done to Connie. What difference did it make who'd left the womb first?

I loved hearing about Chloe's close relationship with Sam as children and the fun they'd had together. She also talked about the tricky moments for them because of the favouritism Debs showed towards Chloe over her own daughter. I still needed to open up the favouritism discussion with Connie, but there'd been so much to discuss last night that I'd made a conscious decision not to throw that into the mix. It was interesting hearing the other side from Chloe. Until now, I'd mainly thought about how Mum's disappointment in me and pride in Connie affected me, and hadn't really considered how difficult it could be for 'the favourite'. When I did have that conversation, I'd approach it a little differently.

Before I set off back to Chapel View late that afternoon, I found 'Mr Blue Sky' on my phone and set it away playing. This time, there were no sweary lyrics from me. There probably weren't many correct ones either, but I felt relaxed and uplifted. I'd had a great day today, unexpectedly discovering a few new skills. I'd never have imagined myself as someone who'd enjoy crafting. Connie would be shocked. She used to knit and do cross-stitch kits, but it had never appealed to me before.

I also felt a lot more positive about the work situation today. I didn't have a plan but, as Chloe had pointed out to me, I had time on my side. The only pressure to leave college at the end of term with a job lined up was self-imposed. I needed to cut myself a little slack and enjoy the financial security I had.

28

SAMANTHA

On Sunday afternoon, Zayn and I were hunched over the microscope, looking at poo samples from a female adult hedgehog which had been dropped off this morning. Blossom had been found in the courtyard of Amblestone Chapel near Lauren's house and had arrived presenting with severe fly strike and dehydration.

'What's your verdict?' I asked Zayn.

He glanced again at the folder beside him where I kept laminated pictures of the various parasites when seen under a microscope.

'Fluke and roundworm,' he said.

'Spot on. Poor Blossom.'

All internal parasites were nasty, but fluke was particularly grim if not caught early enough. Caught either from drinking contaminated water or a host like a slug or snail – which hedgehogs would only eat if they couldn't find their preferred food sources – this parasite feeds on the liver, often proving fatal. Before getting to that point, it can cause excessive hyperactivity.

'Check that final sample, will you?' I asked Zayn. We usually took three samples to ensure we caught everything. There was a third common parasite – lungworm – and a really poorly hedgehog might have all three. I hadn't seen any evidence of lungworm in the first two samples but wanted to check the final one to be sure.

'Fluke and roundworm again,' Zayn said, 'but definitely no lungworm.'

He stepped aside so I could see for myself. 'That's one bit of good news. Can you remember the treatment?'

After we'd discussed and given Blossom her treatment, Fizz arrived.

'I wasn't expecting to see you today,' I said as she hung her bag up near the door. 'I thought you were at Bumblebee Barn for the afternoon.'

'I've been for lunch, but Barney's new girlfriend was there.' She scrunched up her face and shuddered. 'I hate being nasty but, oh, my word! She has to be the worst so far. I swear I have no idea where he keeps finding them.'

She was making a round of drinks as the door opened. Darcie ran across the room clutching Twizzle and Tango, her furry unicorns, and launched herself at Fizz.

'We spotted your car outside,' Phoebe said, following behind with Josh.

'How was lunch?' I asked. I'd dropped Phoebe and Darcie off at Rosemary's new place in Fimberley around mid-morning, and Josh had been to pick them up.

'I had four Yorkshire puddings!' Darcie declared. 'And so did Trixie.'

'That's a lot,' I said. 'They must have been very tasty.'

'They were awesome. Rosemary let me mix the batter.'

'Clever you. You'll have to make us some Yorkshire puddings over half-term.'

'We've got a new hedgehog,' Zayn announced. 'Her name's Blossom...'

When we finished updating everyone, Zayn took Darcie across to show her which crate was Blossom's. He was so good with her and never seemed to mind being bombarded with questions.

I took my mug over to the sink to wash. As I was drying it, I watched Fizz and Phoebe huddled over one of their phones, laughing at something. They really would make a lovely couple given half a chance.

'What are you smiling at?' Josh asked, putting his arms round me from behind and nuzzling my neck.

'All of this. When Thomas left me the farm, I only thought about all the spikey creatures who'd enter my life and touch my heart. I had no idea that so many humans would do the same. I think he knew.'

Josh tightened his hold and kissed my neck. 'He probably did. And how are you feeling about the possibility of another one on its way?'

'Much calmer now that you know.'

My period was due today, although me stopping my pills mid-cycle could have messed with that, so we'd decided to wait until tomorrow to take the test. Whatever happened in the next few days, I was blessed to have my found family. Watching Zayn giving a piggyback to Darcie, I felt a warm glow inside me. *Thank you, Thomas.*

I spotted Riley's convertible when I pulled into the college car park on Monday morning and the butterflies in my stomach stirred, just like they did every time I thought about him which, for some strange reason, had become a regular thing.

We'd spent so little time together and he was the man responsible for taking my job away, but he'd somehow got under my skin and into my head. Why?

Last week, the butterflies had fluttered every time I saw him, and my heart leapt whenever someone mentioned his name. I'd found myself calling by his office to ask questions instead of phoning him, and he'd dropped round some paperwork which he could easily have emailed. I sensed he wanted to talk, but there was always someone around, so the conversation had to remain work-based.

Shortly after the first classes of the day started, I went to the staffroom and my stomach went into spin cycle. Riley was beside the coffee machine, wearing my favourite shirt. He was concentrating on tapping something into his phone, a frown creasing his brow, and he obviously hadn't noticed me.

I didn't want to disturb him but I needed a drink, so I reached for a mug, but he turned and reached for one at the same time. Our hands touched and electricity zipped through me, making me feel a little lightheaded. I looked up into those intense eyes and was sure he'd felt something too. My heart raced as I imagined him taking my hand, pulling me towards him and lowering his lips to mine.

'Lauren! Hi!'

'I didn't mean to creep up on you,' I said.

'You didn't. It's me. I was miles away.'

'Everything okay?'

'Problems with my ex. We have an eleven-year-old son, Kai, who lives with her but...' He shook his head. 'Let's just say it's messy. How was your weekend?'

'It was okay. I still don't—'

But I didn't get to finish my sentence as the door opened and Judith joined us, grabbed a coffee, then whisked Riley away to a meeting.

He turned back to me at the door and gave me an apologetic shrug while mouthing 'sorry'. I leaned back against the cabinet, my heart racing. I hadn't imagined it. There was definitely something sparking between us.

The thing with Jonathan had been fleeting – caught up in a moment – but my draw towards Riley seemed to strengthen by the day and I couldn't help thinking he felt the same.

* * *

Around mid-morning, one of the admin assistants handed me my department's post. I wandered round the office, dropping the envelopes onto the appropriate desks then stopped dead, staring at the next envelope in the pile.

My heart thumped and beads of sweat prickled my forehead and upper lip. The rest of the post slipped onto the floor, leaving that one envelope in my hands. Holding onto the desks for support, I staggered back to my chair and sat down heavily. I'd recognise that handwriting anywhere.

My mouth was dry, and I felt like I was clawing for air as the room closed in on me.

'Are you all right?'

Alice's voice sounded distant, as though she was underwater.

'Lauren?'

'Yeah. Erm... I need to get something from my car.'

'You're sure you're all right?'

'Yeah.' I attempted a smile as I grabbed for my bag. 'I'll be back soon.'

Outside, despite grey skies and a cool breeze carrying light drizzle, my hands felt clammy. I unlocked my car and sank into the driver's seat, staring at the envelope.

'Rip off the plaster,' I muttered. 'One, two, three...' Rip!

L,

I'm so sorry to write to you out of the blue like this, especially after the way I left without explanation. I'm also sorry to write to you at your workplace. I found you on LinkedIn and looked up the address.

A final apology (for now) is that I have some bad news and there's no way to soften the blow. Mum is dying. They've given her until the end of summer at the very most. She has two dying wishes:

To see you again. Losing touch is her greatest regret

For me to explain why I left. This is my greatest regret

I handled everything badly and can only begin to imagine the pain my actions caused you. I wouldn't even know where to start writing it all down and feel I owe you an explanation in person anyway.

The next step is up to you. Mum and I are both aware we have no right to ask you for anything. If you wanted to see Mum but not me, I completely understand, although she's likely to tell you why I left and I'm sure that will lead to questions which she'll be unable to answer.

My email is the-lost-osprey@gmail.com but I have one final request. If you would like me to explain, please, please, please can we do that face to face?

S x

A shiver ran through me. Not one but two ghosts from the past had just caught up with me. Feeling chilled to the bone, I started the car and turned up the heating to full. The light drizzle turned to rain, tapping on the windscreen, and I shivered again, pulling my jacket tightly across my body.

All this time, I'd longed for Shaun to make contact and, now that he had, I had no idea how to feel. Shocked? Angry? Delighted? All I had right now was numb, even at the news that Ivy was dying.

I scanned down the letter once more before stuffing it back in the envelope and into my bag. My workload might have lightened, but I still had a job to do, and I was going to remain the consummate professional until the end.

I dashed across the car park in the increasingly heavy rain, cursing that I hadn't had the sense to grab my golf brolly out of the boot but knowing I'd get wetter going back for it than I would if I kept going.

In the reception, I shook my arms, flicked my sodden hair back and looked up to see Riley, a few paces away, watching me intently. My stomach did an enormous backflip, and my heart began to race.

'It's raining,' I said, feeling that words were needed and managing to land on the two most pointless ones.

He smiled, exposing that one gorgeous dimple.

'I can see that,' he said, stepping closer. 'I'd offer you a towel if I had one.'

'Quick blast under the hand dryer and I'll be sorted.'

He steered me away from the reception desk. 'Sorry I had to rush off earlier. Are you free later today? I've got a job proposal I want to run by you.'

I shook my head. 'I've already signed on the dotted line. Nine weeks and counting.'

'It's not a job here. I've got a conference call shortly, but are you free in an hour?'

My diary was clear but there was no way I'd be able to concentrate on anything he had to say today, not with that letter burning a hole in my handbag. I was struggling to have a coherent conversation right now. I needed a quiet day with just me and some easy paperwork.

'Today's tricky,' I said.

'That's a shame. I'm going to struggle with the next couple of days. How about ten on Thursday?'

'Okay. It's a date. Obviously not a date date, but a date in the diary.' Yep, definitely struggling with words. I winced at the hole I was digging. 'I'm going to find a hand dryer and I'll see you on Thursday. You can propose to me then.'

His eyes twinkled. 'I was thinking of presenting a business idea rather than an engagement ring.'

I looked at him blankly.

'You just said "you can propose to me then",' he said, clearly struggling to hold back his laughter.

'I never did!' But as I replayed the conversation, I realised I had. 'Sorry! No more words. Thursday. Bye.'

Cringing, I took off down the corridor. Of all the people who could have been in reception just now, why had it had to be Riley Berry and why had he wanted to talk to me when the power of coherent speech had been snatched from me by the ghost of husbands past?

Alice had gone by the time I returned to my office via the hand dryers, which was a relief as I couldn't face any questions. I sat in front of my emails but didn't take in a single word I read, too busy glancing at my handbag on the floor beside me.

'Sod it!' I muttered, grabbing the letter after managing roughly fifteen minutes of work in an hour. Connie would have advised me to at least give it overnight before replying to allow for thinking time, but what was there to think about? This was my opportunity to finally get answers. As for Ivy, of course I'd grant her dying wish. I was devastated when we lost touch, but I understood she'd had little choice. It was her son or me, and which mother wouldn't choose their son?

I typed in a response, stabbing the keys with such ferocity that I'm surprised I didn't break the keyboard.

To: The-Lost-Osprey

From: Lauren Harbuckle

Subject: Where do I even start?

Got your letter. Only 26 years overdue. Damn right you owe me an explanation. I can shift a few things and be free this weekend to get it over with.

As for your mum, I'm genuinely sorry to hear that. Ivy meant the world to me
and I also regret that we lost touch. My sympathy to you too. It's hard losing
parents. My mum died ten years ago.

Yes, of course I'll see Ivy. This situation wasn't of her making and I bear no
ill-feeling towards her. I agree it would be best to do that after I've seen you
as it's not fair to expect her to do your dirty work for you.

I await confirmation of a time and place and I trust you will not change your
mind having written to me on a whim.

I read it back several times. I might have felt numb in the car but
now I was angry, and every single word clearly reflected that, but I
didn't care. When I met him, I wouldn't be rushing to hug him and
shower him with forgiveness, and it was best that he be prepared for
that.

Satisfied I had the tone how I wanted it, I sent the email and went
to the staffroom to make myself a strong coffee. When I returned, I was
surprised to see he'd already responded.

From: The-Lost-Osprey

To: Lauren Harbuckle

Subject: RE: Where do I even start?

Great to hear from you and I'm very sorry about your mum.

How about 10am on Saturday at April's Tea Parlour in Great Tilbury?

I replied to confirm I'd be there and to reiterate that he'd better
turn up, and he responded immediately.

I will be there. I promise. A heads-up that I've changed a lot since I last
saw you.

I rolled my eyes at that pointless comment. So what if he was bald, bearded, overweight or whatever? We were in our fifties now. Of course we'd changed. I didn't want to prolong the email conversation by making that observation, so I closed it down and attempted to do some work.

This next week was going to crawl by slower than snail's pace, but at least I'd finally have that much-needed closure on Saturday. I'd better see if Connie was free again because I could well need her that night.

30

SAMANTHA

Mornings at Hedgehog Hollow were wonderfully chaotic – especially Mondays with the return to school, college and work after the weekend.

My period hadn't returned yesterday and while that didn't mean I was pregnant, it made it a greater possibility than before, and I was trying to stay calm about it. In the midst of the Monday morning chaos wasn't the right moment for taking a pregnancy test, so Josh and I agreed to wait until the end of the day when we'd eaten, when Darcie, Archie and Lottie were asleep, when we could be alone to discuss what happened next.

'If you want to take the test while everyone's out rather than waiting for me to get home, I understand,' Josh said as he kissed me goodbye.

'We agreed to do it together.'

'But you're anxious about it and I'm sure you'd rather know either way. The only problem is I've got back-to-back surgeries, so you'll be on your own with the news until I get home.'

'I'll think about it.'

A few hours later, I stood in the en-suite with the pregnancy testing kit in my hands, Josh's words ringing in my ears. The farmhouse was silent. Paul and Beth had taken Archie and Lottie to the playground in

Great Tilbury followed by lunch in April's Tea Parlour, so I really was on my own if I took the test now. It wasn't ideal, but not knowing was too stressful.

Heart thumping, I unwrapped the test. 'Okay. I'm ready. Let's do this.'

I closed my eyes while I waited for the result, focusing on keeping my breathing slow and steady as I counted two minutes in my head.

Taking a deep breath, I opened my eyes and looked at the result window.

Not pregnant.

I blinked and looked again.

Not pregnant.

I expected to feel happy or at least relieved, but I didn't feel either of those things as I stared at the stick in my hand, frowning at those two words. A couple of tears splashed onto my hands and I swallowed hard on the lump in my throat. Why was I crying? That made no sense. This was the result I'd hoped for, wasn't it?

The stick slipped onto the tiles as I slumped back on the toilet, tears trickling down my cheeks. The phrase *you never know what you've got till it's gone* swirled round my mind. For me, there'd never been a baby but there'd been a possibility of one, and now that had gone. After all that worry, all that fear that it was too soon, had I actually been looking forward to having a baby? The tears and the overwhelming feeling of disappointment suggested I had.

I was in the barn and had just finished feeding the hoglets when Josh arrived back from work. Phoebe and Darcie were in the farmhouse, preparing our evening meal, and I'd been texted with a twenty-minute warning for food.

'You look tired,' Josh said, sitting down beside me after he'd kissed me.

'I feel it.'

'Did you take the test?'

I nodded. 'It was negative. I'm not pregnant.'

'*Not* pregnant?' He took my hand in his. 'Are you relieved?'

'You'd think I would be after all that fuss but I'm not. I'm gutted, actually.'

'Aw, Sammie.'

'I cried for an hour.'

He stood up and wrapped his arms round me as the tears flowed once more.

'Could it have been too early?' he asked when I pulled away to grab a tissue. 'Might it be worth taking another test in a couple of days?'

'My period returned a few hours ago. I'm definitely not pregnant.'

He drew me back into a hug and we stood in the barn for several minutes, holding onto each other.

'How do you feel?' I asked him.

'A bit choked up,' he said after a moment, his voice thick with emotion. 'I know you weren't sure, but...' He sighed.

'I know,' I said, tightening my hold. 'You wanted this and it seems I did too. I wasn't expecting that.'

'You know what I think you should do now?' he said. 'Have a long, hot bubble bath and an early night. We can talk about it, we can watch a film to take our minds off it or we can both try to get some shut-eye.'

'Sounds good. I'm sorry about all the stress.'

'Hey, we've talked about this and there's nothing to be sorry about. Come on, let's clear up in here and get some food.'

* * *

Dad was on hoglets duty, so I nipped over to the barn to see him after we'd eaten.

'You look tired,' he said.

'Josh said the same. I think the wedding and honeymoon excitement has caught up with me, so I'm going to have a bath and an early night. How are you?'

'Not too bad. There's something I want to talk to you about, but it's not urgent, so I can catch you later in the week.'

I sat down on the sofa bed. 'You know you can't leave me hanging like that. Spill.'

Dad smiled as he sat beside me. 'It's about your mum and me.'

Butterflies fluttered inside me. Was he about to tell me they were back together and he was going to return to Whitsborough Bay? I hoped not, but I'd be supportive of him, whatever decision he'd made.

'We had a moment at your wedding and, on the back of that, we spent some time exploring whether we could have a future together. While you were on honeymoon, I went over to Whitsborough Bay a few times and we agreed that, if anything happened, we had to take it slowly.'

He sighed and his gaze drifted away from me towards the window. 'I went across again yesterday and we had a long chat.' He turned back to me, his eyes sad. 'It's not going to work. We're still getting divorced.'

'Aw, Dad, I'm sorry. Was that a joint decision?' I'd only just stopped myself from asking if it was Mum's decision, which had been my worst fear for Dad.

'Pretty much. I went across to tell her I didn't think it was going to work and she admitted she'd been feeling the same.'

'You sound disappointed.'

'I am, but I know it's the right decision. At your wedding, I really thought we could make it work, but it was the romance and nostalgia...'

'And the champagne?' I suggested.

Dad smiled. 'Very likely. Neither of us regret that we tried again. I think we'd have both always wondered if we hadn't, but our future is as friends – nothing more.'

Misty-Blue wandered through the cat flap and jumped up, stretching out between us both for maximum attention.

'I'm glad you've found friendship,' I said, stroking the cat's belly. 'It's been great seeing you two chatting and laughing together.'

My cheeks coloured and I decided that, as he'd been honest, I might as well be. 'Although it was a bit of a shock to see you kissing each other at the wedding.'

Dad stopped stroking Misty-Blue for a moment. 'You saw us?'

'Josh, me and this little one were in the gazebo. I was worried about you trying again and getting hurt, so it's a bit of a relief to hear it's not going anywhere.'

'I can't believe you saw us. Lauren did too. We could have sworn we were alone.'

I wanted to offer some platitudes about him meeting someone else and finding love again, but that was probably something I wanted for him more than he wanted for himself right now. He'd been a caring and devoted husband and I knew how difficult it had been for him to end things with Mum in the first place. I suspected he'd wondered if he'd done the right thing then, so it was good that they'd tried again and confirmed that divorce was the right route to take. They had full closure now.

A little later, in the bath, my thoughts turned to Lauren. Would she ever be able to get the closure she so badly needed so that she could move on and potentially find love again? I really hoped so.

LAUREN

On Tuesday morning, I gulped back down the last mouthful of my second coffee, picked up my bag and drove to the college. Hopefully I'd have a busy day ahead of me but without anything too taxing to do, as I didn't feel like I had any brain power left.

I'd barely slept last night, my thoughts flitting between what it would be like to see Shaun again on Saturday and the sad news that Ivy was dying. I wished there'd been a way we could have stayed in each other's lives. Pulling away would have hurt her as much as it had hurt me.

Seeing her just to say goodbye would be one of the most painful things I'd ever do, but I had to do it for her and for me. Not taking that opportunity could eat away at a person, as I'd seen first-hand.

About a year after Shaun and I married, his biological father Max contacted Ivy, asking to meet them both. He wanted to apologise but, after a lifetime as a single mum with no contact and no financial support from Max, Ivy wasn't interested. She told Shaun she'd respect his decision either way, but he said no too. As far as he was concerned, Max was merely a sperm donor and meant nothing to him. A year later, the shock news came of Max's death. He'd been terminally ill and had wanted to die having righted his many wrongs, his greatest being how he'd treated Ivy and Shaun, although he'd never said that when he made contact.

Unfortunately that very act of reaching out created another 'wrong' because of the guilt it laid at Shaun's door for not granting a dying man the opportunity to make peace. It hit him so hard that he had to take a few days off work. I felt awful because we were short-staffed at the hospital and I couldn't get the time off to be with him, but he reassured me that the solitude was good for him while he worked through his emotions.

When I pulled into the car park, my heart leapt at the sight of Riley's car. He'd said he'd be busy for the next couple of days so I might not see him around, but knowing he was in the building felt comforting.

I went straight to the staffroom for another strong coffee and took it to my office. There was a box of chocolate shortbread biscuits from Bloomsberry's in the middle of my desk with a Post-it note stuck to it:

Heard these were your favourites – R

'Riley,' I whispered, smiling.

I moved the box to one side and laughed as another Post-it was revealed:

Save one for me!

I grabbed the Post-it pad and scribbled something on it, then opened up the packet and placed the note behind one of the biscuits. It read 'Riley's shortbread' with a downward arrow. I took a photo and emailed it to him with the subject line: *If you want it, you'll have to come and get it*

As soon as I pressed 'send', I had a moment's panic that the message might sound suggestive, but the photo of the biscuits would surely negate that. A reply came back containing three crying-with-laughter emojis.

I've got a meeting with Judith in 1 minute otherwise I'd be there. I'll try to drop by later.

It was lunchtime when he appeared, and Alice was in the office so we couldn't chat, but his fingers brushed against mine as he reached for his biscuit, sending butterflies swarming as usual.

'He's a nice bloke,' Alice said after he left the office.

'Yeah, he seems to be.'

'I don't think he likes making people redundant. I bet some people get a kick out of it – it's a power thing – but I get the impression it hurts him.'

'What makes you think that?'

'When I had my one-to-one with him, I told him how disappointed I was about the college letting you go. He said something like "It often works out for the best for the people leaving, although I don't usually get to see that part. I just see the hurt." He seemed to drift off into his own world for a moment.' She picked up an armful of files. 'No rest for the wicked. I'll see you later.'

When the door closed, I reflected on what she'd said and it endeared Riley to me even more.

'Oh, my gosh!' I exclaimed, my eyes darting across the beautiful display that Chloe and Lauren had created upstairs in the rescue centre on Tuesday evening. 'How have you managed to make all of this?'

'Two hours' sleep for the past fortnight,' Chloe deadpanned before lightly nudging me. 'Joking! This is a mix of work from me, Lauren and the enthusiastic and excited members of the Bentonbray Craft Club. They've embraced the hedgehog theme and have tried new patterns or brought in samples they've had lying around at home.

What you see here is a fairly representative selection of what we can do, but there's so much scope using the same crafting techniques. Take the humble felt hedgehog, for example...'

She picked up a brown felt hedgehog and handed it to me. It was a little larger than the palm of my hand, with a cream hanging ribbon at the top.

'You can hang that little fella up anywhere in your house, any time of year, right? But do this...' She picked up another hedgehog which looked very similar except it was sporting a red and white Santa hat, '... and we have a Christmas tree decoration.'

'It's gorgeous. You realise I'm going to need several of these for my tree?'

'Thought you might.' She reached for another item but kept it hidden in the palm of her hand. 'This is still felt but we've tweaked the design, changed the colour and made it smaller to get this.' She opened up her palm, revealing a cerise pink hedgehog keyring.

'Cute!'

'We can replace the ribbon with a suction cup,' she continued, 'or use material instead of felt like this one...'

Chloe barely paused for breath as she talked me through the different designs on the table including bunting, felt garlands, baby comforters and bibs, cushions, purses, aprons and pencil cases. There were knitted, crocheted and needle-felted hedgehogs which she said could be made in an array of sizes, styles and colours. I could feel the excitement emanating from her and it was obvious to me she was in her element.

'I've just had a thought about this one,' she said, picking up the Christmas decoration. 'I don't think we should sell these at the Family Fun Day. How about a Christmas craft fair? We could hold it in Wildflower Byre and have food stalls and activities for the kids. We could still sell non-Christmas crafts – great present ideas – but also make a load of special Christmas ones, maybe with a few other animals on them to cater to wider tastes. We could invite some other crafters to have a stall and charge them for it and we...'

She paused, looking a bit sheepish. 'I'm talking too much. And I'm taking over. Sorry.'

I smiled reassuringly. 'The crafts are superb, so are your ideas, and I don't think you're taking over. In fact, I couldn't be more grateful to you. This is exactly what I envisaged but I don't have the time or talent to pull it off myself, so you taking it on like this is a gift.'

'It's been fun.'

'I can tell. I haven't seen you so passionate about something in such a long time and it's lovely. Yes to a Christmas Fair. Another brilliant idea and potentially a great fundraiser which could become an annual thing. I'll check the diary when we go downstairs, and I can sound Natasha out about catering and check her availability too.'

'Tell her about the face-painters,' Lauren said.

I listened, grinning, as Chloe filled me in on the booking she'd made with Lauren's approval and showed me the pictures of the animals they could paint. Relief flowed through me. With the worry about being pregnant and then the disappointment of not being pregnant, I hadn't given much more thought to the Family Fun Day and had resigned myself to not having the time or headspace to run anything bigger and better than last year, but Chloe had thought of everything.

'I'm so glad you like it all,' she said.

'Chloe, you've excelled yourself. I just wish I could pay you for all the time and effort.'

'I'm loving it. It's keeping me busy, my brain's ticking over again and you were right about getting out there and joining in. I'd never have done it without that kick up the backside from you, which was exactly what I needed.'

'I'm so pleased to hear that. You're not regretting moving after all?'

She shook her head. 'Not anymore. Ooh, I've had a couple more ideas for the Family Fun Day too.' She scrolled through her phone and showed me a photo of a beautiful hedgehog cake.

'One of the leaders at Beavers runs a cake-decorating business from home. She's offered to donate something like this either as a raffle prize or for a guess the weight of the cake competition.'

She scrolled onto a photo of hedgehog cupcakes. 'If we reimburse the cost of the ingredients, she can make a load of cupcakes to sell too.'

The final photo was of some hedgehog biscuits. 'And I had a go at these while you were away. I'd have brought you a sample, but James was a bit partial to them. I think he was shocked to see me in the kitchen. He now knows I can actually cook – I just choose not to – and he's agreed to continue with the lion's share of the cooking as long as I promise to do more baking, which is a win-win all round. I was thinking I could make some biscuits to sell, but we can also have some that aren't decorated and run a table where children – or adults if they want – get to decorate a plain hedgehog, obviously paying for the privilege.'

'Another brilliant idea. Yes, please.' I looked across the table, picking up and stroking various objects, feeling quite tearful at how much pressure this took from me. 'I can't thank you both enough.'

'It was all Chloe,' Lauren said graciously. 'I've just cut out and sewn a few bits. She's the creative genius.'

'Thank you, Chloe. I've been getting really worked up about it and along you come and save the day. Hug?'

'Always!'

We hugged each other tightly, laughing.

'It's what Chloe came to talk to you about on Friday,' Lauren said.

'Aw, Chloe! I'm so sorry.'

She shrugged. 'It's my fault. I should have known you'd be busy and not just turn up like that.'

'But you were turning up to help me and I shouldn't have shouted at you.'

Chloe shook her head. 'I understand why you did it and I deserved it for all the previous times, but I listened to you and I got involved.' She pointed to her Beavers leader uniform. 'Still doing Pilates, too. Member of the craft club. I'm quite the joiner now!'

I walked to the door with them a little later, after helping pack everything away.

'Did you spot Hogmeo and Hogliet on your way in?' I asked Lauren, pointing to where I'd positioned them either side of the barn door.

'You can't separate them!' she cried, picking one up and moving it next to the other, noses close together. 'They're star-crossed lovers. They're meant to be kissing like that.'

Her eyes sparkled and she was all giggly as she said it. I swear she blushed too – something I'd never seen her do before.

I waved them off, still smiling. I'd wanted bigger and better than last year, but I'd never have expected my cousin would be the person who enabled that. I'd never have imagined Lauren embracing the world of crafting either, but Chloe had pointed out which items were

Lauren's and I could barely tell them apart from Chloe's. And Lauren and Chloe joining forces was another surprise, but they'd been bouncing off each other tonight. I was sure Lauren had only tolerated Chloe in the past to avoid making things difficult for me, but it sounded like they'd had a great time together on Sunday.

'As for putting you two together kissing,' I said, looking at Hogmeo and Hogliet. 'Why has Lauren suddenly morphed into a romantic? Come on! Fess up! I'm sure you two know something.'

33

SAMANTHA

On Wednesday afternoon, Paul and Beth took Archie and Lottie over to Alder Lea to meet with Dave to discuss some work on the house. Fizz and Phoebe were in the barn, and I dropped Darcie off with them after school so I could prepare our evening meal.

I was in the kitchen peeling potatoes when the doorbell rang. I frowned as I wiped my hands. Nobody ever came to the door. Any deliveries – spiky or otherwise – went straight to the barn.

'Mum!' I said, surprised to see her on the doorstep.

'I texted to say I was in the area, but you mustn't have seen it. I can go if it's not convenient.'

'No, come in!' I took my phone out of my pocket and rolled my eyes at her. 'I've forgotten to knock it off silent. Drink?'

'A coffee would be great.'

'Go through to the lounge. I'll bring it through.'

'You said you were in the area?' I prompted when I handed Mum her coffee.

'Yes. I was owed a lieu day, so I decided to check out Bloomsberry's. Your dad said that Lauren recommended it. What a fabulous garden centre.'

'So do you have a car full of plants?'

Mum smiled as she shook her head. 'My garden's done so I don't have the space but, if I had, I could have spent a small fortune. Remember when you visited, I was thinking about studying landscape gardening, but I wasn't sure I could go back to college? I thought about what you said about me being capable of studying again and decided to go for it. I filled in the enrolment form for Claybridge Agricultural College and I'm starting there in September.'

'That's fantastic news! Are you excited?'

'Nervous, apprehensive but, yes, mainly excited. The thing is, I need another garden to work on. I've looked into allotments but they're practical spaces for growing food and I want to be creative with flowers, shrubs and water features. I could dig up what I've already done at home and start over, but that's a waste of money and effort and I'd prefer a new challenge.'

She reached into her handbag and removed a folded piece of A4, which she handed to me. 'I viewed this today.'

It was an estate agent's details for a stone cottage called Orchard House which appeared to be in need of some TLC. Wooden shutters were hanging off their hinges, the front door was covered in peeling paint and the front garden was a jungle of weeds.

'It's in Little Tilbury,' I said, noticing the address. Nanna and Gramps's former home, Meadowcroft, was in that village.

'It's at the other end of the village to Meadowcroft. I remember the woman who lived there when Louise and I were little. She used to stand in the front garden with her arms outstretched with bird seed in her palms and birds of all varieties would sit on her hands and eat the seed. We called her Bird Lady. Not very imaginative. Anyway, she died years ago, and the house was tied up in all sorts of legal wranglings due to no clear next of kin. It's ended up with a very distant relative who lives abroad and just wants rid of it. Nobody's interested because it's a wreck and, as you can see, the price reflects that.'

I glanced down at the low figure. Definitely priced to sell.

'What's it like inside?'

'Everything needs ripping out and re-fitting but, despite looking unloved, it's structurally sound. There's no obvious damp or anything like that, although I'd get a full survey to make sure. The house could be incredible, but it's the land that excites me. The back garden is enormous. It's got an orchard and a stream, and it would be a wonderful project to develop my skills and use as a showcase if I did set up my own business.'

She'd become animated as she talked, but suddenly her expression darkened and she bit her lip. 'But it all depends on you.'

'How?'

'I know you moved to the Wolds because of Chloe and James, but I'd imagine you were relieved to get away from me too. You're so happy here with Josh and your new life and I don't want to jeopardise that, so if you have even the tiniest reservation about me living nearby, please say and I'll search for a project closer to home.'

I tapped the picture of the cottage. 'You'd really give this up if I was uncomfortable about you living closer to me?'

'Of course I would! I've done so much damage to you already. I don't want to encroach on the wonderful life you have here.'

I studied her face and could tell she was deadly serious. This wasn't an attempt at making me feel guilty or manipulating me into saying it was fine. Although it was fine. Better than fine. Mum had made so many inroads this year and having her front row at my wedding had been a special moment. I wanted her to be part of my life and get to know any children we might have, which would be so much easier if she was living in Little Tilbury rather than Whitsborough Bay.

'You know what I think?' I said. 'I think you should phone that estate agent and tell them you're interested and, if you haven't already done so, get your house on the market. This is too good an opportunity to miss out on and, as for living closer to me, I'd love it.'

'Thank you.' She reached across for a hug, and it felt natural to be in Mum's arms.

'Does Dad know?' I asked.

'I spoke to him about it last night. He says he told you about our little thing.'

'Yeah, I'm sorry about that.'

She batted her hand. 'It's fine. It's the right decision for both of us. I think we just needed to have a little more time together to absolutely confirm that. Obviously I didn't want to encroach on his new life either, and I wouldn't even have viewed it if he thought it was a bad idea, but he said to go for it too.'

'Does he know how the viewing went?'

'Not yet. I wanted to tell you first.'

'Do Auntie Louise and Uncle Simon know?'

Mum steepled her fingers against her lips and grimaced. 'Not yet. I'm dreading telling them. They know I want a new project and that I've struggled to find anything suitable in Whitsborough Bay, so they know I was widening the net but with you, Jonathan, Chloe and James and now me moving over here, I don't think they're going to be too impressed.'

'It's not like it's a million miles away,' I said gently. 'You've got to do what's right for you and I'm sure they'll see that.'

'I hope so.' She took the details back and smiled at the house. 'It's going to be so beautiful.'

'Do you think it will feel strange living back in Little Tilbury?'

'I wondered that at first, but I don't think it will. It's so long since I left home, and I didn't get back as often as I should have. I walked around after the viewing and there was so much I didn't recognise.'

'Why don't you give the agent a call now? I'll finish peeling the potatoes. Find me in the kitchen when you're done.'

* * *

'Sorry for being so long,' she said, joining me at the kitchen table about fifteen minutes later. 'I phoned an estate agent back home too. A house round the corner sold really quickly and I'd heard there'd been a bidding war, so I contacted them and they're confident the people who missed out will be interested in mine.'

'That's brilliant news. And Orchard House?'

'They've noted my interest. Nobody else has enquired about it for months, and they've promised to let me know if anyone does. So if the Whitsborough Bay agent can sell mine fast, I'll put an offer in and it's all go. If you're sure.'

'I'm sure. I'm really happy for you, Mum, and I think Nanna and Gramps would be too.'

Her eyes glistened. 'Thank you. That means a lot.'

We chatted about her college course while I finished preparing the vegetables. When she left, I wandered outside and over to the meadow.

'Lots of exciting changes ahead,' I said, leaning on the fence. 'Who'd have thought it? I ran away to escape from most of my family and they end up following me here and we're stronger than ever. Thomas and Gwendoline, this really is a magical place. But I think you always knew that, didn't you?'

34

LAUREN

Riley had emailed me to say we were going off-site on Thursday morning but hadn't said where. As agreed, I met him in reception and my stomach did somersaults.

'I feel like I'm playing truant,' I said as we walked to the car park. 'I'm not used to going off-site during the day.'

'Did you ever play truant from school?'

'Never. I enjoyed school and college and, even if it had crossed my mind, I'd have been terrified of my mum finding out. Wouldn't have been worth it.'

'Strict upbringing?'

'Not strict, but it had its moments. Mum thought the sun shone out of my twin sister Connie's backside, but I think she saw storm clouds gathering round mine.'

I had no idea why I'd just shared that with Riley. What was it about him that made me blurt things out that I never shared with anyone else?

'Did you and your sister get on, or did that cause friction?'

'We're close, but we could be closer. I sometimes keep her at a distance.' Again, something I'd never discussed until I told Sam about it last week, so why had I just shared it with Riley?

The conversation paused while we got in his car and set off.

'Do you have siblings?' I asked, eager not to give him an opportunity to question me further about Connie.

'I have an older brother, Nathaniel, but it's been over two decades since I last saw him.'

'Family fall-out?'

'I wish it was. No. He went out to get a cheeseburger for his pregnant girlfriend one November night and never came back. He's officially a missing person.'

'Oh, Riley. How do you deal with that?'

'The first few years were tough on all of us but especially his girlfriend, Susie. She took on so much guilt for being the one with the cravings, thinking he'd maybe had a car crash because of her, but there was no evidence to suggest that's what happened. The police searched the route and there were no signs of anyone coming off the road. There weren't any cliffs for him to go over or lakes for him to plunge into. We're talking a ten-minute easy drive in suburban Derby.'

'So you think he chose to disappear?'

'It's a possibility, although it's hard to imagine why, because he and Susie were happy together. They were planning a Christmas wedding, were excited about the baby, he loved his job and they had no money worries. He was one of those naturally bubbly people who everyone warmed to and was great fun to be around. I know we're so much more aware these days about mental health and that there may be things going on beneath the surface that men in particular might struggle to share, but I'd swear that wasn't the case with him.'

Shaun disappearing had been horrendous, but at least I'd discovered after a couple of months that he was alive. It had to be unbearable never knowing.

'Eventually we had to conclude he'd died because that was almost easier to deal with than acknowledging that he'd intentionally walked out on his girlfriend, his unborn child and the rest of the family who loved him.'

'Do you still see his girlfriend?'

'Yeah. Susie's part of the family. She had a boy – Dylan – who's twenty-two now and the spitting image of Nathaniel at that age. Susie eventually met and married someone else – Dale. He already had a son and they've had two girls together and they're all part of our extended family, so we've lost a lot, but we've gained a lot too. I wish we knew what happened with Nathaniel, but we've had to come to terms with the strong likelihood that we never will.'

'I'm so sorry.'

Riley gave me a sideways glance. 'Thank you. And I'm sorry for just blurting all that out. I don't normally do that.'

'I'm happy to listen.' It was on the tip of my tongue to say I understood the need for closure and, had it not been for Shaun's letter arriving on Monday, I probably would have shared why I felt that way too. But I stayed quiet. It was still too raw.

'So where are you taking me?' I asked.

'The place we met. I thought we could pull off a rhubarb and custards heist.'

'Throw in some white mice and I'm with you all the way. They won't break your teeth.'

Riley glanced at me again, smiling widely.

We pulled into the car park at Bloomsberry's. I'd only ever visited on weekends or during school holidays, and it was always busy then, but I hadn't expected to see it so packed first thing on a school-day Thursday.

'It's because of the café,' Riley said when I shared my observation with him. 'Ever been in?'

'No. I've always visited on my own, so I've shopped and left.'

'It's the best, as you're about to discover.'

I followed him into the garden centre, past the tills, and through a wide wooden arch strewn with realistic-looking artificial flowers. I'd imagined the café to be small, but a short corridor decorated with a floral painted mural opened out to an enormous space. There were several sections, some on higher levels, each decorated to appeal to different clientele. I smiled at the colourful flowers with smiling faces painted onto what was clearly a family section.

'It's counter service,' Riley said, 'but anyone who needs table service can sit at that end instead.'

'That's a good idea.'

'Thank you.'

I followed him to the counter and ordered a black coffee and a piece of carrot cake. It was only after he'd paid that I registered what he'd said.

'Why did you thank me when I said the table service was a good idea?'

'That's connected to what I want to talk to you about. We'll get settled and I'll explain.'

He led us to a table in the far corner decorated with a calming sunrise theme.

'Remember the day we met here and I said I knew the owners? I know them very well. They're my parents.'

I gasped. 'Bloomsberry's! Your surname's in the name. How did I miss that? I was thinking of strawberries and berries on trees.'

'Which is exactly why we chose it.'

'It's clever. Have your parents owned it for long?'

'Nearly eighteen years. We're from Derbyshire originally and they started off with a smaller garden centre there. This place came up for sale and they were partway through the purchase when Nathaniel went missing so they pulled out and someone else bought it. Five years later, it was back on the market, and I convinced them to go for it. They couldn't keep their lives on hold in the hope that Nathaniel would turn up. They transformed the place and I think it was the best thing that could have happened to them because it gave them a focus.'

'I can imagine. Did they sell the Derbyshire one?'

'No. They still have that and Susie manages it, so it's a proper family business. Which brings me onto my job proposal. My parents are in their mid-seventies now and they're finally ready to retire. Christmas is huge here, so the original plan was to have one more Christmas, stick around for the big January sale and then they'd be done.'

While he spoke, I'd been tucking into my carrot cake, which was mouth wateringly delicious.

Riley glanced around him as though making sure nobody was in earshot, then leaned forward.

'The staff here all know about my parents' retirement plan, but they don't know the next part. Mum hasn't been feeling well for a while and she's had difficulty swallowing. They've found a tumour in her larynx. It's benign, but she's having surgery to remove it soon. Dad's booked in for a knee replacement in late July so their retirement has come forward.'

'Is your mum okay?'

'A bit weak, but she'll be fine once she's had the op. As I'm sure you can imagine, we've had lots of conversations about the future of the business and the one thing we all agree on is we want to keep it in the family. Susie wants to stay in Derbyshire. Dylan's settled there and the girls are still at school, so I'm going to take over here.'

'You're leaving your job?'

'Yes, but please can you keep that to yourself? Nobody knows yet, not even my boss. I've got transition commitments up until the end of next summer, so I don't want to hand in my notice just yet.'

'I won't tell anyone.' It was touching that he felt able to trust me with such big news.

'Thank you. I appreciate that. Which finally brings me onto my proposal. I'm looking for someone to manage the transition between my parents leaving and me starting, and I think you'd be perfect.'

'But why? I've never worked in retail before.'

'You don't need to and, for what I've got in mind, it's an advantage that you haven't. I'm after someone with good people management skills, which you have, and someone who's great with customers, which you are. But, more than anything, I'm after someone who can step back and see problems and inefficiencies. We're all too close to the business now and a lot of what we do is how we've done it for years. There may be better ways, and a fresh pair of eyes would see that.'

I frowned at him. 'Sounds like someone feels guilty about turfing me out and has made up a job for me so they can feel better about it.'

Riley laughed. 'If I created a job here for everyone who's been displaced by a restructure I've been involved in, there'd be more staff than plants and we'd be bankrupt. Susie had agreed to the role. She doesn't want to leave Derbyshire but, as it was a short-term transition role, she was happy to do it. However, Dylan's girlfriend has discovered that the weight she'd been gaining recently wasn't her addiction to Mars bars and she's actually seven months pregnant and, understandably, Susie wants to be around for her first grandchild. So I can assure you it's not a made-up job. But do I feel guilty about what's happened to you?'

His gaze intensified and his voice softened. 'Yes, I do. It's the toughest part of what I do. These are people's lives I'm changing and no matter how many times I tell myself that old gem of *it's not personal, it's business*, I know it's personal. There are some who welcome the news. For them, it's an opportunity to take early retirement with a bigger pay-out or to leave a job they no longer love and get paid to do so. But for each of them, there's someone like you who it hits like a ton of bricks and it's heart-breaking seeing how upset some people are. So, yes, I feel guilty every single time. I'm not a machine. And for a reason I can't fathom, I feel more guilty about you than anyone else I've ever displaced. Maybe it's because we'd met outside of work and I already liked you.'

Those butterflies soared and I gulped. Nobody spoke for what felt like an eternity. I knew that if I opened my mouth something stupid and flippant would spurt out, so I bit my lip and kept schtum.

'You're very quiet,' he prompted.

'Just taking it all in. Still not seeing why you'd want me.'

'Because I do.'

I wasn't sure we were talking about work any longer and I didn't know how to respond. The only words that came to mind were: *The feeling's mutual.* No way could I say that. But was it how I felt?

It was Riley who broke eye contact, clearing his throat then taking a gulp of his drink.

He unzipped the portfolio he'd brought with him and placed a piece of paper headed 'Job Description' on the table.

'Let's go through it and I'll explain why I think you're perfect... for the role.'

The butterflies swirled once more at the unmistakable pause.

* * *

As we left the garden centre an hour or so later, I opened my bag of white mice and offered it to Riley before popping one into my mouth. I let it rest on my tongue, the sweet chocolate melting and tantalising my taste buds.

'Mmm, I'd forgotten how good these were.'

'I'll let you into another secret,' Riley said, holding his mouse in front of him. 'I've never had one.'

'How's that possible?'

'When I was little, my dream job was to be the Milky Bar Kid. I had a cowboy outfit and cowboy boots and would strut around with a hat full of Milky Bars.'

'No! I hope there's photographic evidence of this.'

'There is somewhere. Anyway, this one time I decided the Milky Bars weren't on me and I scoffed the lot and was very sick that night. It was actually a stomach bug and nothing to do with Milky Bars, but it put me off white chocolate.'

'I'm not surprised!'

He popped the mouse into his mouth.

'What's the verdict now?' I asked. 'Bad memories?'

'It's actually really delicious. Very sweet, so I'm not sure I could eat many.'

We got back in his car and set off towards college.

'Have you eaten it already?' I asked, still sucking mine.

'Yeah. Haven't you?'

'No. I let it melt in my mouth. You've got to try it. I'll finish mine and I'll give you another one and we'll see who can last the longest.'

I pushed a mouse up to the top of the bag so he could grab it – putting it in his mouth for him while he was driving felt far too intimate.

We hadn't travelled far before Riley released a frustrated cry. 'I've just bitten it! This is impossible!'

'To be fair, you are up against the master, although I've messed up because I should have said the loser has a forfeit.'

It felt good to have a few moments of light relief while there was so much heavy stuff to face right now.

'You promise me you'll give the job offer some serious thought,' Riley said as we drew closer to college. 'We can talk some more about it, I can give you a tour, I can even introduce you to my parents. I genuinely think that, with your skill set and your track record of all the amazing changes you've implemented at the TEC, you would excel in this role, but the decision has to be yours and I'm not going to pressure you to say yes. I'm conscious that the lack of teaching was one of the reasons you didn't want the principal or VP roles here and, while our role includes staff training, I'm not going to mislead you by saying it's a regular thing.'

'I appreciate you thinking of me, and I'll admit you've piqued my interest, so a tour would make sense, maybe over half-term if that works for you.'

'I'm sure I can arrange something for then.'

We said goodbye in reception and headed to our respective offices, and I found myself wishing that our trip to Bloomsberry's could have lasted all day. I wanted to know more about his missing brother, and I wanted to talk about my family too. That wasn't like me at all.

35

SAMANTHA

I'd arranged for Natasha to meet Chloe and me at Hedgehog Hollow on Friday morning while Samuel was at nursery. We'd decided on a date of Sunday, 21 November for the Christmas Fair and wanted to discuss tentative arrangements for that, as well as plans for the Family Fun Day.

'Four weeks tomorrow,' Natasha said as we wandered over to Fun Field. 'I can't wait. I've got a box of flyers and posters for you in the back of the car, and I'll distribute mine over the weekend.'

As well as crafting this week, Chloe had jumped into the role of chief communications officer. Online, she'd found a list of villages with noticeboards, noting which were accessible for adding our own posters and the contact for the locked ones. She'd also compiled a list of shops, pubs, cafés and other businesses willing to display a notice and/or carry flyers. Fizz, Natasha and Chloe were doing the drop-offs over the weekend. All I'd needed to do was share the freshly designed graphics on our social media accounts.

Chloe had told me several times how much she was enjoying herself, but that I must say if I thought she was taking over and needed reining in. She was welcome to do it. Yes, I was excited about the event but what gave me a buzz wasn't the planning and organising – it was knowing money was coming in to keep Hedgehog Hollow running and educating the public about how to help hedgehogs. It was therefore the ideal partnership and an added bonus for me was seeing Chloe happier than I'd seen her in a long time.

Natasha was supplying the stalls and I zoned out as the pair of them discussed where best to position them. I was happy to go with whatever they decided between them. I'd be tucked away in the rescue centre anyway, giving talks to small groups about hedgehog care, just like I'd done last year.

I followed them down to Wildflower Byre so they could continue their conversation in there. Talk turned to the Christmas Fair.

'Twenty-five weeks till the fair,' Natasha said. 'That might sound ages away, but it's never too early to start planning these things.'

I drifted off again. Twenty-five weeks away? If I'd returned from our honeymoon pregnant, I'd have been well into my third trimester by then. I experienced a stab of longing. I'd had several of those since discovering I wasn't pregnant on Monday and had welcomed the opportunity to talk through my jumble of emotions with Lydia at my counselling session this week. She'd helped reassure me that it wasn't unusual for a woman to have mixed emotions about pregnancy – even those who were desperate for a child and didn't have any of my baggage – because it was such a big life-changing event. Beth sharing that she'd had a panic when pregnant with Lottie had helped too, but I had to be 100 per cent sure I was ready – no way could I go through that panic again – so I was back on the pill for now.

* * *

'Are you okay?' Chloe asked when we sat on Thomas's bench with glasses of pink lemonade after Natasha left. 'You drifted off a couple of times earlier.'

Chloe and I used to talk about everything, but that changed when she got together with James. Obviously I couldn't talk to her about how I felt about her being with my ex-boyfriend, but that set off a pattern of me pulling away from her. When she'd discovered on their wedding day that I still loved James, she'd severed ties with me. Since getting past that, our relationship hadn't been the same, and I missed that closeness. She'd shared a huge secret about her past when she stayed last summer, but I hadn't opened up to her. It couldn't go back to exactly how it used to be between us – too much had happened – but Chloe had put in so much effort recently to make amends, and this was the perfect opportunity for me to give a little too.

'When we came back from honeymoon, I thought I might be pregnant. I'm not, but it's all a bit confusing...'

'I agree with your counsellor,' Chloe said when I'd finished. 'You know how much I longed for a family, but I had so many moments of doubt when I was expecting Samuel. I had the fear too. After abandoning Ava, I thought I was unfit to have another baby. I think I said before that I kept expecting something to go wrong with the pregnancy as a punishment, especially when I was so poorly. And you saw how that continued once Samuel was born.'

When Chloe left James last summer and stayed at Hedgehog Hollow, she'd been struggling. She had moments where she dumped Samuel on me, as though absolving herself of all responsibility, but most of the time, she wouldn't let him out of her sight for fear of something happening to him. It was all tied up with a combination of undiagnosed post-natal depression and that enormous secret from her past – that she'd secretly had baby Ava when she was a teenager and had left her at the hospital, convinced she wouldn't be a suitable mother.

'We both come with a lot of baggage,' she continued, 'but I remember a woman in my pre-natal class who had a panic midsession. No baggage. Just a sudden realisation of how much her life was about to change and a fear she wasn't ready. It's completely normal.'

I gave her a grateful smile.

'I was going to say you're nothing like your mum, but your mum can be kind and caring, just like you are. You and Josh will be amazing parents, but part of being a parent is constant doubt about doing the right thing and making the right decisions. The way I see it now, there is no right or wrong way to deal with any of it and most of us make it up as we go along. Children don't come with manuals, they're all different, and you can tie yourself in knots reading all the parenting guides because they contradict each other. I'm learning to go with gut instinct a lot more.'

'You sound so much happier.'

'I feel it, and it's all thanks to you. I'd never have got the help I needed without your support. James and I have even been talking about whether to try for another baby.'

'Do you feel ready for that?' I asked tentatively, trying hard to keep any concern out of my voice. It was their decision, not mine.

'Not at the moment. But maybe next year, once Samuel's two. We'll have been in Bentonbray for a year then, so we should be fully settled. We'll see how we feel then. It's got to be right for both of us.'

How lovely to hear Chloe say something like that, finally accepting that the world didn't revolve solely round her and that something as major as another child had to be a joint decision.

'As for fitting a baby around your commitments here,' Chloe continued, 'you just have to roll with that. Having a baby disrupts everything and there'll never be a perfect time for it. You and Josh will make adjustments and you'll work it out somehow. It won't be easy. It'll be messy and complicated at times, but it'll be worth it. And you have lots of people who love you and will help out as much as they can.'

'Thank you. That's really helpful.'

My phone beeped with a text message:

✉ From Mum

Orchard House is mine! That couple who missed out on the house round the corner have just viewed mine and put in an asking price offer & I've had mine accepted on Orchard House. Can't wait to get started on that garden. Thank you for all your support xx

I showed Chloe the message, feeling warm inside at the kisses. I'd never have believed my relationship with Mum would reach the point of kisses on texts.

'That's brilliant news,' Chloe said, 'although I still can't believe your mum's moving to the area too.'

'How did your mum and dad take it?'

Mum had phoned me yesterday to check I was still okay about the move after reflecting on it overnight, which I thought was lovely of her and another sign of how seriously she was taking moving our relationship forward. When I confirmed I was looking forward to it, she said she'd set up a viewing on her house and would speak to Auntie Louise and Uncle Simon that evening.

'Mum FaceTimed me this morning,' Chloe said. 'They'd known Auntie Debs was house-hunting and that she was struggling to find the sort of project she wanted in Whitsborough Bay. They were surprised she chose Little Tilbury and it's further away than they'd have hoped, but they think it'll be a good move for her. Mum joked they might even move here themselves.'

'Do you think they would?'

'I'm not sure. Their jobs are in Whitsborough Bay, and they love it there. But their family will all be living in the Wolds, so who knows?'

Chloe stayed for another hour or so and we talked some more about pregnancy and motherhood. When she left, I felt lighter. She'd been understanding, encouraging, full of great advice and it had felt like a significant step forward in our new – and hopefully improved – relationship.

✉ To Chloe

HOT TIP: There's a woman in Bentonbray brimming with ideas and talent. Crafter, mother, listener, hugger, friend. It's great to have her back xx

36

LAUREN

✉ From Connie
Are you sure you don't want me to come with you?

✉ To Connie
For my protection or Shaun's?

✉ From Connie
Ha ha! Thought you might appreciate the moral support x

✉ To Connie
Ta but I need to do this on my own. But stay on standby with wine tonight! x

✉ From Connie
Good luck xxxxxxxxx

I twisted and turned in front of my mirror on Saturday morning. What did you wear to face your past? What sort of outfit said: *You hurt me badly but you didn't break me. Well, not quite.* Other than the odd occasion where I consciously chose the power suit, I normally didn't give a damn how I looked.

Feeling comfortable was the main priority today – especially when the situation itself would be anything but that – so I settled on my current favourite outfit of jeans with a loose royal blue top and a silver pendant.

I reached for my watch but stopped myself. It had been my twenty-first birthday present from Shaun and remained my most treasured possession. We'd both saved like mad to buy each other an expensive watch and have it engraved. Even though 'Forever yours, S xx' had turned out to be a lie, I hadn't been able to stop myself from wearing it. Connie had challenged me on that when the divorce came through and I'd snapped at her: 'It's a nice watch, so why wouldn't I? Don't see why I should have to buy another one and it's not like I'm still wearing my rings.' She didn't need to know that I still wore my wedding band to bed, always hoping that 'Forever yours' hadn't been a lie after all.

Jonathan was downstairs scrolling through something on his phone. He looked up and smiled.

'You look good. How are you feeling?'

'Sick.'

'I'm not surprised. Are you sure you don't want reinforcements? I don't have to come in. I can drive you there and wait in the car.'

It was touching how supportive Jonathan and Connie had been. 'Connie's offered too but I need to do this myself.'

'Good luck.'

'I'm going to need it.' I wasn't normally one for nerves, but this morning I was bricking it.

Jonathan hugged me and kissed the top of my head. 'You've got this.'

* * *

I didn't want to be late – that would be churlish – but that meant I'd arrived in Great Tilbury way too early. What if Shaun arrived and saw me sitting in my car outside April's? I might look desperate. I was, but I didn't want him to know that. I pulled away and parked down a side lane for ten minutes then returned to the café with a minute to go.

Deep breath, you can do this! Time to finally get some answers.

I heaved my bag onto my shoulder and glanced along the row of cars. Assuming he was already here, which one was Shaun's? He hadn't been into cars, but that was then and this was now. Was he a gleaming red sports car person or someone who drove a Mini with a union flag roof? My eyes rested on a family saloon with child seats in the back and my stomach lurched. He could have a family and even be a grand-parent by now. I was about to find out.

April's Tea Parlour consisted of two shop units knocked into one with a double door in the middle. I couldn't bring myself to look in the first window as I strode past, needing a few more seconds to compose myself before looking into the eyes of the man who'd broken my heart.

'Good morning,' chirped a young blonde woman wearing a mint green apron with the name Daisy embroidered on it. 'Do you have a booking?'

I glanced to my right – the unit I'd walked past. There were several tables taken but no lone diners. No Shaun. He must be in the other room, which I couldn't see into past Daisy. Unless he wasn't here yet. Unless he'd bottled it.

'I'm meeting my...' I paused, finding myself unable to finish the sentence. 'It's Shaun Marfell.'

'Lovely. If you'd like to come with me...'

I followed her into the other room. There weren't any customers in there but there was a serving of tea for one on a table in the corner.

'I think your friend might be in the bathroom,' Daisy said, indi-cating for me to sit at that table and handing me a menu. 'I'll be back shortly to take your order.'

'Can I order a black coffee for now?' I asked, my mouth suddenly very dry. I'd heard the food here was delicious, but I wasn't convinced I'd be able to stomach anything.

I was still alone when Daisy returned with my drink, my eyes fixated on the louvred doors to the toilets. What was taking him so long? Had he done a runner? Found a back door or climbed out through a window?

Finally the doors opened and I prepared myself to come face to face with Shaun, but it was a woman who stepped through them. Dressed in cropped navy trousers, a loose white blouse and a sheer navy scarf, she looked effortlessly classy.

I turned my attention back to my coffee, but my stomach lurched and something made me turn my gaze back towards the toilets. The woman was only a few paces away and staring at me, her brow furrowed, her hand pressed to her chest. My eyes were drawn to the watch on her wrist, which looked like the one I'd given to Shaun for his twenty-first.

It can't be! My mouth dropped open as I lifted my gaze and my eyes met hers. The warm brown. The gold flecks.

'Shaun?'

'I told you I'd changed a lot since I last saw you.'

37

LAUREN

I was aware that I was staring, but I couldn't tear my eyes away. I recognised so much of the man I loved in the woman standing before me, yet there was much that was unfamiliar too.

'Am I okay to sit?' she asked.

'Yes! Sorry! This is...' I shrugged. What was it?

'Unexpected?' she suggested, sitting down opposite me.

I nodded slowly.

'You look amazing, Lauren. I'm Sasha, by the way. Sasha Bailey.'

The voice was unfamiliar – softer, higher – and the regional accent had gone. I thought I detected a north-west twang, maybe from Manchester.

'Bailey?' I repeated, the surname holding a familiarity I couldn't place for a moment.

'Like Tom Bailey from the Thompson Twins.'

'Oh. Okay.'

She'd named herself after the lead singer of our song? What did that mean? I had no idea what to say next. I'd come here for answers about why Shaun left, and I'd psyched myself up for coming face to face with an older-looking version of my husband, hoping I'd be able to push aside my feelings for him and remain strong. But this wasn't an older-looking version of my husband. This was like looking at Shaun's sister, if he'd had one.

Why had he left? The reason was staring me right in the face – or presumably this was the reason – but it led to a million more questions.

I opened my mouth and closed it again. There were so many words swirling round my mind, but I seemed to have lost the ability to pull any of them into a coherent sentence.

'You really do look fantastic,' Sasha said, smiling. 'I always knew you'd age well. The highlights suit you.'

I self-consciously ran my fingers down a lock of hair. Should I return the compliment? Sasha's hair was a similar colour to mine now – blonde with honey highlights – but worn shorter in a smooth fringe-less bob. It was very glossy. Mine never looked like that.

'Blonde,' I said. Not exactly a compliment, but at least it was a word.

'That hideous mousy brown was one of the first things to go.'

I'd loved the mousy brown.

'Are you ready to order?' Daisy asked, joining us.

Sasha picked up her menu and quickly glanced down it. 'Another tea and a fruit scone, please.'

Daisy looked at me expectantly. 'Glass of tap water,' I mumbled.

'Coming right up.'

'Not hungry?' Sasha asked when she'd gone.

'Not really.'

Silence.

'Thanks for meeting me today,' she said.

I nodded, still lost for words.

'Should I just talk?' Sasha suggested after a few moments. 'You can interrupt. You can ask questions.'

'Okay.'

She sipped on her tea. 'How about I tell you a bit about who I am today, so I can lay those cards on the table and we can work back from there?'

'Okay.'

'As I said, my name's Sasha Bailey now and I'm a trans woman. I had gender-affirming surgery twenty years ago. I live in Bramhall in Stockport and I'm one of two directors of a charity in Manchester called Whole Moon, which I set up with a friend. We work with young people – teenagers to early thirties – from the LGBTQ+ community but predominantly those who are trans. We offer a range of services from advice to counselling to a safe space to be themselves.'

Our order arrived, so we momentarily paused the conversation while Daisy unloaded everything.

As Sasha topped up her tea and buttered her scone, I gulped down my water, trying to process what she'd just said about her new life. I'd barely registered the stuff about the charity. All I could focus on was the part about the surgery twenty years ago. That was six years after Shaun disappeared. When had he first considered surgery? At the point he left? Before that? Afterwards?

Sasha took a bite of her scone and made some appreciative sounds as she chewed. That initial feeling of shock turned into anger. How could she casually sit there looking calm and relaxed with her shiny hair, big hoop earrings and immaculate make-up eating a scone? That was how best friends behaved on a weekly meet-up, and we were far from that.

'When did you decide to turn into a woman?' I blurted out, immediately wincing at my choice of words.

'That was badly worded,' I said, lowering my voice. 'I'm sorry. I don't know—'

Sasha placed her hand over mine and I automatically glanced down, tears rushing to my eyes with memories of the thousands of occasions when Shaun's hands had entwined with mine, run through my hair, caressed my body. Now the skin was softer and the bitten nails were manicured and painted a soft pink. She gave my hand a light squeeze then let go.

'I'd rather you say what you're thinking than leave with unanswered questions because you're worried about how to phrase them. Nothing you say will offend me. You'll probably call me Shaun at some point, and I'm not going to get annoyed if you do. I know it's a lot to take in. You can ask me whatever you like.'

'Okay. Have you always known?'

'No. There are trans women who talk about dressing up as princesses, playing with dolls from a young age and having this sense of not being at one with their birth-assigned gender, but that wasn't me. It was in our first year at senior school, before we met, when I started to have this feeling that something wasn't quite right. My two best friends from primary school had gone to the Catholic school so I'd lost my friendship group and, even though I made an effort with the other kids, I felt as though I didn't quite fit in. Mum would ask me if I'd made new friends and I'd tell her I preferred my own company.

'I spent hours on my skateboard, trying to work out why I felt like such an outsider. I wondered if I'd been trying to get in with the wrong kids – ones I didn't have anything in common with. I loved skateboarding so thought maybe I should find others who shared that passion so, one day in the summer holidays when I was twelve, I told my mum I was going to the park but decided to brave the skatepark – somewhere I'd previously avoided because the kids who hung out there actually scared the hell out of me. I stood by the railings for ages watching this beautiful girl with long blonde hair psyching herself up to go down the ramp while the kids around her laughed and made chicken sounds. She seemed like an outsider too and I felt drawn to her. When she fell and the other kids laughed again, I helped her up, took her home to my mum, cleaned her wounds and felt like I'd found the missing part of my life.'

Her voice softened and her eyes glistened. 'When I met you, everything finally clicked into place. I found my best friend and that deepened into love.'

I had to look away as I was welling up again. Shaun and I had often reminisced about the day we met and how Ivy had been right about destiny bringing us together. And that was the reason I didn't believe in fate or destiny anymore as a positive thing. Not after what I'd been through.

I sipped my coffee, trying to work out what any of that had to do with Shaun's transition into Sasha.

'I'm not getting the connection, Shau... Sasha. Loads of kids never find their place at school. I didn't.'

'Sorry,' she said. 'Let me try again. You asked when I decided to be a woman, but it wasn't a decision. Obviously the surgery was a decision, but identifying as a woman was more of an eventual realisation. The feeling I'd had throughout school that something wasn't quite right didn't go away and, a couple of years into our marriage, it felt stronger than ever, which made no sense to me. I was married to the woman of my dreams. We were really happy together and we loved each other, so why did I still have this niggling feeling of some sort of disconnect in my life? I had this sense that it was something inside of me and I couldn't get a handle on what it was or why. Until Max died.'

I frowned, intrigued as to what his biological dad's death had to do with it.

'While I took those few days off after we heard about Max, I had this overwhelming desire for everything around me to be about comfort. I watched back-to-back romantic films, cuddling your fluffy lamb, and I gorged on chocolate and ice cream. I had a couple of deep bubble baths every day. During my second bath that first day, I was drying off when I spotted your satin robe hanging on the back of the door. I remember thinking, *ooh, that looks comfy*. I slipped it on and the material was so soft. I could smell your perfume on it and everything about the feel and scent of it was like a big hug, so I kept it on until just before you were due home. It was the first time I ever wore women's clothes.'

I didn't have the robe anymore, but I remembered it well. Calf-length, cream, with a tie-waist and an embroidered red heart on the pocket, Ivy had bought me it as a Christmas gift. She'd been mortified to discover that the wrong size robe had been put onto the right size hanger and had offered to exchange it, but I'd wanted to keep it. We'd joked at the time that it was so big, it would probably fit Shaun. Little did we know.

'I wore your robe for the next two days,' Sasha continued. 'I tried to convince myself that it was about being close to you when you couldn't be there in person but I found myself reaching for it every time you were on a night shift or working late and I couldn't ignore this increasing realisation that I felt more me wearing your robe than I did wearing anything else.'

'Did that scare you?'

'Not really. It was like, *Ah! That's the disconnect. Now I get it!* I did some research – not easy when there was so little information about transgender people back then – and that confirmed for me that I wasn't a man who liked dressing in women's clothes. I was a woman whose physical form was not in alignment with who I was. I didn't know what to do with that realisation. It was the early nineties and Yorkshire wasn't exactly a thriving hub of LGBT activity.'

It blew my mind that Shaun had come to that realisation – seemingly calmly – and those first steps towards becoming a woman had been undertaken alone while I hadn't had the slightest inkling about any of it.

'Why didn't you talk to me? Or your mum? Paul? Connie?'

'It was one thing having that conversation with myself, but I had no idea how to even begin to explain it to anyone else. And, as I said, the realisation that I was a woman didn't scare me. But what that might mean for my relationship with you terrified me.'

'So you hid it for five more years and then decided to just up and leave one day because having no conversation was easier for you than having a difficult one?' I could hear the bitterness in my voice as the volume rose and I fought to lower it. 'You knew who you were for most of our marriage, but you lied to me about that. How could you do that? How could you tell me you loved me every day when you obviously didn't?'

'I never lied about how I felt about you. My feelings for you never wavered through any of it. I loved you completely and utterly.'

'How does that work?' I demanded, immediately kicking myself for such a stupid statement. Of course!

'Because I'm a gay woman,' she confirmed. 'Part of my journey of self-discovery was realising I was a woman who loves women – well, one woman. I loved you so much that I thought I could push aside my gender dysphoria – how I felt about the mismatch between my birth-assigned sex and my gender identity – to be with you.'

Sasha paused to take a sip of her tea while I tried to make sense of that.

'And you managed to do that for five years?'

'Yes, but it was killing me.'

My feelings were so jumbled. There was still anger but there was empathy too.

'But five years?' I repeated, trying to imagine how Shaun could have kept it hidden for all that time. There'd been no mood swings. There'd been nothing. 'I just can't get my head around it. That's so long.'

'I know. And when you're pretending to be someone you're not, it feels like even longer.'

'I honestly don't know how you managed it and I don't know how I didn't know you were hiding something.'

'You didn't know because you were the one part of my life that made sense. I fell more deeply in love with you every day. I never gave you any reason to think there was anything going on.'

'So what happened to stop the pretence and why then? Why plan a holiday with me and bugger off the day before? None of it makes sense to me, but the holiday thing – especially when you'd known who you were for five years – really messes with my head.' I gasped as a thought struck me. 'Was it an apology? Did you expect me to go on my own and that a week in the sun would miraculously heal my broken heart?'

She shook her head. 'I'm sorry. The holiday wasn't an apology. We were meant to go together, and it seemed like a good idea, but things happened and...' She paused and took a sip of her tea. 'Let me back-track a bit. I wanted it all. I wanted to fully live my life as a woman, and I wanted to stay married to you, and I was desperate to find a way of making both those things happen. I managed to convince myself that we could have this amazing holiday and, when we came home and I told you the truth, the holiday would remind you of how good we were together and you'd stay with me. I had this little fantasy of you telling me that you'd fallen in love with me as a person, not a gender, and you'd support me through my transition and still be with me on the other side.'

Sasha's cheeks flushed. 'Hearing me say that out loud, I do realise exactly how naïve and selfish it sounds. That's desperation for you.'

'That's manipulation for you,' I snapped. I'd never have thought that Shaun was capable of being so devious, desperate or not. The man I knew would have sat down and said *There's something I need to tell you...* It didn't matter how difficult that conversation was for both of us. We'd had plenty of tricky conversations in our lives, including the one about not wanting children.

I narrowed my eyes at Sasha. Had Shaun lied to me about children too? We'd skirted around it in our teens, but the proper deep conversation happened about eighteen months after Josh was born. Connie had suffered another miscarriage and I sat down with Shaun and categorically told him that I didn't see children in our future. I was happy to be a hands-on auntie, but motherhood didn't appeal to me, and no way did I want to experience what Connie and Paul had gone through in their efforts to become parents – far too risky and heart-breaking. I'd got really worked up about having that conversation and had started to imagine all sorts of worst-case scenarios like Shaun deciding he wanted to become a dad more than he wanted to be with me. He'd hugged me and said he agreed wholeheartedly. It would have been about six months after Max died, so he'd known who he really was at that point. Had that influenced his decision?

'I'm sorry,' Sasha said, bringing my attention back to her. 'I can see why you'd think that. I wasn't hopeful it would work, so I put preparations in place in case you wanted out. I found a place to live, quit my job and—'

'I know. The day you went missing, I phoned the council and Eddie told me. Those surprises just kept on coming. Although the biggest surprise was the note itself which, by the way, I thought was a suicide note. It was fun going round the house, pushing open each door, wondering if I'd find your body.'

I didn't care how sarcastic I sounded as I glared at her, wanting her to understand the repercussions of her actions.

She gasped and pressed her hand across her mouth. 'You must have... I'm so sorry. I never thought.'

'No, you didn't. Not at all. You know what? All I've heard so far this morning is how *you* felt and what *you* wanted. I know this is about your journey, but did you ever pause to think about the phenomenal impact you leaving would have not just on me but on all the other people who loved you? Your poor mum! Our friends! You left carnage behind, Shaun... Sasha. Complete and utter carnage.'

'I'm sorry. I wasn't thinking straight. I know I messed up. If I could go back, I'd handle it all so differently.'

'Good. I'm glad you've learned that because what you did was just about the shittiest thing anyone could ever have done. You say you loved me and that you fell deeper every day, but nothing you've told me sounds like what I understand love to be. Love is about partnership, sharing, communicating. You did none of those things.'

'But I was going to. I'd decided to tell you after our holiday.'

'The holiday we didn't go on because you'd already thrown in the towel.'

'I hadn't!'

'Bullshit! Of course you had. You were convinced that, when you told me the truth, I'd send you packing. Why else would you have left your job and found somewhere else to live? You'd already made the decision that we had no future, and you didn't give me any say in it. That wasn't fair. Whether we stayed together was *my* choice to make and you took that from me.'

The café had filled up and I was aware of people glancing in our direction. I didn't want to mute the conversation. I wanted to understand what Sasha had gone through, but I needed her to understand the hurt that Shaun had caused in order to become the woman sat opposite me today.

'It's getting busy,' I said. 'I think we should go somewhere where we can talk properly – shout, cry, stomp about if we want – and this isn't the place for it.'

Sasha nodded. 'Where do you suggest?'

While she rummaged in her purse and dropped a £20 note on the table, I searched my mind for a suitable location.

'There's a crossroads between Great Tilbury and Little Tilbury and there's a bench on one corner. We can park near there.'

We traipsed outside in silence, leaving Sasha's scone with only a couple of bites out of it, and got into our separate cars. She set off towards the crossroads and I closed my eyes for a moment, fighting the urge to speed off in the opposite direction.

When I opened them again, a man and woman were each securing a child into the back of the family saloon I'd seen earlier. The idea that it could have been Shaun's car, representing his new family life without me, had filled me with dread earlier. Now I wished it had been his. It would be a hell of a lot less confusing than the truth.

* * *

As I stopped near the crossroads, Sasha sat down at one end of the bench and shook out her hair. The way she sat carried an air of confidence and it struck me that Shaun had never sat like that. He'd always slumped forward or fidgeted. Had that been because he felt so uncomfortable in his own skin?

I removed my jacket from the back seat and pulled it on.

'It's lovely here,' Sasha said as I joined her, sitting at the opposite end. 'Very peaceful. Good choice.'

'I half-expected to get here and find you'd done a runner.'

She smiled – a facial movement so familiar yet unfamiliar. 'I half-expected to be here on my own.'

'I *was* tempted to flee,' I admitted.

'I can understand that. As I said before, it's a lot to take in. As for me, before I came, I promised myself that the only way I'd leave without giving you a full explanation was if you asked me to. I was prepared for it to get uncomfortable. I should have suggested somewhere less busy.' She pushed a strand of hair behind her ear. 'You were saying I took your choice away from you.'

'Yes! You made the decision and walked out without giving us the opportunity to explore it together. What about what I wanted?'

'It might not seem it, but I did what I did for both of us. Hand on heart, what would you have done if I'd told you I wanted gender-affirming surgery and that, if you chose to stick by me as my wife, you'd be married to a woman?'

'I'd have supported you.'

She smiled warmly. 'I don't doubt that for a minute, Lauren. You were my best friend and the most amazing woman I'd ever met. You'd absolutely have been there to support me as I transitioned and as I recovered from surgery. But what would happen then? You'd have been a cisgender woman married to a lesbian. Think about that for a moment. It would have been life-changing for both of us.'

I sank back against the bench. She was right. It would have been life-changing, and I'm not sure I could have done it. My husband would have become my wife. I'd have still loved *him*, but would I have been attracted to *her*?

Sasha adjusted her position on the bench so she could hold better eye contact.

'In April's, you asked whether something happened to trigger me leaving. It did. Two nights earlier, we were watching TV and a trailer came on for a documentary about people whose partners had transitioned. It showed our situation – a married couple where the husband identified as a woman and the wife was faced with whether to stay married, end the marriage and remain friends, or walk away. You said, "Poor woman. How much strength would you need to cope with a bombshell like that?" Then you asked me if I wanted a cup of tea.'

I clapped my hand across my mouth, imagining what must have been going through Shaun's head when I said that.

'I don't remember it.'

'Why would you? It was a two-minute trailer and, as far as you were aware, that documentary had no connection to your life and you'd made a throwaway comment that I'm sure people were making up and down the country. But it *was* depicting my life and I panicked. I'm not mentioning this to guilt trip you. What you said wasn't offensive, but it was a wake-up call to me. My little plan to have the holiday of a lifetime was flawed because I was going to bring you back home with a bump by dropping a bombshell on you. A bombshell that – as you'd rightly identified – would take considerable strength to deal with and I couldn't do it to you. My initial instinct was to run, but I forced myself not to do anything rash. We had some enforced time apart because you were on night shift the following night, which meant I had time to rethink my plan. But then I couldn't help myself. I watched the documentary and it all seemed pretty hopeless.'

'It didn't work out for them?'

Sasha shook her head. 'It followed four trans women who were all married to or in a long-term relationship with a straight woman when they came out as trans. Only one relationship survived, but that was just as friends, and even that was touch and go at first. I know every couple would be different, but that documentary laid bare the reality of what very likely lay ahead for us. At best, we might make it out the other side with some semblance of friendship. At worst, you'd hate me and be fairly messed up.

'I'd placed so much stock on how strong our friendship was and how much I loved you, but I hadn't thought about the practicalities of it. You're not physically attracted to women, so why would you be physically attracted to me as a woman? So I packed my cases, loaded them into the boot, and waited for you to come home from the hospital so I could tell you and give you some space to think about it.' She looked down at her hands joined loosely in her lap. 'I'd forgotten you were going shopping on your way home. With each passing minute, I got myself more and more worked up until I lost my nerve. I scribbled a quick note and bolted.'

A cabbage white butterfly fluttered past us, paused briefly on one of the tall grasses, then continued on its way. The symbolism of that struck me – Shaun the caterpillar emerging from a chrysalis as the beautiful butterfly Sasha.

'When you left, you broke me,' I said, the words forced out over the constriction in my throat.

I wouldn't have admitted that to Shaun – or I don't think I would – but this wasn't him. This was Sasha – a woman who bore a resemblance to an aged version of my ex-husband, but who was otherwise a different person. It wasn't just her physical appearance and voice that had changed. Her personality had altered. In the short time we'd been together today, I could already see a strength and confidence that could have come with age but was far more likely to have been the result of living life as her true self.

'I'm sorry. If it's any consolation, leaving you broke me too. Please don't ever doubt how much I loved you.'

Her voice cracked and I looked away, trying to force back the tears that begged to fall. Across the years, I'd convinced myself that Shaun hadn't really loved me and it had been easy for him to walk away. I'd been angry at him for being able to do that when I couldn't, but it broke my heart all over again to think of him hurting as much as I had.

'Lauren,' Sasha said gently. 'Please look at me.'

'I need a minute.' I leapt up from the bench and, head down, rushed to the back of my car, out of view. I rested my head in my arms on the rear windscreen while silent tears soaked into my jacket.

The conversation with Riley two days earlier sprung into my mind. He'd talked about his brother as a missing person and how the hardest part was not knowing what had happened – something I'd wholeheartedly been able to relate to. Now I knew why Shaun had left and it was like the call Riley's family had dreaded – the news that their beloved brother/son/boyfriend was dead – because, to all intents and purposes, Shaun Marfell was dead. The boy who'd cleaned my bloody knee when I'd fallen off my skateboard, become my best friend, my boyfriend and finally my husband, was gone.

'Lauren.'

I hadn't heard Sasha approach. I glanced up but could barely see her through my tears. I opened my mouth to speak but emitted a sob instead.

'It's all right,' she whispered, easing me off the windscreen and into her arms. I stiffened initially, unsure about being held by Shaun after all these years. But she felt nothing like Shaun because she was Sasha and, right now, she was the comfort I so badly needed.

* * *

After the tears subsided, I knew I didn't want to talk anymore. Not today. Sasha said she understood and was grateful for the time I'd given her so far. I resisted the urge to snap that it hadn't been for her. Today had been for me and my desperate need for an explanation, although, now that I had it, I was more confused than ever.

Standing on the road behind my car, we exchanged phone numbers and I gave her my personal email address. I told her I'd be in touch about meeting again when I'd had time to process what I'd learned so far. I still wanted to meet with Ivy this week while I was off work, very much aware that time wasn't on her side.

'You'll definitely get in touch?' Sasha asked as she put her phone away in her bag.

'I don't play games and I don't let people down.' I stared at her pointedly and she nodded, presumably accepting the dig. 'When I say I'll get in touch, I mean it. Might take a few days, but it'll happen.'

'Okay. I'll head back to Stockport and look forward to hearing from you soon.' She walked towards her car, and I opened the door of mine.

'Lauren!' She turned to face me. 'Thanks for being kind today.'

'I'm not sure I was.'

'Believe me, you were. Some people would have...' She tailed off and smiled. 'Ignore me. You were never *some people*. You were always you, seeing the best in people, facing the storm head on. Thank you.'

I didn't know how to respond, so I gave her a weak smile and nodded. My legs felt shaky, and I wanted Sasha to drive off first so I could compose myself. I slipped off my jacket and laid it across the back seat, feeling relieved when I heard her car start.

With a quick toot of her horn and a wave, she pulled away and soon disappeared from sight. I closed the door and rested my back against the car, gulping in deep breaths and willing myself not to break down.

Kind? Was that really what she'd thought of my reaction? I'd felt anything but kind. Shock, denial, anger. Not kindness. And a whole pile of confusion because I'd had two items on my agenda today: to find answers and to kick ass. I'd wanted to hurt Shaun. I'd wanted him to know that the impact of him disappearing like that had stayed with me for life and I didn't care if that made me seem weak. I wanted to guilt trip him, make him apologise a million times and beg for my forgiveness. I'd even had a little fantasy of walking out on him and seeing how he felt when there was no closure, although I'd known I wouldn't really do that, even if Ivy hadn't been involved.

But Shaun hadn't been here today.

Another butterfly flew past – a painted lady – and rested on a stem of cow parsley. I watched it for a moment, flitting from flower to flower before flying off again and disappearing from view.

Sighing, I clambered into my car and started the engine. I needed 'Mr Blue Sky'. I scrolled through my phone and was about to press 'play' when I paused and scrolled down a little further. My finger hovered over the track I'd played on constant repeat when Shaun left – 'Don't Walk Away'. It was probably the only song I knew every single lyric to – the real ones rather than my made-up version. I'd curl up on our bed facing the empty space Shaun used to occupy, cuddling my lamb, twiddling my wedding ring round my finger and wondering, as the lyrics said, how I was going to go on without him. A year after he left, I listened to it one last time and had avoided both that track and our song, 'Hold Me Now', ever since.

I turned up the volume in the car, placed my head against the head rest, closed my eyes and whispered along to the lyrics, tears streaming down my cheeks.

38

SAMANTHA

It was the start of the half-term break and time to fulfil our promise to take Phoebe and Darcie to Whitsborough Bay.

'Look at that smile!' I linked Josh's arm as we stood on the beach at South Bay, watching Darcie on the return leg of her first ever donkey ride.

Phoebe had walked alongside her so she could take photos, and her smile was as wide as Darcie's. For years, she'd been forbidden from taking Darcie anywhere other than their 'seriously scabby' local playground, so it meant the world to Phoebe that Darcie had opportunities like this. Over the summer, Phoebe would have driving lessons and, unbeknown to her, Josh was keeping his eye out for a small car for her so she could have the independence to take Darcie places on her own.

'That was epic!' Darcie exclaimed as Phoebe lifted her down from the grey donkey. She paused to stroke the donkey's mane and neck. 'Thank you for my first ever donkey ride, Talulah.'

Tears pricked my eyes as she gave Talulah a kiss on her neck, and I noted Phoebe quickly looking away, likely feeling as emotional as me.

'What do you want to do next?' Josh asked.

'Pleasureland!'

I'd thought Darcie might want to go to the fair first, but I should have known that she'd be drawn to the animals as a priority. She held onto Phoebe's hand, skipping, as we walked along the seafront towards Pleasureland.

'Does it feel strange to be back?' Josh asked.

'It feels strange to be here when it's so busy,' I said as we dodged round a family walking five abreast across the promenade as though they owned the space. 'One of the things about living in a seaside resort is that, when you get older, you tend to avoid the most touristy parts at the height of season. Chloe and I came down to the beach loads when we were kids, but I don't think I've been down to South Bay on a bank holiday weekend for at least a decade.'

'Is it too busy for you?'

I looked round me at the packed beach and the sea of people on both the promenade and the other side of the road in front of the arcades, shops and cafés.

'There's an exciting buzz and I feel like I'm on holiday, but one day is enough for me.'

'Same here,' Josh agreed. 'I love the coast, but my heart's in the country. We're lucky we have easy access to both.'

We continued our walk, taking it all in – excited squeals of children playing on the individual rides outside the arcades, cries of dismay as a greedy seagull swooped down and helped itself to a sausage from someone's tray of sausage and chips, pirate calls from the edge of the harbour to join the pirate cruise.

We swerved out of the path of a family coming towards us – a teenaged girl licking an ice cream, a woman pushing a buggy, and a man with a girl of about Darcie's age on his shoulders, eating candyfloss. The family mirrored how we'd have looked this time next year if I'd been expecting, and I felt that longing once more. My worries about finding time to run the rescue centre alongside having a baby hadn't gone away, but talking to Beth and Chloe had reassured me there was rarely a 'right' time to have a baby. If you want something badly enough, you'll always find a way to make it work.

39

LAUREN

I checked my face in the sun visor mirror. What a wreck! My eyes were puffy and bloodshot, my cheeks streaked with tears.

I'd been aware of several cars passing as I sat near the crossroads listening to 'Don't Walk Away' on repeat. If anyone had noticed my distress, they hadn't stopped, and I'd been grateful for that. I didn't want to involve any strangers. I didn't even want to involve my sister until my head was clear.

I ignored Connie's text, not feeling able to articulate any of it just yet. I couldn't go back home to Chapel View as Jonathan would be there, and I couldn't go to Hedgehog Hollow either – too many people. I'd drive for a bit instead.

* * *

I picked up the packet of white mice, then hesitated and grabbed another two. I hadn't planned to come to Bloomsberry's but I'd felt the need for sugar.

'I hope you're going to pay for those.'

I spun round to face Riley.

'Your car wasn't outside.' I'd checked the car park before coming in, not wanting him to see me like this.

'I left it at my parents' place in the village. I fancied some fresh air and a sugar fix.'

'Me too.' I held up the three bags.

He narrowed his eyes at me. 'Are you okay, Lauren?'

I opened my mouth to make some dismissive comment but the concern in his voice was too much and I couldn't get any words out over the lump in my throat. The tears which I thought surely had to have dried up earlier flowed again.

'Come with me.'

He placed his hand gently on my elbow and led me to the back of the garden centre and through a door marked 'staff only', taking us into a corridor with more doors. He pushed one open. Inside was a small office with two desks facing each other and a low round coffee table with a couple of comfy chairs.

'Sit down and I'll be back in a minute.' His voice was gentle and reassuring, but the sympathy was too much, and the tears flowed faster as I lowered myself to the chair, dropping the bags of white mice onto the table. I'd already used the full packet of tissues in my bag and was relieved to see a box on one of the desks.

I'd just about got my tears under control when the door opened and Riley placed a collection of soft drinks on the table – water, fruit and fizzy.

'I wasn't sure which you'd prefer,' he said, sitting down on the other comfy chair.

I reached for the blackcurrant drink and gratefully took a couple of gulps. 'Thank you.'

'You're welcome. Do you want me to leave you in peace for a bit?'

'No, it's okay.' I dabbed my cheeks again.

'Do you want to talk about it?'

'I'm not sure.'

'Would a white mouse help?'

I smiled weakly. 'It might.'

We each took one and I felt a little more relaxed as the chocolate melted on my tongue.

'I'm not sure if we were doing the competition thing,' Riley said. 'But I've failed at the first hurdle. Mine's now headless.'

'It takes a lot of willpower,' I said. 'Try again.'

We sat in companionable silence, sucking on our sweets, and I marvelled at how Riley alleviated the stress from any situation by allowing me breathing time.

'I met my ex-husband earlier,' I said. 'I haven't seen him in nearly twenty-six years.'

Riley raised his eyebrows but didn't say anything.

'You know what you were saying about your brother's disappearance and how the hardest thing was the not knowing? I've some understanding of how that feels. Shaun walked out the day before our seventh wedding anniversary and we were meant to be going to Tenerife the following day. I got home from work to a note saying he couldn't do it anymore.'

I paused and took another sip of my drink.

'Nobody knew where he'd gone, and his mum was beside herself. We only knew he was safe when he sent her a birthday card seven weeks later, but I never heard from him again – other than via his solicitor with the divorce papers – until a letter from him arrived at work on Monday.'

I held his gaze and saw the realisation dawn.

'You'd just read it when I saw you in reception,' he said.

'I recognised his handwriting, so I took it out to my car. It wasn't raining heavily at that point.'

'And I take it that was to ask you to meet him?'

'Yes. So I met him this morning, except he's not a him anymore.

Shaun's now Sasha. Over the years, I've imagined all sorts of scenarios, but I have to say, that particular one never entered my head.' My voice cracked and I dabbed at the ready tears.

'You had no warning?'

'He... she'd told me she looked a bit different, so I was thinking overweight, bald or bearded. I wasn't thinking female. Who would?'

'Why did she want to see you after all this time?'

'Her mum's dying. Ivy and I were really close, but we lost touch when Shaun reconnected with her, and she wouldn't tell me what was going on. She said it wasn't her story to tell and that made me angry at the time, but I get it now. She wants to see me to make peace before she goes.'

'And you found that out today too?'

'No. That part was in the letter. We didn't actually get round to talking about Ivy today. I cut it short. I couldn't...'

'Does it feel any better knowing why he left?'

'That's the really confusing part. I've longed for answers for so long, and now I have answers, but I have more questions than ever so I'm still angry and frustrated but for different reasons. I thought Shaun and I knew everything about each other. No secrets. We used to say that we could survive anything because we knew each other inside out. Turns out there was only one of us doing the sharing.'

Considering I hadn't wanted to talk, I couldn't seem to stop myself. Out it all came – the entire history of our relationship, from the day I met Shaun through to the conversation with Sasha today, including my disastrous relationship with Glen in the middle.

'Oh, my God!' I said, noticing a clock on the wall and blanching at the time. 'Is that clock right? It's never twenty past three, is it?'

He checked his phone. 'It's correct.'

'I've talked at you for hours. Why didn't you shut me up?'

'Because I didn't want to. You needed to talk and I wanted to listen.'

'You're a good listener.'

'I try to be. I know how it feels to need to talk and how helpful it is to be listened to.'

'Nathaniel?' I asked.

'Among other things.' He stood up and stretched out. 'These comfy chairs don't feel so comfy anymore. My parents are away and I'm not needed here. Do you want to come back to theirs for a coffee and better seating?'

'Okay. But you're the one doing the talking this time. Deal?'

'Deal.'

I picked up my bag and the rest of the white mice and followed Riley through the garden centre. He picked up a few more bags of sweets on the way and insisted on paying for mine as well as his. I didn't have the energy to object. I didn't have any energy at all. My eyes felt sore and heavy, and I just hoped I could stay awake long enough to hear Riley's story.

* * *

'It's this one on the right,' Riley said. 'Pull onto the drive next to my car.'

'It's stunning,' I said as we climbed out.

Overlooking Cherry Brompton village green, the house was a large old stone L-shaped building with stone window frames and ivy cladding. As I'd have expected for a couple who owned a garden centre, the front garden was immaculate and bursting with colour.

Riley directed me into the lounge while he made coffee. The room was large but cosy with two sofas flanking an inglenook fireplace. I was drawn towards a set of shelves displaying family photos.

A large wooden frame contained a photo of a smiling older couple who were presumably Riley's parents. There was another photo of them looking much younger with two young men and a woman. I recognised Riley and, from the family resemblance, guessed the man with his arm round the woman was Nathaniel.

I picked up the photo, feeling melancholy as I noticed the woman was cradling a baby bump. That had to be Susie, taken shortly before Nathaniel disappeared. They were all smiling for the camera, none of them with any idea of what lay ahead.

'He disappeared three weeks after that photo was taken,' Riley said, confirming my thoughts. 'It's the last photo any of us have of him.'

'It's a good one. You all look happy.'

'We were. We'd been out for Mum's birthday, and there was lots to look forward to.' He sighed and shook his head. 'That's my parents, Diane and Roy, and Susie, obviously.'

As I put the frame back, he pointed to a double one. 'That's my nephew Dylan as a baby and on his twenty-first birthday last year.'

He pointed to a couple of group photos. 'That's Susie with her husband Dale and their family. Dylan's in that one too. And that's them on their wedding day. That was a mixed day for everyone. Celebrations but sadness too.'

'I can imagine.' I spotted another wedding photo and squinted at it. It looked like a twenty-something Riley, but it was odd that his parents would display a photo of his wedding day if he'd been through a messy divorce.

'That's Clara, my first wife. We were a few months off our third anniversary when she died.'

'Oh, Riley! I'm so sorry. When was this?'

'Twenty-eight years ago now. Long time.' He pointed to another double photo frame with a baby boy on one side and a young boy on the other. 'That's my son, Kai.'

'Who lives with your ex-wife?' I asked, remembering what he'd said in the staffroom.

'Yeah, Rachael. He'd rather live with me, and it's been fraught, but we're working on it.'

We sat at either end of a squishy brown leather sofa and sipped coffee while Riley fulfilled his end of the deal by doing the talking.

'I'll start from the beginning with Clara, as that helps make sense of the Rachael situation. Listening to you talking about Shaun and Glen earlier, there are some spooky parallels. Like Shaun, Clara was my perfect match. We met on our first day at university and became immediate friends. We got together at the start of our second year and married the day after graduation when we were twenty-one. Three years later, I got the sort of phone call nobody ever wants. She'd nipped out from work at lunchtime and got mugged. Witnesses say a couple of kids grabbed her bag and she gave chase. She was no match for them, so she sat down on a bench to get her breath back, but that's not so easy when you're asthmatic and your bag containing your inhaler has just been stolen.'

'Oh, Riley!' I pressed my hand to my throat, tears filling my eyes.

'They did their best, but it was too late. Her bag was found down a nearby side street, the contents emptied onto the floor, only her purse taken. It kills me that her inhaler was only a few hundred metres away while she took her final breaths.'

'Did they catch the kids?'

'Yes, but they were never sentenced. Thirteen and fourteen. Can you believe that? Clara's parents were livid and were constant visitors down the police station and to their local MP demanding justice, but what justice was there? Would sending them to juvie bring Clara back? I dealt with it the only way I knew how – by throwing myself into my career. I qualified as a project manager and took what I'd learned into property management, picking up wrecks at auction and turning them round. I made time each week for my family but spent the rest of the time either working or networking to make more contacts. It was relentless.'

'I'm surprised you didn't burn out.'

'I think I would have done if Nathaniel hadn't disappeared. Susie needed someone. She wasn't particularly close to her parents and mine were struggling to come to terms with it themselves, so I took some time out to be there for her. She got me to open up about Clara and we became really close. When Dylan was born, I moved in to help her, but that caused gossip. She fell out with a couple of her friends who were convinced there had to be something going on which, of course, there wasn't. People can be so twisted. The people who counted knew neither of us would ever do that to Nathaniel.'

'How long did you stay?'

'Dylan was about eighteen months when Susie told me she felt ready to face life as a single mum. I'd always known that day was coming and how important it was that she took that step, but it hit me hard. I missed the company and I missed playing dad, so I threw myself back into work again.'

It was exactly what I'd done after breaking up with Glen. I'd needed a focus in my life, to feel useful, and work had been the only thing I could control. I'd put in ridiculous hours, but it had been exactly what I needed at the time.

'When did you meet Rachael?' I asked.

'It was Christmas, a decade after Nathaniel disappeared, and I wasn't in a good place. Susie had married Dale and they'd had their first daughter, Mum and Dad were doing brilliantly with the garden centres and they were stronger than ever. Nobody had forgotten Nathaniel, everyone was still hurting, but they all had someone in their lives to move forward with and I didn't. I was rapidly approaching forty, single, childless, angry that Clara had been taken from me and I was still struggling to deal with it. In my darkest moments, I was angry at Susie for re-marrying. A Declaration of Presumed Death had been issued for Nathaniel after seven years, but none of us really knew if he was dead, yet she'd managed to move on. I categorically knew Clara was dead, but I couldn't let go.'

'So many echoes of how I felt about Shaun,' I said. 'It's hard to let go when you've loved and lost.'

'So hard,' he agreed. 'When you were telling me about Shaun and Glen earlier, the circumstances were different, but I could feel every emotion because I'd been there myself.'

He held my gaze and my heart started to pound. Talking to Sam, Connie and Jonathan had helped me tremendously, but talking to Riley was on a whole different level. He'd been there. He'd experienced the pain.

'You were telling me about how you met Rachael,' I prompted.

'Oh, yeah! A client invited me to an event, Rachael was there, and we got talking. She was recently divorced and not looking for anything serious and I was thinking about dipping my toe in the water again, so a no-strings relationship was exactly what we both needed. Then a year later, she announced that she was pregnant and presented me with an ultimatum – to marry her or never see her or our baby again.'

I winced. 'That's not a very nice ultimatum.'

'She's not a very nice person, although I didn't realise that at the time. I should have done. Who else presents marriage and a baby as though it's a business deal? She made it clear that she didn't love me and never would, but she wasn't getting any younger and this was probably her last chance to have the baby she desperately wanted. She told me she'd chosen me because she thought I'd make a good dad and a bearable husband.'

'Wow! And they say romance is dead.'

'Tell me about it! Even though I agreed with her that it would never be love, we got on well so I thought we could make it work, especially when we were both getting the child we longed for. Kai came along and I was smitten with him, but Rachael seemed detached and disinterested. She'd made up that stuff about longing for a baby. Already twice-divorced, she'd realised she could get a better pay-out if there was a child involved – something which she took great delight in telling me when Kai was five and she gave me divorce papers for Christmas.'

'If she's not interested in Kai, why's he still living with her?'

'To get more money out of me. It's her one and only motivation, which I discovered when she lined up husband number four, Matisse, shortly after we split. His parents owned a château in the Loire Valley which had been running as a successful business for years. His dad died a few years back and his mum passed away a couple of weeks ago, so Matisse has just inherited everything and Rachael's getting ready to start her new life in France.'

'Without Kai?'

'That's the hope. Rachael assumed he'd be excited about the fresh start and, because he's bilingual, thanks to Matisse, he'd easily fit into school. Kai doesn't want to live abroad and he's really dug his heels in about it, so they're always arguing, which has led to Rachael and

Matisse arguing. Matisse has a few health issues and the stress isn't doing him any good. He's threatened to move to France without her, so it's been suggested that Kai might like to stay with me during term time and visit her during the holidays. I've got my solicitor working on something more secure.'

'No wonder you said it had been fraught.'

'It's been a shocker. The week I made the announcement about the takeover, the plan was to be there for all the questions, but Rachael phoned me at midnight to say that Matisse's mother had been rushed to hospital, didn't have long left and she was on her way to the airport to join Matisse. She'd left Kai in the house asleep, all alone, so I had to phone Susie and ask her to go round while I raced down to Derbyshire in the early hours. It was lucky I'd sneakily had a key cut for her in case of emergencies. I stayed for a couple of days because Kai had his SATs. Susie offered to look after him, but it wasn't fair on Kai to have both parents abandon him, especially during exam time.'

I thought about the email Judith said he'd sent at stupid o'clock telling her about his emergency and felt guilty at my initial reaction that nothing could be urgent enough to have abandoned us at our time of need. His eleven-year-old son had been left alone and needed him. Some things *were* more important than work.

'When you came back in that Friday and we had our meeting about the new structure, you were on the phone when I arrived. It didn't look pretty.'

Riley grimaced. 'You saw that? No, it wasn't pretty. Matisse's mother died the night before, so Matisse was busy making arrangements. Rachael can still only speak pidgin French so she was feeling helpless and thought it would be a good idea if I put our son on a plane to France, on his own, to keep her company for the weekend and be her translator. You can probably imagine how that conversation went.'

'How did you manage to hold it together to talk restructures with all that going on?'

'How do we manage to hold anything together?' he said. 'Some-times we just have to take a deep breath, close off all the hassle and distractions, and focus on what's right in front of us. Tell you what, though, when I saw how upset you were, I nearly lost it myself. I thought I'd give you some space but, as soon as I closed the door, I realised I needed some space too.'

'I really appreciated you leaving me for a moment,' I admitted. 'But I'm sorry you were hurting too.'

'And I'm sorry you're hurting now.'

Our eyes met and I felt something crackling between us once more, but neither of us moved. I'd been confused as to why I'd felt so drawn to Riley when I barely knew him. Could this be the reason – a deep-down connection of past experiences?

'How do things stand now?' I asked.

'Lots of heated discussions and solicitor appointments, but Rachael's coming round. She does love Kai in her own way and, surprisingly, I think she loves Matisse too and is scared of losing him, so I think she'll ultimately do what's best for them both. In the meantime, some long runs are helping me work out the frustration.'

'I hope you get things sorted soon.'

'Me too,' Riley said. 'Here's an idea. I've skipped lunch and I suspect you have too. Why don't I knock together a bowl of pasta and we open a bottle of wine? The château has a vineyard, so Rachael brought me back some samples and they're very good. We can call you a taxi later and sort out getting your car back to you tomorrow. No pressure if you've had enough talking and just want to get home.'

If I went home, I'd need to go through it all with Jonathan and probably Connie too and I couldn't face it. I didn't want to cry again. If I stayed, Riley and I might continue talking about it, but it was the starting from scratch *Shaun is a now a woman and, no, I had no idea at all* conversation that I wanted to avoid.

'Pasta sounds good,' I said, smiling at him. 'I just need to text my sister to let her know I'm okay.'

'Come and find me in the kitchen when you're ready.' He stood up. 'There's a toilet under the stairs and the kitchen's at the far end. See you shortly.'

With a flash of that dimple, he left. I stayed where I was for a moment, trying to calm the butterflies in my stomach, then picked up my phone and texted Connie and Jonathan:

✉ To Connie & Jonathan
Quick message to let you know I'm okay. Seeing Shaun again was nothing like I expected but I now know why he left. Loads to tell you but not tonight. I bumped into a friend and we're having dinner. I might be home late so I'll have to keep you in suspense until tomorrow xx

Jonathan would accept that and probably reply wishing me a good evening, but Connie would likely push for more detail. I switched my phone off.

40

LAUREN

Despite having every intention of getting a taxi home last night, I'd somehow managed to fall asleep on the sofa. Riley covered me with a spare duvet, and I had no idea I'd crashed out there until he woke me up with a mug of coffee this morning and an apology for turfing me out because he needed to drive to Derbyshire to spend the day with Kai.

There'd been several texts and missed calls from Connie, so I texted her as soon as I got back to Chapel View to say I was having a shower and could she give me forty minutes. She must have set off immediately because I found her in the kitchen making coffee as soon as I'd showered and dressed.

'I've been so worried about you,' she said. 'Are you okay?'

I ran my hands through my damp hair and shrugged. 'Yesterday was tough.'

'You said you found out why he left.'

'Yep. Brace yourself, because all the explanations we came up with weren't even close. Shaun is no longer Shaun. Shaun is now Sasha.'

Connie dropped the teaspoon into the mug with a clatter. 'What?'

'She's a trans woman.'

'But... oh, wow, that's... oh, my goodness, Lauren. How did he... she look? How did you feel? So many questions!'

'Tell me about it. Finish making that coffee and I'll tell you what I know...'

I thought I'd be able to get through it, but it was all still too raw and I ugly-cried again, as did Connie.

I'd wondered if she might be upset that I'd told Riley first and assured her it hadn't been planned, but she said not to give it a second thought, she was glad he'd been there for me, and it had probably helped me to talk it through in the first instance with someone who hadn't known Shaun and could be completely objective. She was right that it had been. Over dinner, Riley and I had delved a little deeper into our relationships and I felt it had helped him as well as me.

'How have you left it with Sasha?' she asked.

'I said I'd get in touch when I'd had a chance to digest everything but, unfortunately, I don't have much time to do that with Ivy being terminally ill. I feel bad. We didn't even get as far as talking about her.'

'Don't kick yourself,' Connie said. 'You've had a shock and you needed some space to process that first.'

'I'm going to suggest Sasha meets me tomorrow and, depending how that goes, maybe I'll travel to Stockport to see Ivy on Wednesday or Thursday.'

'If you want company for the journey, I'm all yours.'

'I'd like that. Thank you.'

* * *

I arranged to meet Sasha at 10.30 a.m. the following morning in Purple Paws Gardens, just south of York. I hadn't visited for several years but there was a café where we could talk and stunning gardens to wander round if the café was too crowded, which was fairly likely on a Bank Holiday Monday.

As I drove closer, the knot in my stomach tightened and I turned up ELO's greatest hits. A track called 'Confusion' was playing – exactly how I felt now that I'd met Sasha. I was confused about how my best friend Shaun could have hidden who he really was from me for so many years. I was confused about his logic for walking away instead of talking to me. And I was confused about what I'd have done if he had told me the truth back then. I'd never know. I hadn't been given that chance and I was still angry with him, and now her, for that.

I was early, but Sasha was even earlier and had secured a secluded table on a large decked terrace outside the café. She stood up as I approached and I couldn't help notice how effortlessly stylish she looked once more in a pair of white linen trousers, a red and white striped T-shirt and a thin navy cardigan.

'Thanks for meeting me again,' she said, smiling. 'How're you doing?'

'Still trying to get my head round it all. I'm not sure I took it all in on Saturday.'

'That's understandable.'

'I've got a stack of questions.'

'Also understandable.'

I sat down and we made small talk about our journey lengths and the beautiful weather before Sasha went inside to place our order.

'Fire away,' she said, returning a little later with drinks and scones.

'Okay. Can I ask why you cut your mum out?'

'I didn't mean to. I was going to tell you the truth then drive to Mum's and tell her while you had some time to digest it, but that all went wrong when I bottled it and did a runner.'

'You could have still phoned her and let her know you were okay.'

'I know, and I should have, but I was...' Sasha bit her lip and gazed down into her drink. 'Okay, I wasn't going to say this because I didn't want you to think I was trying for the sympathy vote, but I promised you the truth. I had a breakdown. I'll spare you the details, but I was in hospital for a while and in no state to contact anyone. When I sent Mum her birthday card, I was in a really bad place. The card was completely inadequate, but it was all I could manage at the time. Christmas wasn't much better but, by Mother's Day, I felt strong enough to speak to her and ask her to meet me.

'When I told her, she was amazing about it, but she gave me a hell of a lecture for not telling you. She begged me to get in touch with you, but I couldn't do it. I was scared that if I saw you again or even just heard your voice, I'd try to cling onto the life we had as Lauren and Shaun and it would destroy us both.'

We talked for a couple more hours but, when the café filled with customers wanting lunch, we vacated our table and ambled round the gardens. There were a few overwhelming moments where I had to fight the urge to run, but I kept telling myself that I'd longed for answers for years so I needed to pull up my big girl's pants and hear them, no matter how uncomfortable it was.

'Tell me about Ivy,' I said as we sat on a bench in the rose garden.

'She has a glioblastoma multiforme brain tumour – GBM for short. She had it removed and had chemo and radiotherapy, but GBMs diffuse themselves to other cells so it's almost impossible to remove it entirely. It grows back, like it did with Mum. It's aggressive and she couldn't face more treatment, especially knowing it was likely to return again. It's in a part of her brain affecting her mobility, so she's bedridden but at home.'

'I'm so sorry.'

'She had a good life. She settled in Stockport really well and made lots of friends. She says she's ready to go, or at least she will be when she's seen you.' Tears pooled in Sasha's eyes. 'I don't mean to pressure you.'

'Wednesday,' I said. 'I'll come down and see her on Wednesday.'

Sasha took my hand in hers and squeezed it. 'Thank you,' she whispered.

We sat in silence for several minutes. I couldn't imagine Ivy confined to a bed, although it was also hard to picture her in her eighties. She'd been this petite powerhouse of strength and enthusiasm and it was going to hurt to see her this way. I could have suggested tomorrow but I felt the need for an extra day to psyche myself up.

'What about you?' Sasha asked. 'You're teaching now?'

As Sasha asked me about my life, I kept my answers vague. I didn't feel ready for casual chit-chat, as though we were the best of friends again. Friends didn't hurt each other in the way Shaun had hurt me, although, from what Sasha had told me, I hadn't been the only one hurting deeply.

* * *

Jonathan was in when I arrived home late that afternoon, feeling drained from five hours of talking. Over dinner, I brought him up to date and shed a few more tears as I talked about Ivy.

I asked him not to say anything to Josh or Sam for the moment. I wanted to see Ivy before anyone else knew and it would be easier to tell them when I'd assembled all the puzzle pieces instead of giving them dribs and drabs of information. It would give time for my emotions to settle too.

41

SAMANTHA

In typical school holiday fashion, the weather had turned, with steady rain since 5 a.m. on Wednesday, expected to continue for the next few days. Phoebe and Darcie had been planning a trip to the playground in Great Tilbury this morning but were instead over in the farmhouse.

Paul and Beth had gone homeware-shopping ready for their Alder Lea move and Phoebe had offered to look after Archie and Lottie while watching Darcie's favourite film – *The Princess and the Frog*.

With Fizz being at university, she didn't have a half-term break, but she'd be joining us after lunch for her usual afternoon off and I was fairly sure Phoebe would bring everyone over to the barn when Fizz arrived, so I was hoping to catch up on my emails before it got busy.

Around mid-morning, I'd finished feeding the hoglets and logged onto my laptop to check my emails. There was one from Zayn.

'Zayn Hockley, you absolute star,' I said, smiling after I'd opened the attachment.

He'd been looking at Gwendoline's drawing of the elephant Terry had given me and had asked why it was so creased. I explained the origins and that I'd attempted a cool iron, but it hadn't made much difference and I feared anything hotter might burn the paper. He'd said he was 'pretty useful' at Photoshop and had offered to give it a go. Looking at the image he'd sent over, he was more than 'pretty useful'.

I'd already bought a photo frame in the hope that Zayn would be able to work his magic on the creases and couldn't wait to present Terry with it on Sunday. I'd asked him when and where he'd like to go out for his thank you meal with Josh and me and he'd said his preference was for a Sunday carvery. Phoebe and Darcie had arranged to go to Rosemary's this coming Sunday, so we were dropping them off then picking up Terry.

I'd managed another half an hour of admin when Terry arrived.

'I wasn't expecting to see you until Sunday,' I called to him as he pulled the barn door closed.

'I've got summat for you but it's not a hedgehog. I weren't sure whether to take it to Josh instead. Is Wilbur safe?'

'Yes, he's fine.'

Terry released the lead and Wilbur padded down the barn, pausing to let me briefly stroke him.

'Wilbur found this,' Terry said, placing a cardboard box on the treatment table.

'A fox cub!' I cried. 'Aw, it's gorgeous. But that looks painful.' I winced at the barbed wire tangled round one of its back paws.

'I went home for some cutters so I could free it, but I were scared to take it off fully in case it tried to run off.'

'You did the right thing.' I peered a little closer. 'It looks like one of the barbs is sticking into the flesh, so you'd have needed to be ready to apply pressure as soon as you removed it.'

I washed my hands, pulled on some gloves, and laid a fresh towel on the treatment table. Terry wanted to watch and help if he could.

'I'll need to weigh him so I can administer the right level of antibiotics,' I told Terry, 'so if you could grab that pad and pen and write his weight down, that would be helpful.'

A little later, our fox cub was curled up in one of our large hedgehog crates with the barbed wire removed, his wounds cleaned and a shot of antibiotics inside of him. He'd gobbled down a bowl of cat food and eagerly slurped some water.

With some online assistance, I'd identified that he was male and discovered that cubs were typically born in March or April. Looking at the photos, I reckoned ours was roughly eight weeks old and likely to be fully weaned. He'd probably got tangled while out playing with his litter and the vixen had been left with no choice but to abandon him.

'I'll ask Josh's advice on the best plans for release,' I told Terry as I wiped down the table. 'I'd imagine we're talking the same as a hedgehog release – ideally the place they were found.'

I took a couple of dog biscuits over to Wilbur. 'Who's a clever boy?' I said. 'You're a life-saver again.'

'I love foxes,' Terry said. 'I know some folk think they're a nuisance, but I say folk are a nuisance.' He smiled at me. 'Not all of 'em, mind.'

'I know what you mean, Terry. I love foxes too, although I do feel for anyone with chickens as I've seen the aftermath of fox attacks on a chicken coop and it's not pretty. I sometimes saw foxes crossing the road at night when I lived in Whitsborough Bay, but I've seen loads since I moved here, and it always gives me a thrill. They're mesmerising.'

'Aye, that they are. I remember Gwendoline rescuing a fox once...'

I made us a drink as Terry reminisced about the occasion. The story sounded familiar, but I wasn't going to let on that he'd already told me. I had no problem hearing stories about Gwendoline a dozen times and each tale clearly took Terry to a happy place. I'd always have time for that.

* * *

'Awwwwww! He's sooooo cute.'

I smiled at Darcie's reaction that afternoon when I introduced her to our newest patient.

'Can I get him out and give him a cuddle?'

'I'd love to say yes but, just like our hedgehogs, he's a wild animal and not a pet, and what does that mean?'

'Only handling him when it's essential for medicine and cleaning.'

'Exactly. He'll be returned to the wild as soon as he's well and will hopefully go back to his family, so we need to have as little contact with him as we can to make that transfer easier for him.'

'But Luna's not a wild animal, so I can cuddle her?'

'Luna might have been living wild at Barney's farm, but cats are domesticated animals, so that's fine.'

'Can I name him?' she asked.

'If you like.'

She thought for a while. 'What's the name of the fox in *The Fox and the Hound*?'

I shrugged, unable to remember the last time I'd watched that film.

'Tod, I think,' Phoebe said.

'That's it! I'll call him Tod.' She blew him a kiss. 'I love you, Tod. We'll make you all better and you can soon get back to your family.'

Fizz had been leafing through one of the colouring books I kept in the barn. 'There's a picture of a fox in here, Darcie, if you want to colour it in.'

Darcie didn't need to be asked twice. She lay down on the floor with the colouring book and a pot of felt-tips with Misty-Blue tucked in beside her. She'd happily colour in for hours.

* * *

Paul and Beth returned around mid-afternoon after going via Alder Lea to drop off their purchases. They said hello then made a dash across to the farmhouse, each holding a child under a golf brolly.

'I'm so excited we have a fox cub,' Fizz said as we fed the hoglets shortly afterwards.

'I know. Me too.'

'Have you ever thought about running Hedgehog Hollow as more than a hedgehog rescue centre?' Phoebe asked.

'Thomas left me the farm on the proviso I fulfilled Gwendoline's wish, which was all about hedgehogs, so I never considered going wider. When I was getting prepared, I spent a few days at a wildlife rescue centre between Whitsborough Bay and Whitby, which was pretty special. The owner, Pauline, was so inspiring and I helped her release a badger while I was there.'

'That's awesome,' Fizz said. 'You should do it. Turn this into a rescue centre for all animals.'

'In theory it's a lovely idea, but having more animals needs extra funds and additional volunteers. Pauline worked even more hours than I do, and it worked for her because she was older and single and not interested in meeting anyone, but I've got Josh, all of you, and other friends and family I want to spend time with. This place means the absolute world to me but it's not my entire world.'

The rescue centre, much as I loved it, did take a lot of time and attention. As well as helping me with my PTSD and my relationship with Mum, I'd found my counselling sessions with Lydia invaluable for reminding me of the importance of keeping that balance between work and life. That statement about Hedgehog Hollow meaning the world but not being my entire world had come from her and was a sentiment which Josh echoed. I often reminded myself of it when I was unable to save hedgehogs and could easily let that loss impact on other parts of my life. It also fed into my fears about having a family and finding that balance between the two.

'My dream job would be working in a wildlife rescue centre full-time,' Fizz said, sounding wistful. 'But sadly that isn't going to pay the bills, so it'll have to be a regular veterinary practice. At least I can still get my fix of wildlife by volunteering here.'

'Look at my badger!' Darcie announced, rushing up to us with her colouring book. She'd already coloured in the fox, followed by an owl and a butterfly.

'It's brilliant,' Phoebe said.

We all congratulated her on her neat colouring in and helped her decide whether to colour in a farmyard scene or a peacock next.

The rain continued to tap against the window. Phoebe had put some music on low and it was warm and snug inside the barn. I smiled as I watched Fizz giving Phoebe some advice on an alternative way to hold a particularly wriggly hoglet. Rescuing hedgehogs wasn't my whole world, but it had created the world I loved, and I was very fortunate.

42

LAUREN

'Are you sure you don't want me to drive?' Connie asked as we got back into my car on Wednesday morning after a stop for coffee at a service station on the M1, roughly halfway to Stockport.

'I might need you to drive the whole way back,' I said. 'So I'll continue for now. Thanks again for coming.'

'Where else would I be?'

* * *

Around late morning, I pulled up outside Ivy's bungalow on a leafy street. It was part of a small new-build development on the outskirts of Stockport, which Sasha said Ivy had moved into five years ago when she'd developed some mobility challenges.

The plan was for Connie to find a café or go shopping until I called her to pick me up. We hugged and Connie was about to settle into the driver's seat when the front door opened and Sasha stepped out.

Connie stopped, her hands on the door, staring at Sasha.

'Hi, Connie,' Sasha said, smiling at my sister.

'Hi. Sorry. I'm staring. That's rude.'

'It's all right. Just ignore the crow's feet.'

'You haven't got crow's feet. Your skin's gorgeous.'

'Thank you.'

They stared at each other for a moment longer, both a little dewy-eyed.

'Connie's going to find a café,' I said.

'You don't have to do that. You can come in.'

'I wouldn't want to encroach,' Connie said. 'Pretend you haven't seen me.'

'You really don't have to go,' Sasha insisted, but then she frowned. 'But if it's uncomfortable...'

'It's not that.' Connie glanced at me.

'I've got no problem with you coming in,' I reassured her.

Connie switched off the ignition, grabbed her bag and we both followed Sasha inside.

'Mum's asleep at the moment,' Sasha said, 'but she knows you're coming. I'll make us some drinks. The lounge is through that door if you want to make yourselves comfortable.'

We gave our drinks preferences and went into the lounge.

'I wasn't expecting to see her,' Connie whispered. 'Did I make a mess of it?'

'No. What did you think?'

'It's like looking at Shaun's twin sister. That thing you were saying about familiar but unfamiliar is spot on. She's very pretty.'

Connie sat down in a reclining armchair, but I was too agitated to sit, nervous about seeing Ivy again after all these years.

The room was L-shaped and painted in a soothing pale green. The furniture was white and the upholstery grey – much more modern than her house in Wilbersgate had been, and I couldn't help thinking it suited her. I scanned round for anything I might recognise from her old life and felt momentarily disappointed that there wasn't a photo of me on the large shelving unit - a sign that I'd always been in her thoughts. I didn't have any photos of her on display, though. Too hard. Maybe she'd felt the same.

'Mum's awake now,' Sasha said, handing Connie a mug. 'I've taken your drink through, Lauren. Are you ready?'

'I think so.'

'She looks a lot different too. Not as different as I do, but... well, you can see for yourself.'

Ivy had been fifty-eight when I last saw her. At eighty-three and terminally ill, I was prepared for a significant difference, but it was still shocking to see her shrunken form eclipsed by a hospital bed, a face covered in liver spots and little more than wispy tufts of silvery hair on her head.

'Hi, Ivy,' I said, forcing down the lump in my throat as I stepped closer to her bed. It had been raised so she was semi-upright, propped up on a couple of pillows.

Her hand twitched and I took hold of it as I sat down on a padded dining chair beside her.

'It's been a long time,' I said.

'Too long,' she whispered, her eyes searching mine. 'I've missed you.'

Feeling her slender fingers tighten round mine, tears pooled in my eyes. 'I've missed you too.'

'I'm so sorry. I shouldn't—'

I shook my head, stopping her mid-flow. 'Don't. It doesn't matter.' As I said it, I realised it really didn't. This woman who'd championed whatever I'd done – unlike my own mother – was dying and I didn't want her to spend her final days or weeks begging for my forgiveness. She already had it. She'd faced an impossible choice and had done the only thing a mother could have done. We could have stayed in touch, but I'd pushed and pressured her before shutting her out of my life completely.

'Tell me about you,' she said, smiling weakly. 'Husband? Children?'

I glanced up at Sasha, who nodded. 'I'll leave you two to get reacquainted. Lauren, there's a button by the bed. Buzz if you need me.'

Sasha left the room, closing the door behind her.

'Well?' Ivy asked.

'No. I never wanted kids, remember? I did remarry and it didn't work out, but it's fine.'

I'd tried to keep my voice positive, but she was the one person who'd always been able to see through my protective shield.

'I have a brain tumour,' she said. 'It's affecting my mobility, not my mind. Tell me the truth, little lamb.'

The use of my former nickname nearly broke me. I looked away for a moment, trying to compose myself. The curtains were open, and the bed was angled to face the patio doors, which looked out at a pretty garden full of bird feeders. I focused on a grey squirrel scampering up the iron stem of one.

'Okay, it's been hard,' I admitted when I felt able to speak. 'You saw how I was after Shaun left. I never got over it. It took me a lot of years before I dated again, and the marriage was a mistake. It wasn't just that I wasn't over Shaun. He had issues too. I resolved not to get involved again after that until...'

I paused, frowning. Where had the 'until' come from and why had Riley's face popped into my mind?

'Until...?' Ivy prompted.

'I've met someone recently. Nothing's happened. Not even close. But there's a possibility that, somewhere in the distant future, perhaps it could.' I smiled and shook my head. 'It probably won't and I'm reading too much into his kindness but, if it did, I don't feel like I'd run a mile. That's a first for me.'

'What's his name?'

'Riley.'

'How did you meet?'

'When I pulled into a garden centre playing "Mr Blue Sky" far too loud on the radio. He was sitting in his car listening to the same song and we had a bonding moment.'

'Tell me more...'

On the way over, Connie had asked me what I thought we might talk about. Telling Ivy all about Riley Berry certainly hadn't been one of my predictions, but it felt so right to share it.

'You have so much love to give,' she said, her words slow and hoarse, her eyes flickering as though she was fighting sleep. 'You gave your heart to Shaun so fully and completely and I know how badly he crushed it. I hope Sasha has returned it to you.'

'I think she's trying.'

'Give her a chance. She did what she thought was best for you.'

'I know.'

Ivy's eyes closed and I watched the slow but steady rise and fall of her chest before turning to watch the birds in the garden.

Sasha poked her head round the door a little later.

'She's asleep,' I whispered.

'You didn't drink your coffee.'

'She was interrogating me. It went cold.'

'She'll probably sleep for a couple of hours. Do you want a fresh drink?'

I nodded and stretched as I stood up. 'I might stick around until she wakes up again. Is that okay?'

'Of course.'

As I followed her out of the room, I noticed some photo frames hanging on the wall and tears pricked my eyes. I featured in several of them.

'She's never stopped thinking about you,' Sasha said, gently. 'She wanted those opposite her bed so she can see you every day.'

* * *

'She's not going to make it until the end of the summer, is she?' I said to Sasha as we sat in the lounge with a fresh round of drinks.

She closed her eyes and shook her head slowly. 'They said weeks, but she's going downhill fast. I think it could be days.'

'I'm so sorry,' I said, at the same time as Connie.

'Could even be as soon as tonight,' Sasha said. 'I can't help thinking she's just been hanging on to see you and make her peace. Did she do that?'

'She started and I interrupted her and said it didn't matter and we were fine.'

'She'll be grateful for that, but I think she'd still have liked to say her piece. I'm not criticising...'

'No, that makes sense. When she wakes up, I'll make sure I hear her out. It didn't seem important to me anymore, but I can see it would be important to her.'

'Thank you.'

A few minutes' silence followed as we sipped on our drinks. I could hear the birds chirping outside and the ticking of a clock somewhere.

'I can't leave her,' I said eventually. 'Especially not if we're talking days. Can I stay?'

Sasha pressed her fingers to her lips. 'You'd do that for Mum?'

'I'd do it for both of you,' I said, my voice cracking. 'Connie...?'

'I can get a train home. Alex can pick me up from the station.' She dug her phone out of her bag. 'Let me look up some times.'

* * *

I dropped Connie off at Stockport train station an hour later and stopped off at a supermarket on the way back to buy toiletries and clothes. I knew Sasha would have loaned me something from her wardrobe, but I wasn't at the sharing clothes with my ex-husband stage yet.

'The doctor came while you were out,' Sasha said when I returned to the bungalow. 'He's upped her pain control and confirmed what I thought – days rather than weeks.'

'Oh, no! I'm so sorry.'

'I'm so grateful to you for coming to see her. She can go peacefully now.' Sasha's voice cracked and tears glistened in her eyes.

'I wouldn't be anywhere else. I'm sorry I shut her down before.'

'When she wakes up again, you can talk to her then. *If* she wakes up again.'

43

LAUREN

Ivy woke up shortly after six on Thursday morning. Sasha had just made me a coffee and had gone for a shower to freshen up.

'Morning,' I said softly, reaching for Ivy's hand.

'Still here?' she murmured.

'Can't get rid of me now that I've found you,' I said, smiling at her.

'Good girl.'

I was about to apologise for cutting her off yesterday, but she spoke again.

'How's your mum?'

'She died ten years ago.'

'I'm sorry. How?'

'Heart failure, although Connie and I think it was a broken heart. Kelvin died from pneumonia a month earlier and she was lost without him.'

'Poor Bev. Looked so happy with Kelvin when I saw them. Nice couple.'

'When was this? Before you left Reddfield?'

'Eleven years ago, maybe. Back for a funeral. Saw them in town.' She closed her eyes for a moment, and I thought she'd drifted off, but they flickered and opened again. 'She was so proud of you.'

'Of me? No. Mum was proud of Connie, never of me.'

'No. You. Proud of you for nursing. Proud of you for teaching.'

'You're sure?'

'Certain. She loved you, lamb. May not have shown it, but it was there. So proud.'

Her eyes closed once more and this time she'd definitely drifted off.

'Everything okay?' Sasha asked, wandering into the room wearing a fluffy dressing gown and a towel turban and eyeing me curiously.

'Your mum woke up and said something strange. She said she'd bumped into Mum and Kelvin in Reddfield and Mum told her how proud she was of me. Mum was never proud of me. I was the perpetual disappointment.'

Sasha sat down opposite me. 'Mum went back to Reddfield for the funeral of a colleague she'd kept in touch with. She wondered about getting in touch with you but was worried too much time had passed and it might do you both more harm than good. She bumped into them in town and asked after you, and your Mum said you'd left nursing and gone into teaching and she was so proud of you for trying something new and for making something of your career.'

'I can't believe it! I wish she'd told me that when she was alive. You know how it was with us. She could be so lovely, but there'd always be this undercurrent of disappointment.'

'I remember. I hated how upset it made you. I'm sorry she never told you how she really felt.'

'I must be so hard to talk to.' I looked up at Sasha and shook my head. 'Sorry. Pity party moment.'

'You were never hard to talk to,' Sasha said softly. 'It was me and your mum who had the problem, not you.'

I sipped on my coffee, stunned at the revelation.

'She didn't have a chance to say sorry,' I said. 'She said the stuff about Mum then fell back to sleep.'

'She might wake up again, but she might not. Promise me one thing: do *not* beat yourself up if you don't have that conversation. She knows you forgive her. Why else would you be here?'

44

SAMANTHA

I was on hoglets duty on Thursday night when, shortly after nine, Phoebe joined me in the barn, carrying a couple of mugs of hot chocolate.

'I thought I'd keep you company for a bit,' she said, handing me one of the drinks.

Thanking her, I pushed my chair back, intending to move to the sofa bed.

'Probably easiest to stay here,' she said. 'There's something I want to show you on your laptop.'

'Okay. Sounds intriguing.'

I moved aside so she could open something on her memory stick. A spreadsheet appeared on the screen, but she lowered the lid before I could see the content. I'd assumed she'd wanted to talk about Fizz, but I couldn't imagine she needed a spreadsheet to do that.

'So, I've been thinking about Tod the fox cub and the conversation we had yesterday about this place becoming a rescue centre for more than hedgehogs. Would you like to do that?'

'I can't afford to and there aren't enough hours in the day.'

'Forget about any financial or staffing issues for the moment. If all that was resolved, hand on heart, would you like to take in more Tods?

Badgers? Owls? Rabbits? Don't answer it immediately. Think about it for a moment.'

I sipped on my hot chocolate, thinking about my amazing three days at Redcliffe Rescue last year. I'd stayed in touch with Pauline and had even invited her to our evening do, but she'd been away on a rare holiday so hadn't been able to come. I regularly checked her website and I loved reading about all the other animals.

I glanced across at the noticeboard and Gwendoline's drawing of the elephant. The many stories Terry had told me about her love of animals whirled round my mind. He'd affectionately nicknamed her Snow White, picturing the scene in the film where she was surrounded by woodland animals. Gwendoline hadn't just loved hedgehogs; she'd loved *all* animals. I was pretty sure that, if she'd lived long enough to fulfil her dream of setting up the hedgehog rescue centre, it would only have been a matter of time before she accepted other animals.

'Yes, I would,' I admitted. 'Hedgehogs would always be my number one priority, but it would be great to help other wildlife.'

'Thought you might say that.' Phoebe beamed at me as she opened the laptop. 'I've been doing some number crunching and I think I've found a way of making it happen.'

I listened, rapt, as Phoebe presented her thoughts on turning Hedgehog Hollow into a wildlife rescue centre run by two full-time salaried staff members – me and Fizz once she was fully qualified as a veterinary nurse next summer – as well as support from willing volunteers. Food and medication would predominantly be paid for from a mixture of funds raised from the Family Fun Day and Christmas Fair, the wish list, and donations from the public.

She proposed that we massively step up our presence in the community, educating the public while securing donations. We could speak to groups such as the Women's Institute as well as going to schools and libraries, and could ask for physical or financial contributions in lieu of any appearance fees offered.

The income generated from the holiday cottages and the events held in Wildflower Byre once they were fully established would more than cover the two salaries.

'Plus I can continue to access grants,' Phoebe said. 'Widening the type of animal we support will likely open up additional funding opportunities. So what do you think?'

I scanned down the projected figures, my heart racing with excitement. Phoebe had been conservative with her estimates, appreciating that the holiday cottages wouldn't be at full occupancy all year and that Wildflower Byre might only host a dozen or so events. She'd also factored in a budget for wear and tear and the figures still worked.

'I think you're a financial genius,' I said. 'We could really do this.'

'I'd suggest another year to build up to it.'

'Which would nicely coincide with Fizz graduating,' I said, smiling at her.

Her cheeks tinged pink. 'Pure coincidence. Okay, no, it's not. I'd do anything to make her happy, but it's not just about Fizz. I'd do anything to make you happy too. Darcie and I owe you and Josh our lives.'

Her voice cracked and I wrapped my arms round her slender body.

'Neither of you owe us anything,' I whispered.

We both grabbed tissues when we pulled apart and laughed as we dabbed our eyes.

'I mean it,' I said. 'Knowing you and Darcie are safe and happy is the only repayment we need.'

'We're both very happy here.'

'Good. Long may that continue.' I pointed to the spreadsheet. 'Josh needs to see this. Are you up to briefing him now if I ask him to come over?'

With Phoebe's agreement, I rang Josh, who said he'd be over in ten minutes.

'I thought you'd come over to talk about Fizz,' I said, deciding to put it out there in case Phoebe did still want that opportunity.

'I thought about it but there's not much more to say. Like I said at the barbeque, she's with Yasmin and she seems happy, so I'm not going to do anything to mess that up for her. She probably doesn't even know I'm gay.'

'You've never told her?'

'I don't know how to.' She shrugged. 'I've known who I am since I was fourteen. I know some teenagers find it a struggle but, for me, it was about the only thing in my teens that actually made sense. If it had still just been me and Dad against the world, I'd have told him. We used to be so close until Tina snared him. After they got married, I didn't feel I could say anything to him that wouldn't get back to Tina, and there was no way I wanted her to know. She and Jenny didn't need another reason to hate me.'

From what I'd seen and heard, I could well imagine homophobia featuring among the Grimes sisters' many undesirable traits.

'I had to keep it hidden for my own safety, but that means I've never had the conversation with anyone – until you – and I do struggle a bit with the concept of coming out. If someone's straight, they don't need to come out, so why should someone who's gay? It's not like it completely defines me, so I'd prefer for people to discover it naturally.'

'Makes sense to me.'

'You can tell Josh,' she said. 'The only planned conversation I'll have is with Darcie and I don't want to do that yet. She's had so much change already this year and our focus needs to be on us establishing our relationship now that I've adopted her. I don't want anything to cloud that. It's another reason why I'm chilled about the Fizz thing. The timing's wrong for her because she's with Yasmin, but it's wrong for me too. Darcie's my number one priority. A relationship with anyone, whatever their gender, would complicate that, so it's not even an issue right now.'

She swept her dark hair back from her face and my heart glowed, thinking about how the timid young girl I'd met last summer had blossomed into a wise, mature, confident young woman.

'To use a Fizz-ism, you're awesome, Phoebe Corbyn.'

'You think so?'

'I know so. And one day, when the timing is right for you both, I'm sure Fizz will see that too but, if she doesn't, someone else will and she'll be very lucky to have you.'

* * *

'What are you looking at?' I asked Josh as we fed the hoglets together a couple of hours later. He kept looking up from the one he was feeding to gaze at different parts of the barn.

'I'm imagining how the barn would look with different animals in it.'

Josh had thought Phoebe's proposal was brilliant and had stayed with me after she returned to the farmhouse so we could discuss it further.

'I've had a thought,' he said. 'What if we did set up a full rescue centre but, instead of running it as a separate charity, it became part of the practice?'

'Could we still get donations if we did that? I wouldn't want the rescue centre to absorb all the practice's profits.'

'I don't know. Tariq still hasn't decided whether to stay in the UK or go abroad again, so I'll offer him a few days' consultancy work to look into it. He loves stuff like this.'

Before turning the lights off, I had a final check on Tod, curled up in his crate, fast asleep.

'Your arrival has certainly stirred things up,' I whispered.

When I'd visited Redcliffe Rescue, I'd felt so overwhelmed at the massive undertaking ahead of me but, having run Hedgehog Hollow for a year, the idea of expansion didn't unnerve me. It felt like a natural transition. We had the space, we had the willing – I had no doubt that Fizz was serious about working here if we could pay her – and we potentially had the financial means.

And if the rescue centre did come under the veterinary practice, the staff there could cover holiday, sickness and maternity leave, which would take away my final worry about starting a family. It felt like everything was coming together once more.

45

LAUREN

I feared I'd missed the opportunity to let Ivy say her piece, but she awoke again around ten on Thursday evening. I'd been in the lounge watching the TV on low but not taking anything in when Sasha said Ivy wanted to see me.

I took Ivy's cold hand as I sat beside her bed. 'How are you feeling?'

'Calm,' she whispered. 'I'm ready.'

I swallowed down the instant lump in my throat and tried to draw the strength I'd found during my years as a nurse, but it was so much harder when the person dying was somebody you loved.

'Sasha says you want to say sorry. I cut you off yesterday and I should have let you talk. I'm listening now.'

'Very sorry. Broke my heart losing you.' Her breathing was shallow, and her words slurred. 'Shaun needed me. He was broken... deeply troubled... full of regrets... was scared he'd not make it.'

Tears rained down my cheeks as I stroked her hand. 'I understand. You were in an impossible position.'

'Not strong enough for both of you... hated choosing... should have got in touch when Shaun became Sasha... was too late... too many years gone.'

'I'm here now.'

'Still loves you,' she murmured, her eyes flickering with her struggle to stay awake. 'Try to forgive... be friends again... help each other heal.'

'I'll do my best,' I said, kissing her hand.

'I love you, little lamb.'

I could barely see her through the tears. I wiped my face on my sleeve and leaned over and kissed her cheek. 'I love you too, Ivy. Find your peace.'

When Sasha joined me a little later, I shared Ivy's wish for us to be friends and asked if that was what she wanted.

'I'd love it, but I don't know if it's possible. So long has passed and, although you haven't gone into the details, I'm pretty sure I hurt you more than I'd imagined.'

'You did, but I think we can get through it if we both want to. Only if we share everything – the anger, the fears, the dark places. A friendship won't work if there's anything left simmering.'

So that's what we did, leaving no stone unturned. We laughed, cried, stormed outside needing a time out, and cried some more. And we were honest. Brutally so.

'I never fell out of love with you,' I admitted. 'I thought I never would, but I don't feel that way anymore.'

'Because I'm a woman now.'

'It's not just that. I'm not going to lie and say that's not a major part of it, but I can't help feeling now that if I'd met you at April's and you'd still presented as and identified as male, I'd feel the same. Our time was then, and I've had you up here as this impossible benchmark that no other man could ever reach because, if they did, I'd be risking getting my heart broken all over again. Does that make any sense at all?'

Sasha smiled. 'Perfect sense, because I might have done the same thing.'

She shared how she'd had a few short-term relationships post-transition but had found reasons to end them all because they weren't me. She remained single for several years after that until she met Kristi.

They were together for five years, but Kristi ended it, unable to deal with living in my shadow any longer. Sasha had known the only way she'd be able to move forward was to make peace with me but thought it too selfish to ask that after how she'd treated me. Then Ivy fell ill and wanted to make amends, and there was no way she couldn't grant Ivy her dying wish, especially when it was because of her that Ivy and I had lost contact.

'It sounds like it's Kristi you love now – not me,' I told her. 'Is it too late?'

'I don't know. I see her around from time to time. She's still single.'

'Then tell her how you feel. We've both wasted too many years chained to our pasts instead of living for the present and building a future. Oh, my God! I sound like Connie. What have you both done to me?'

We laughed and, deciding there was no time like the present, Sasha texted Kristi to tell her about Ivy. Her phone rang minutes later and I went back into Ivy's bedroom to give Sasha some space. I couldn't hear the conversation but was pretty certain from the tone of it that Kristi and Sasha had a future together. Which made me surprisingly happy.

* * *

On Saturday morning, I opened my eyes with a start. 'Ivy?'

'She's still with us,' Sasha whispered from the other side of the bed.

I rolled my stiff shoulders. 'What time is it?'

'Quarter past three.'

The last time I'd noticed, it had been a little after 2 a.m.

'I'm nipping to the loo. Do you need anything?'

'A fresh water would be good.' She handed me a half-drunk glass as I passed.

In the bathroom, I splashed some cold water over my face. I hadn't meant to drift off like that, but it had been so warm and peaceful in Ivy's bedroom with only the gentle glow from a bedside lamp, and my eyelids had grown heavier. Three nights sitting beside a dying woman's bed was going to take its toll. She'd awoken in the early hours of Friday morning and I'd slipped out of the room so she and Sasha could say their goodbyes. She'd been asleep ever since.

I returned to Ivy's bedroom and placed Sasha's fresh drink beside her. She caught my hand as I passed.

'I'm glad you're here.'

'Me too.'

Over the next hour, Ivy's breathing pattern changed from a slow but regular rhythm to shallow with the occasional deep gasp, as though Ivy was fighting the inevitable. I'd seen this in hospital so often.

Sasha looked up at me, her eyes red.

'Keep talking to her,' I said gently. 'Let her know she isn't alone and that she's loved.'

At 4.33 a.m., Ivy stopped breathing. I stroked her cold hand and raised it to my lips for a final kiss. 'Goodbye, Ivy,' I whispered. 'I love you.'

I rounded the bed and wrapped my arms round Sasha. I didn't think I'd ever be able to forgive Shaun, but it turned out that I could. Ivy had always believed in our friendship and its ability to endure anything. She'd been right.

46

LAUREN

The doorbell rang around mid-morning. Sasha hadn't wanted to leave Ivy on her own, so we'd taken turns to get showered and changed.

'That'll be the funeral director,' she said.

'Do you want me to get it? Leave you to say your last goodbye.'

Sasha nodded and I patted her shoulder as I left the room.

I opened the door, but it wasn't the funeral director.

'You must be Kristi,' I said, smiling at the stunning auburn-haired woman on the doorstep. Sasha had shown me photos of them together.

She bit her lip as she looked me up and down. 'I nearly didn't come. I wasn't sure about meeting you. But I thought...'

She looked so vulnerable. 'Believe me, Kristi, I'm no threat. I loved Shaun and Shaun loved me, but there is no Shaun anymore. Sasha loves you.'

'Thank you.'

I stepped back. 'She's in the back bedroom with her mum. I think she'll be pleased to see you.'

Pulling on a jacket and grabbing my phone, I went into the garden. The curtains were still closed in Ivy's bedroom, giving them all some privacy.

I stood on the patio for a moment, breathing in the cool air. The sky was grey and there was a light breeze, although no immediate threat of rain.

✉ To Connie

Ivy died at 4.33. Waiting for the funeral director. Sasha's trying to be strong but it's hard. I'll call you later when I know my plans xx

✉ From Connie

That's so sad. Sending you both hugs. Speak soon xxx

I clicked into the WhatsApp conversation I'd had with Riley yesterday after I'd asked for a rain-check on the tour round the garden centre and re-read his reply.

✉ From Riley

I'll keep my phone switched on. If you need me, call. Whatever the time x

I hadn't registered the kiss yesterday.

'I do need you,' I whispered. And I didn't just want to speak to him. I wanted to see him. My heart thudded as I waited for the FaceTime call to connect.

'Hey,' he said, giving me a weak smile. 'How's it going?'

I'd been determined to stay strong, but the tears flowed again. 'She died just after half four.'

'I'm so sorry.'

I wiped my cheeks with my sleeve. 'I don't know why I keep crying. I haven't seen her for so long.'

'Time apart makes no difference when you care about someone. How's Sasha doing?'

'Struggling. Her ex-girlfriend's here now so she's got a friend and I want to give them some space. I'm not sure if I'll be back today or tomorrow but it'll definitely be one of them, although I'm not sure I can face college on Monday.'

'Don't worry about that. I can arrange bereavement leave for you next week. Did you say you have your car there?'

'Yeah, Connie caught the train back.'

'Don't think about doing the drive on your own. You're upset and your head must be about to explode with everything that's happened this week.'

I tapped my forehead then splayed my fingers out and made an explosion noise to show him it was.

'Give me half an hour. I'll check some train times and come and meet you this afternoon. If you need to stay until tomorrow, I'll check into a hotel overnight.'

'I can't expect you to drop everything just like that, Riley. It's too much.'

'You're right. It's a *huge* ask, so it's going to cost you at least three bags of sweets, but I know somewhere that has them on a three-for-two deal.'

I laughed through my tears. 'Thank you.'

'Send me the address and I'll let you know which train I'll be on, but do what's right for you. If you want to stay another night, that's fine by me.'

'I think I'll be ready to leave today. It's been an emotional few days and I need a bit of space.'

'I can imagine. Take care and I'll see you soon.'

He pressed his fingers to his lips and blew me a kiss before disconnecting. It felt so natural and so comforting. I pressed my fingers to my lips and blew a kiss back at the blank screen.

These past few weeks had been packed with the unexpected. Including falling a little bit in love with Riley Berry.

* * *

Riley had texted his train times, so I was expecting him around mid-afternoon. Sasha and Kristi nipped out to the shops, saying we were out of coffee. I'd already spotted a spare jar in the cupboard but appreciated their attempt at subtlety.

As I paced the floor in the lounge, watching for him, I glanced at the time on my phone and my stomach lurched as I spotted the date on the screen. Saturday, 5 June. I sank down onto the sofa, my heart pounding. Today was the thirty-year anniversary of my dad's death. Of all the days for Ivy to die!

I heard a car pulling away and rushed to the door as I spotted Riley walking up the path.

'How are you doing?' he asked when I opened the door.

I stood aside, shaking my head, unable to find any words.

He closed the door behind him, pulled me into his arms and held me as more tears fell.

'I've just realised what date it is,' I cried, my voice coming out in short bursts. 'My dad died thirty years ago today.'

'Oh, Lauren, I'm so sorry.'

We stood in Ivy's hall, locked together, as thirty years of pent-up grief poured out of me. Riley didn't speak. He just held me as my body shook and I gasped for air.

When the sobs eased, he led me into the lounge and sat beside me on the sofa, holding my hand.

'Water?' he asked, once again giving me that breathing space he seemed to instinctively understand was needed.

'I didn't cry when Dad died,' I said when Riley returned with two glasses of water. 'Or at his funeral or any time since. I think I might have saved it all for you. Last thing you needed after a couple of hours on the train.'

'I didn't mind. I'm sorry about your dad. You never mentioned him last weekend.'

'It's usually easier not to. He was an alcoholic, and it was heart failure that took him, although he had liver damage too. Connie and I were both eighteen when we got married. Dad was hammered at her wedding, and my stepdad Kelvin had to step in and do a father of the bride speech. I feared it would be the same at mine, but he never even showed up. I didn't see him much after that. Too painful.'

'That's awful.'

'That's families for you. Can't choose them, although, if I could, I'd have chosen my dad from before. When I was little, he was the absolute best, but bad things happen and different people deal with it in different ways. Dad was a maintenance manager in a factory. He loved it but they stripped out the entire layer and he never got over it.'

'And then the same thing happened to you,' he said, grimacing.

'Yeah, but the difference is I sang loud sweary ELO lyrics instead of drowning my sorrows.'

'Mr Shit Sky?' he suggested.

'Exactly that!'

When Sasha and Kristi returned, it could have been strange introducing my ex-husband to my... whatever Riley was... but only if I made it that way. I didn't need to use the labels from the past and could focus instead on the future. Sasha wasn't 'my ex-husband'. She was my new friend.

We stayed for another hour or so then, after hugs all round, Riley drove my car home. He asked if I wanted to talk about Ivy or Dad, but I surprised myself by talking about Mum instead. I'd never have imagined that my time with Sasha and Ivy would help me find some peace in my relationship with Mum too.

Riley hugged me when we arrived back at his parents' house.

'I could do with a couple of days to get my head together so I won't come into college on Monday,' I said, 'but I'll be back on Tuesday. I'll need the distraction.'

'Let me or Judith know if you change your mind and you need longer, and give me a call if you need me.'

'I think I'll be all right now.'

'You say that, but you haven't just lost Ivy. You're grieving for Shaun and your parents too. And because somebody rudely took the job you loved from you. Hate him.'

'Yeah, but that same person offered me another job and has gone out of his way to be there for me recently. Impossible to hate him, especially when he has such good taste in sweets and music.'

Riley laughed as he gave me another quick hug. 'Take care of yourself.'

I got into my car and wound the window down.

He crouched down. 'I hope you're going to play "Mr Blue Sky" on the way home.'

I smiled. 'It's the perfect lift.'

I scrolled through my phone and set it away playing.

'Turn it right up,' he said. 'Someone once told me life's too short for quiet music.'

As I pulled off his parents' drive, 'Mr Blue Sky' blaring out, I did feel surprisingly lifted. And it wasn't just from the music.

47

SAMANTHA

Late on Sunday morning, Josh and I dropped Phoebe and Darcie off at Rosemary's then picked up Terry to take him out for a carvery at the Fox and Badger in North Emmerby.

'You really didn't need to thank me,' Terry said when we'd finished eating. 'But that were delicious. Thanks for the treat.'

'Our pleasure.' I removed a package from my bag. 'We've got something else for you.'

'A present?' Terry frowned as he took it from me. 'But it's not my birthday till November.'

'It's not a birthday gift. Open it and you'll see.'

He unwrapped the photo frame and his mouth dropped open. 'You've fixed it.'

'Zayn did some computer wizardry,' I said. 'I've got the original on the noticeboard.'

He adjusted his glasses and peered closer. A print-out of Gwendoline's drawing took pride of place in the middle of the frame and there were four smaller images round it: two of Terry's favourite elephant photos from our honeymoon, printed off in black and white, and a couple of black and white photos Terry had found from his youth featuring him and Gwendoline, which Zayn had cropped and tidied up.

'I'll treasure this.' He grasped my hand and kissed me on the cheek, then shook Josh's hand across the table.

'We've got some news for you as well,' Josh said. 'Tod the fox cub is ready for release so we wondered if we could do it together this evening.'

'Aye, that'd be grand.'

* * *

Wilbur joined us for the release and Josh held his lead while I opened the door of the carry crate in the area where Terry had originally found Tod.

'What if he doesn't find his family?' Terry asked me as Tod emerged from the crate, sniffing the air. 'Or what if they reject him?'

'We have to take that chance. We can't keep a wild animal in captivity. Hopefully he's big enough to fend for himself.'

Tod took a couple more tentative steps, then shot through the undergrowth and out of sight.

'Good luck, Tod,' Terry called.

Josh handed him Wilbur's lead and walked up to the barbed wire tangle from where Terry had rescued Tod.

'Looks like a spot of fly-tipping,' he called back to us. 'Might take a couple of journeys but we can clear it between us.'

There was nothing heavy – a few coils of barbed wire, some cables, a broken bike and a couple of empty paint tins – so we carefully transported the items back to Josh's jeep to add to the skip Dave had outside Alder Lea.

'We've been thinking about how Gwendoline loved all animals,' I said to Terry on our second journey back to the jeep. 'And we've been thinking about Tod and all the other wildlife who might need help, so we're looking into expanding Hedgehog Hollow to include other animals.'

'Oh, lass, that's brilliant news.'

'We've still got a lot to explore and we're probably not talking until next year,' Josh said.

'If it's money stopping you, you can have more of your inheritance now.'

'Terry! It's *your* money.'

'I don't need it and I've got no family to give it to so, like I told you before, Hedgehog Hollow gets the lot when I pop me clogs. How much do you need?'

'We don't,' I said gently. 'But thank you. It's just a proposal at the moment but we'll hopefully make it happen.'

'Don't struggle. The money's there whenever you need it.'

* * *

When we pulled back into the farmyard after dropping Terry and Wilbur back home, it was getting dark. Josh took my hand.

'There's something I want to show you in the garden,' he said, 'but I need you to close your eyes.'

'What are you up to?' I asked, smiling at him.

'Do you trust me?'

'Always.'

'Then close your eyes. We're going into the garden, so you'll feel the surface change.'

I closed my eyes and allowed him to lead me across the farmyard and onto the grass.

'Going down the lawn,' he whispered, tightening his hold as the grass inclined a little.

'Stop, open your eyes, and turn round.'

I did as instructed, turning to face the back of the house. My heart leapt at the flickering candles arranged in the shape of a large heart on the lawn.

Josh took both my hands in his. 'One year ago today, I asked you to marry me, and you made me the happiest man alive by saying yes. I wanted to remind you that I'm still the happiest man alive and always will be as long as I've got you by my side.'

'I'll always be by your side,' I said. 'I'll love you forever.'

He kissed me tenderly, making my heart race.

'When did you arrange this?'

'Beth picked up the candles for me when they were shopping at the weekend and put them out earlier. I texted her and asked her to switch them on when you were saying goodbye to Terry.'

'It's so lovely.'

'What's that?' Josh asked, pointing towards the dip at the top of the heart.

I squinted. 'I can't see anything.'

'I'm sure there's something up there.'

We stepped into the heart and walked to the top. I bent down and picked up a small jewellery box. Expecting it to be earrings, I flicked it open and gasped. I looked up at Josh questioningly.

'They say an eternity ring can be given at any time and lots of couples choose a wedding anniversary. It's a symbol of everlasting love and commitment, and you've got that from me, whether we have a family or not, so I thought, why wait until our first wedding anniversary? Why not our engagement anniversary? The jeweller said it can be worn on the right hand.'

He took it out of his box and slipped it onto my finger.

'It's so beautiful, Josh. Thank you.'

'Thank you for saying yes.'

I gazed at the heart-shaped platinum band with the row of diamonds, my heart bursting with love for Josh in making such a romantic gesture. What a perfect end to a special day.

48

SAMANTHA

I'd been dreading Monday – Paul and Beth's moving out day. As soon as I woke up, I felt tearful.

'We'll still see loads of them,' Josh said, hugging me.

'If I'm this bad when they're only moving a few miles away, could you imagine what a wreck I'd be if they were moving to another country?'

'I agree it'll be strange without them. We've been through a lot together in the space of a year.'

Downstairs, Phoebe dished out hugs then rushed out, saying she'd be late for college if she didn't go. She was going to be very early, but I knew she was as sad as I was about them leaving. Even Darcie was unusually sombre on the journey to school, so I assured her we'd see them really soon, just like Josh had assured me.

Dave's van was parked outside the farmhouse when I got back, which set me off again. Rich was between shifts in his role as an ambulance paramedic and, as there wasn't much to move, they'd said it would be quicker and easier if they did it between them. I said hello then left them to it, grateful to have hoglets to feed to keep me distracted.

When the van left, I headed over to the farmhouse with a heavy heart. Paul was doing one last check to see if they'd missed anything while Beth was on the floor in the lounge with Archie and Lottie.

She looked up at me, her eyes puffy and her cheeks stained with tears.

'It's not just me, then,' I said, pointing to my face.

'It's like the end of an era,' she said, scrambling to her feet and hugging me close.

Paul wandered into the lounge with one of Lottie's cardigans and a plastic duck while I was cuddling Archie goodbye.

'Where were they?' Beth asked as he held them up.

'Airing cupboard. The cardigan makes sense. Not so sure about the duck.'

I swapped Archie for cuddles with Lottie.

'We've got you a thank you gift,' Paul said. 'It's in the kitchen. It's for you and Josh but mainly you.'

Still cuddling Lottie, I followed them across the hall. In the middle of the kitchen table was a gorgeous traditional wicker picnic basket and a rolled-up picnic blanket in a carry-strap.

'Oh, my gosh!'

Paul took Lottie from me so I could open the basket, which contained plates, cutlery, glasses, napkins, a corkscrew and salt and pepper shakers.

'It's gorgeous. Thank you.'

'A reminder of your grandparents,' Beth said. 'And we're already looking forward to our first picnic invite.'

'First of many,' I said, hugging them both.

'We'd best get going,' Paul said. 'Thank you for everything.'

'Honestly, Paul, it has been an absolute pleasure having you all here. Don't be strangers.'

* * *

Dad paid an unexpected visit at lunchtime, bringing a couple of baguettes with him. The recent rain had left the air fresh but a bit too cool for eating outside, so we wandered over to the farmhouse and I showed him my picnic basket.

'You should have seen Beth and me earlier,' I said. 'The pair of us were blubbing messes.'

'That's the reason I stopped by for lunch. Josh and I thought you might be a bit upset and appreciate the company. Josh would have come but he's been called into emergency surgery.'

'You two are the best. I've been sobbing most of the morning, but I think I'm over the worst of it now. I keep reminding myself how important it is for them to have their own home and their own lives now that Paul's pretty much back to full health.'

'It'll be good for all of you.'

It would be, but it would take some getting used to. The house was going to be very quiet without them all, especially Archie and Lottie. Once more, that feeling was there that I might be ready to fill the house with our own children after all.

* * *

Later that afternoon, I met Mum in Little Tilbury.

'What do you think?' she asked as we stood in the overgrown front garden, looking up at Orchard House.

'You're right. It's got the potential to be so special.' It was oozing with charm and character and all it needed was someone to show it some care and attention. I'd put Mum in touch with Dave and he was up for the work. Converting unusual buildings and restoring old ones were his favourite types of project, and it helped that this was so close to home.

'Come and look round the back,' Mum said, 'but bring that vision with you.'

Once more, I could see why she'd been smitten. Like the front garden, it was an overgrown mess, but the space was incredible. There was even a secret garden.

'I'd never have spotted it if I hadn't had the plans,' Mum said as we peered through the tiniest of gaps in the hedge. 'I could see there was another chunk of land and I paced up and down before realising the hedges were off-set. They've grown into each other as you can see, but how wonderful will that be when I've trimmed them back and cleared the garden?'

'There's a swing,' I said.

'Probably rotten, but I can have another one put in. It would be brilliant for any grandchildren.' She stepped away from the hedge, cheeks pink. 'Sorry. None of my business.'

I smiled at her. 'We'll have to see what the next year or two brings. In the meantime, you've landed yourself a project and a half, but I love it.'

'Thank you. I can't wait to get started.'

We peered through the windows at the back of the house but they were dirty so I couldn't see much. Same with the front ones.

'Do you have time for a wander round the village?' Mum asked.

I glanced at my watch. 'Darcie's gone to a friend's for tea, so I'm all yours for a bit longer. You can tell me more about your childhood haunts and whether there were any other characters in the village like Bird Lady.'

'There were a couple,' Mum said as we set off walking. 'You see that house over there? The man who lived there used to sit in a wheelbarrow in his front garden, knitting.'

'You're making that up!'

She held her hands up in a surrender pose, laughing. 'I swear I'm not. Ask Louise.'

As we wandered round the village, with Mum reminiscing about her childhood there, I felt like we'd made another major breakthrough in our relationship. I felt closer to her but also to my grandparents. They'd been such a major part of my life but all of my memories featuring them and Mum were strained, so it was lovely to hear her talking so fondly about them.

'I enjoyed this,' Mum said when we returned to the cars. 'I've been talking to my counsellor about my parents and how close we used to be. She's encouraging me to move my energy away from the regrets and onto the happy times. I feel much lighter for it.'

'I loved hearing your stories. And I love seeing you like this.'

'I'd never have got help if it hadn't been for you. Thanks, Sammie.'

Sammie? She'd never called me that before. Only the most important people in my life – Dad, Josh and Chloe – used that version of my name.

'Thank you for going,' I said gently. 'Because it means I can do this.'

My throat burned and my eyes blurred as I hugged my mum.

49

LAUREN

On the Tuesday, ten days after Ivy's passing, it was her funeral. Riley offered to accompany me but so did Connie and, as Connie had known Ivy and seemed keen to pay her final respects, it felt right to accept her offer.

'How are you holding up?' Connie asked once we were settled into our seats on the train.

'One minute I'm sad she's gone, and the next I'm so grateful that I had a chance to see her again and say what needed to be said. I never got that chance with Mum or Dad.'

'No, me neither.'

'I haven't told you what Ivy said about Mum being proud of me...'

I intentionally hadn't told Connie immediately, as I'd felt I needed some time to reflect on it and how it had affected me over the years. The main impact had been my relationship with Connie due to her being the clear favourite but, if I stood back from that objectively, had it affected us that significantly? I hadn't opened up to her about still being in love with Shaun, but there'd been so many other reasons for that, so I'm not sure I'd have confessed it even if there hadn't been that undercurrent. As for the undercurrent, I couldn't help wondering if it was only me who'd felt it. Had it all been in my head?

'I can't believe you didn't think Mum was proud of you,' Connie said after I'd told her what Ivy and Sasha had said. 'I know Mum and I did more together when I was younger, but I always thought she preferred you when we were older. She'd say things to me like, "Have you never thought about getting yourself a career like our Lauren?"'

'She never did!'

'I swear she did.'

'But she thought a woman's place was in the home and that I should be focusing on keeping my husband happy instead of pursuing a career. And as for making an active choice not to have children...'

Connie smiled. 'She was a funny onion sometimes. It sounds like the things she had a go at you about were the things she told me she was proud of you for and vice versa. She wanted us both to be happy and because she hadn't found happiness with Dad, she didn't know what that looked like, and she didn't know how to guide us.'

'You really thought she favoured me?' I asked.

'Absolutely!'

'All these years, I thought you were her favourite.'

'What? Why?'

I'd thought it was going to be a difficult discussion, but it ended up being a hilarious conversation as we both remembered more and more occasions when Mum had held one of us up as a role model to the other. It was amazing what you could discover when you let people in. I'd learned a valuable lesson.

50

SAMANTHA

✉ From Chloe
HOT TIP: The family event of the year is happening over at Hedgehog Hollow today and the mother of hedgehogs, the unicorn of friends, the amazing Sammie Alderson, is going to be phenomenal. See you soon xx

'That's one sick outfit!' Phoebe cried. 'You look amazing!'

'Mickleby!' Darcie squealed, launching herself at Josh and stroking the curved spines down the back of the furry costume of Mickleby, our mascot.

Three weeks had whizzed past, and it was the morning of the Family Fun Day on what would have been Thomas's eighty-fifth birthday. I couldn't stop laughing as I took photos in the lounge and the back garden of Phoebe and Darcie with Josh. Those oversized paws on his hands and feet cracked me up every time.

When he'd first worn the costume last May on our official opening weekend, he'd said to me, 'If at any point in the future, you have even the tiniest doubt about how much I love you, picture me wearing this costume and know that I did it just for you. This right here? This is what true love looks like.' As it happens, I'd never for one minute doubted how much Josh loved me. I felt it emanating from him every day. But I did like to picture him in the costume from time to time because it instantly lifted me.

'We need some with you in,' Phoebe insisted, taking my phone from me.

After our photo shoot, we made our way over to Wildflower Byre and I looked up at the sky. We'd been blessed with sunshine, but a few fluffy clouds trailing lazily across the sky made the temperature pleasant rather than uncomfortable.

'Josh couldn't get out of the costume last year,' I told Phoebe and Darcie. 'We came back to the farmhouse and I got held up outside. Josh tried to pull the costume off on his own but he got stuck.'

'I couldn't breathe,' he cried, 'and all Sammie could do was laugh. See! She's still laughing about it now!'

'Oh, my gosh! It was the funniest thing I've ever seen.' I patted his arm. 'Don't worry. We'll make sure there are plenty of people around to help you this year.'

We'd only opened half an hour ago, but the farmyard was already full of cars and there were dozens parked in the field out the front of the farmhouse where we'd built snowmen at the start of the year.

'We're going to be busy,' I said, seeing a steady stream of vehicles coming along the farm track. Rich and Dave, wearing yellow high-vis jackets, waved to us. They'd volunteered to take the first shift on car park duty.

Last year, we'd set up an area outside the barn for a meet and greet with Mickleby using props borrowed from the performing arts department at Reddfield TEC. We'd borrowed the woodland backdrop and wooden red and white spotted toadstools again but had added in some wooden trees and set it up in Wildflower Byre instead. Poor Josh had been sweltering in the costume last year and it was fairer to him and the queuing children to be out of the sun.

Hannah and Toby were running it, like last year, but Chloe had drawn up a detailed rota using several of our volunteers to ensure everyone helping had a decent break to wander round the event themselves or rest if they preferred.

Chloe had been such a godsend. I had no idea she had such strong organisational skills, and I couldn't have been more grateful to her for taking it all on so that I could focus on running the rescue centre.

We'd had a change of heart about the location of my talks, holding them in Wildflower Byre rather than the rescue centre so that I could speak to a larger audience without worrying about any noise disturbing the hedgehogs. I had a voice amplifier this time, so my voice hopefully wouldn't be quite as hoarse as last year. I'd show the resources and equipment we used every day with the assistance of soft toy hedgehogs. There were bound to be some attendees who were disappointed about not seeing real hedgehogs, but my talk started by explaining the importance of minimal handling and avoiding noise around them, which should appease them. If they wanted their fix of real hedgehogs, they could study the enlarged photos of patients past and present displayed on project boards borrowed from the TEC.

A queue had already formed ready for Mickleby, and excited squeals echoed round the building as the children spotted him approaching, running up to him and trying to hold his paws.

'I'll leave him in your capable hands,' I said to Hannah and Toby.

Darcie wanted to watch for a while, so I left her and Phoebe there and went on a final circuit round Fun Field, welcoming and thanking any volunteers I'd missed while I'd been helping Josh into his costume.

I was touched by how much help we had today. All my family and friends were helping, nearly everyone who volunteered at the rescue centre had offered some of their time, most of the members of the Bentonbray Craft Club were here, and Fizz had enlisted some of her university friends. Even Terry was helping Dad and Uncle Simon with the barbeque, much to Wilbur's delight, as the occasional sausage got 'accidentally' dropped.

My face was already aching from smiling. The face-painting was going down a storm and it was lovely to see how many children had chosen hedgehogs. I'd been stunned by the volume of crafts Chloe, Lauren and the craft club had managed to make in a relatively short space of time, and the stall was proving really popular. The children's clothes and accessories made by some of the TEC's costume design students were adorable and Hannah had bought the cutest pinafore dress and matching sunhat for Amelia, which she was wearing already.

Chloe had set up the art stall in Wildflower Byre using more display boards from the TEC. She'd said that having it in there would avoid the risk of the flyers blowing across the field if it was windy. I'd never have thought of that. A sweet stall, cake stall and the 'guess the weight of the hedgehog' cake were also in the byre to keep them out of the sun.

I couldn't help but reflect on the same event last year, how much had changed since then, and how much exciting change still lay ahead.

'You look deep in thought.'

I turned and smiled at Dad. 'I was just thinking about how much has changed since the Family Fun Day last year, not just for me and Hedgehog Hollow, but for everyone.'

'It's been a year for it,' Dad agreed. 'Thankfully mainly positive. It's amazing what you've achieved in the past year.'

'It is, but none of it would have been possible without so many people volunteering their time and donating funds and supplies.' I looked over to the barbeque where Terry was chatting to Uncle Simon. 'Terry said recently that he prefers animals to people, and I get where he's coming from, but I think people can be pretty amazing too.'

51

LAUREN

✉ From Riley

Hope it goes well today. Kai and I will probably be over by late morning. Can I buy you lunch if you have time for a break? x

✉ To Riley

Chloe has planned things with military precision! I'm on lunch at 1.30pm. Look forward to seeing you later and to meeting Kai x

'Are you sure you're okay?' Chloe asked as I knocked over a display of needle-felted hedgehogs on the craft stall for the third time in the space of an hour.

'I'm fine. Thank you.'

I wasn't fine at all. I'd never been so nervous in my life. I'd never experienced the 'meet the parents' trauma because I'd got to know Ivy when Shaun and I were just friends, and Glen had been estranged from his parents, so I hadn't met them. I'd heard it was nerve-wracking but couldn't imagine it was worse than how I felt about 'meet the child'. And it wasn't like I was even dating Riley. I didn't know what we were. Friends? Colleagues?

Since driving me back from Ivy's, we'd spent plenty of time

together, but he'd never made a move. We'd hugged but never kissed. We'd talked but never about 'us', and it was killing me, but I couldn't bring myself to make the first move in case what I felt building between us was all in my imagination.

I'd arranged for him to give me an out of hours tour round Bloomsberry's on Wednesday and there'd been several moments when we were standing really close together, eyes locked, and I was convinced he was building up to saying something. Then he'd stepped away and talked shop instead.

The passion he clearly had for the family business was infectious. I'd been wary about what I could contribute but I could finally see it and had bounced a few initial ideas off him, which he'd loved. My gut feeling was that I was interested but only because it was a short-term opportunity which would bring in some income while I decided where my future really lay. I was meeting his parents tomorrow and would make the final decision after that. If they were anything like their son, it wouldn't be a difficult decision to make, but I had to be sure.

I anticipated some 'meet the parents' nerves tomorrow but I didn't imagine they'd be as strong as today's. Having Kai's approval felt very important. Could that have been why nothing had happened between Riley and me? Had he wanted to introduce me to his son first? No pressure!

'Ouch!' Chloe squealed a little later. 'What was that for?'

'Sorry!' I hadn't meant to grab her arm, but I'd just spotted Riley.

'Who's that?' she asked, following my eyeline.

'Riley Berry.' My voice came out all husky.

'He's hot. Are you and him...?'

'In my dreams.' I bit my lip. Had I just said that out loud?

'You must have very pleasant dreams,' she said, giggling.

Riley spotted me, waved, and headed over to the stall.

'You won't say anything?' I whispered.

'Of course not. But if he's single, I think *you* should before anyone else gets in there.'

'Hi,' Riley said, reaching the stall.

'Hi.'

My heart raced as he smiled at me.

'Lauren, this is my son Kai. Kai, this is Lauren.'

Kai had the same bright blue eyes as Riley but had dark hair, almost black, rather than blond like his dad.

'So you're the one my dad fancies,' he said.

Chloe snorted with laughter as Riley clamped his hand across Kai's mouth.

'Kids, eh?' he said, those eyes of his twinkling with mirth. 'Didn't you want to get your face painted, Kai?'

'Dad! I'm eleven, not six. But if you give me a tenner, I'll get some sweets.'

'A fiver,' Riley said, taking a note from his wallet. 'And I expect change.'

'Thanks, Dad!' He ran off, laughing.

'Sorry about that,' Riley said. 'I don't know where he got—'

'It's okay,' I said, keen for him not to finish that sentence and dash my hopes.

'Why don't you take your lunch break now?' Chloe said. 'I'm Chloe, by the way. Sammie's cousin, Lauren's friend. Nice to meet you.'

She stretched her hand across the crafts and shook Riley's.

'I'm not scheduled for lunch until half one,' I said.

'And I'm the schedule-master and I say you can go now, so shoo!'

It would only get more uncomfortable if I argued further so, with a playful scowl in Chloe's direction when Riley wasn't looking, I retrieved my bag from under the table.

We wandered away from the stall and I grappled for something to say, but all I could think about was Kai's statement. He wouldn't just come out with something like that, would he? Riley had to have said something to prompt it.

I hated that Riley occupied most of my waking thoughts – and a lot of my sleeping ones too. This wasn't who I was. I was a strong, independent woman who didn't go all dreamy over the opposite sex. But was that because I hadn't met Riley Berry before?

We joined the queue for the barbeque, making small talk about the weather, how busy it was, and what a great fundraiser it would be for Hedgehog Hollow. Kai joined us, clutching a striped carrier bag.

'Your change,' he said, and I laughed as he placed a five pence piece in Riley's outstretched palm.

'Kai!'

'I didn't spend it all on me.' He reached into the carrier and handed Riley a paper bag containing rhubarb and custards.

'And I got these for you,' he added, handing me a bag of white mice. 'Dad said they're your favourites.'

'Thank you, Kai. They are and that's very kind of you. Would you like one while we're queuing?'

Kai thanked me as he took one and Riley caught my eye and smiled. Had I passed my first test?

* * *

I kicked off my sliders and wriggled my toes as I sat on the bench in my back garden early that evening, sipping on a chilled glass of rosé. My feet were aching from standing all day, but what a brilliant fundraiser it had been. Jonathan was still up at the farm helping count the money, but early indications were more than double last year.

The doorbell rang and I reluctantly shoved my feet back in my sliders and went to answer it.

'Riley?' My heart started racing.

'Do you have a minute?'

'Sure. Come in.'

He stepped past me and I breathed in his body spray. No idea what it was, but it did it for me. As did the shirt he'd changed into.

'I was having a glass of wine in the garden if you want to join me,' I said.

'That would be great, thanks.'

I poured him a glass and indicated he should follow me over to the bench.

'I recognise the pots,' he said, nodding towards the ones I'd put together the day we met. 'They look good.'

'Are you okay?' I asked. He seemed nervous, tapping his leg and running his hand through his hair.

'Yeah! No, actually...' He exhaled deeply. 'There's something I want to say to you – something I should have said ages ago – and I'm no good at this sort of thing. Dry throat.'

He grabbed his wine off the wooden table and took a swig of it.

'So, erm, what Kai said earlier... I could have killed him for blurting that out but, the thing is, it's true.' He put his glass down and twisted to face me. 'I really like you, Lauren. Really, really, *really* like you and I know it's probably rubbish timing with everything you've been going through, but Kai said I had to tell you before you friendzone me. He seems to know an alarming amount about these things for an eleven-year-old and definitely way more than me. I know we're colleagues and you might take the job at the garden—'

He stopped as I lightly pressed my fingers against his lips.

'I really, really, *really* like you too,' I said, shuffling closer to him. 'And your timing couldn't be better.'

My heart raced once more as his lips met mine. The soft but sensuous kiss stirred sensations inside me I didn't think I'd be capable of feeling again. He ran his fingers through my hair, and I did the same to him as our kiss intensified.

The timing really was perfect because I was finally ready. I'd spent far too long chasing dreams of a life with Shaun, but I was now ready to let go of the past, ready to embrace the future, ready to love again.

52

SAMANTHA

✉ To Chloe

Wishing you and James a happy 2nd wedding anniversary. Give my love to Brussels! xx

Today – 10 August – was a very special day. Chloe and James's second wedding anniversary also meant two years since I'd met Thomas, triggering so many positive changes in my life. I'd stumbled across the farm after getting hopelessly lost on the way to the wedding reception, where I'd found Thomas collapsed. I'd saved his life that day, but he'd also saved mine.

Rosemary and her best friend Celia had booked a static caravan in North Wales and had taken Phoebe and Darcie with them for a week so, with the house empty, Josh and I had planned a picnic by the meadow to celebrate everything Thomas and Gwendoline had brought to our lives.

It was Riley's birthday next month but it fell on the same day as Connie and Alex's wedding, so Lauren had organised a surprise early birthday present of a hot air balloon flight. If the wind direction was right, their balloon and two others would pass over Hedgehog Hollow.

'Aw, look at those two!' I said, pointing to Misty-Blue and Luna chasing each other along the edge of the meadow as I billowed out the picnic blanket on the lawn.

'Best friends forever,' he said.

Darcie's wish had come true and, when the hoglets were too big (and spiky) to feed from her, Luna had seemed happy to make the farm her home. She didn't venture inside for a couple of weeks, but Darcie persisted with treats and now Luna was officially a family pet.

Josh placed the picnic basket – our gift from Paul and Beth – on one corner and poured us both a glass of wine before settling down onto the blanket.

'Cheers,' he said, clinking his drink against mine.

'Cheers,' I said, smiling back at him. 'To Thomas and Gwendoline.'

We raised our glasses towards the meadow.

Josh breathed in the fresh air and sighed contentedly. 'We couldn't have picked a better evening.'

The baby-blue sky was tinged with streaks of peach and orange – so warm and restful. Butterflies flitted across the meadow and birds sang their evening lullaby in the trees. I could smell the sweet aroma of strawberries growing nearby and looked forward to picking a few later.

In the distance, a red tractor and trailer moved slowly across one of our fields – our neighbouring farmer Bill Davis or one of his team working on the land he rented from us. How lucky were we to live in such a stunning place?

We'd just finished our picnic when Josh cried out, 'Balloon!'

Three hot air balloons – a red and white striped one, a blue and white striped one, and a rainbow-coloured one – floated over the farm-house, ever so slowly.

'I wonder which one Auntie Lauren and Riley are in,' he said.

'I'm guessing the one with blue stripes. She said something about them having names and putting in a special request to be on the one called Mr Blue Sky.'

I loved Lauren and Riley's story, how they'd met while both listening to that ELO song, and how he'd helped her through a challenging couple of months. I'd thought that Lauren and Dad would make a good couple but now that I'd seen Lauren with Riley, I realised I'd been wrong about that. Dad and Lauren had an amazing friendship, but the connection between Riley and Lauren was something else.

Lauren had told me that she and Riley had agreed to take things slowly because they'd both been hurt before, but I wouldn't be surprised if they'd moved in together by the end of the year.

'This reminds me of our honeymoon,' Josh said, resting back on his elbows. 'That sunrise balloon trip was magical.'

'So was that evening,' I said, winking at him.

We lay down side by side, gazing up at the sky, hands held, my other hand resting on my stomach. When the balloons disappeared, I glanced down at my eternity ring, sparkling in the low evening sun, then turned my head towards the meadow and smiled. It was time. *We're going to fulfil your other dream, Thomas and Gwendoline. We're going to fill this farmhouse with children.*

I propped myself up on my side and gazed down at Josh. 'I'm ready to try for a baby.'

His lips curved into a smile. 'Are you sure?'

'Completely and utterly positive.'

'Are you really, *really* sure?'

'A million per cent. Is it still what you want?'

'Yes, but only if it's right for you.'

'It is. If it happens for us, I can't guarantee that I'll be relaxed and panic-free for the whole of the pregnancy, but I promise to tell you any time I have a moment.'

'And how perfect that we have an empty house all week.' He ran his fingers into my hair and pulled me close as his lips met mine.

53

LAUREN

Connie and Alex's wedding

I fastened the ankle straps on my sandals and stood up, but I didn't need to curse my ridiculously high footwear for this wedding. When we'd been dress shopping, Connie had picked up the sparkly flats off the display.

'They're far more you than a pair of stilettos.'

'I'll wear heels for you.'

'No. You be you.'

Riley knocked on the bedroom door. 'Are you ready?'

'Just about.'

I took one last look at myself in the mirror and smiled. Surprisingly, I loved my maid of honour dress – a plain ankle-length heather dress with a fitted bodice and dropped sleeves.

'Stunning!' Riley exclaimed when I opened the door. 'Happy birthday to me!'

I laughed as I gave him a twirl then gently kissed him.

We were staying in Snuffles' Den again, sharing the cottage with

Jonathan. I'd been nervous about introducing Riley to Jonathan, but they'd hit it off immediately. After Glen's jealousy, I was also wary of any negative reaction Riley might have to me sharing my home with another man, but his only feedback was how lucky I was to have such a great cook living with me.

Riley and I stopped outside Meadow View, where Connie and Alex were spending the night.

'I'll see you over there,' he said, giving me another gentle kiss.

I rapped on the door when he left. Connie answered it in her dressing gown and ushered me inside.

'I thought you were meant to be putting your dress on,' I said. We'd had our hair and make-up done together in Meadow View and had separated to change.

'I was, but I realised I can't fasten it without help so I thought I'd wait for you.'

I followed her into the master bedroom where her dress was hanging on the outside of the wardrobe. She stepped into it and I fastened the delicate buttons up the back.

Connie hadn't wanted a big white dress, having done that before, but she still wanted to look bridal. This ivory beaded dress with flutter sleeves and a wrap-style bodice was the perfect compromise, being ankle-length and without a train. I'd loved it when she tried it on in the wedding boutique, but seeing it now with her hair and make-up done took my breath away. She'd grown her bob out and her hair was fastened back in a loose knot with a heather flower, matching the colour of my dress and the ribbon round the waist of hers.

'Absolutely stunning,' I said, standing behind her as she looked in the full-length mirror. 'Ready to say "I do" to your one true north?'

'I am. What about you and yours?'

I shook my head.

'Don't do that! He *is* your true north.'

'Yes, he is,' I admitted, 'but it's a no to marriage.'

'Third time lucky?'

I smiled. 'I think it will be for both of us. But not as a married couple. Come on. Let's find you a groom.'

Riley and I had spoken about it a few nights ago and had been in full agreement that neither of wanted to walk down the aisle again. We'd both been there, done that, twice. We carried the emotional scars of the loss of our first spouse and were still licking our wounds from the second attempt. This relationship would be different.

* * *

Connie and Alex's wedding ceremony was lovely – even more relaxed and informal than Josh and Sam's had been – and Chloe and I surprised the bride and groom with a ring cushion we'd made together. I'd done the sewing and Chloe had embroidered their names and dates on it.

We'd also decorated the front of the top table in Wildflower Byre with some personalised bunting we'd made. Crafting had become my new addiction. I'd invested in a sewing machine, had converted the spare bedroom into a small craft room, and always had several projects on the go. I'd developed a love for knitting and crocheting and was constantly trying out new things.

In the pause between the day and evening events, Riley and I went for a wander round the farm.

'It's beautiful,' he said as we leaned against the fence beyond the stables, a little way behind Wildflower Byre, looking up over the fields which Sam's neighbour farmed. 'I can see why you love coming here.'

'It's my happy place. Which is weird because I had no idea I was into nature or an animal lover before.'

'Would you like to live somewhere like this?'

'It's my idea of heaven. I love Chapel View and Amblestone, but this view!'

He took his phone out of his pocket and scrolled through it for a moment before handing it to me. 'What do you think of this view?'

I glanced down at a photo showing a farmhouse set in miles of rolling countryside, dotted with trees. 'Stunning. Where is it?'

'It's a farm not too far from here and it's a similar set-up to Hedgehog Hollow, in that another farmer rents the land. I was going to buy it when I first moved back here. Kai loved it and I'd had my offer accepted and everything, but the owners pulled out at the eleventh hour.'

'That's frustrating.'

'I was gutted. That day we met, when I'd viewed a couple of rentals, it was because the farm had fallen through. I didn't really want to move back in with my parents but I'm glad I did. Since their ops, they've both needed my help and I'd never have known that if I hadn't been living with them because they'd have been too proud to ask.'

'Everything *does* happen for a reason,' I agreed. 'Maybe the farm will come back on the market when the timing's better for you.'

'Maybe it will.'

He held my gaze and my heart raced as it so often did around Riley. It was too soon to talk about moving in together, but I knew what he was thinking – if the farmhouse did come back on the market, it could make a great home for us and for Kai. I couldn't agree more.

'We'd better get back to the wedding,' I said eventually. 'Sasha and Kristi will be here soon.'

The pair of them were fully back together and Connie and I had met up with them several times over the summer, including going away for a gorge walking and white-water rafting weekend. Ivy would have been proud of my new friendship with Sasha and Kristi, and I suspected Mum would have been proud of how much closer Connie and I had become.

'Do you mind if we look in the stables?' Riley asked as we set off back.

I followed him in, curious to see the inside.

'They're bigger than I expected,' I said, looking up at the vaulted ceiling. There were four stalls either side of a wide corridor. I suspected 'corridor' wasn't the word, but I knew nothing about horses.

'Do Josh and Sam have plans to do anything with them?' Riley asked.

'I don't think so. Neither of them ride. Why?'

'You love crafting, right? And you love teaching?'

'Yes to both.'

'And so does Chloe?'

'Also yes to both.'

'This may be completely random, but what if you and Chloe joined forces and set up a crafting school in here? You'd need to reconfigure the space, but it's a good size.'

'A crafting school?'

'Yeah. It could be a real winner. You'd make an income from it, you'd both be doing something you love, you'd be using the skills you love the most, it would be rewarding, and you'd help the rescue centre because you'd be paying rent.'

I stared up at the ceiling, my mind racing. 'That sounds like my dream job and I'm pretty sure it would be Chloe's too. But do you think people would be interested in something like that?'

'I know someone back in Derbyshire who set up something similar with a few friends. They started small and they're phenomenally successful now. I'm sure she'd be happy to talk you through how they did it and any pitfalls to avoid.'

I gazed around me, trying to picture it. I'd need to talk to Sam and Chloe, but I couldn't imagine either of them being against the idea.

'You know what?' I said, snaking my arms round his neck and drawing him into a kiss. 'I think destiny knew what she was doing when she crossed our paths.'

'I thought you didn't believe in that.'

'I did once and, thanks to you, I do again.'

54

SAMANTHA

The 1980s-themed disco was underway, and the dance floor was buzzing. The DJ had started playing Michael Jackson's 'Thriller' but, after spotting that Sasha and Kristi knew the dance routine, had organised everyone into lines to copy them while he started the track again.

Fizz called me up to join her, but it was far more fun watching and capturing it on video. Yasmin didn't look too impressed at the organised dancing. She exchanged a few words with Fizz and pointed towards the bar. Fizz shook her head and did a 'Thriller' move as though she wanted to stay and dance. Yasmin stormed off the dance floor, leaving Fizz looking dejected, but Darcie grabbed her hand and she was soon laughing as she acted like a zombie, sandwiched between Darcie and Phoebe.

I wasn't convinced by Yasmin. Fizz claimed they were having a great time together, but I didn't see it. She always seemed a little more subdued and on edge when Yasmin was around, and so much more natural and relaxed in Phoebe's company. Still, it wasn't my place to interfere.

'Thriller' came to an end and the DJ clearly wasn't done with the group dancing, playing 'Come On Eileen' which had everyone in circles, arms round each other, kicking their legs in time to the music.

Josh put his arm round me and I snuggled against him, watching them all. It was only four months since our wedding, but so much had changed during that short period of time. Our family had extended once more with the addition of Riley and Kai, Sasha and Kristi. My relationship with Mum had never been better. Her house sale and purchase had gone through, and Dave had started the work on converting Orchard House. She'd decided that it would be impossible to live there while the work was ongoing and was living in a caravan out the back instead. We'd invited her to stay at the farmhouse, but it would have made for a longer commute to agricultural college – starting on Monday – so she'd declined. It was probably for the best, as living together again was risky and I didn't want to do anything to damage the amazing progress we'd made.

'Happy?' Josh asked, kissing my forehead.

'I think all my dreams have come true this year,' I replied.

Hedgehog Hollow continued to thrive and Tariq's research into joining forces with Josh and Dad's veterinary practice while widening our wildlife rescue efforts had been extremely encouraging. Paul, Beth and the children had settled into Alder Lea, and Paul had accepted the veterinary nurse position and would be easing in with a couple of half days from Monday.

There were no tensions or family rifts, and the Grimes family remained behind bars and out of our lives. Phoebe had passed her accountancy diploma with top marks and secured her first paid role with an accountancy firm in Reddfield, and Darcie was excited about school returning, having stayed in touch with various new friends across the summer.

Yes, all those dreams had come true.

'Except one,' I said, placing my hand on my stomach. But Josh and I were working on that. A lot.

I looked around the room, smiling. There were still a few people I loved who were chasing their dreams and hopefully they'd come true too. If the romance of another wedding didn't work its magic,

Christmas was less than four months away. I knew what was on my Christmas list...

ACKNOWLEDGMENTS

Thank you for reading *Chasing Dreams at Hedgehog Hollow*, the penultimate book in the Hedgehog Hollow series. I hope you enjoyed Lauren's story. I've been itching to tell this one for ages, but other things kept happening at the end of the books like Chloe turning up announcing she'd left James and the unexpected theft of all that money! Lauren has been waiting (fairly impatiently) to have her tale told.

I have a little confession. I found this the hardest of all the books in the series to write and there were two unrelated reasons for this. The first was the overwhelmingly positive reaction I received for *A Wedding at Hedgehog Hollow*. It's an emotional story which covers an extremely difficult subject, but the sensitive handling of this had so many readers citing this as my best book so far and questioning how on earth I could top that. The simple answer was I wasn't sure I could! I went into full-on panic mode that I'd reached my pinnacle with that book and that readers would hate everything else I wrote. That inner voice – the one that afflicts me with imposter syndrome – stopped me in my tracks and I couldn't write for several days. Fortunately, I have an amazing husband, great friends and a fabulous editor who all managed to reassure me. Thank you, Mark, Sharon, Sarah and Nia. I'm particularly grateful to fellow author Samantha Tonge, to whom I dedicate this book, for an amazing piece of advice: *You don't have to set out to write the best book every time; just the best book you're capable of at that time.* I love it! Do check out Samantha's books – they're brilliant.

The second struggle was with the rescue centre setting – or lack of it! With Samantha and Josh on their honeymoon and this being

Lauren's story, the first half of the book needed to be set away from Hedgehog Hollow, and I had another panic that readers might not like that. I really hope you enjoyed your trip to Tanzania, seeing the elephants that Gwendoline loved so much and meeting a native hedgehog.

As always, considerable research has gone into this book to ensure accuracy and authenticity on everything from going on safari in Tanzania to a brain tumour diagnosis to being a transgender woman. A range of online sources, videos and conversations have been used, and I'm very grateful to Claire from the LGBTQ+ community for undertaking sensitivity reading on the chapters between Lauren and Sasha. Please note that in these chapters I have intentionally used he/him pronouns to refer to Shaun in the past and the present day because this is Lauren's story and she had only known Shaun presenting as a man. I've used she/her pronouns for Sasha. Therefore, any time I mix the pronouns or refer to Sasha as Shaun, it is deliberate, to distinguish between Shaun from Lauren's past and Sasha in the present.

We didn't run a 'name the hedgehog' competition for this book, but I did ask my reading community, Redland's Readers (please do join us on Facebook), for inspiration for the garden centre. Thank you to Tricia Thorne for the fabulous Bloomsberry's, which inspired me to change Riley's surname to Berry.

Thanks to the wonderful Ann and Angela from Wolds Hedgehog Rescue Centre – a real-life Hedgehog Hollow in the Yorkshire Wolds – who I'm delighted to support. They introduced me to the delightful phrase 'poop soup'.

Thank you to everyone in the Boldwood Books family and our partners who have played their part in releasing *Chasing Dreams at Hedgehog Hollow* – copy-editor Cecily Blench, proofreader Sue Lamprell, cover designer Debbie Clement (for a new favourite!), Rachel Gilbey for the blog tour, Claire Fenby for the marketing support, and my amazing editor Nia Beynon, who I can never thank enough for such valuable insights to enhance the story.

If you've listened to the audiobook, a huge thank you to Emma

Swan, who has brought Samantha to life for a fifth outing, Gloria Sanders for narrating Lauren's chapters, ISIS Audio and Ulverscroft for the recording and distribution.

Thanks as always to my amazing husband Mark, daughter Ashleigh, bestie Sharon and brilliant Mum for all the support.

And a final thanks to you wonderful readers/listeners. There's one more book to come in this series – *Christmas Miracles at Hedgehog Hollow* – and then we say goodbye to Hedgehog Hollow for now, but not forever. The series ends, but it won't be the last we hear from the rescue centre. Please spread the word if you've loved this series and do try my Whitsborough Bay books if you haven't already done so.

Big hugs,

Jessica xx

HEDGEHOG TRUE/FALSE

Hedgehogs are born with spines

FALSE - Imagine poor mum giving birth if they had spines! Ouch! When hoglets are born, their skin is covered in fluid and, after a few hours, this is reabsorbed and soft white spines erupt from the skin

Hedgehogs are good swimmers

TRUE - They're really good swimmers and, perhaps even more surprisingly, can climb trees. They do sometimes drown, though. It's not the swimming that's the problem; it's the getting out again and they can perish due to the exhaustion of trying to escape. It's therefore important that ponds have the means for a hedgehog to get out if they accidentally fall in

Baby hedgehogs are called hoglets

TRUE - Isn't it cute? They're sometimes known as piglets, pups or kittens but the official term is hoglets

Hedgehogs are nocturnal

TRUE AND FALSE – We tend to think of hedgehogs as being nocturnal which would suggest they're only out at night but, while they are most active at night time, the technical term for hedgehogs is 'crepuscular' which means they can be active at twilight too. We often see hedgehogs moving around in summer when it's still light because the days are longer and they need to search for food

Hedgehogs can run in short bursts at speeds of up to 3mph

FALSE - They're even faster than that. They are surprisingly nippy and can reach top speeds of 5.5mph in short bursts. Go hedgehogs!

Hedgehogs lose half their body weight during hibernation

FALSE - It's actually just over a third but that's still a significant amount and hedgehogs fresh from hibernation are going to need some major feasts to build up their strength quickly

Hedgehogs got their name in the Middle Ages from the word 'hygehoge' which translates today as 'hedge' and 'pig' combined

TRUE - The name does what it says on the tin! They snuffle round hedges for their foot and this snuffling/grunting is just like a pig

Hedgehogs have good eyesight

FALSE – Eyesight is the weakest of the hedgehog's senses and they are very susceptible to visual conditions. They have a keen sense of smell, taste and hearing and it's these senses they will use far more than their eyesight so one-eyed hedgehogs and even blind ones can survive in the wild thanks to their other senses

Hedgehogs are quiet eaters

FALSE - They're very noisy when they eat. They love their food and will slurp, crunch and lip-smack with their mouths open. Not the ideal dinner guest!

HEDGEHOG DOS AND DONT'S

Food and Drink

DO NOT give hedgehogs milk to drink. They are lactose intolerant. Dairy products will give them diarrhoea which will dehydrate them and can kill them

DO give hedgehogs water but please have this in a shallow dish. If it's in a deep dish, the risk is that they'll fall in and be unable to get out again

DO give hedgehogs dog or cat food - tin, pouch or biscuit format - they can eat both meaty and fishy varieties. It's a myth that they can't have fishy varieties of food but they may prefer meaty varieties because they prefer the smell

DO try to create a feeding station for a hedgehog so that other garden visitors (including cats) don't beat the hedgehog to it. You don't need to buy anything expensive. There are loads of tutorials and factsheets online around creating your own simple station

Your Garden

DO avoid having fences with no gaps under them. Hedgehogs can travel a long way in an evening and they rely on being able to move from one garden to the next. Or you can create a hedgehog highway in your fence

DO place a ramp by a pond so that, if a hedgehog falls, it can easily get out

DO NOT let your dog out into your garden without checking it's hedgehog-free. This is especially important during babies season (May/June and Sept/Oct) when there may be hoglets out there

DO build a bug hotel and DO plant bug-friendly plants. It will attract all sorts of delicious food for your hedgehogs

DO NOT use slug pellets. Hedgehogs love to eat slugs so pellets reduce their food supply and/or poison hedgehogs

DO have a compost heap or a messy part in your garden. If you can have some sticks/wood piled up in a safe corner, this makes a perfect habitat for hibernating

DO check your garden before strimming or mowing. Garden machinery can cause horrific accidents or fatalities

DO NOT leave netting out as hedgehogs can become trapped in it. If you have football goals in your garden, lift the netting up overnight and secure it safely to avoid injury or fatalities

DO always check bonfires before lighting as there may well be hogs nestling in there

Finding Hogs

DO NOT assume that a hedgehog out in the daylight is in danger. They usually are but watch first. It could be a mum nesting. If it's moving quickly and appears to be gathering food or nesting materials, leave it alone. If this isn't the case, then something is likely to wrong. Seek help

DO handle hedgehogs with gardening glove - those spines are there to protect the hogs and hurt predators - but keep handling to a minimum. Stay calm and quiet and be gentle with them. Transfer them into a high-sided box or crate with a towel, fleecy blanket or shredded news-paper (and a thick layer of paper on the bottom to soak up their many toilet visits). This will help keep them warm and give them somewhere to hide. Make sure there are plenty of air holes

DO NOT move hoglets if you accidentally uncover a nest but, if mum isn't there, do keep an eye on the nest and seek help if mum doesn't return. Hoglets won't survive long without their mother's milk. Put some water and food nearby so mum (assuming she returns) doesn't have far to travel for sustenance. If the hoglets are squeaking, this means they are hungry and you may need to call help if this continues and there's no sign of mum

MORE FROM JESSICA REDLAND

We hope you enjoyed reading *Chasing Dreams at Hedgehog Hollow*. If you did, please leave a review.

If you'd like to gift a copy, this book is also available as an ebook, digital audio download and audiobook CD.

Sign up to Jessica Redland's mailing list for news, competitions and updates on future books.

http://bit.ly/JessicaRedlandNewsletter

ABOUT THE AUTHOR

Jessica Redland writes uplifting stories of love, friendship, family and community set in Yorkshire where she lives. Her Whitsborough Bay books transport readers to the stunning North Yorkshire Coast and her Hedgehog Hollow series takes them into beautiful countryside of the Yorkshire Wolds.

Visit Jessica's website: https://www.jessicaredland.com/

Follow Jessica on social media:

facebook.com/JessicaRedlandWriter

twitter.com/JessicaRedland

instagram.com/JessicaRedlandWriter

bookbub.com/authors/jessica-redland

ALSO BY JESSICA REDLAND

Welcome to Whitsborough Bay Series

Making Wishes at Bay View

New Beginnings at Seaside Blooms

Finding Hope at Lighthouse Cove

Coming Home to Seashell Cottage

Other Whitsborough Bay Books

All You Need is Love

The Secret to Happiness

Christmas on Castle Street

Christmas Wishes at the Chocolate Shop

Christmas at Carly's Cupcakes

Starry Skies Over The Chocolate Pot Café

The Starfish Café Series

Snowflakes Over The Starfish Café

Spring Tides at The Starfish Café

Hedgehog Hollow Series

Finding Love at Hedgehog Hollow

New Arrivals at Hedgehog Hollow

Family Secrets at Hedgehog Hollow

A Wedding at Hedgehog Hollow

Chasing Dreams at Hedgehog Hollow

ABOUT BOLDWOOD BOOKS

Boldwood Books is a fiction publishing company seeking out the best stories from around the world.

Find out more at www.boldwoodbooks.com

Sign up to the Book and Tonic newsletter for news, offers and competitions from Boldwood Books!

http://www.bit.ly/bookandtonic

We'd love to hear from you, follow us on social media:

facebook.com/BookandTonic

twitter.com/BoldwoodBooks

instagram.com/BookandTonic

Printed in Great Britain
by Amazon